An Irish Country Doctor

Patrick Taylor

A Tom Doherty Associates Book

New York

AN IRISH COUNTRY DOCTOR

Copyright © 2004, 2007 by Ballybucklebo Stories Corp.

This book was previously published in 2004 under the title *The Apprenticeship of Doctor Laverty* by Insomniac Press, Toronto.

Excerpt from "Storm on the Island" from Poems 1965–1975, by Seamus Heaney. Copyright © 1980 by Seamus Heaney. Reprinted by permission of Farrar, Straus and Giroux, LLC.

Excerpt from "The Host of the Air" from *The Collected Poems of W. B. Yeats*, Macmillan New York, 1956. Reproduced here by kind permission of A P Watt, Ltd., on behalf of Michael B. Yeats.

Maps by Elizabeth Danforth

A Forge Book
Published by Tom Doherty Associates
120 Broadway
New York, NY 10271

www.tor-forge.com

Forge® is a registered trademark of Macmillan Publishing Group, LLC.

The Library of Congress has cataloged the hardcover edition as follows:

Names: Taylor, Patrick, 1941– author.
Title: An Irish country doctor / Patrick Taylor.
Description: First edition. | New York : Forge, 2007. | Series: Irish country books ; book 1 | "A Tom Doherty Associates book."
Identifiers: LCCN 2006033708 (print) | ISBN 9780765316233 (hardcover) | ISBN 9781429920629 (ebook)
Subjects: LCSH: Laverty, Barry (Fictitious character)—Fiction. | O'Reilly, Fingal Flahertie (Fictitious character)—Fiction. | Physicians—Fiction. | Country life—Northern Ireland—Fiction. | Northern Ireland—Fiction. | GSAFD: Pastoral fiction.
Classification: LCC PR9199.3.T36 (print) | DDC 813/.54—dc22
LC record available at https://lccn.loc.gov/2006033708

ISBN 978-1-250-86898-5 (trade paperback)

Our books may be purchased in bulk for promotional, educational, or business use. Please contact your local bookseller or the Macmillan Corporate and Premium Sales Department at 1-800-221-7945, extension 5442, or by email at MacmillanSpecialMarkets@macmillan.com.

Second Forge Paperback Edition: 2022

Printed in the United States of America

0 9 8 7 6 5 4 3 2 1

Praise for Patrick Taylor's Irish Country novels

"Wraps you in the sensations of a vanished time and place."

—Vancouver Sun

"The author laces his heartwarming moments with liberal doses of whiskey and colorful Ulster invectives."

—Chicago Sun-Times

"Taylor's Ireland is always a pleasure to visit."

—Shelf Awareness

"Hilarious and heartwarming."

—The Roanoke Times

"Heartwarming . . . The stories, shenanigans, and essential goodness of the doctors and townspeople continue to provide a welcome balm for their souls, and, in these tough times, for ours."

—Booklist on *An Irish Country Welcome*

"This book is written with compassion and hilarity about a community whose inhabitants are as wonderful and loony as any on earth. A grand read from a grand man."

—Malachy McCourt, *New York Times* bestselling author, on *An Irish Country Doctor*

"Deeply steeped in Irish country life and meticulous in detail, the story is the perfect companion for a comfy fire and a cup of tea. . . . A totally wonderful read!"

—Library Journal (starred review) on *An Irish Doctor in Peace and at War*

To Sarah and David, with love

ACKNOWLEDGMENTS

Doctor Fingal Flahertie O'Reilly made his first appearance ten years ago.

His gradual development was gently supervised by Simon Hally, editor of *Stitches*.

O'Reilly's growth to maturity has been nurtured by three re-markable people:

Carolyn Bateman, who edits, advises me about, and polishes all my manuscripts before submission.

Adrienne Weiss, editor at Insomniac Press of Toronto, which first published this book in 2004 under the title *The Apprenticeship of Doctor Laverty*.

Natalia Aponte of Tor/Forge Books, New York, who has had unswerving faith in the inhabitants of Ballybucklebo and has con-stantly encouraged me.

And since the acquisition by Forge I must also recognize, with enormous gratitude, Tom Doherty, Paul Stevens, Irene Gallo, Gregory Manchess, Patty Garcia, Alexis Saarela, Don Kalancha, Joe Maier, Susan Crawford, and Jessica and Rosie Buckman.

To you all, O'Reilly and I tender our unreserved thanks.

AUTHOR'S NOTE

Doctor Fingal Flahertie O'Reilly and the denizens of Ballybuck-lebo first appeared in 1995 in my monthly column in *Stitches: The Journal of Medical Humour*. It was suggested to me that these characters might form the foundation for a novel.

I had just finished *Pray for Us Sinners*, and hesitating to delve once more into the misery of the Ulster Troubles, I found the idea of something lighter to be appealing. *An Irish Country Doctor* began to take shape.

Like *Only Wounded* and *Pray for Us Sinners*, the book is set in the northeast corner of Ireland, but unlike its predecessors, which I strove to make historically accurate, this story has taken some liberties with geography and time.

The setting is a fictional village, the name of which came from my high-school French teacher who, enraged by my inability to conjugate irregular verbs, yelled, "Taylor, you're stupid enough to come from Ballybucklebo." Those of an etymological bent may wish to know what the name means. *Bally* (Irish, *baile*) is a townland—a mediaeval geographic term encompassing a small village and the surrounding farms, *Buachaill* means "boy," and *bó* is a cow. In *Bailebuchaillbó*, or Ballybucklebo—the townland of the boy's cow—time and place are as skewed as they are in Brigadoon.

Little Irish is spoken in the North, but I have been at pains to use the Ulster dialect. It is rich and colourful, but often incomprehensible to one not from that part of the world. For those who may have some difficulty, I have taken the liberty of appending a glossary (page 345).

My attention to the spoken idiom is as accurate as I can make it; however, the purist will note that in 1964, the Twelfth of July fell on a Sunday, not a Thursday, and Seamus Heaney's first book of poetry was not published until 1966. No salmon river called the Bucklebo flows through north County Down. The nearest is the Shimna River in the Mourne Mountains. But everything else is as accurate as extensive reading and memory permit.

The rural Ulster that I have portrayed has vanished. The farms and villages still look much as they did, but the simplicity of rural life has been banished by the Troubles and the all-pervasive influence of television. The automatic respect for their learning shown to those at the top of the village hierarchy—doctor, teacher, minister, and priest—is a thing of the past, but men like O'Reilly were common when I was a very junior doctor. And on that subject, may I please lay to rest a question I am frequently asked by readers of my column in *Stitches*? Barry Laverty and Patrick Taylor are *not* one and the same. Doctor F. F. O'Reilly is a figment of my troubled mind, despite the efforts of some of my expatriate Ulster friends to see in him a respected—if unorthodox—medical practitioner of the time. Lady Macbeth *does* owe her being to our demoniacally possessed cat, Minnie, and Arthur Guinness owes his to a black Labrador, now long gone but who had an insatiable thirst for Foster's lager. All the other characters are composites, drawn from my imagination and from my experiences as a rural GP.

PATRICK TAYLOR

N

North Channel

• portmuck

County
Antrim

• whitehead

carrickfergus •

newtownabbey •

Belfast lough

• Bangor

• Ballybucklebo

Belfast •

The Kinnegar

• newtownards

County
Down

Strangford lough

County Antrim
and North Down

danforthos

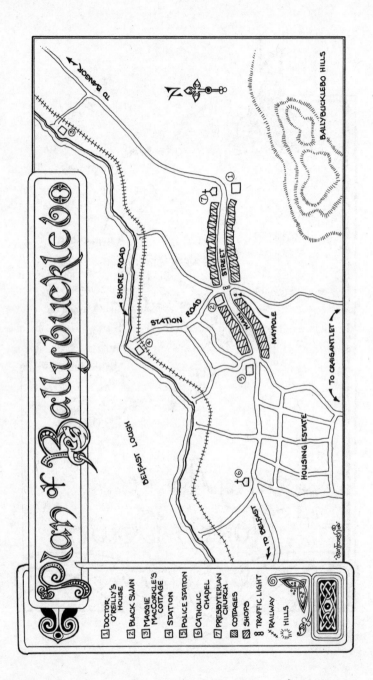

Plan of Ballybucklebo

TO BANGOR

N

BALLYBUCKLEBO HILLS

SHORE ROAD

STATION ROAD

STREET

MAIN

MAYPOLE

TO CRAIGANTLET

BELFAST LOUGH

HOUSING ESTATE

TO BELFAST

1 DOCTOR O'REILLY'S
   HOUSE
2 BLACK SWAN
3 MAGGIE
   MACCORKLE'S
   COTTAGE
4 STATION
5 POLICE STATION
6 CATHOLIC
   CHAPEL
7 PRESBYTERIAN
   CHURCH
   COTTAGES
9 SHOPS
8 TRAFFIC LIGHT
   RAILWAY
   HILLS

1

You Can't Get There from Here

Barry Laverty—*Doctor* Barry Laverty—his houseman's year just finished, ink barely dry on his degree, pulled his beat-up Volkswagen Beetle to the side of the road and peered at a map lying on the passenger seat. Six Road Ends was clearly marked. He stared through the car's insect-splattered windscreen. Judging by the maze of narrow country roads that ran one into the other just up ahead, somewhere at the end of one of those blackthorn-hedged byways lay the village of Ballybucklebo. But which road should he take? And, he reminded himself, there was more to that question than simple geography.

Most of his graduating classmates from the medical school of the Queen's University of Belfast had clear plans for their careers. But he hadn't a clue. General practice? Specialize? And if so, which speciality? Barry shrugged. He was twenty-four, single, no responsibilities. He knew he had all the time in the world to think about his medical future, but his immediate prospects might not be bright if he were late for his five o'clock appointment, and though finding a direction for his life might be important, his most pressing need was to earn enough to pay off the loan on the car.

He scowled at the map and retraced the road he had travelled from Belfast, but the Six Road Ends lay near the margin of the paper. No Ballybucklebo in sight. What to do?

He looked up, and as he did he glimpsed himself in the rearview mirror. Blue eyes looked back at him from a clean-shaven oval face. His tie was askew. No matter how carefully he tied the thing, the knot always managed to wander off under one collar tip. He understood the importance of first impressions and did not want to look scruffy. He tugged the tie back into place, then tried to smooth down the cowlick on the crown of his fair hair, but up it popped. He shrugged. It would just have to stay that way. He wasn't going to a beauty contest—it was his medical credentials that would be scrutinized. At least his hair was cut short, not like the style affected by that new musical group, the Beatles.

One last glance at the map confirmed that it would be of no help in finding his destination. Perhaps, he thought, there would be a signpost at the junction. He got out of the vehicle, and the springs creaked. Brunhilde, as he called his car, was protesting about the weight of his worldly goods: two suitcases, one with his meagre wardrobe, the other crammed with medical texts; a doctor's medical bag tucked under the bonnet; and a fly rod, creel, and hip waders lying in the backseat. Not much to show for someone possessing a medical degree, he thought, but with any luck his finances would soon take a turn for the better—if he could just find Bally-bucklebo.

He leant against the car door, conscious that his five-foot-eight, slightly built frame barely gave him enough height to peer over Brunhilde's domed roof, and even standing on tiptoe he could see no evidence of a signpost. Perhaps it was hidden behind the hedges.

He walked to the junction and looked around to find a grave deficiency of signposts. Maybe Ballybucklebo's like Brigadoon, he thought, and only appears every hundred years. I'd better start humming "How Are Things in Glocca Morra?" and hope to God one of the little people shows up to give me directions.

He walked back to the car in the warmth of the Ulster afternoon, breathing in the gorse's perfume from the little fields at either side of the road. He heard the liquid notes of a blackbird hiding in the fuchsia that grew wild in the hedgerow, the flowers drooping purple and scarlet in the summer air. Somewhere a cow lowed in basso counterpoint to the blackbird's treble.

Barry savoured the moment. He might be unclear about what his future held, but one thing was certain. Nothing could ever persuade him that there was anywhere, anywhere at all, he would choose to live other than here in Northern Ireland.

No map, no signpost, and no little people, he thought as he approached the car. I'll just have to pick a road and . . . He was pleasantly surprised to see a figure mounted on a bicycle crest the low hill and pedal sedately along the road.

"Excuse me." Barry stepped into the path of the oncoming cyclist. "Excuse me." The cyclist wobbled, braked, and stood, one foot on the ground and the other on a pedal. For a moment Barry wondered if his hopes of meeting a leprechaun had been fulfilled. "Good afternoon," he said.

He was addressing a gangly youth, innocent face half hidden under a Paddy hat, but not hidden well enough to disguise a set of buckteeth that Barry decided would be the envy of every hare in the Six Counties. He carried a pitchfork over one shoulder and wore a black worsted waistcoat over a collarless shirt. His tweed trousers were tied at the knees with leather thongs that the locals called "nicky tams."

"Grand day," he remarked.

"It is."

"Och, aye. Grand. Hay's coming along fine, so it is." The youth picked his nose.

"I wonder if you could help me?"

"Aye?" The cyclist lifted his hat and scratched his ginger hair. "Maybe."

"I'm looking for Ballybucklebo."

"Ballybucklebo?" His brow knitted, and the head scratching increased.

"Can you tell me how to get there?"

"Ballybucklebo?" He pursed his lips. "Boys-a-boys, thon's a grand wee place, so it is."

Barry tried not to let his growing exasperation show. "I'm sure it is, but I have to get there by five."

"Five? Today, like?"

"Mmm." Barry bit back the words "No. In the year 2000." He waited.

The youth fumbled in the fob pocket of his waistcoat, produced a pocketwatch, and consulted it, frowning and muttering to himself. He looked at Barry. "Five? You've no much time left."

"I know that. If you could just—"

"Ballybucklebo?"

"Please?"

"Och, aye." He pointed to the road that lay straight ahead. "Take that road."

"That one?"

"Aye. Follow your nose 'til you come to Willy John Mc-Coubrey's red barn."

"Red barn. Right."

"Now you *don't* turn there."

"Oh."

"Not at all. Keep right on. You'll see a black-and-white cow in a field—unless Willy John has her in the red barn for milking. Now go past her, and take the road to your right." As he spoke, the youth pointed to the left side of the road.

Barry felt a mite confused. "First *right* past the black-and-white cow?"

"That's her," he said, continuing to point to the left. "From there on, it's only a wee doddle. Mind you, sir . . ." He started to mount his rusty machine. Then he delivered the rest of the sentence with the solemnity of a priest giving the Benediction: ". . . if I'd been you, I wouldn't have tried to get to Ballybucklebo from here in the first place."

Barry looked sharply at his companion. The youth's face showed not the least suggestion that he had been anything other than serious.

"Thank you," said Barry, stifling his desire to laugh. "Thank you very much. Oh, and by the way, you wouldn't happen to know the doctor there?"

The youth's eyebrows shot upwards. His eyes widened, and he let go a long low whistle before he said, "Himself? Doctor O'Reilly? By God, I do, sir. In soul, I do." With that, he mounted and pedalled furiously away.

Barry climbed into Brunhilde and wondered why his advisor had suddenly taken flight at the mere mention of Doctor O'Reilly. Well, he thought, if Willy John's cow was in the right field, he'd soon find out. His appointment at five was with none other than Doctor Fingal Flahertie O'Reilly.

2

He Flies Through the Air
with the Greatest of Ease

Dr. F. F. O'Reilly, M. B., B.Ch., B.A.O.
Physician and Surgeon
Hours: Monday to Friday, 9 a.m. to noon.

Barry read the lines on a brass plate screwed to the wall beside the green-painted front door of a three-storey house. A glance at his watch told him that by the grace of Willy John McCoubrey's black-and-white cow, he had arrived with five minutes to spare. He tightened his grip on his brand-new, black leather bag, stepped back, and looked around.

On either side of the doorway, bow windows arced from grey, pebble-dashed walls. To his right, through the glass, the furniture of a dining room was clearly visible. So, Barry thought, like many country general practitioners, Doctor O'Reilly must run his practice from his home. And if the man's voice, raised and hectoring, that Barry could hear coming from behind the drawn curtains of the left-hand window was anything to go by, the doctor was in and at his work.

"You're an eejit, Seamus Galvin. A born-again, blethering, bejesusly bollocks of a buck eejit. What are you?"

Barry could not hear the reply. Somewhere inside, a door

banged against a wall. He took a step back and glanced over his shoulder at a gravel walkway leading from the front gate, rose-bushes flanking the path. He sensed movement and swung back to face a large man—huge in fact—standing, legs astraddle, in the open doorway. The ogre's bent nose was alabaster, the rest of his face puce, presumably, Barry thought, because it must be tiring carrying a smaller man by the collar of his jacket and the seat of his moleskin trousers. As the small man wriggled and made high-pitched squeaks, he waved his left foot, which Barry noticed was quite bare.

The large man swung the smaller one to and fro in ever-increasing excursions, then released his grip. Barry gaped as the lit-tle victim's upward flight and keening were both cut short by a rapid descent into the nearest rosebush.

"Buck eejit," the giant roared and hurled a shoe and a sock after the ejectee.

Barry flinched. He held his black bag in front of himself.

"The next time, Seamus Galvin, you dirty little bugger . . . The next time you come here after hours on my half day and want me to look at your sore ankle, wash your bloody feet! Do you hear me, Seamus Galvin?"

Barry turned away, ready to beat a retreat, but the path was blocked by the departing Galvin, clutching his footwear, hobbling toward the gate, and muttering, "Yes, Doctor O'Reilly sir. I will, Doctor O'Reilly sir."

Barry thought of the cyclist who had given the directions to Ballybucklebo and who had fled at the mere mention of Doctor O'Reilly. Good Lord, if what Barry had witnessed was an example of the man's bedside manner . . .

"And what the hell do *you* want, standing there, both legs the same length and a face on you like a Lurgan spade?"

Barry swung to face his interrogator.

"Doctor O'Reilly?"

"No. The archangel bloody Gabriel. Can you not read the plate?" He pointed at the wall.

"I'm Laverty."

"Laverty? Well, bugger off. I'm not buying any."

Barry was tempted to take the advice but he held his ground. "I'm Doctor Laverty. I answered your advertisement in the *British Medical Journal*. I was to have an interview about the assistant's position." I will not let this bully intimidate me, he thought.

"*That* Laverty. Jesus, man, why on earth didn't you say so?" O'Reilly offered a hand the size of a soup plate. His handshake would have done justice to one of those machines that reduce motorcars to the size of suitcases.

Barry felt his knuckles grind together, but he refused to flinch as he met Doctor O'Reilly's gaze. He was staring into a pair of deep-set brown eyes hidden under bushy eyebrows. He noted the deep laugh lines around the eyes and saw that the pallor had left O'Reilly's nose, a large bent proboscis with a definite list to port. It now had assumed the plum colour of its surrounding cheeks.

The pressure on Barry's hand eased.

"Come in, Laverty." O'Reilly stepped aside and waited for Barry to precede him into a thinly carpeted hall. "Door on your left."

Barry, still wondering about Galvin's ejection, went into the room with the drawn curtains. An open rolltop desk stood against one green wall. Piles of prescription pads, papers, and what looked like patients' records lay in splendid disarray on the desktop. Above, O'Reilly's framed diploma dangled from a rusty nail. Barry stole a quick peep. "Trinity College, Dublin, 1936." In front of the desk were a swivel chair and a plain wooden chair.

"Have a pew." O'Reilly lowered his bulk into the swivel seat.

Barry sat, settled his bag on his lap, and glanced round. An examining table and a set of folding screens jostled with an instrument cabinet against another wall. A dusty sphygmomanometer was fixed to the wall. Above the blood-pressure machine an eye-testing chart hung askew.

Doctor O'Reilly pushed a pair of half-moon spectacles onto his bent nose and peered at Barry. "So you want to be my assistant?"

Barry had thought so, but after the ejection of Seamus Galvin he wasn't so sure.

"Well, I—"

"Course you do," said O'Reilly, pulling a briar from his jacket pocket and holding a lighted match over the bowl. "Golden opportunity for a young man."

Barry noticed that he kept sliding forward on his seat. Try as he might, he had to brace his feet firmly on the carpet and keep shoving his backside upwards.

O'Reilly wagged his index finger. "Practising here in Ballybucklebo. Most satisfying thing in the world. You'll love it. Might even be a partnership in it for you. Course you'll have to do as I tell you for a while until you get to know the ropes."

Barry hitched himself back up his seat and made a quick decision. He might work here if he were offered the job, but he sensed—no, he *knew*—that if he didn't establish his independence immediately, Doctor O'Reilly would walk all over him.

"Does that mean I'll have to hurl patients into the rosebushes?"

"What?" A hint of pallor returned to the big man's nose. Was that a sign of temper? Barry wondered.

"I said, 'Does that mean—'"

"I heard you the first time, boy. Now listen, have you any experience with country patients?"

"Not ex—"

"Thought not," said O'Reilly, emitting a puff of tobacco smoke like the blast from the funnels of RMS *Queen Mary* when she blew her boilers. "You'll have a lot to learn."

Barry felt a cramp in his left calf. He shoved himself back up his seat. "I know, but I don't think a physician should chuck patients—"

"Rubbish," said O'Reilly, rising. "You saw me pitch Galvin into the roses. Lesson number one. Never, never, never"—with each "never" he poked at Barry with the stem of his pipe—"*never* let the customers get the upper hand. If you do, they'll run you ragged."

"Don't you think dumping a man bodily into your garden is a little—?"

"I used to . . . until I met Seamus Galvin. If you take the job and get to know that skiver as well as I do . . ." O'Reilly shook his head.

Barry stood and massaged the back of his leg. He was going to carry on the debate about Galvin, but O'Reilly began to laugh in great throaty rumbles.

"Leg stiff?"

"Yes. Something's wrong with this chair."

O'Reilly's chuckles grew deeper. "No, there's not. I fixed it."

"Fixed it?"

"Oh, aye. Some of the weary, walking wounded in Ballybuck-lebo seem to think when they get in here to see me it's my job to listen to their lamentations 'til the cows come home. A country general practitioner, a single-handed country GP, doesn't have that sort of time." He pushed his spectacles further up his nose. "That's why I advertised for an assistant. There's too much bloody work in this place." O'Reilly had stopped laughing. His brown-eyed gaze was fixed on Barry's eyes as he said softly, "Take the job, boy. I need the help."

Barry hesitated. Did he really want to work for this big, coarse man who sat there with a briar stuck in his wide mouth? Barry saw O'Reilly's florid cheeks, the cauliflower ears that must have been acquired in the boxing ring, and a shock of black hair like a badly stooked hayrick, and he decided to play for time. "What have you done to this chair?"

O'Reilly's face broke into a grin that Barry thought could only be described as demonic. "I fixed it. I sawed an inch off the front legs."

"You what?"

"I sawed an inch off the front legs. Not very comfortable, is it?"

"No," said Barry, pushing himself back up the seat.

"Don't want to stay long, do you?"

Barry thought, I'm not sure I want to stay here at all.

"Neither do the customers. They come in and go out like a fiddler's elbow."

How could a responsible physician ever take a proper history if his practice ran like a human conveyor belt? Barry asked himself. He rose. "I'm not sure I do want to work here. . . ."

O'Reilly's laugh boomed through the room. "Don't take yourself so seriously, son."

Barry felt the flush begin under his collar. "Doctor O'Reilly, I—"

"Laverty, there are some *really* sick people here who *do* need us, you know." O'Reilly was no longer laughing.

Barry heard the "us" and was surprised to find that it pleased him.

"I need help."

"Well, I—"

"Great," said O'Reilly, putting another match to his pipe, rising, and marching to the door. "Come on, you've seen the surgery. . . . Why our American cousins insist on calling it the office is beyond me. . . . I'll show you the rest of the shop."

"But I—"

"Leave your bag there. You'll need it tomorrow." With that, O'Reilly vanished into the hall, leaving Barry little choice but to park his bag and follow. Immediately opposite he could see into the dining room, but O'Reilly charged along the hall, past a staircase with an ornate mahogany balustrade. Then he stopped and flung a door wide open. Barry hurried to catch up.

"Waiting room."

Barry saw a large room, wallpapered with god-awful roses. More wooden chairs were arranged around the walls. A single table in the centre of the room was covered with old magazines.

O'Reilly pointed to a door in the far wall. "Patients let themselves in here; we come down from the surgery, take whoever's next back with us, deal with them, and show them out the front door."

"On their feet, I hope." Barry watched O'Reilly's nose. No pallor.

The big man chuckled. "You're no dozer, are you, Laverty?"

Barry kept his counsel as O'Reilly continued. "It's a good system . . . stops the buggers swapping symptoms, or demanding the same medicine as the last customer. Right . . ." He swung round and headed for the staircase. "Come on."

Barry followed, up a flight of stairs to a broad landing. Framed photographs of a warship hung on the walls.

"Sitting room's in there." O'Reilly indicated a pair of panelled doors.

Barry nodded but looked more closely at the battleship. "Excuse me, Doctor O'Reilly, is that HMS *Warspite*?"

O'Reilly's foot paused on the first step of the next flight.

"How'd you know that?"

"My dad served in her."

"Holy thundering Mother of Jesus. Laverty? Are you . . . are you Tom Laverty's boy?"

"Yes."

"I'll be damned."

So, thought Barry, will I. His father, who rarely talked about his wartime experiences, had from time to time alluded to a certain Surgeon Commander O'Reilly who had been welterweight boxing champion of the Mediterranean Fleet—that would account for O'Reilly's cauliflower ears and bent nose. In his dad's opinion, O'Reilly had been the finest medical officer afloat. This man?

"I'll be damned. Laverty's boy." O'Reilly held out his hand. His handshake was firm, not crushing. "You're the man for the job. Thirty-five pounds a week, every other Saturday off, room and board all in."

"Thirty-five pounds?"

"I'll show you your room."

"What'll it be?" O'Reilly stood at a sideboard that bore cut-glass decanters and ranks of glasses.

"Small sherry, please." Barry sat in a big armchair. O'Reilly's upstairs sitting room was comfortably furnished. Three Milliken watercolours of game birds adorned the wall over a wide fireplace. Two walls were hidden by floor-to-ceiling bookcases. From Barry's quick appraisal of the titles—from Plato's *Republic*, Caesar's *De Bello Gallica*, *Winnie-the-Pooh* and its Latin translation *Winnie Ille Pu*, to the collected works of W. Somerset Maugham, Graham Greene, John Steinbeck, Ernest Hemingway, and Leslie Charteris's *The Saint* books—O'Reilly's reading tastes were wide ranging.

His record collection, stacked haphazardly beside a Philips Black Box gramophone, was equally eclectic. Beethoven's symphonies on 33⅓ rpm LPs were jumbled in with old 78s by Bix Beiderbecke and Jelly Roll Morton, along with the Beatles' most recent LP.

"Here you are." O'Reilly handed Barry a glass, sat heavily in another armchair, and propped his stoutly booted feet on a coffee table. Then he lifted his own glass, which Barry thought could have done service as a fire bucket if it hadn't been filled to the brim with Irish whiskey. "I don't go much for sherry myself," O'Reilly announced, "but each to his own."

"I'd have thought it was a bit early for whiskey."

"Early?" said O'Reilly, taking a gulp. "It's never too early for a decent drop."

My God, Barry thought, looking more closely at O'Reilly's ruddy cheeks; don't tell me he's a raging drouth.

O'Reilly, clearly oblivious to Barry's scrutiny, nodded to the picture window. "Would you look at that?"

Barry looked past the moss-grown, lopsided steeple of a church across the road from O'Reilly's house, down over the rooftops of the terrace cottages of Ballybucklebo's main street, and out over the sand dunes of the foreshore to where Belfast Lough, cobalt and white-capped, separated County Down from the distant Antrim Hills, hazy against a sky as blue as cornflowers.

"Jesus," said O'Reilly, "you couldn't beat that with both sticks of a Lambeg drum."

"It's lovely, Doctor O'Reilly."

"Fingal, my boy. Fingal. For Oscar." O'Reilly's smile was avuncular.

"Oscar, er, Fingal?"

"No. Not Oscar Fingal. Wilde."

"Oscar Fingal Wilde, Fingal?" Barry knew he was getting lost. He saw a hint of pallor developing on O'Reilly's nose.

"Oscar . . . Fingal . . . O'Flahertie . . . Wills . . . Wilde."

Barry stifled the impulse to remark that if you put an air to that you could sing it.

"You look confused, son."

Confused, baffled, bewildered, utterly at sea.

The pallor faded. "I was named for him. For Oscar Wilde."

"Oh."

"Aye," said O'Reilly. "My father was a classical scholar, and if you think I got a mouthful, you should meet my brother, Lars Porsena O'Reilly."

"Good Lord. Macaulay?"

"The very fellah. *Lays of Ancient Rome*." O'Reilly took a deep drink. "Us country GPs aren't all utterly unlettered."

Barry felt a blush start. His first impressions of the big man sitting opposite might not have been entirely accurate. Lowering his head, he sipped his sherry.

"So, Laverty," O'Reilly said, clearly ignoring Barry's discomfort. "What's it to be? Do you want the job?"

Before Barry could answer, a bell jangled from somewhere below.

"Bugger," said O'Reilly, "another customer. Come on." He rose. Barry followed.

O'Reilly opened the front door. Seamus Galvin stood on the doorstep. In each hand he carried a live lobster. "Good evening, Doctor sir," he said, thrusting the beasts at O'Reilly. "I've washed me foot, so I have."

Barry thought of a grubby Eliza Doolittle saying to Professor Higgins, "I washed me 'ands and face before I come."

"Have you, by God?" said O'Reilly sternly, passing the squirming creatures to Barry. "Come in and I'll take a look at your hind leg."

"Thank you, Doctor sir, thank you very much." Galvin hesitated. "And who's this young gentleman?" he asked.

Barry was so busy avoiding the crustaceans' clattering claws he nearly missed O'Reilly's reply. "This is Doctor Laverty. He's my new assistant. I'll be showing him the ropes tomorrow."

Morning Has Broken

Barry woke to the jangling of his alarm clock. His attic room had just enough space for a bed, a night table, and a wardrobe. Last night he'd unpacked, put his few clothes away, and propped his fishing rod in one corner near a dormer window.

He rose, drew back the curtains, and looked out over what must be O'Reilly's back garden. Then he picked up his toilet kit from the bedside table and headed for the bathroom. As he shaved, he thought about the events of last night. O'Reilly had strapped Seamus Galvin's ankle, put the lobsters in the kitchen sink, taken Barry back up to the sitting room, and poured more drinks. He'd explained that for the first month they'd work together so Barry could get to know the patients, the running of the practice, and the geography of Ballybucklebo and the surrounding countryside.

Somehow the evening had slipped by, and despite O'Reilly's steady intake of Old Bushmills Irish whiskey the man might as well have been drinking water. He had given no sign of any ill effects. After two sherries Barry had noticed a certain laxity in his knees and a gentle cotton-woolly feeling in his head, and he had been grateful to be shown to his quarters on the third floor and wished a very good night.

He rinsed his razor and looked in the mirror. Just a tad of red in the whites of his eyes. Had the sherry affected his judgement so much? Certainly he had no recollection of actually agreeing to take the job, but it seemed that once O'Reilly made up his mind, lesser mortals had no choice but to go along. Well, in for a penny. . . . He dried his face, went back to his garret, and dressed. Best pants, best shoes, clean shirt . . .

"Move yourself, Laverty. We haven't got all day," O'Reilly roared up the stairwell.

Barry ignored the command. This was a medical practice, not the navy, and the sooner Doctor Fingal Flahertie O'Reilly, lately surgeon commander, recognized that Barry was not there to be ordered about like some able-bodied seaman, the better. He knotted his Queen's University tie, slipped on a sports jacket, and headed for the stairs.

"Eat up however little much is in it, Doctor Laverty dear."

Barry looked up from his plate of Ulster mixed grill—bacon, sausages, black pudding, fried eggs, tomatoes, lamb chop, and slices of fried soda bread—into the happy face of Mrs. Kincaid. He saw silver hair done up in a chignon, black eyes like polished jets set between roseate cheeks. A mouth smiled above her three chins.

"I'll do my best."

"Good lad. You'll be having this for breakfast a lot," she said, setting a plate in front of O'Reilly. "Himself here is a grand man for the pan, so."

Barry heard the soft Cork lilt of her voice, with the habit Cork folk had of adding "so" at the end of a sentence.

"Go on with you, Kinky." O'Reilly lifted his knife and fork and dug in with obvious gusto.

Mrs. Kincaid left.

O'Reilly muttered something through a mouthful of black pudding.

"I beg your pardon?"

O'Reilly swallowed. "I forgot to warn you about Kinky. She's a powerful woman. Been with me for years."

"Oh?"

"Housekeeper, cook, and Cerberus."

"She guards the gates of Hades?"

"Like the three-headed dog himself. The customers have to get up very early in the morning to put one past Kinky. You'll see. Now get stuck into your grub. We've to be in the surgery in fifteen minutes."

Barry ate.

Mrs. Kincaid reappeared. "Tea, Doctor?"

"Thank you."

She poured from a Belleek teapot and nimbly moved her fourteen stone to where O'Reilly sat mopping up the last of an egg with a slice of fried bread. She poured his tea and gave him a sheet of paper.

"That's your afternoon calls for today, Doctor," she said. "Maggie wanted you to drop round, but I told her to come into the surgery."

"Maggie MacCorkle?" O'Reilly sighed and dabbed at an egg stain on his tie. "All right. Thanks, Kinky."

"Better she comes here than you drive ten miles to her cottage." Mrs. Kincaid cocked her head and studied the mess on O'Reilly's tie. "And take off the grubby thing, and I'll wash it for you, so."

To Barry's surprise, O'Reilly meekly undid the knot and handed the tie to Mrs. Kincaid, who sniffed, turned, and left, remarking, "And don't forget to put on a clean one."

O'Reilly finished his tea, rose, and said, "I'll be back in five minutes; then it's into the salt mines for the pair of us."

"Jesus," whispered O'Reilly, "would you take a look? You'd need five loaves and two small fishes to feed that bloody multitude."

Barry, who had no doubt that O'Reilly would be perfectly happy to cast himself in the role of the Deity, craned round the big man and stared through the gap where O'Reilly held ajar the door to the waiting room. It was standing room only. How on earth was O'Reilly going to see so many patients before noon?

O'Reilly opened the door wide.

"Morning."

A chorus of "Morning, Doctor O'Reilly" echoed from the waiting room.

"I want you all to meet Doctor Laverty," he said, propelling Barry forward. "My new assistant."

Barry smiled weakly at the mass of enquiring faces.

"Doctor Laverty has come down from the Queen's University to give me a hand."

A voice muttered, "He looks awful young, so he does."

"He is, James Guiggan. The youngest doctor ever to take the first prize for learning at the university."

Barry tried to protest that he was no such thing, but his mumbled denial was drowned by a chorus of oohs and ahs. He felt O'Reilly's hand grip his forearm and heard him whisper, "Remember lesson number one."

Never let the customers get the upper hand echoed in Barry's head as O'Reilly said, "Right. How many's here for tonics?"

Several people rose.

O'Reilly counted. ". . . Five, six. I'll take you lot first. Hang on a minute." O'Reilly turned and headed for the surgery. Barry followed.

He watched as O'Reilly produced six hypodermics, filled them with a pink fluid from a rubber-topped bottle, and laid them in a row on a towel on top of a small wheeled trolley.

"What's that, Doctor O'Reilly?"

O'Reilly grinned. "Vitamin B_{12}."

"B_{12}? But that's not—"

"Jesus, man, *I* know it's not a tonic . . . there's no such thing. *You* know it's not a tonic, but . . ."—his grin widened—"*they* don't know it's not a tonic. Now, go get 'em."

"All of them?"

"Every last one."

Barry headed for the waiting room. Heavens, this was hardly the kind of medicine he'd been taught. He avoided the stares that greeted him and said, "Would all those for tonics please follow me?"

The six victims did so meekly, silently.

His little procession trooped into the surgery where O'Reilly waited by the trolley.

"Along the couch."

Three men and three women dutifully faced the examination couch.

"Bend over."

Three trousered and three calico-dressed backsides were presented.

Barry watched, mouth agape, as O'Reilly moved his trolley to the start of the line. He stopped and grabbed a syringe in one hand, a methylated spirits–reeking cotton-wool ball in the other. He dabbed the calico over the first derrière with a ball. "Listerian antisepsis," he intoned, as he jabbed the needle home.

"Ouch," yelped a skinny woman. The process was rapidly repeated down the line—dab, jab, "Ouch"—dab, jab, "Ouch"—until O'Reilly stood before his final victim, a woman of massive proportions. He dabbed and stabbed. The hypodermic flew across the room as if propelled by a giant catapult and stuck in the wall, quivering like a well-thrown dart.

O'Reilly shook his head, filled another syringe, and said, "Jesus, Cissie, how many times have I to tell you, don't wear your stays on tonic day?"

"Sorry, Doctor, I forgo . . . ouch!"

"Right," said O'Reilly. "Off you go. You'll all be running around like spring chickens when that stuff starts to work."

"Thank you, Doctor sir," said six voices in unison. The patients filed out and left by the front door.

O'Reilly retrieved the syringe-dart, laid it with the others, turned to Barry, and said, "Don't look so bloody disapproving, boy. It'll do them no harm, and half of them will feel better. I know it's only a placebo, but we're here to make folks feel better."

"Yes, Doctor O'Reilly." There was some truth to what the older man said, and yet . . . Barry shrugged. For the moment he would keep his counsel.

"Now," said O'Reilly, planting himself in the swivel chair and putting on his half-moon spectacles, "be a good lad, nip along, and yell, 'Next.' "

Barry spent the morning acting as a runner between the waiting room and the surgery, and sitting on the examining couch watching and listening as O'Reilly dealt with a procession of men with sore backs, women and their runny-nosed children, coughs, sniffles, and earaches—the myriad minor ailments to which the human race is heir. Occasionally, O'Reilly would seek Barry's opinion, always, at least in front of the patients, treating the advice with great solemnity.

Barry noticed that O'Reilly knew every patient by name, rarely consulted a medical record, yet had an encyclopaedic knowledge of every supplicant's medical history.

At last. The waiting room was empty.

O'Reilly sprawled in his chair, and Barry returned to what now was his familiar place on the couch.

"So," asked O'Reilly, "what do you think?"

"Not much about you injecting people through their clothes,

and I won no prizes at university." Barry glanced at O'Reilly's nose tip. No paleness.

O'Reilly produced his briar and lit it. "You've a lot to learn, Laverty." He stood up and stretched. "Country folk are a pretty conservative lot. You're a young lad. Why should they trust you?"

Barry stiffened. "Because I'm a doctor."

O'Reilly guffawed. "You'll find out. It's not what you call yourself, *Doctor* Laverty; it's what you do that counts here. All I did was give you a head start."

"I suppose that's what you were doing every time you asked for my advice?"

O'Reilly looked over his half-moons at Barry and said nothing.

Someone knocked on the door.

"See who that is, will you?"

Barry walked stiffly to the door. Head start, he thought. As if he wasn't fully qualified. He opened the door to a woman in her sixties. Her face was as weathered as a piece of dried dulse. Her upper lip sported a fine brown moustache. Her nose curved down, her chin curved up like that of Punch in a Punch-and-Judy show, and when she smiled he could see that she was as toothless as an oyster. Her ebony eyes twinkled.

She wore a straw hat with two wilted geraniums stuck in the hatband. Her torso was hidden under layers of different coloured woollen cardigans, and under the hem of her rusty ankle-length skirt peeped the toes of a pair of Wellington boots.

"Is himself in?"

Barry felt a presence at his shoulder.

"Maggie," he heard O'Reilly say. "Maggie MacCorkle. Come in."

Barry remembered Mrs. Kincaid mentioning the name at breakfast. The new arrival pushed past him. O'Reilly ushered her to the patients' chair and went and sat on the examining couch.

"This is my assistant, Doctor Laverty. I'd like him to see to you today, Maggie. Nothing like a second opinion."

Barry stared at O'Reilly, nodded, and strode to the swivel chair. "Good morning, Mrs. MacCorkle."

She sniffed and smoothed her skirt. "It's *Miss* MacCorkle, so it is."

Barry glanced to where O'Reilly sat, arms folded. Expressionless.

"Sorry. Miss MacCorkle. And what seems to be the trouble?"

It was her turn to glance at O'Reilly before she said, "The headaches."

"I see. When did they start?"

"Lord Jesus, they've always been acute, but last night they got something chronic, so they did. They were desperate." She leant forward and said with great solemnity, "I near took the rickets."

He stifled a smile. "I see. And where exactly are they?" Barry followed the classical history-taking protocol like a minor bureaucrat hewing to his rulebook.

She whispered conspiratorially, "There." She held one hand above the crown of her flowery hat.

Barry jerked back in his chair. No wonder O'Reilly had sighed when Mrs. Kincaid announced that Maggie was coming. He wondered where O'Reilly kept the necessary forms for certifying that someone was insane.

"Above your head?"

"Oh, aye. A good two inches."

"I see." He steepled his fingers. "And have you been hearing voices lately?"

She stiffened. "What do you mean?"

"Well, I . . ." He looked helplessly at O'Reilly, who slipped down off the couch.

"What Doctor Laverty means is, do you have any ringing in your ears, Maggie?"

"Ding-dong or brrring?" Maggie asked, hitching herself up in the uneven chair and turning to O'Reilly.

"You tell me," he said.

"Ding-dong, Doctor dear."

O'Reilly smiled at her over his half-moon spectacles.

Clearly encouraged, she continued. "Ding-dong it is. Dingy-dingy-dong."

An apt description of the woman herself, Barry thought.

"Mmm," said O'Reilly, looking wise. "Mmm. Ding-dong and two inches above. Now are the pains in the middle or off to one side?"

"Over to the left, so they are."

"That's what we call 'eccentric,' Maggie."

That's what I'd call the pair of you, thought Barry.

"Eccentric? Boys-a-dear. Is that bad, Doctor?"

"Not at all," said O'Reilly, laying a comforting hand on her shoulder. "Fix you up in no time."

Her shoulders relaxed. She smiled up at her medical advisor, but when she turned to Barry, her stare was as icy as the wind that sweeps the lough in the winter.

O'Reilly leant past Barry and grabbed a plastic bottle of vitamin tablets from the desk. "These'll do the trick."

Maggie rose and accepted the bottle.

O'Reilly gently propelled her towards the door. "These are special, Maggie."

She nodded.

"You have to take them exactly as I tell you."

"Yes, Doctor sir. And how would that be?"

O'Reilly held the door for her.

"Half an hour." His next words were delivered with weighted solemnity: "Exactly half an hour before the pain starts."

"Oh, thank you, Doctor dear." Her smile was radiant. She made a little curtsey, turned, and faced Barry, but she spoke to O'Reilly. Her departing words stung like the jab of a wasp. "Mind you," she said, "this young Laverty fellow . . . he's a lot to learn."

4

In a Pig's Ear

Barry sat back in his dining-room chair and pushed his lunch plate away. Certainly, he thought, O'Reilly's clinical methods might leave something to be desired, but, he burped gently, he was willing to forgive the man's eccentricities as long as Mrs. Kincaid's cooking stayed at its current level.

"Home visits," said O'Reilly from across the table. He consulted a piece of paper. "Anyone who's too sick to come to the surgery phones Kinky in the morning, and she gives me my list."

"The one she gave you at breakfast?"

"Aye, and she tells me to add any who call during the morning." O'Reilly folded the paper and stuck it into the side pocket of his tweed jacket. "We're lucky today—just one. At the Kennedys'." He rose. "Let's get moving. There's a rugby game tonight on the telly. I want to get back in time for the kickoff."

Barry followed down the hall and into the kitchen where Mrs. Kincaid, up to her elbows in a sink full of soapy water, greeted them with a smile and said, "Would you like them lobsters for supper, Doctor dear?"

"That would be grand, Kinky."

Barry savoured the prospect.

O'Reilly's forward progress stopped. "Kinky, is tonight your Women's Union night?"

"Aye, so."

"We'll have the lobsters cold. Leave them with a bit of salad and get you away early."

He charged on, ignoring Mrs. Kincaid's thanks, opened the back door, and ushered Barry through.

He found himself in a spacious, fenced garden, the one he'd seen from his bedroom window. Vegetables grew in a plot by the left-hand hedge. Some apple trees, heavy with early apples, were bowed over a well-kept lawn—he recognized a Cox's Orange Pippin and a Golden Delicious. A tall chestnut tree at the far end drooped branches over a fence and shaded a dog kennel.

"Arthur!" yelled O'Reilly. "Arthur Guinness!"

A vast black Labrador hurled himself from the kennel, charged over the grass, and, tail wagging so hard that his backside swung ninety degrees, leapt at O'Reilly.

"Who's a good boy then?" O'Reilly said, thumping the dog's flank. "I call him Arthur Guinness because he's Irish, black, and has a great head on him . . . just like the stout."

"Aryouff," said Arthur.

"Arthur Guinness, meet Doctor Laverty."

"Arf," said Arthur, immediately transferring his affections to Barry, who fought desperately to push the animal away. "Ararf."

"Arthur Guinness is the best bloody gundog in Ulster."

"You shoot, Doctor O'Reilly?"

"Fingal, my boy, Fingal. Yes. Arthur and I enjoy a day at the ducks, don't we, Arthur?"

"Yarf," said Arthur, as he wound his front paws round Barry's leg and started to hump like a demented pile driver. Keep that up, dog, Barry thought, as he tried and failed to hold the besotted beast at bay. Keep that up, and your next litter will be Labrador-corduroy crossbreeds. "Down, Arthur." He might as well have kept his mouth shut as the animal redoubled his efforts.

"Get on with you, sir," said O'Reilly, pointing to the kennel. "Go home."

Arthur Guinness gave one last thrust, disengaged himself, and wandered off in the general direction of his abode.

"Affectionate animal," said Barry, as he unsuccessfully tried to brush the mud from the leg of his best trousers.

"If he likes you," said O'Reilly, as he walked on, "and he obviously does."

"I'd never have guessed." Barry made a mental note to avoid the back garden.

"Garage is out here," said O'Reilly, opening the back gate. He crossed a lane to a dilapidated shed and swung an overhead door upwards. Barry peered inside and saw a black, long-bonnet Rover, one of a line of cars that had not been produced for at least fifteen years.

O'Reilly climbed in and started the engine. It grumbled, spluttered, and backfired. Barry hopped into the passenger seat. O'Reilly put the car in gear and nosed out into the lane. Barry gagged. The car stank of damp dog and tobacco smoke. He wound down a window.

O'Reilly turned left onto the street and drove past his house, past the church with the lopsided steeple, and on along Ballybucklebo's main thoroughfare. Barry looked around. Terraces of whitewashed, single-storey cottages, some thatched and some with slate roofs, lined the route. They came to a crossroads and halted at a red traffic light. A large maypole, paint peeling, leaning to the left, stood like a huge barber's pole on the far corner.

"It's fun here on *Beltane*—that's the old Celtic May Day," said O'Reilly, pointing to the pole. "Bonfires, dancing, the pursuit of young virgins . . . if there's still one or two around. The locals aren't far removed from their pagan ancestors when there's the chance of a good party." He revved the engine and gestured at the road to the right. "Go down there, and you'll end up at the seashore; left takes you up into the Ballybucklebo Hills."

Barry nodded.

The light changed to amber. O'Reilly slipped the clutch and roared ahead. "Amber," he remarked, "is only for the tourists." He paid no attention to a tractor that had been coming in the other direction and now stood with its trailer slewed across the intersection. "Got to get home in time for the game." He gestured vaguely around. "The throbbing heart of Ballybucklebo," he said.

Two-storey buildings now. Greengrocer, butcher, newsagent, and a larger building, outside of which hung a sign: The Black Swan. Barry noticed a familiar figure, left ankle bandaged, limping towards the front door.

"Galvin," said O'Reilly. "Jesus, that one'd drain the lough if it was Guinness."

Barry turned to watch as Galvin pushed his way into The Black Swan.

"Never mind him," said O'Reilly, shifting up with a grinding of gears. "I'm meant to be showing you the way around. Now. You can take this road we're on to Belfast, or if you take a look to starboard . . . see? You can always take the train."

Barry glanced to his right to see a diesel train moving slowly along a raised embankment. Interesting, he thought. He might just do that on his day off. It would be cheaper than driving up, and he'd like to visit one of his friends from medical school because—

He was hurled forward as O'Reilly braked. "Bloody cow!" O'Reilly growled.

Barry saw a single black-and-white bovine, eyes soft, reflecting the utter vacuity behind, ambling along the centre of the road, chewing its cud with delicate deliberation.

O'Reilly wound down his window. "Hoosh on, cow. Hoosh. Hoosh."

The animal lowered its head, emitted a single doleful moo, and budged not one inch.

Barry sat back and watched O'Reilly to see just when the man's already demonstrated short fuse would burn down. O'Reilly dismounted, slammed the door, and walked to face the cow. "Look, cow, I'm in a hurry."

"Moo," replied the cow.

"Right," said O'Reilly. He took a horn in one hand and pulled. To Barry's amazement the beast took two paces forward, clearly unable to withstand the force being applied to its head. "Move your bloody self," O'Reilly roared.

The cow flicked its ears, lowered its head, and skittered to the side of the road. O'Reilly climbed into the car, slammed it into gear, and took off with a screeching of rubber on tarmac. "Jesus Murphy," he said. "Animals. They're one of the delights of country practice. You just have to get used to dealing with them."

"All right," said Barry. "Fine." He was quite unaware of how soon Doctor O'Reilly's words would be shown to be true.

O'Reilly grunted and then ground the gears. Barry listened to the grumbling of the engine as the rear tires whined and spun—and spun.

"Bugger it," said O'Reilly. "We'll have to walk." He leant over, reached into the back seat, and grabbed his black bag and a pair of Wellington boots. "Out."

Barry stepped out—and sank to his ankles in a sheugh. He hauled each foot loose from the mud and squelched to the lane's grassy verge. Blast! His shoes and best pants, already stained from the attentions of Arthur Guinness, were filthy. Barry wondered how much it would cost to have them dry-cleaned.

He turned and stared at a farmhouse at the end of the rutted lane. "Is that where we're going, Fingal?"

"Aye, that's the Kennedys' place."

"Is there some other way to get there? My shoes . . ."

"Always bring wellies." O'Reilly pointed to his own footwear. "Don't worry about your shoes."

"But these shoes cost—"

"Christ Almighty! All right, we'll cut through the fields." Barry noticed just a hint of pallor in the tip of O'Reilly's nose. "Get a move on. The match starts in half an hour." O'Reilly hefted his bag, pushed open a rusting five-bar gate in the blackthorn hedge, and strode off. "Close the bloody gate after you," O'Reilly yelled over his shoulder.

Barry struggled to haul the gate shut, scratching his hand on the wire loop that had to be used to secure the gate to the gatepost. He sucked his bleeding hand and stared at the ruin of his shoes—his only pair of good shoes. He heard O'Reilly yelling, "Is it today you were coming?"

"Bugger off," Barry muttered, as he walked to where O'Reilly stood. The grass in the pasture was knee-deep, lush, feathered with seeds. And damp, very damp. As Barry walked purposefully ahead, he knew that the grass seeds would cling to his pant legs, and already he could feel his shins growing moist. Oh, well, he thought, at least the dew would wash off some of the mud.

"What kept you?"

"Doctor O'Reilly," Barry began, refusing to be intimidated, "I came as fast as I could—"

"Huh."

"And my shoes and pants are ruined."

"What," asked O'Reilly, "do you know about pigs?"

"I fail to see what pigs have to do with my clothes."

"Suit yourself, but there's one coming." O'Reilly started to walk rapidly.

Barry hesitated. Coming towards them was a pink something

with the dimensions of a small hippopotamus. It had the same rolling gait as the African animal, but as Barry reckoned such beasts were rare round Ballybucklebo, the creature in question must be a pig, and its eyes—he could see them now that it was appreciably closer—were red and distinctly malevolent. Barry set off at a canter in pursuit of O'Reilly and caught up with him halfway between the gate and the end of the field.

"It *is* a pig."

"Brilliant," said O'Reilly, lengthening his stride. "I've read somewhere that domesticated boars can turn ugly."

"Ugly?"

"Right." O'Reilly was breathing heavily. "Bloody big teeth." O'Reilly's gait moved up to a fully developed trot and opened a fair gap between Barry and himself.

Barry, quite aware that glancing back had cost several Olympic hopefuls a gold medal, nevertheless risked a backward glance. The beast was gaining, and if it had intentions of using its "bloody big teeth," it was reasonable to assume that the victim would be the first one it hunted down. He began to sprint. Ten yards from the far hedge, Barry passed a flagging O'Reilly. The extra helping of Mrs Kincaid's steak-and-kidney pudding must be slowing O'Reilly down, Barry thought, as he himself cleared a low gate.

He almost collided with a small grinning man in a flat cap, who stood in the farmyard. Before Barry could begin to explain, the quiet of the afternoon was shattered by sounds of crashing and rending, and he saw O'Reilly break through the blackthorn like an American tank smashing through the hedges in the *bocage* country of Normandy.

O'Reilly came to a halt, examined the rents in his tweed suit, and tried to control his laboured breathing. Then he marched over to the cloth-capped stranger who, Barry noticed, had a ferocious squint but was laughing heartily.

Although O'Reilly's cheeks were scarlet, despite his recent exertions his nose tip was alabaster.

"Dermot Kennedy," he bellowed, "what's so bloody funny?"

There was no answer. Mr. Kennedy was doubled over, holding his tummy and gasping between hiccups of laughter, "Boys-a-dear, thon was a quare sight to see."

"Dermot Kennedy." O'Reilly drew himself up to his full six-foot-two. "You're a menace to civilized people. What in God's name are you doing keeping a man-eating boar in an open field?"

Mr. Kennedy straightened, took a hanky from the pocket of his trousers, and wiped his eyes.

"I'm waiting for an explanation," O'Reilly roared.

Mr. Kennedy stuffed the hanky back. "Thon's no boar, Doctor dear. Thon's Gertrude, Jeannie's pet sow. She only just wanted her snout scratched."

"Oh," said O'Reilly.

"Right," said Barry, still smarting for being yelled at for being tardy. "Animals are, I believe—and please correct me if I'm misquoting you, Doctor O'Reilly—'one of the delights of country practice. You just have to get used to dealing with them.'"

"You can do that if you like, Doctor sir," said Mr. Kennedy, his laughter quite gone, "but it's really the farmer's job. Doctors keep an eye to the sick and"—he hesitated and glanced down at his boots—"I'm powerful sorry for dragging you out here, so I am, but I'm sore worried about our Jeannie. Would you come in and take a wee look at her, sir?"

5

More Haste, Less Speed

Barry followed Mr. Kennedy and Doctor O'Reilly to the farm-house, a single-storey building, whitewashed and thatched with straw that, judging by the patches of moss, had not been replaced for many years. Smoke drifted upwards from a chimney. Barry could smell the tang of burning peat. Black shutters flanked every window.

He heard O'Reilly ask, "How's the barley coming on this year, Dermot?" and Mr. Kennedy replying, "A treat, Doctor . . . and I still have the contract with the whiskey distillery at Bushmills." That, Barry thought, should make O'Reilly happy.

An open-fronted barn built of grey concrete blocks stood at the far side of the yard, bales of hay stacked against one wall and a Massey-Harris tractor parked under the corrugated-iron roof. Cows peered at Barry from their stalls. Chickens and an arrogant rooster pecked in the straw-strewn mud of the yard. A Border collie peered out of its kennel near the front door.

Barry heard Mr. Kennedy say, "Go on in, Doctors." Barry glanced at his muddy shoes.

"There's a boot scraper there, sir." Mr. Kennedy pointed to the scraper beside the door.

Barry cleaned as much muck off as he could and went in. He

found himself in a bright kitchen. A black-enamelled cast-iron range hunkered against the far wall. A wisp of steam from a kettle drifted up to the varnished ceiling beams. The floor was tiled.

"The doctors is here, dear," Mr. Kennedy called.

A woman stood, pouring tea into a cup patterned with daffodils. By the wrinkles in her neck and the slight twisting of the joints of two fingers in her right hand, Barry took her to be in her early fifties. "Thanks for coming, Doctor O'Reilly."

O'Reilly parked himself at a solid-looking pine table. "It's no trouble. This is my new assistant, Doctor Laverty."

Mrs. Kennedy bobbed her head to Barry.

She wore an apron. Her grey-flecked dark hair was untidy, and although she smiled at him, her smile was only on her lips. Her eyes, dark circles beneath, gave away her forced humour.

"Would you like a cup of tea, Doctor?"

"Please."

"Sit down," she said. "I'll fetch another cup." She moved to a Welsh dresser where blue plates stood in racks and a jam jar filled with scarlet and yellow nasturtiums held pride of place in the centre of the lowest shelf.

Barry pulled out a chair and sat beside O'Reilly. He thanked the woman when she gave him a cup of tea, dark and stewed.

"What do you take?"

"Just milk, please."

She handed him a jug.

"And you say Jeannie's been off-colour since yesterday?" O'Reilly's tone, for the first time in Barry's short acquaintance with the man, had none of its usual brusqueness.

"Aye, Doctor. She'll no' eat nothing. Says her wee tummy hurts."

"Has she boked?"

Barry smiled at O'Reilly's use of the country vernacular for "vomited."

"Just the once. All over the sheets. Jeannie was all embarrassed, so she was. Me and Bridget's been up with her all night." He glanced at his wife.

"And she's burning up, so she is," Mrs. Kennedy said softly, as her hands gripped the hem of her apron.

"Did you not tell all this to Mrs. Kincaid when you phoned, Bridget?" O'Reilly said. "I'd have come sooner."

"Och, Doctor dear, we know how busy you are." Mrs. Kennedy's hands twisted and crumpled the cloth. "Sure, it's only a wee tummy upset, isn't it?"

"Mmm," said O'Reilly through pursed lips. "Maybe we'd better take a look at her." He rose.

Mr. Kennedy looked up at his wife. "You go, Bridget."

"This way, Doctor," she said, walking to a door.

"Come on," said O'Reilly, lifting his bag and standing aside to give Barry room. Barry walked after Mrs. Kennedy into a hall and through the door of a small bedroom. Bright chintz curtains framed the window. A beam of sunlight fell on the counterpane of a child's bed, where a little girl, black hair tied up in bunches, teddy bear clutched to her flushed cheek, lay listlessly against two pillows. She stared at him from overbright, brown eyes.

"This is Doctor Laverty, Jeannie," Mrs. Kennedy explained.

Barry moved to the corner of the room and watched as O'Reilly grinned at the child and sat on the edge of the bed. The springs creaked under his weight.

"So, Jeannie," he said, "not so good?"

She shook her head. "My tummy's sore."

O'Reilly laid the back of his right hand on the child's forehead. "Hot," he remarked. "Can I take your pulse, Jeannie?"

She gave him her right arm.

"Hundred and ten," said O'Reilly.

Barry mentally added that fact to the rest of the information.

With the twenty-four-hour history of abdominal pain, the child not wanting to eat, vomiting, a fever, and a rapid pulse rate, he was already quite sure she had appendicitis. He glanced at Mrs. Kennedy as she stood at the foot of the bed trying to smile at her daughter.

"Can I see your teddy, Jeannie?" O'Reilly asked.

She handed him the stuffed bear, its orange fur worn in places to the net backing, one ear half chewed away. "Now, Teddy," said O'Reilly, laying the toy on the counterpane, "put out your tongue and say ah." He bent and peered at the bear's face. "Good. Now let's have a look at your tummy." He nodded his head wisely. "Too many sweeties," he said.

Jeannie smiled.

"Your turn," said O'Reilly softly, returning the bear. "Put out your tongue."

The child obeyed. He bent forward and sniffed. "Have a look at this, Doctor Laverty."

Barry stepped forward. The tongue was furred, and the child's breath fetid.

"Can we pull the bedclothes down, Mummy?" O'Reilly asked.

Mrs. Kennedy turned back the covers.

Barry watched as Jeannie's gaze flickered from her mother to her own stomach and up to O'Reilly's face.

"Can you point to where the pain started?"

Her finger hovered over her epigastrium, where her lower ribs flared out.

"And is it there yet?"

She solemnly shook her head and pointed to her lower right side.

Barry flinched. The next part of the examination would not be pleasant. One of the signs of appendicitis was rebound tenderness. When the abdominal wall was pushed in and then suddenly let go, the movement of the inflamed layers of the peritoneum would cause intense pain. Worse, the textbooks called for the doctor to examine the patient rectally. He had always disliked paediatrics, the terror of the little patients, the tears, the anguish of the parents who did not understand. He particularly hated having to inflict pain on small people, but understood that it was sometimes necessary.

"Right," said O'Reilly. To Barry's surprise, O'Reilly gently pulled the bedclothes up over the small body, covering the Peter Rabbit nightgown. "Jeannie, would you like to go for a ride to Belfast?"

The little girl looked at O'Reilly and then to her mother, who nodded. Jeannie stared into O'Reilly's craggy face. "All right," she said. "Can Teddy come?"

"Oh, aye," said O'Reilly. "Now you just lie there like a good girl. I need to have a wee word with your mummy." He rose, bent, and smoothed the child's hair from her forehead; then he straightened and headed for the door.

Barry hesitated. This wasn't right. O'Reilly had not been thorough. He'd barely examined the patient. The bloody man was in such a hurry to get back to watch his rugby game that he was cutting corners. It wasn't good enough.

"Are you coming, Doctor Laverty?"

Barry looked once more at the little girl, trying to decide whether he should complete the examination.

"Laverty."

No, he decided, he'd do nothing at the moment, but he'd have this out with O'Reilly later. Standing by while O'Reilly gave injections of useless medication through patients' clothes and fobbed off a crazy old lady with vitamins—a woman who in Barry's opinion needed a thorough psychiatric examination—was one thing. But this cavalier treatment of a little girl who was obviously ill . . . ?

"Bye-bye, Jeannie," he said, as he left and returned to the kitchen.

Mr. Kennedy stood with one arm around his wife's shoulder. She dabbed at her eyes with the hem of her apron.

O'Reilly had the phone clapped to one ear. He'd be arranging for an ambulance. That's it, Barry thought. Send the child to hospital; they'll take over, and you can get back to your bloody rugby match.

O'Reilly's voice echoed from the roof beams. "What the hell do you mean, you've no beds? I've a kiddie with appendicitis here. She'll be at Sick Children's in half an hour. . . . Balls, young man. You get hold of Sir Donald Cromie. . . . I don't give a bugger if it is his day off; you tell him that Doctor Fingal Flahertie O'Reilly called . . . no, not O'Rafferty, you buck eejit. O'Reilly. O . . . bloody . . . Reilly . . . from Ballybucklebo." He slammed the receiver into the cradle. "Bloody junior medical staff."

"You've called the ambulance already?" Barry asked.

"Don't be ridiculous," growled O'Reilly. "We'll take her up to Belfast in my car."

"I thought you wanted to get home to see—"

"Don't be bloody well daft. Jeannie needs her appendix out. And quick. We haven't time to wait for an ambulance."

Once the Kennedys had been delivered to the Royal Belfast Hospital for Sick Children, and O'Reilly was satisfied that Sir Donald Cromie agreed with the diagnosis and would operate immediately, he spoke once more with Mrs. Kennedy, grabbed Barry by the arm, and hustled him to the car.

"Come on, Laverty. If we get a move on, we'll still be able to watch the second half."

So, thought Barry, as they walked across the car park, he hasn't forgotten about the game, nor have I forgotten about what I watched back in the farmhouse. Admittedly, despite his sloppy practices, O'Reilly had been right about Jeannie Kennedy's appendix, and it had been above and beyond the call of duty to drive the Kennedys to Belfast, but that did not alter how Barry felt.

As O'Reilly drove from the hospital grounds onto Falls Road, Barry said, "Doctor O'Reilly, I think you were very lucky to make the right diagnosis."

"Oh?" said O'Reilly mildly, "and why would you think that?"

"You didn't examine the child properly because you were in a hurry."

"Was I?"

"That's what it looked like to me."

O'Reilly swerved to avoid a cyclist. "Daft bugger," he muttered.

"Are you calling me daft?"

"No," said O'Reilly, "but I will if you want me to." He stopped at a red light and turned to Barry. "Son, the diagnosis was as clear as the nose on your face from the minute we walked into the room. You could smell her halitosis."

Barry looked at O'Reilly's nose expecting to see the telltale pallor. There was none.

"Did you want me to prod her belly and stick a finger up her backside just because that's what the book says?"

"Well, I—"

"Well, nothing," said O'Reilly, driving on. "That wee girl was terrified; there was no need to hurt her anymore."

"I suppose . . ." Barry could see O'Reilly's logic. He also knew that there had been no real need for O'Reilly to take the family to Belfast.

"You just suppose away," said O'Reilly, "and stick with me, son. You'll learn a thing or two the books don't teach you."

6

Forty Shades of Green

Barry sat quietly in the passenger seat. Neither he nor O'Reilly had spoken during the drive through Belfast since their brief discussion about why O'Reilly had decided not to complete the examination of Jeannie Kennedy. And damn it, the more Barry thought of O'Reilly's explanation, the more he recognized that the older man, the experienced man, was probably right not to have inflicted unnecessary pain. Perhaps under his rough façade O'Reilly had a softer side.

Barry's ruminations were interrupted as the car moved past the redbrick wall of Campbell College, his old school. It didn't seem like seven years had passed since he'd left there to go to medical school. He'd been a boarder for four years at Campbell, the school that the inmates used to say was run on the lines of Nelson's navy: rum, sodomy, and the lash—without the solace of the rum. Not altogether true, of course, although there had been times when he had been beaten by a prefect for some infringement of the rules.

And he had made one good friend there, Jack Mills—he was training as a surgeon in the Royal Victoria Hospital. Jack and Barry had shared a study at Campbell in their senior year, stuck together as medical students, been housemen together. Barry decided he'd give Jack a call and see if they could get together when he had his first Saturday off. He'd be interested to hear his friend's opinion of O'Reilly.

The car left the city traffic. O'Reilly slammed his foot onto the accelerator and hurled the Rover at the twisting Craigantlet Hill Road. Barry stared ahead as the hedgerows ripped past the window, and he tensed as the car lurched when a wheel bounced off the verge.

O'Reilly was saying something.

"I beg your pardon?"

"I said, 'We'll be home in no time.'"

Or upside down in the ditch, Barry thought.

"Goes like a bird," said O'Reilly. "We're coming up to The Straight. I can really let her out there."

I wish to God you'd let me out here, Barry thought. He glanced at O'Reilly, who had one hand on the wheel and with the other held a match over the bowl of his pipe.

"Aren't we going a bit fast, Doctor O'Reilly?"

"Nonsense, my boy." O'Reilly puffed smoke like a labouring, coal-fired tank engine and threw the car into a turn.

Barry ducked as they scraped past a hay wagon coming from the opposite direction. When he slid back up in his seat he could see that the road stretched straight ahead to the horizon. He wondered how many times his dad had driven him over this road after collecting him from or delivering him back to Campbell College. The road's tarmac surface followed the undulations of the hills on either side. This was drumlin country, the rounded mounds left behind by the last ice age.

He knew that off to his right was one of the great neolithic hill forts, built thousands of years ago by the original Celtic inhabitants of this corner of Ireland. *Dúndonald,* Irish for "Donal's fort," was a complex of earthen ramparts and burial mounds. And if O'Reilly didn't slow down—the car was rocketing over the contours like an out-of-control roller coaster—there might be a sudden need for two more graves.

Barry took a deep breath and hoped that the queasy feeling in the pit of his stomach would pass. At least, he tried to comfort himself, they'd soon come to the end of The Straight, and O'Reilly would have to slow down.

And he did, slightly. The car rocked as it headed into the next curve.

"Exhilarating," remarked O'Reilly. "Bloody marvellous. I love that bit of road."

"Poop, poop," Barry muttered under his breath, as he had a sudden vision of Mr. Toad of Toad Hall roaring through the English countryside, in a stolen car.

"Not far now," said O'Reilly, turning into a lane. "Over the Ballybucklebo Hills and home." He glanced at his watch. "Ten minutes to the second half."

He drove steadily, under elms with leaf-laden boughs that blocked the sun and gave the lane the sombre dignity of an old church, past drystone walls that bordered the lane and set the boundaries of little fields where sheep and cattle grazed and yellow-flowered whin bushes stood bold against green grass.

The car crested a rise. Below, Barry saw Ballybucklebo, where the edges of the village straggled up the hillside and the railway line—he *would* take the train to Belfast as soon as he was free—and the houses and terraces of the centre of the village clustered round the maypole. He noted the single traffic light and the road past it that O'Reilly said led to the seashore. Above the dunes and silver scutch grass, a flock of white birds wheeled and dipped, then flew out over the whitecapped waters of the lough.

A single freighter butted through the chop, making its way to the port of Belfast, and past its bow he could make out the gantries of the Harland and Wolff shipyard. They stood proud against the backcloth of industrial haze that hung over the city and stained the sky as it drifted to the Knockagh Memorial obelisk, a granite finger on the crest of Cave Hill.

He wound down his window and breathed the clean country air.

From overhead he heard a skylark, and from a field nearby the rattle of a corncrake; the classical music and the rock and roll of the bird world, he thought.

The car passed the first outlying cottage.

"Nearly home," said O'Reilly.

"Home?" For you all right, Doctor O'Reilly, Barry thought, and yet will it be for me?

O'Reilly stole a sideways glance at his passenger. "Aye," he said quietly, "it is. Just around this bend and past the light." He turned the corner onto Ballybucklebo's main street and braked behind a red tractor waiting for the light to change.

Barry thought there was something familiar about the tractor's driver. He'd seen that angular form and shock of ginger hair somewhere.

The light turned to green, and presumably to encourage the driver ahead, O'Reilly blew his horn. The tractor driver turned in his seat. Barry recognized the cyclist who had given directions at Six Road Ends and who, at the mention of Doctor O'Reilly, had fled. Now the bucktoothed youth stared through the car's windscreen, shuddered, turned back—and stalled the tractor's engine.

The light flashed back to red.

"Bugger it," said O'Reilly. "Get a move on."

The tractor's starter made a *nurgley-nurgley-nurgley* sound, but the engine didn't catch.

Green went the light.

Nurgley-nurgley-phut went the starter.

"Damnation," went O'Reilly.

Red went the light.

The starter's note rose two full octaves, *nurgling* and *phutting* to no avail.

Green went the light. Barry looked behind. A line of cars and lorries stretched up the main street. More horns started to blow.

O'Reilly got out as the light changed back to red. He strode up to the tractor. As green once more appeared ahead, Barry heard O'Reilly's bellow over the rumbling of engines and the honking of horns.

"Tell me, Donal Donnelly, you miserable apology for a human being, tell me so I'll understand . . . *was there a particular shade of green you were waiting for?*"

Barry changed out of his muddy best pants and shoes as soon as they arrived at O'Reilly's house, and then joined him in the upstairs lounge to watch television. The Ireland under-twenty-three rugby football squad had beaten the Scots.

He finished the last of Mrs. Kincaid's cold lobster salad and put the plate on a coffee table beside his armchair.

O'Reilly belched contentedly, stared through the bay window, and said, "She's a dab hand in the kitchen is Kinky."

"Agreed." The cold meal had been delicious.

"Don't know what I'd do without her." O'Reilly wandered over to the sideboard. "Sherry?"

"Please."

Barry waited as O'Reilly poured a small sherry for him and a gargantuan Irish whiskey for himself. "Here." He gave the sherry to Barry. "Seems like she's been with me forever." He sat in his armchair. "I'd not have the practice if it hadn't been for Kinky."

"Oh?"

"I came here in nineteen thirty-eight, assistant to Doctor Flanagan. Crusty old bugger. I was just out of school, reckoned I was no goat's toe, and he was pretty out of date, and I'll tell you, some of the things he did were very unorthodox, even for back then."

"Really?" Barry hoped that his smile would go unnoticed.

"His big concern . . . he warned me about it . . . was a strange condition that he'd only ever seen in Ballybucklebo. Cold groin abscesses."

"What?"

"Cold groin abscesses. He said he saw a lot of them in labouring men. He always lanced them."

"He did surgery here, in the village?"

"GPs did before the war. That's all changed now. We have to re-fer surgical cases to the hospital. Maybe it's for the best . . . the last time I took out an appendix was on the old *Warspite*." He took a long pull on his drink. "Anyway, 'Cold groin abscesses,' says Flanagan to me, 'when you lance them, you never get pus. Just wind or shit . . . and the patient dies about four days later.' "

Barry sat bolt upright. "He thought inguinal hernias were ab-scesses?"

"He did. And when he sliced into the rupture he always cut into—"

"The bowel. Good God. What did you do?"

"Tried to suggest to him that maybe he didn't have it quite right."

"And?"

"I only ever tried to correct Doctor Flanagan that once. You've no idea how cantankerous some old country GPs could be, and I needed the money. Jobs were hard to come by back then."

"Not like today," Barry said, holding his glass to his lips to hide his expression. "I'm surprised you stayed."

"I didn't. I volunteered for the navy as soon as war broke out."

"What brought you back?"

"When the war was over I'd had enough of the navy, so I wrote to Doctor Flanagan. I got a letter back from his housekeeper, Mrs. Kincaid, to say that he'd died and the practice was up for sale."

"You bought it?"

"You had to in those days, and I had my gratuity as an ex-serviceman. That, and a bank loan, bought me the house and the goodwill of the practice and Mrs. Kincaid agreed to stay on. We've been here since nineteen forty-six." O'Reilly looked at his now empty glass, grabbed Barry's, and announced, "A bird can't fly on one wing."

"I really shouldn't. . . ."

"Here," said O'Reilly, handing over a refilled glass. "Sit down." Barry sat.

O'Reilly followed suit. "Where was I?"

"You bought the practice."

O'Reilly held his glass in both big hands. "And damn nearly lost it in the first year."

"What happened?"

"Country folk," he said. "You've got to get used to them. My mistake was to try and change things too quickly. One of my first patients was a farmer with the biggest hernia you ever saw."

"A cold groin abscess." Barry laughed. "Did you lance it like Doctor Flanagan?"

O'Reilly did not laugh. "Maybe I should have. When I refused to, the man spread the word that I was a young pup who didn't know his business. The customers stopped coming." He took a long drink. "The mortgage payments didn't."

"You must have been worried."

"Worried sick. I told you I'd have gone under if Kinky hadn't saved my bacon. She's a Presbyterian, you know."

"From County Cork?"

"They're not all Catholics in Cork."

"I know."

"She made me go to church with her. Let the locals see that I was a good Christian man."

"That's important here?"

"Back then it was."

"You mean even in this wee village they still fight the old sectarian wars?"

"Not at all," said O'Reilly. "They just liked to think that their doctor was a churchgoer. Didn't much matter if he went to church or chapel as long as he went."

"That's a relief. I spent enough time sorting out the casualities of the Protestant-Catholic street battles when the Divis Street riots hit Belfast. It was pretty ugly."

"You'll not see any of that here," said O'Reilly. "Father O'Toole and the Reverend Robinson play golf together every Monday." He hauled out his pipe and started to stuff the bowl with Erinmore Flake tobacco from a tin lying on the table in front of him. "On the Twelfth of July . . . that's next Thursday . . . the Orange Lodge has its parade, and half the Catholics in Ballybucklebo'll be lined up, waving Union Jacks. They've even let Seamus Galvin . . . mind you, he's what you'd call a lapsed Catholic . . . into the pipe band." He struck a match. "Anyway," he said, "I was telling you about Kinky."

"Right."

"Off to church the pair of us trotted, Kinky in her best hat and gloves, me in my only suit."

Barry thought ruefully of his own mud-spattered corduroys.

"Turned a few heads when we took our pew. I'd no doubt who the congregation were muttering about. I heard someone say that I was the young doctor who didn't know his arse from his elbow. Some of them kept turning round to stare at me during the sermon. Very uncomfortable."

"I can imagine."

"Do you believe in Divine Providence?"

Barry looked at O'Reilly to see if he was joking. By the way the big man held his eyes, he clearly was not.

"Well, I didn't. Not until that particular Sunday. In the middle of the last hymn a big fellow in the front row let a wail out of him like a banshee, grabbed at his chest, and fell over with a hell of a clatter. The singing stopped, and the minister said, 'I believe there's a doctor here.' Kinky gave me a ferocious nudge. 'Go and do something.' "

"What did you do?"

"I grabbed my stethoscope out of my bag . . . back then you never went anywhere without it . . . and rushed down the aisle. Your man was blue as a bloater. No pulse, no heartbeat. He'd popped his clogs."

"Was CPR invented back then?"

"Not at all. We hardly even had any antibiotics except the sulphonamides."

"So you were stuck?"

O'Reilly chuckled. "Well, yes and no. I reckoned it was my one chance to make my reputation. 'Someone get my bag,' says I, unbuttoning your man's shirt. Kinky arrived and gave me the bag. I grabbed whatever injection was handy, filled a syringe, and stuck the victim in the chest. I clapped my stethoscope on. 'He's back,' says I. You could have heard the gasps of the congregation all the way to Donaghadee. I waited for a couple of minutes. 'He's gone.' I stuck him again. More gasps all round. 'He's back.' "

"Was he?"

"Not at all. He was stiff as a stunned mullet, but I gave him one more injection."

"I don't see how losing a patient in church in front of half the village saved your practice."

"Kinky did that for me. I heard someone sniff that the demise of the recently departed just went to show what a useless doctor I was. I thought I was as dead as your man in the aisle."

"I'm not surprised."

" 'Just a small, little minute,' says Kinky. She stared at the minister. 'You have to agree, your reverence, that our Saviour brought Lazarus back from the dead.' The minister agreed. There was a hush in the place like at the eleventh hour of the eleventh day of the eleventh month. That's when Kinky said, 'And Jesus only did it once, so. Our doctor, our Doctor O'Reilly, himself here, did it twice.'" O'Reilly finished his drink. "I've been run off my feet since."

"You wily old—"

The doorbell clanged in the hall.

"See what I mean?" said O'Reilly. "Be a good lad, and nip down and see who that is."

Barry opened the front door. He was confronted by a man standing on the step, legs astraddle, arms folded. He was short and sufficiently rotund to warrant being described as spherical. He wore a black three-piece suit, a bowler hat, and a scowl that Barry reckoned would have served Ivan the Terrible on a bad day.

"Where the hell's O'Reilly?" The visitor forced his way into the hall. "O'Reilly, come 'ere; I want ye," he bellowed, like the master on his quarterdeck hailing the masthead lookout in a force-ten gale. "O'Reilly, get down here. Now."

Barry could hear movement overhead. Perhaps the newcomer didn't recognize that yelling at O'Reilly would have the same effect as poking a stick into the eye of a rabid Doberman pinscher.

"Perhaps I can—"

"I've heard about you, Laverty." The newcomer half turned to face Barry, who was thinking, I'm only one day in the place. News travels fast.

"I want himself."

Barry stiffened. Here was a patient who was well on the way to breaching Doctor F. F. O'Reilly's first rule of medical practice. Barry glanced up to see O'Reilly approaching; he knew that

O'Reilly would sort this man out, but Barry was quite willing to fight his own battles. "It's *Doctor* Laverty, and if you have something wrong—"

"*Doctor*, is it? Huh!" The little round man's eyes flashed. "Do you know who I am?"

Barry decided that replying, "Why? Can't you remember?" would not go down well.

"I'm Councillor Bishop, worshipful master of the Ballybucklebo Orange Lodge, so I am."

"Good evening, Councillor," said O'Reilly from behind the man. "What can I do for you? I do hope it's not a cold groin abscess." His tone was solicitous; his wink at Barry demonic.

Councillor Bishop spun to face O'Reilly, who towered over the rotund man. O'Reilly was smiling, but Barry recognized the telltale paleness in his bent nose.

"My finger's beelin', O'Reilly." He thrust his right index finger under O'Reilly's nose. Barry could see the skin, red and shiny round the nail bed, the yellow pus beneath.

"Beelin' sore, so it is."

"Tut," said O'Reilly, donning his half-moon spectacles.

"Well, what are you going to do about it?"

"Come into the surgery." O'Reilly opened the door. Barry followed them inside and watched as O'Reilly lifted instruments from a cabinet, dumped them into a steel sterilizer, and switched it on. "Won't be a minute."

"Get on with it. I'm a busy man." Councillor Bishop planted his ample behind in the swivel chair.

"And how's Mrs. Bishop?" O'Reilly enquired.

"Look, would you get a move on?"

"Certainly." O'Reilly pushed the trolley towards the councillor. Its wheels squealed. The sterilizer bubbled, wisps of steam jetting from under its lid. He went to a cabinet, brought out a cloth-wrapped pack, and placed it on the trolley. "Open that, please, Doctor Laverty."

Barry peeled off the outer layer. Inside lay green sterile towels, sterile swabs, sponge forceps, stainless-steel gallipots, a kidney basin, and a pair of surgical gloves. He heard water running as O'Reilly washed his hands. Barry knew what was going to happen and what would be needed. Antiseptic, the instruments from the sterilizer, and some local anaesthetic, at least—O'Reilly would use a local, wouldn't he? He wouldn't just stick a scalpel into the abscess?

He heard the *snap, snap* as O'Reilly donned the gloves. "Dettol and Xylocaine are on the bottom of the trolley," he said.

Barry retrieved the local anaesthetic and a bottle of brown disinfectant, relieved that O'Reilly was not going to incise the abscess without deadening the pain. He poured some Dettol into a gallipot on the trolley, then set the bottle on the trolley's lower shelf.

"Thank you." O'Reilly stuffed a couple of swabs between the jaws of the sponge forceps. "Now, Councillor, if you'd hold your finger over this basin."

"Just hurry up."

The ringing of the sterilizer's bell to indicate that the instruments were now ready almost muffled Councillor Bishop's "*Yeeeowee!*"

Yes, indeed, Barry thought, Dettol does bite. He retrieved the now sterile forceps, scalpel, and hypodermic, carried them over, and set them on O'Reilly's trolley. "Local?"

"Of course," said O'Reilly, lifting the hypodermic.

Councillor Bishop made little whiffling noises as he puffed short breaths through pursed lips and stared wide-eyed at the needle.

"I'm going to freeze your finger," said O'Reilly. He stabbed the bottle's rubber stopper and filled the syringe's barrel.

"This'll sting," said O'Reilly, pushing the needle into the skin of the web between the index and middle finger.

"*Wheee, arr, wowee,*" howled the councillor.

"Sorry," said O'Reilly. "Other side." He injected Xylocaine at the outside of the first knuckle.

"*Whooeee, owww.*" The councillor writhed in his chair.

"I know you're in a rush, but we'll have to wait for that nerve block to work."

"All right," whimpered Councillor Bishop. "Take your time."

"How long has the finger been bothering you?" O'Reilly asked.

"Two, three days."

"Pity you didn't come in sooner . . ." O'Reilly looked directly into Barry's eyes. "The surgery's always open in the mornings."

"I will next time, Doctor. Honest to God, I will."

Barry noticed the merest upward tilt of O'Reilly's mouth, the tiniest twinkle in his eyes, as he said, "Do." He picked up the scalpel. "Right," he said. "You won't feel a thing." He sliced into the flesh. Barry watched blood and yellow pus ooze out, as the swollen tissues shrank.

"Better an empty house than a bad tenant," O'Reilly remarked. "Oh, dear," he said, "the councillor seems to have fainted."

Barry looked at the little round man, who lay crumpled in the chair.

"Nasty man," said O'Reilly, as he swabbed the mess away. Then he used two clean gauze squares to dress the wound. "Thinks he's the bee's knees because he owns half the property in the village." He pointed to his rolltop desk. "There's a bottle of smelling salts in there. Get them, will you? We don't want to be here all night."

Barry went to the desk, aware that he had seen Doctor O'Reilly perform minor surgery with all the skill of one of the senior surgeons at the Royal. And somehow he had let Councillor Bishop know that while patients might have certain expectations of their physician, courtesy was a two-way street. Get the upper hand? Barry thought Councillor Bishop hadn't, in local parlance, come within a beagle's gowl.

7

By the Dawn's Early Light

A telephone rang. Barry fumbled for the receiver. The night sister must want him up on one of the wards. His hand, the one he had cut on Mr. Kennedy's gate, smacked into an unfamiliar bedside table. "Ow." The pain brought him to full wakefulness, and he remembered he wasn't in his room in the junior staff quarters of the Royal. He was in the attic in O'Reilly's home.

The door opened and a beam of light from the landing spilled into his room. A large figure stood in the doorway.

"Up," said O'Reilly, "and be quiet. Don't disturb Kinky."

"Right." Barry knuckled his eyes, got out of bed, dressed, and crept downstairs to find O'Reilly, black bag in hand, waiting in the hall.

"Come on." He headed for the kitchen. Barry followed out through the back garden, which was illuminated only by the dim rays of a distant streetlight. Arthur Guinness stuck his head out of his doghouse.

"I'm not going shooting," O'Reilly said.

"Umph," said Arthur, eyeing Barry's trouser leg. The dog must have decided that love at this hour was too much trouble. He retreated into his kennel, muttering something in Labradorese.

Barry climbed into the Rover. "What time is it?"

"Half one," said O'Reilly, backing into the lane.

Barry yawned.

"Mrs. Fotheringham called. Says her husband's sick, but I doubt it." He headed for the road. "Major Basil Fotheringham's had every illness known to man, and a few that only the Martians have dreamed of. He always takes a turn for the worse after midnight, and as far as I can tell, he's fit as a bloody flea. It's all in his mind." He turned left at the traffic light.

"So why are we going out into the Ballybucklebo Hills at this hour of the morning?"

"Do you know about the houseman and the surgeon?" O'Reilly asked, turning the car's lights to full beam.

"No."

"Surgeon comes in to make rounds in the morning. 'How is every one?' says he. 'Grand,' says the houseman, 'except the one you were certain was neurotic, sir.' 'Oh,' says the great man, 'gone home has he?' 'Not exactly, sir. He died last night.' Once in a while even the worst bloody malingerer does actually get sick."

"Point taken."

"Good. Now be quiet. It's not far, but I've to remember how to get there."

Barry sat back and watched the yellow headlights probe the blackness ahead. Now that Ballybucklebo lay behind, the dark enveloped them as tightly as a shroud. He peered up and saw the Summer Triangle: Altair, Vega, and Deneb high in the northwest, each star set in a jet sky, backlit by the silver smudge of the Milky Way. His dad had been a keen amateur astronomer, probably because he'd been a navigating officer in the war. He'd taught Barry about the constellations.

Barry's dad and mum would be seeing different stars now, he thought. The Southern Cross would sparkle over their heads. Their last letter from Melbourne, where his dad was on a two-year contract as a consulting engineer, had been full of their enthusiasm for Australia, had hinted that there were all kinds of opportunities for doctors there. Barry watched a meteor blaze through Orion, and knew he was quite at home with the northern stars.

The car braked in a driveway, and Barry came back to earth.

"When we get in there I want you to agree with everything I say, understand?" said O'Reilly.

Barry hesitated. "But doctors don't always agree. Sometimes a second opinion—"

"Humour me, son."

"Humour you?"

"Just open the gate."

Barry climbed out and opened a gate, waited for O'Reilly to drive through, closed the gate, and crunched along a gravel drive-way to a two-storey house. An imitation coach lamp burned in the redbrick porch. "Agree with everything I say. Humour me." What if O'Reilly made a mistake? Barry looked ahead. There O'Reilly stood, dark against the light from an open door, talking to a woman wearing a dressing gown.

"Mrs. Fotheringham, my assistant, Doctor Laverty," he said when Barry arrived.

"How do you do?" she said, in a poor imitation of the accent of an English landed lady. "So good of you both to come. Poor Basil's not well. Not well at all. Not at all."

Barry heard the harsh tones of Ulster beneath her affected gentil-ity. That, he thought, is what I'd call the buttermilk coming through the cream. He followed as she led them through a hall, expensively wallpapered and hung with framed prints of hunting scenes, up a deeply carpeted staircase, and into a large bedroom. Drawn pink velvet curtains covered the window and clashed with the pale orange tulle drapings of a four-poster bed.

"The doctors have come, dear," Mrs. Fotheringham said, as she stepped up to the bed and smoothed the brow of the man who lay there.

Major Fotheringham sagged against his pillows and made a mewling noise. Barry looked for any obvious evidence of fever or distress, but no sweat was visible on the patient's high forehead; there was nothing hectic about his watery blue eyes, nor any drip from a narrow nose that hooked over a clipped military moustache.

"Right," said O'Reilly, "what seems to be the trouble this time?"

"He is very poorly, Doctor," Mrs. Fotheringham said. "Surely you can see that?"

"Oh, indeed," said O'Reilly, making space among the ranks of salves and unguents on the glass top of an ornate dressing table and setting his bag among the bottles. "But it would help if Major Fotheringham could describe his symptoms."

"Poor dear," she said, "he can hardly speak, but I think it's his kidneys."

"Indeed," said O'Reilly, pulling his stethoscope from his bag. "Kidneys, is it?"

"Oh, yes," she said, twitching at the front of her silk dressing gown. "Definitely. I think he needs a thorough examination."

"I'd better take a look then," said O'Reilly. He stepped to the bed. "Put out your tongue, Basil."

Here we go again, Barry thought. O'Reilly had not made the remotest attempt to elicit any kind of history, and here he was barrelling ahead with the physical examination. *Agree with everything I say.* Well, we'll see.

"Mmm," said O'Reilly, pulling down the patient's lower eyelid and peering at the inside of the lid. "Mmm-mmm." He grasped one wrist and made a great show of consulting his watch. "Mmm."

Barry watched Mrs. Fotheringham's narrow face as she stared intently at every move O'Reilly made, heard her little inhalations each time he muttered, "Mmm."

"Open your pyjamas please." O'Reilly laid his left hand palm down on the patient's hairless chest and thumped the back of his hand with the first two fingers of his right. "Mmm." He stuffed the earpieces of his stethoscope in his cauliflower ears and clapped the bell to the front of the chest. "Big breaths."

Major Fotheringham gasped, in out, in out.

"Sit up, please."

Major Fotheringham obeyed. More thumpings; more stethoscope applications, this time to the back; more huffing and puffing; more *mmms.*

Mrs. Fotheringham's little eyes widened. "Is it serious, Doctor?"

O'Reilly pulled his stethoscope from his ears and turned to her. "I beg your pardon?"

"Is it serious?"

"We'll see," said O'Reilly, turning back to Major Fotheringham. "Lie down." O'Reilly quickly and expertly completed a full examination of the belly. "Mmm, *huh.* I see."

"What is it, Doctor?" Mrs. Fotheringham's voice had the same expectancy that Barry had heard in children's voices when they wanted to be given a treat.

"You're right," O'Reilly said. "It *could* be his kidneys."

And how in the world had he arrived at that diagnosis? Barry thought. No one had said anything about fever, chills, or difficulties or pain urinating, and nothing O'Reilly had done had come close to examining the organs in question.

"Told you so, dear," said Mrs. Fotheringham smugly, as she fluffed her husband's pillows. The major lay languidly, unspeaking as ever in the four-poster bed.

"Then again, it might not be," said O'Reilly, grabbing his bag. "I think a test's in order, don't you, Doctor Laverty?"

Barry met O'Reilly's gaze, swallowed, and said, "I don't quite see—"

"Course you do." O'Reilly's eyes narrowed, his tone hardened.

"But—"

"In a case like this we can't be too careful. You'd agree, Mrs. Fotheringham?"

"Oh, indeed, Doctor." She smiled at O'Reilly. "Yes, indeed."

"That's settled then." O'Reilly glared at Barry, who looked away. O'Reilly rummaged in his bag and produced a bottle that Barry recognized immediately. It would contain thin cardboard strips used to detect sugar or protein in a urine sample. What the hell was O'Reilly up to?

"I'll need your help, Mrs. Fotheringham." O'Reilly handed her several of the dipsticks.

"Yes, Doctor." Her eyes were bright, her smile barely concealed.

"I want you to . . ." He looked at his watch. "It's two fifteen now . . . so start the test at three. Make Basil drink one pint of water."

"A pint?" she echoed.

"The whole pint. At four give him another pint, but not until he's passed a specimen."

"Specimen?"

"Of urine."

"Oh."

"Dip one of those dipsticks in it, and put the stick on the dressing table."

Mrs. Fotheringham looked dubiously at her handful of cardboard, sniffed, and said, "Very well." She sounded, thought Barry, like an English memsahib who'd been asked to clean up a heap of elephant manure from the streets of colonial Bombay—and who would do so, but only for the sake of the empire.

"And," O'Reilly bored on, "I want you to repeat the test every hour on the hour until Doctor Laverty and I come back to read the results."

"Every hour? But—"

"It's a terrible imposition, Mrs. Fotheringham, but . . ."
—O'Reilly put one large hand on her shoulder—"I know I can rely on you."

She sighed.

"Should give us the answer, don't you think, Doctor Laverty?"

Barry nodded, knowing his earlier attempts to stand up to O'Reilly had been ineffective, sure that any protest he might make would be rolled over with the force of a juggernaut, and despising himself for his lack of courage.

"Good," said O'Reilly to Barry. He turned to Mrs. Fotheringham, who was sorting out the little pile of cardboard. "Get started at three, and remember, this test will sort out once and for all just how sick your husband is. Mind you, I'm pretty sure I know what's wrong with him."

She nodded meekly.

"Don't bother to see us out," said O'Reilly, striding to the door. "You're going to have a busy night."

Barry sat stiffly in the Rover. He was angry about O'Reilly's hocus-pocus and angrier at his own inability to intervene. He watched as streaks of yellow made pastel shadings in the grey of the false dawn, and fidgeted in the seat.

"Go on," said O'Reilly, "spit it out."

"Doctor O'Reilly, I—"

"Think your history taking stinks, and you're up to no good with all that buggering about with the dipsticks."

"Well, I—"

O'Reilly chuckled. "Son, I've known the Fotheringhams for years. The man's never had a day's real illness in his life."

"Then why didn't you just tell them to wait until the morning?"

"Would you have?"

"If I knew the patient as well as you obviously do, I might."

O'Reilly shook his head. "It's another little rule of mine. If they're worried enough to call at night, even if I'm damn sure it's nothing, I go."

"Always?"

"Lord, aye."

Nothing in O'Reilly's tone suggested pride to Barry. There was no hint of smugness, simply a matter-of-fact statement of how things were in the big doctor's particular universe. "I see," Barry acknowledged grudgingly, "but what was all that nonsense with the test? I've never heard of any such procedure."

"Ah," said O'Reilly, turning into the lane at the back of his house. " 'There are more things in heaven and earth, Horatio, / Than are dreamt of in your philosophy.' "

"You'll not put me off by quoting *Hamlet*, Doctor O'Reilly."

"No," said O'Reilly, as he braked, "I didn't think I would, but you'll have to wait until we go back to the Fotheringhams' if you want to find out the answer. Now be a good lad, hop out, and open the garage door."

While O'Reilly parked the car, Barry waited in the lane. He looked past the lopsided steeple of the church to where the clouds were being lit by the rising sun.

"Begod," said O'Reilly, standing by Barry's shoulder and staring up. "Red sky in the morning, sailor, take warning. I wonder what the rest of today's going to have in store for us?"

8

Water, Water, Everywhere

Never mind sailors taking warning; anyone caught out in the summer gale that had blown up in the early hours would be getting drenched. Barry listened to the rain clattering off the surgery's bow windows. He glanced at his watch. Even at almost noon the lights were still needed in the room. Barry stretched and ran a hand over the back of his neck. He was feeling the effects of a broken night. He watched O'Reilly usher an older man with arthritis to the door. The morning had been busy, and yet O'Reilly showed no signs of fatigue.

A fresh gust shook the panes.

"Jesus," said O'Reilly, "I wonder if there's an old lad wearing a long gown and a beard running round the Ballybucklebo Hills looking for gopher wood and trying to keep all the animals together two by two?"

"He'd not be doing that. He'd have Shem, Ham, and Japheth to do all the running around for him," Barry muttered.

"Sensible man, Noah," said O'Reilly with a grin. "Trot along and see who's next."

Barry shook his head and went to the waiting room to discover that only one patient remained, a young woman with long auburn hair that had a sheen like a freshly shelled horse chestnut, and green eyes set in a freckled face. "Good morning," he said. "Will you come through, please, Mrs. er . . . ?"

"Galvin," she said, standing with some difficulty, one hand supporting the small of her back, the other holding her swollen belly.

"I'm a bit slow getting about," she said, giving him a weak smile.

"That's all right; take your time." Barry stepped aside as she waddled past.

"Doesn't look as though it'll be long now."

"Just a week more." She went into the surgery. "Morning, Doctor O'Reilly."

"How are you, Maureen?" O'Reilly asked.

"Grand." She rummaged in her handbag and gave him a small plastic urine-sample bottle.

O'Reilly took it and handed it to Barry. "Pop a dipstick into that, would you?"

Barry took the specimen over to the sink and tested the urine. He found nothing wrong. As he worked, he heard O'Reilly say, "Can you get up on the couch, Maureen?"

She turned her back to the table and sat. "Are you sure there's only the one in here, Doctor O'Reilly? I feel like the sidewall of a house."

"It was only a week ago when I examined you," he said, "but if it'll make you happier, we'll get Doctor Laverty to lay on a hand."

"I heard you'd a new assistant," she said.

O'Reilly bent and put one arm under her legs. "There you go," he said as he lifted her legs onto the couch. He reached past her. "Stick that pillow under your head."

She lay down, and Barry watched and listened as O'Reilly asked the routine late antenatal questions, took her blood pressure, and palpated her ankles to make sure there was no swelling. "Right, let's see your bump."

She lifted the skirt of her maternity dress. The blue of the material was bleached, and a small patch was neatly sewn on one side.

O'Reilly pulled the top of her underwear down until Barry could just see a wisp of pubic hair at the bottom of her distended abdomen. He noted the silver snail tracks of stretch marks on her flank, her umbilicus turned inside out from the pressure of the uterus that filled the abdominal cavity. He stepped back and waited while O'Reilly examined her. Maureen's green eyes never left O'Reilly's face. Barry saw her concern, watched as O'Reilly's face betrayed no expression.

"Doctor Laverty?"

Barry moved to the table. As he did so, he rubbed his palms rapidly together trying to warm them. "This won't take long."

"Take your time, Doctor." She flinched as he began his examination.

"Sorry."

"Cold hands is the sign of a warm heart." She smiled at him.

He examined the belly, felt a single baby's back on her right side, the hardness of the head just above the pubic symphysis. He grasped the head between the outstretched thumb and finger of his right hand. It refused to budge when he tried to move it from side to side.

"Here," said O'Reilly, handing Barry a fetal stethoscope.

He laid the wide end of the aluminium trumpet over the abdominal wall and bent to put his ear to the flattened earpiece.

Tup-tup-tup-tup. . . . Barry listened, counted, and looked at his watch. "A hundred and forty." He saw the narrowing of Maureen's eyes and the questioning lines appear in her forehead. "Absolutely normal," he said, pleased to see the little furrows disappear.

"So?" said O'Reilly.

Barry trotted out the formula he had been taught. "There's a singleton, longitudinal lie, vertex presentation, right occipito-anterior, head's engaged, heart rate . . ."

"A hundred and forty," said O'Reilly. "The rest's right too."

Barry felt smug.

"So are you worried now, Maureen?"

Barry looked at the woman's face. The furrows were back and were keeping company with three deeper ones that ran upwards from the bridge of her nose. She glanced from O'Reilly to Barry, then back to O'Reilly. "Not if *you* say so, Doctor."

"Just like Doctor Laverty said, Maureen, there's one baby, just the one . . ."

Some of the furrows flattened.

". . . Straight up and down, the back of its head is on the right—that's the most normal way—and the head's dropped. The little divil's halfway out already."

Her forehead became smooth, a twinkle shone in her green eyes, laugh lines appeared at the corners. She gave a contented sigh. "That's great, so it is."

Barry cleared his throat. He saw how he'd baffled the woman with his jargon. She hadn't understood a word of his "singleton, right occipito-anterior" talk, but O'Reilly had gone right to the heart of the matter in plain English.

"Come on." O'Reilly helped her off the couch. She adjusted her underwear and straightened her dress. "Right," he said, "same time next week."

"And if the waters break or the pains start, I've to phone you."

"You'll be fine, Maureen," O'Reilly said. "By the way, how's Seamus?"

"His ankle's on the mend, Doctor, and he hopes you liked the lobsters."

"We did." O'Reilly took her elbow and began to steer her to the door. "Tell him to pop in next week, and I'll take another look at his hoof."

She stopped and looked him in the eye. "Seamus means well. He's a heart of corn, but sometimes—"

"Don't you worry about Seamus," said O'Reilly. "I'll take care of him." He winked at Barry, who had a vivid mental picture of an airborne supplicant with a dirty foot. That Galvin was this young woman's husband?

"You'll not need to much longer," she said in a whisper. "You'll not tell no one, Doctor, but my brother—"

"The builder in California?"

"Aye. He's got a job out there for Seamus, and we've saved up for the tickets. We're going after the baby's born."

"Wonderful," said O'Reilly, and Barry wondered whether his colleague's delight was due to the Galvins making a fresh start or to the practice losing one of his less favourite patients.

"Now don't you tell."

"I promise."

"I'll be in next week." She left.

"I'll be damned," said O'Reilly. Moving to the desk, he sat and wrote the results in Maureen Galvin's record. "Maybe the worthy Seamus'll have to do an honest day's work in America. I wonder where they got the money? He's a carpenter by trade, but to my knowledge he's hardly done a hand's turn here." He looked up. "One of life's little mysteries. By the way," he asked, "was her urine clear?"

"Yes," said Barry. He hesitated. "I'm sorry I didn't explain things to her better."

O'Reilly fished out his pipe and lit it before he said, "Ah, but you will the next time, won't you?"

"I will."

"Grand," said O'Reilly. "Now tidy up those urine-test kits. We've another test to go and read after we've had lunch."

"Wonderful, Kinky," said O'Reilly, pushing away his plate, "and those lobsters last night? They'd have brought a tear to a glass eye."

"Get on with you, Doctor O'Reilly," Kinky said. Barry saw the corners of her eyes wrinkle and dimples appear in her ample cheeks. "It was only a shmall little thing, so."

"They were delicious, Mrs. Kincaid."

"Aye, so, well you need to keep up your shtrength, Doctor Laverty. Judging by the shtate of your corduroys, you'd been running a race through the Bog of Allen yesterday."

"Very muddy," Barry agreed.

"Don't you worry," she said. "I've them washed and hung up to dry."

"Thank you."

She bustled away, calling over her shoulder, "And I think the good Lord's looking out for you today. There's no calls in at all, and it roaring down out there like water from a fire hose, so."

"It is that," said O'Reilly, "but there's no peace for the wicked. We've to go back to the Fotheringhams'."

"We wouldn't have to," Barry ventured, "if it wasn't for that weird 'test' of yours."

"Patience, son," O'Reilly said. "I'm sure the major and his lady are having a wonderful time."

Not even the passing of Barry's legs would tempt Arthur Guinness to stick his muzzle out of his kennel into the downpour that thrashed the back garden, knocked young apples to the sodden grass, and stung Barry's face as he followed O'Reilly to the car.

"Nice day for ducks," O'Reilly remarked, as he swung out of the garage.

Barry listened to the drumming on the car's roof, heard the rhythmic back-and-forth squealing of the windscreen wipers as they fought a losing battle against the downpour, saw drops ricochet from the steaming surface of the road. O'Reilly, refusing to make any concession to the poor visibility, hurled the car round the twists and turns.

Barry, to distract himself from O'Reilly's kamikaze attitude to driving, muttered, " 'Water, water, everywhere, / And all the boards did shrink, / Water, water, everywhere . . .' "

" 'Nor any drop to drink.' " O'Reilly finished the verse. "Coleridge, Samuel Taylor, 1772 to 1834, poet and opium addict. Water," he continued, turning into the Fotheringhams' drive, "I wonder how these folks have been getting on with it?"

Barry scuttled after O'Reilly and sheltered in the porch until a bleary-eyed Mrs. Fotheringham, hair in disarray, dressing gown dark from scattered damp patches, opened the door.

"Thank goodness you've come," she said, holding the back of her forearm to her brow in a gesture that reminded Barry of the hyperemoting Norma Desmond in the old movie *Sunset Boulevard*. He wondered if Mrs. Fotheringham was going to swoon. "Do come in. Take off your coats." He took off his drenched raincoat, hung it with O'Reilly's on a clothes stand in the hall, and followed the two upstairs.

Major Fotheringham sat up against his pillows, black circles under his bloodshot eyes. "Doctor O'Reilly," he croaked, "it's been a hellish night. Hellish."

"Oh, dear," said O'Reilly in his most solicitous voice. "Well, let's see how the test went. Come and take a look at this, Doctor Laverty."

Barry stood beside O'Reilly at the dressing table. Neatly arranged as a rank of the guards lay fourteen soggy dipsticks. There was a faint aroma of ammonia. Not a single stick had changed colour.

"Oh-oh," said O'Reilly, "oh-oh."

Barry was baffled. No colour change meant that nothing untoward had appeared in the patient's urine.

"What's wrong with him, Doctor O'Reilly?" Mrs. Fotheringham begged.

"Can I stop the test now?" The pleading tone that Barry heard in

Major Fotheringham's voice would have softened Pharaoh's hard heart.

"Certainly," said O'Reilly, "and you are to be commended, Mrs. Fotheringham, on your meticulous devotion to duty."

She simpered, "Thank you, Doctor. But what's wrong with him?"

"Ah," said O'Reilly, "you remember I told you last night I was pretty sure that I knew?"

"Yes."

"Well, now I'm certain, and I'm sure Doctor Laverty here would agree with me completely."

You old bugger, Barry thought. Couldn't resist having a little go at me, could you? But he decided to play along. "Absolutely," he said, looking solemn.

"What's wrong with you, my dear Major Fotheringham?" O'Reilly took a three count. "I'm very much afraid it's nothing. Absolutely nothing. Nothing at all."

Barry saw Mrs. Fotheringham's jaw drop. "Nothing?" she whispered. "Nothing?"

"Well," O'Reilly allowed, "he might be a bit waterlogged, but other than that? Not a thing."

Barry had great difficulty controlling a laugh.

O'Reilly pointed to the soggy sticks. "You can keep the test sticks, and of course, if you think you need me, anytime, anytime at all, day or night, don't hesitate to call."

"Yes," said the weary Mrs. Fotheringham.

"Fine," said O'Reilly, "and now we'd better be running along. We've more calls to make."

That was news to Barry. Kinky had said there were none, but by now there was little that Doctor Fingal Flahertie O'Reilly could do that would come as a surprise.

9

Cats on a Cold Tile Roof

"I thought that was the only call we had to make." Barry slammed the car door.

"Just a couple more," said O'Reilly as he reversed out of the driveway. "I don't think," he said, with a huge grin, "that the major or his lady will call us out again for a while. Do you?"

"I doubt it." In spite of himself Barry chuckled. "Mind you, it's not the sort of medicine I was taught, but it seems to work." He had a mental image of six backsides being injected through their clothes.

"Like a charm, my boy." O'Reilly fished in one pocket for his pipe. "D'you see, there's more ways of killing a cat than drowning it in cream. When I started out, I thought that every patient would behave like a civilized human being, that they'd all treat their doctor with respect. Twenty years ago I'd have read the Fotheringhams the riot act for wasting my time."

Barry glanced down. His own thoughts exactly.

"Didn't take me long to find out that consideration for other people can be one of the lesser attributes of some members of the species *Homo sapiens*."

"I've noticed."

"And yelling at them does no good."

"It seemed to work with Seamus Galvin."

O'Reilly laughed. "Seamus? You couldn't get an idea into that one's thick head with a two-pound hammer. He's one of a kind." He lit his briar, filling the car with pungent smoke. "For most of the other bolshie ones, the trick is to treat their medical complaints to the very best of your ability, but you don't have to dance attendance on them all, and you can make your point like the serpent in Genesis."

" 'Now the serpent was more subtle than any beast'?"

"Exactly. Something they didn't teach you at medical school." O'Reilly braked at the traffic light. The car rocked as a gust of wind screeched up the road that led to the seafront. "What got you into medicine anyway?" he asked.

Barry hesitated. That decision had been a personal one, and he was always reticent about giving the real reasons. He tried to deflect the question. "When I left school, my dad said I was too dim to read physics or chemistry, would never make a living with an arts degree, wasn't a Catholic—so the priesthood was out—and I didn't look like a soldier. So, there was nothing left for me but medicine."

O'Reilly guffawed. "Sounds like the sort of thing Tom Laverty would say." He turned and looked into Barry's eyes. "But there was more to it than that, wasn't there?"

"The light's changed, Doctor O'Reilly."

"Right." The Rover charged across the intersection, tires shrieking as O'Reilly hauled the big car into a right turn. He steadied on course. "You still haven't answered me."

"Well, I—"

"Don't like talking about it, but you'd a half-notion you'd like to help people. Do something useful—"

"How the hell did you know that—?"

"Didn't make many friends at school, so you hoped if you went into medicine people would like you. . . ."

Barry's mind went back to his boarding-school days. He'd had no close friends apart from Jack Mills. Barry had been a good scholar, and as a result he was shunned by the in-crowd of his closed-in little world. His four years had been lonely.

"Thought so," said O'Reilly. "Well, most of the customers aren't going to love you. They'll say thank-you if you get it right, and treat you like dirt if you don't—and you *will* make mistakes, never doubt that."

Barry wondered how the big man sitting beside him could have understood so completely.

"A few will have no consideration for the fact that you're on call twenty-four hours a day, and some like Councillor Bishop are bloody rude and totally demanding. That man Bishop? There's enough acid in his veins to recharge the batteries of a submarine." O'Reilly shoved his pipe back into his jacket pocket. "You simply don't let the Bishops get on your wick. And there's a good side too. When you *do* get a diagnosis right, make a difference in somebody's life, find you *do* fit into the local scheme of things, it is all worth it."

"You really think so?"

"I know so, boy. I bloody well know so." O'Reilly clamped his hands onto the steering wheel. "You just have to keep pounding away."

Barry hesitated, then asked, "What made you pick medicine?"

"Huh," O'Reilly grunted, "your friend Galvin once ran an electric sander over his hand just to find out what it felt like. Do you know what he said when I asked him why?"

Barry shook his head.

"He said, 'Seemed like a good idea at the time.'" O'Reilly shook with laughter and used the back of one hand to wipe the condensation from the inside of the windscreen. "I think," he said, "the rain's going to clear up."

Barry realized that O'Reilly's flippancy was as much his personal camouflage as was the dazzle paint on the hull of his old ship in the pictures that hung on his landing walls. Barry decided to let the matter drop and stared out through the car window.

The Rover ran along the shore of the lough where a grassy verge dotted with sea pinks was all that separated the road from jagged rocks, black in the driving rain. Obsidian-green combers pounded against the shore, breaking and hurling spume across the roadway. What had O'Reilly said? *You just have to keep pounding away.* Barry smiled.

The car slowed, and O'Reilly parked it with two wheels on the grass. "Come on." Barry climbed out and saw a cottage with grey walls, slate roof, mullioned windows, and boxes full of bright pansies on the sills. The cottage sat squarely beside the road. A short stretch of coarse grass ran down to the shore from behind the cottage. O'Reilly stood and knocked on the front door. Barry joined him and immediately recognized the woman who opened the door. Maggie MacCorkle was not wearing her hat with the geraniums, but was still swathed in layers of cardigans and her long rusty skirt.

"Come on in out of thon, Doctor," she said. "It would founder you out there, so it would."

She closed the door behind them. A single oil lamp on a small oak table lighted the tiny, low-ceilinged room. Barry saw dishes stacked to dry in a plate rack beside an enamel sink, a small gas stove, and a row of wall-hung cupboards. Two easy chairs flanked a fireplace where coals glowed brightly. On one chair a huge ginger cat lay curled in a ball. Its tail covered its nose, but Barry could see that one ear was missing and the animal's left eye was scarred shut.

"Would you take a cup of tea in your hand, Doctor?"

"No thanks, Maggie. We just popped in for a minute," O'Reilly said. "How's the headaches?"

Barry noticed that as O'Reilly spoke, his gaze darted round the room.

"I couldn't have done better at Lourdes," she said, crossing herself. "It's a miracle, so it is. Them wee pills—"

"Good," said O'Reilly, glancing at Barry.

"Away to hell out of there, General." Maggie pushed the protesting cat out of its chair. "Sit down by the fire, Doctor."

O'Reilly sat. "How is the General, Maggie?" He fondled the cat's head. "Up to his usual tricks?"

"That one," Maggie's wrinkled face split into a toothless grin, "that one would sow dissension in a deserted house." She turned to Barry. "Have a seat."

He shook his head, but out of curiosity asked, "Why do you call your cat the General, Miss MacCorkle?"

She chuckled. "That's his pet name. His full name is General Sir Bernard Law Montgomery; isn't it, you wee divil?" The cat turned its good eye to the sound of her voice. "He's just like the man he's named for. He's an Ulsterman, and he loves a good fight, don't you?"

The General made a deep growling noise, laid his only ear back along the side of his head, and glowered at Barry.

"He understands everything I say, you know," Maggie said.

Barry was not sure he liked the way the cat was glaring at him. He took one step back.

"Don't you worry your head about him," she said. "You're not big enough for him to go after."

O'Reilly rose. "We'll have to be getting on, Maggie." He crossed the room. "Now remember"—O'Reilly paused as he opened the door—"if you're out of sorts, come and see me."

"I will," she said, "and thanks for popping by."

"No trouble," said O'Reilly, "we were on our way to see Sonny."

"Sonny?" Maggie cackled, "Poor ould Sonny. He's not too well pleased with me."

"Oh?" said O'Reilly.

"Aye. His spaniel came round here yesterday, but the General saw to that dog, didn't you, General?"

It seemed to Barry that at the word "dog," the cat's growl deepened. He arched his back and spat.

Maggie held the door. "Sonny'll tell you all about it, but pay no heed to him. He's only an ould goat anyway."

"I didn't know that Miss MacCorkle had asked you to call," Barry said, as he shut the car door.

"She didn't," said O'Reilly, driving off. "On slow days I try to visit one or two of the ones that I worry about."

"You were looking for something back there. What was it?"

"Little things. Dishes washed, no half-filled saucepans on the stove, clean floors." O'Reilly turned onto a narrow road. "Maggie's a bit different, but she's independent, and I need to know that she's looking after herself. If she starts to neglect the place, we may have to think about some kind of home care for her." O'Reilly's voice softened. "I'd not like to think of Maggie in a home, so if I can keep an eye on her . . ."

"That's very decent of you."

"Not a bit," said O'Reilly tersely. "There's more to this job than runny noses and hypochondriacs who drag you out of your bed in the middle of the bloody night."

"I see."

"You will," said O'Reilly, "at our next stop."

"Sonny?"

"Sonny. Now there's a story and a half." O'Reilly braked. Barry could see a tractor crossing the road. It was quieter in the car now. In keeping with O'Reilly's earlier prediction, the rain had stopped, and the summer sun was making steam rise in soft tendrils from the road's wet surface. The car moved on.

"I'll tell you about Sonny after we've been there," said O'Reilly. "But if you think Maggie's a bit odd . . ."—he pulled to the side of the road—"what do you make of this?"

"Good Lord."

The opposite verge was cluttered with old cars, television sets, a rusting combine harvester, and folding plastic chairs. Electrical cables drooped from the branches of a larch tree and led to a television set and a glass-fronted spin dryer. Barry could see bundles of clothes inside, whirling and dancing. The yellow-covered extension cords ran from a roofless house that stood back from the road. The roof beams were weather-stained and half caved in. Ivy straggled up the walls and over the windowpanes.

What should have been the front garden was crammed with old cars, motorcycles, farm machinery, and a yellow caravan. A man wearing a brown raincoat tied at the waist with baler twine left one of the rusting motorcars, strode to the caravan, and opened the door. Five dogs piled out, each yapping and vying for the man's attention.

O'Reilly had crossed the road and stood beside the television set. Barry followed.

"How are you, Sonny?" O'Reilly yelled.

"I'm coming." Sonny made his way to a gate and let himself out. "Be good boys now, and stay in there," he said to the dogs that ran along behind a low hedge, yelping and barking. "Hush now," he called, as he strode to where Barry and O'Reilly stood. The noise died away. "Doctor." He offered a hand, which O'Reilly shook.

"Sonny," said O'Reilly, "this is Doctor Laverty."

"Pleased to meet you, Sonny." Barry stared at the man. He was almost as tall as O'Reilly, older, yet stood with the bearing of a regimental sergeant major. He wore a yellow sou'wester from under which locks of iron-grey hair flowed to his shoulders. His eyes were as pale as those of a collie dog, yet his ruddy cheeks told of years of Ulster winds. And, Barry wondered, was there the faintest tinge of blue in the skin above the man's cheekbones?

"Have you any new potatoes?" O'Reilly asked.

"I have." Sonny reached behind the spin dryer and produced a small sack. "Five shillings and sixpence." He gave the sack to O'Reilly, who counted the coins into a hand that Barry could see was bent with the nodules of arthritis.

"I brought you more of these," said O'Reilly, handing over two small plastic medicine bottles.

"How much do I owe—?" Already Sonny was reaching into his trouser pocket.

"Samples," said O'Reilly. "The salesman from the drug company gives them to me for free."

"You wouldn't be having me on? I can pay, you know."

"Not at all," said O'Reilly. "How are the dogs?"

"All grand, except Sandy. The silly bugger got into a fight with Maggie's cat."

"I heard," said O'Reilly.

"And how is the old biddy?" Barry heard tenderness as Sonny spoke.

"Rightly," said O'Reilly.

"I'm glad to hear that." Sonny's pale eyes softened. "Silly old duck."

"Aye," said O'Reilly. "Well, we must be getting along."

"Thank you, Doctor," said Sonny, picking up one of the folding plastic chairs and opening it. "I'll just sit here awhile, now the sun's out." He settled in the chair and looked at the spin dryer. "My clothes are nearly ready." A dog howled from the other side of the hedge. "Wheest now," Sonny called. "I'll be with you in a little minute."

"What on earth was that all about?" Barry asked, as O'Reilly pointed the Rover homewards.

"Pride," said O'Reilly. " 'Pride goeth before destruction, and a haughty spirit before a fall.' Proverbs 16:18."

"Pride?"

"Sonny is the most stiff-necked man I've ever met, and yet he's one of the most contented. He has a Ph.D., you know, used to work for some big chemical company in Belfast, but he'd rather stay at home and live in his car."

"In his car? But I saw a caravan."

"For the dogs," said O'Reilly. "Sonny dotes on his dogs."

"But why does he live in his car? Can he not get the roof of his house repaired?"

"Yes . . . and no. You remember the worthy Councillor Bishop?"

"Yes."

"He's a building contractor. Twenty years ago Sonny hired Bishop to replace the roof. He wanted the house all done up before he got married."

Barry remembered how Sonny had asked about Maggie Mac-Corkle. "Not to Maggie?"

"To Maggie, but—and it's a big but—Bishop . . . and he's a man who'd wrestle a bear for a ha'penny . . . tried to cheat Sonny on the price of a load of slates."

"After the old roof had been stripped?"

"Precisely. Sonny refused to pay Bishop for the work he'd done already. Bishop said Sonny could whistle for his new roof. Maggie wouldn't marry a man who quite literally couldn't keep a roof over her head. Sonny quit his job, moved into his car, supports himself selling vegetables and scrap iron, and there the matter rests."

"I'll be damned. For twenty years?"

"Aye." O'Reilly turned into his back lane. "That's about the length and the breadth of it."

"Sonny's not too well, is he?"

"Why do you say that?"

"His cheeks are a bit blue."

"Smart of you to notice."

Barry smiled. "Heart failure?"

"Only mild." O'Reilly stopped the car.

"What did you give him?"

"Digitalis and a diuretic. They keep it pretty well in control."

Barry frowned. "Can you get those for free from the drug reps?"

"Ah," said O'Reilly, "them as ask no questions get told no lies. Now be a good lad and open the garage door."

Mrs. Kincaid greeted them in the kitchen.

"Any calls, Kinky?" O'Reilly asked.

"Not one, but there is a shmall little matter you should see to, so."

"Oh?"

She glanced down at Barry's trousers. "Have you been in the bogs again so soon? You're clabber to the knee."

"Arthur," said Barry resignedly. "He was pleased to see me back."

O'Reilly laughed. "He's taken quite a shine to you."

Bloody dog, Barry thought.

" 'Tis a good thing I washed your other pants." Mrs. Kincaid looked up.

Barry followed the direction of her glance. Above his head, hanging over a wooden rack that had been hoisted on a system of pulleys, he saw his corduroys.

"Thank you, Mrs. Kincaid."

"Far be it from me to intrude," said O'Reilly, "but you said there was something for me to sort out, Kinky."

Her bright little eyes almost disappeared when she smiled and said, "It's in the surgery." She walked off.

"Lead on, Macduff." O'Reilly followed Mrs. Kincaid.

"Actually, it's 'Lay on, Macduff.' "

" 'And damned be him that first cries "Hold, enough!" ' *Macbeth*," said O'Reilly. "I know that." He went into the surgery where Mrs. Kincaid stood beside the examining table. "You'd just gone out when somebody rang the bell. I found this thing, so." She indicated a wicker basket that sat on the couch.

"Good God," said O'Reilly, "you don't think it's the old waif-in-the-basket number, do you?"

If it is, Barry thought, it's a baby with a most peculiar cry. A low growling, harsh and brittle, with overtones of a small vessel's foghorn, filled his ears.

"Well," said O'Reilly, "I'd better take a look." He tapped on the side of the basket.

Barry watched the basket jerk for several inches along the couch, as if moved by some primal force. The growls increased by about ten decibels.

"Take you care now, Doctor." Mrs. Kincaid made the sign, index fingers crossed, to ward off the evil eye. O'Reilly opened the lid. Barry took a step backwards as a white blur erupted from the container and, with one final eldritch shriek, landed on O'Reilly's shoulder.

"Begod, it's a cat," he said, reaching up and hauling it off its perch. "Push-wush. Pushy-wushy." He held the animal in one big hand and stroked its head with the other. It struggled briefly; then seemingly accepting its lot, it butted its head against O'Reilly's palm. Barry heard a low rumbling. The animal was purring.

"Mmm," said O'Reilly. "I doubt if we'll find out who left it, and we can't just put it out."

"Will I find it some milk, Doctor?"

"That would be grand, Kinky," said O'Reilly, handing her the little feline. "And could you manage a cup of tea for us while you're at it?"

"I will, so. Come on, you wee dote," she said fondly, and headed for her kitchen.

"I don't know about you, Barry," O'Reilly said, "but after last night at the Fotheringhams', I could use a bit of time with my feet up."

Barry yawned.

"Tired?"

"A bit."

"Well," said O'Reilly, "it's only a couple of days 'til your day off."

10

I'm Standing in a Railway Station . . .

Saturday, Barry's first day off, was what the locals would call "a grand soft day." He turned up the collar of his raincoat against the damp that was neither heavy enough to be rain nor light enough to be mist. Mrs. Kincaid had said the train to Belfast would leave Bally-bucklebo at ten fifteen. Half an hour to Belfast, fifteen minutes to walk into the city centre, where he intended to invest a part of his first week's pay in a pair of Wellington boots, half an hour on the bus up Grosvenor Road, and he'd still be in good time to see Jack Mills in O'Kane's Bar opposite the gates of the Royal Victoria Hospital.

He strode along Ballybucklebo's main street, acknowledging the greetings of passersby. Some he recognized. They had been among the many who in the last week had perched on the wooden chair in the surgery. Others were unfamiliar, but all seemed to know who he was. Not, he thought, turning onto the aptly named Station Road, like Belfast where impersonal people ignored each other, and everyone was a stranger, none with as much as a "Good-day." He found the village's familiarity comforting.

He bought his ticket and went to the platform. A pair of tracks, metal shiny from regular use, ran between the raised platforms. On the opposite side of the roadbed a waiting room crouched, its slate roof of granite stone darkened by the drizzle. Old tin advertisements were nailed to its walls. The one for Waverley fountain pens—white letters on a blue background, the message interrupted by streaks of rust—had probably been put up before the First World War, and nobody had bothered to take it down. He read the slogan: "They"—rust blot—"a Boon and a Blessing to men, The"— more rust—"the Owl and the Waverley Pen."

He heard the rattle of an approaching train and could smell its exhaust. The brakes screeched. The train stopped. Barry let himself into a compartment where two upholstered benches faced each other, and was pleased to see that it was unoccupied. He sat in the familiar space and wondered how often as a student he had ridden on this train from his home in Bangor farther down the line to the Queen's Quay terminal in Belfast. How many times had he ridden past Ballybucklebo without even paying attention to its existence?

The train jerked, grumbled, and pulled away from the station. Barry stared through the window and watched the scenery go by. A wide ditch kept company with the track. Families of mallard swam in the ditch, the drakes' heads incandescent green. The ducks dowdy save for the emerald and blue flashes of their wing specula, chivvied their yellow ducklings. A line of Yeats came to mind: "O'Driscoll drove with a song / The wild duck and the drake / From the tall and the tufted reeds / Of the drear Hart Lake." The fragment reminded him that as well as Wellingtons he wanted to buy the most recent book of poetry by this new chap Seamus Heaney. He had an interesting way of using words to describe Ulster life, a way that Barry found resonated with his own thoughts about the place.

He wondered how Heaney would describe the land between the ditch and the lough. A wide, wild bog, where bulrushes and brambles grew with unchecked abandon, was the only way he could think to describe it. The lough was calm, gunmetal grey under a lowering sky, and on the far shore the clouds were so low, so still, that they

Patrick Taylor

might have been nailed to the crests of the Antrim Hills. It was the kind of day that was all too common, that must, he thought, give Ulster folk the dour side to their personalities, although he himself did not feel one bit low. He'd certainly seen a fair bit of how things worked since he joined O'Reilly's practice, and that was why he'd come. He had a great deal to think about, and he was no closer to answering the question, Was he really cut out for rural general practice?

What he had seen had been a revelation. Barry had not understood the diversity of work in a place like Ballybucklebo, and O'Reilly was one of the oddest men Barry had ever met. He was unpredictable, at times bad-tempered, untiring, and given to odd medical practices. He cared deeply about his charges yet was dismissive to the point of becoming angry if anyone hinted that he had a kindly streak. Barry wondered why O'Reilly hadn't married. Perhaps the demands of his practice had not given him time for any social life, or perhaps, Barry smiled, no woman could put up with the man's quirks. He must ask Mrs. Kincaid.

The train shuddered to a halt at Kinnegar Station. Two young women tumbled aboard and sat at the other end of the compartment, one opposite, one on his side. Barry tried to ignore them by turning away and staring out the window. Their chatter intruded. It was impossible to think about anything when one insisted in declaiming her thoughts as if their import was so great that the whole bloody world should be let in on her secrets.

"Away on. Charlie Simpson does *not* fancy Eileen." The speaker's voice was harsh, with the flat accents of Belfast. "That Eileen has a face on her like a sheep."

"He's daft about her. . . ."

"That's not what I heard."

Poor Charlie Simpson, whoever he was, daft about some girl, Barry thought. He himself had been daft about a student nurse. He closed his eyes and pictured her green eyes, auburn hair, slim figure;

thought about the nights in the backseat of Brunhilde, the Volkswagen's windows opaque with the condensation of their breathing, the surreptitious trips to his room in the junior medical staff quarters, the sweetness and the softness . . . and the gnawing emptiness when she had told him, in a voice that was so matter-of-fact that she might have been ordering a pound of bacon in a grocer's shop, that she was going to marry a surgeon. Six months ago. And still it stung.

"Do you know it would serve her right to get stuck with Charlie? He's thick as two short planks, so he is."

Barry wished the young woman would shut up. She had a voice that would cut tin.

The other chuckled. Her laugh was contralto, deep and resonant. Barry glanced at her. She had black hair with a sheen like a healthy animal's pelt. Her face was strong, with a firm chin and full lips that bore the merest hint of pale pink lipstick. Slavic cheekbones. Dark eyes with an upward tilt. They had a deep, unfathomable glow, like the warmth in well-polished mahogany. Her skin was smooth and tanned, and a small dimple showed in her left cheek as she laughed. But for that dimple, she could have been Audrey Hepburn in *My Fair Lady*.

Her laughter died, and Barry found himself wishing that she would laugh again. He didn't want her to see him staring, so he looked away, but soon he found his gaze drawn back. She was looking out the window. He saw her in profile. She wore an unbuttoned white gabardine raincoat.

"Anyway, Patricia," her friend rattled on, "I says to Eileen, says I . . ."

Would she never stop prattling? He glanced down and then stole another look. Patricia, that was her name; Patricia turned, caught him staring, and held his gaze. His hand flew to his head, and he smoothed the damn tuft. "Excuse me," he said, knowing that he was blushing. "I'm awfully sorry. . . ."

She laughed again, warm and throaty. "A cat can look at a king . . . if it doesn't think the king's a mouse."

"I'm sorry."

The train slowed. He saw the sign for Belfast Station glide past the window. The train stopped. They left. Barry closed his eyes and sat back against the cushions. Why in hell had he not had the courage to find out more about Patricia? In the movies she would have left something on the train, something he could use as an excuse to run after her. No such luck. Ships that pass, he thought, and yet, and yet . . .

He left the compartment not expecting to see any sign of Patricia and her chatty friend, but there they were up ahead, Patricia leaning on the noisy one's arm and limping slowly. Must have hurt herself playing hockey, he thought. She certainly looked the athletic type. He took a deep breath, smoothed his hair, and lengthened his stride until he drew level.

"Excuse me," he said, "excuse me."

Patricia stopped and faced him.

"Come away on out of that, Patricia." The friend tugged at Patricia's sleeve and scowled at Barry.

Words tumbled out. "Look. My name's Barry Laverty. I want . . . that is . . . I'd like—"

"Away off and chase yourself." More tugging at the coat sleeve.

"Will you have dinner with me tonight? Please?"

Patricia gave him an appraising look, head-to-toe like a roué undressing a woman with his eyes.

"You've a right brass neck, so you have." The friend glared at Barry. "Anyway, we're busy the night."

Patricia smiled. "That's right. We are."

"Oh." Barry felt that his being able to catch up with the pair had been like a last-minute stay of execution, but by her words Patricia had told him that the warden's midnight call had not come and wasn't going to. His shoulders sagged.

"But I'm taking the ten o'clock train back to the Kinnegar."

He saw the laugh in her dark eyes, and his breath caught in his throat.

Barry sat in a plastic-covered chair at a Formica-topped table in the window alcove of the upstairs room of O'Kane's Bar, the nearest watering hole to the Royal Victoria Hospital. At his feet a pair of Wellington boots lay in a brown paper bag. He glanced at his watch. Jack Mills was late, and that wasn't like Jack.

The curtains behind Barry swayed in the draught coming in through the window. He tried to see out through the smut and drizzle streaks. He leant back and peered up Grosvenor Road to the casualty department, outside which, regal and dignified, the bronze statue of Her Royal Majesty Victoria, *Regina, Dei Gratia, Fid. Def., Ind., Imp.*, sat enthroned. Her sceptre, covered in bird shite, made a convenient perch for a pair of pigeons.

A shadow fell over the table top, and Barry turned to see Jack Mills wearing a long white coat, his usual grin pasted to a country face that would not have been out of place on a farmer from Cullybackey—which was where Jack's folks ran a dairy herd.

"Sorry I'm late." Jack sat. "I'd a bugger of a night on call and this morning was murder." He pulled out a packet of cigarettes. "Fag?"

Barry shook his head. "I quit last year. Remember?"

"Right." Jack lit up. "I'm knackered." He stretched out his legs.

"Pint?" Barry asked, looking forward to spending the afternoon with his old friend.

"Can't. Sorry." Jack inhaled deeply and shook his head.

"Oh?"

"Yeah. The registrar in Sick Kids is sick himself, and they need a hand on a surgical case in about an hour. I got the short straw, damn it." Jack's smile belied his words. "I wouldn't mind a quick bite to eat though."

Barry swallowed his disappointment. It was going to be a long day before the ten o'clock train. He imagined dark eyes and hoped the wait would be worth it.

"Grub," said Jack. He turned and called to the barman, "Brendan, could you manage a steak-and-mushroom pie, chips, and an orange squash?"

"Right, Doctor Mills." Brendan put down the glass he was polishing. "What about you, Doctor Laverty?"

"That would be good." Barry never ceased to be amazed by how Brendan, owner and barman, a man of indeterminate age with a face like a bilious heifer, remembered the names of the generations of students and junior doctors who used his establishment.

"So," Jack asked, "how's the world abusing you?"

"Can't complain."

"And if you did, no one would listen." Jack ground out his cigarette. "So, go on," he said. "How's general practice?"

"It's different. I'm working with a Doctor O'Reilly in Ballybucklebo."

"O'Reilly? Not by any chance Fingal Flahertie O'Reilly? Man of about fifty, fifty-five?"

"That's right."

"Good Lord. Before the war he was one of the best forwards to play rugby for Ireland."

"I didn't know that." Barry was impressed.

"You, brother Laverty, wouldn't know an Irish rugby player from a penny bap." He winked at Barry. "But you saved my bacon in anatomy class, so I'll forgive you."

"Rubbish." Barry remembered the trouble Jack had had when they were students. His Latin was poor, and learning the names of the body's structures, an easy task for Barry, had been a struggle for his friend. Jack's likelihood of progressing through medical school had been in doubt, but with Barry's coaching he'd managed to squeak a pass in the third-year anatomy examinations.

"Here y'are." Brendan set two plates on the table. "I'll get your drinks in a minute."

"Dig in," said Jack, picking up his knife and fork. "Come on, I want to hear about what you're up to."

Barry did his best to describe his first week as O'Reilly's assistant, and the older doctor's habit of riding roughshod over anyone who stood in his way. Jack made sympathetic noises. He chuckled when Barry described O'Reilly's eccentricities.

"But you are enjoying it?"

Brendan reappeared and silently left their drinks.

"I asked you, are you enjoying working in the country?"

"I think so. Mind you, there's an awful lot of routine stuff."

"That's easy," said Jack. "Remember what that plummy English registrar told you when you complained about all the boring things we had to do when we were students?"

"What?"

Jack, always the consummate mimic, declared in the tones of one of the upper class, "Old boy, in this life there will always be a certain amount of shit to be shovelled. I really would urge you to buy a long-handled spade and simply get on with it."

"Right." Barry laughed. "And I have seen some interesting cases." He told Jack how O'Reilly had driven the Kennedy girl to Belfast in his own car. Jack nodded, mouth full, when Barry mentioned that O'Reilly's knowledge of every patient seemed encyclopaedic.

"Now there's a difference," he said. "I never get to know anybody. We're too damn busy. Get 'em in, cut 'em, and get 'em out. Mind you, I really enjoy the cutting bit."

"You would. You always were a bloody sadist."

"Away off and feel your head. It's what Jim Hardy used to say in that TV programme."

"*Tales of Wells Fargo*?"

"That's it, partner." Jack adopted a heavy Texan drawl. " 'Some-times a man's got to do what a man's got to do.' " He reverted to his own voice. "Speaking of which . . . ," he looked up at the clock over the bar, stood, reached into his pocket, and tossed a pound note on the table. "My half. Sorry, mate, but I'd better run on. Sir Donald Cromie is like the wrath of God if his assistant's late."

"Sir Donald who?" Was he the man O'Reilly had consulted on Tuesday?

"Sir Donald Cromie, paediatric surgeon with nimble fingers and a temper like Mount Etna on a bad day. He did an appendix the other night. Now the patient's blown up a pelvic abscess. Sick as a dog."

"You wouldn't happen to know the patient's name?"

Jack laughed. "No. I don't even know if it's a wee boy or a wee girl."

"Oh."

Jack moved toward the staircase. "I'm off. Good to see you, mate. I'll give you a bell next time I'm free. Maybe we could sink a decent pint or two."

"I'd like that."

"And about O'Reilly: *Noli illegitimi carborundum.*"

"I won't," Barry said to his friend's departing back, then took a drink. The Cantrell and Cochrane orange juice was sickly sweet. Barry stood, picked up his parcelled boots, and walked over to the bar. "What's the damage, Brendan?"

"Hang on." Brendan, with great moving of lips and counting on fingers, scribbled with the stub of a yellow pencil on a piece of paper.

As Barry waited, he wondered about the patient with the appen-dix abscess. Could it be Jeannie Kennedy? No way to tell; still the coincidence was a bit worrying.

"Here you are, Doctor Laverty."

Barry paid the bill. "Take care of yourself, Brendan."

"I will, sir."

Barry made his way down the narrow staircase, treads worn concave by the feet of countless patrons. When he stepped out onto Grosvenor Road, the drizzle had stopped. He decided to walk into Belfast. He'd lots of time to kill until the ten o'clock train.

He walked in a world filled with the stink of car exhaust, the constant grumble of traffic, gutters clogged with soggy newspapers. On the pavement, people hurried by, men in Dexter raincoats, one exercising three racing greyhounds, and women in head scarves, their pink and white hair curlers scarcely hidden, their faces pinched and thin-lipped, shopping bags over their arms.

He passed pubs and turf accountants, busy with the comings and goings of men in elbow-patched tweed jackets, cigarettes glued to their lower lips, and then fish-and-chips shops reeking of lard and battered cod, greasy wrappers flung on the pavement to lie among squashed smears of dog turd.

The streets he passed all had familiar names: Roden Street, Distillery Street, Cullingtree Road. They were cramped terraces, sunless and smog-ridden. In his student years he'd seen their inhabitants with chronic bronchitis, rheumatic fever, rickets, head lice, and scabies—all the diseases of poverty and damp, cramped living. He'd delivered babies in tiny bedrooms of "two up, two down" terrace houses, where the bedclothes had been newspapers, the mattress urine-stained and dank, and the woman in the bed, twenty-two going on fifty with her reddened hands, shrunken cheeks, and hair like the strands of a greasy floor mop.

He'd felt so bloody useless. No matter what advances medicine might make, he'd learned the hard way that doctors occupied the last line of trenches in a battle that should have been won at the front. No amount of oxygen for ravaged lungs, vitamins for scrawny kids, or DDT for head lice could have half the effects of a decent diet and a clean, warm home.

Barry lengthened his stride and hurried across the railway bridge to Sandy Row, bastion of Loyalist supremacy. In preparation for next week's great Orange celebration, the Twelfth of July, the kerbstones were freshly painted in red, white, and blue. Union Jacks drooped from every upper window, and street urchins raced about in torn short trousers and half-unravelled Fair Isle pullovers, snail tracks of mucus on their upper lips. Their cries were shrill, harsh: "Hey, silver sleeves? Away on home and wipe your dirty snotters." "Sammy McCandless, yer mammy wants ye." "See you, Bertie? Quit your colloguing, and give us a hand with this here fuckin' tree." This last remark was from a child of eight dragging a dead branch, from God only knew where, to add to one of the bonfires that would rage on the night of the eleventh. The flames would paint the clouds with a glow like that of the blazes that Henry VIII's reforming Protestants set under the flesh of nonrecanting Catholics. The hearty warmth of next week's fires would bring cheer to the drab existence of the inhabitants of Sandy Row, and serve to remind the Fenians in their ghettos on Falls Road and Divis Street, not half a mile away, of their place in the Unionist province of Ulster.

Belfast, he thought, dirty old harridan of a city, and one that I don't miss one bit. There's a lot to be said for Ballybucklebo.

He stopped where Grosvenor Road met the junction of College Square and Great Victoria Street. Two cinemas sat, one on each corner: one marquee read, *Dr. Strangelove*; the other, *The Pink Panther*. Both starred Peter Sellers. Barry looked at his watch. He'd have time to nip over to the bookstore on Donegall Square and come back to the Ritz for the start of *The Pink Panther*. He'd grab a quick bite after the showing. Perhaps, he thought, he'd try the Chinese place on Church Street, and that wouldn't leave him much more than an hour to kill before ten o'clock.

Maybe she wasn't coming. Why would she? Maybe she'd said she'd be on the ten o'clock just to get rid of him.

The train would leave in five minutes, and by arriving too early Barry had given his impatience time to build and his doubts time to grow. For God's sake, why would a young woman who didn't know him from a hole in the ground say she'd meet him on a train—at night? He took one last long look along the Queen's Quay. It was deserted. The cranes on the coal dock stood gaunt and skeletal against a dimming sky. Oh, well. Barry hefted his parcel of boots, turned, and made his way toward the platform. He waited for his turn to surrender his ticket.

"Barry. Barry Laverty."

He turned and saw her limping fast toward him. He almost dropped his package. She stood beside him, panting slightly. "Come on," she said, grasping his arm, "get a move on, or we'll miss the train."

"Just made it," she said, sitting down on a bench as Barry slammed the compartment door.

He sat opposite. "I thought you weren't coming."

She laughed, her dark eyes bright in the compartment's dim light. "So your name's Barry Laverty?"

"That's right. I heard your friend call you Patricia."

"Patricia Spence." He took the hand she offered, feeling the smoothness of her skin, the firmness of her grasp. He knew he was holding on for a moment too long, but he didn't want to let go. He looked into her face. He never wanted to let go.

"I'll have it back, if you don't mind."

He eased his grip, but she let her hand linger just for a moment. He sat forward. Now what? Damn it, why was he always at a loss for words with women?

"You're quiet," she said. "Cat got your tongue?"

The train jolted through the dark night, swaying over the uneven track, rattling where the rails met.

"Not really."

"Don't know what got into you, asking a complete stranger to dinner?"

"That's right."

"If it makes you feel any better, I don't know what got into *me*, telling you I'd be on this train." She tossed her dark mane, highlights dancing in the ebony. "I think it's the way your hair sticks up . . . like a little boy's, and you looked so lost."

His hand flew to that damned tuft. He saw her smile at him. "I washed it this morning, and I can't do a damn thing with it." Christ, he thought, what a stupid thing to say.

She chuckled at the hackneyed line.

Now or never, he told himself. "I just had to meet you, that's all." He swallowed. He felt his fingers digging into his palms. "I've never seen anyone so lovely." He knew he was blushing. The train rattled to a halt. "Sydenham Station," he said.

"Thank you, sir," she said.

"For telling you the name of the station?"

"For telling me you think I'm lovely."

"You are," he said, grateful that no one had boarded, knowing that Kinnegar was only two more stops down the line, happy that the train was on its way again, anxious that his time with her was running out. "Very lovely." He wanted to touch her, to hold her hand, but he was terrified that she might dart away like a startled bird. He sat rigidly. He must keep her talking. "You live in the Kinnegar?" he asked.

"That's right. Number 9, the Esplanade. On the seafront. I love the sea."

"I grew up in Bangor. I know what you mean about the sea. It's never the same. It's . . ." He fumbled in his pocket and pulled out Seamus Heaney's book. "I'm not very good with words but . . ." He opened the book, riffled through the pages, and read:

You might think that the sea is company,
Exploding comfortably down on the cliffs
But no: when it begins, the flung spray hits
The very windows, spits like a tame cat
Turned savage.

He looked into her eyes—cat's eyes—and saw them soften. "That's beautiful," she said gently. "Who's the poet?"

"Chap called Seamus Heaney."

"Never heard of him."

"I think you will. If you like poetry."

"And you do?" Her question was solemn, her gaze never leaving his eyes.

"Oh, yes." He glanced down. He was jerked forward as the carriage stumbled to a halt. He felt the nearness of her. She was wearing a musk that made his head swim. He stared into her face, reached out, and touched her hand. She twined her fingers with his, smiled. He saw her teeth, white, even, against her full lips.

The train jerked. "I get off at the next stop," she said. "I'm sorry."

"I know, but . . . Patricia, I want to see you again."

"My phone number's Kinnegar 657334."

Kinnegar 657334. He repeated the number in his head, over and over. "Can I phone you tomorrow?"

"I'd like that." She squeezed his hand, leant forward, and kissed him gently, little more than a fluttering of butterfly wings. "I'd like that very much."

"Jesus," he whispered. "Oh, Jesus."

"Bangor's not far from Kinnegar," she said, as the train began to slow.

"I don't live in Bangor now. I'm staying in Ballybucklebo."

"You're what?" She sat back and laughed, deep in her throat. He rejoiced in the sound, but what was so amusing about Ballybucklebo?

"Oh, dear," she said. "Oh, dear."

The Kinnegar halt sign appeared in the window. The train stopped. She rose.

He stood and opened the door. "What's so funny?"

"The ten o'clock doesn't stop at Ballybucklebo. You'll have to get off here and walk home."

"What?"

"That's right, and you'd better get a move on if you don't want to go all the way to Bangor."

The train jolted. He hustled her onto the platform and jumped down beside her.

"I'm sorry. I shouldn't have laughed," she said.

"It's all right. At least I can walk you home."

"Come on then. It's not far," she said, as the train's red rear lights vanished round a curve in the track. Damn it. He'd left his new Wellington boots in the compartment.

She took his hand, and boots forgotten, he walked beside her down the steps of the station, out of the weak pools of light thrown from the station windows, and onto a dark country road. After the day's rain the night air was gentle with hay and honeysuckle scents mingled with the tang of the sea. In the distance he could hear the susurration of waves on a shore.

He had to shorten his stride to keep pace with Patricia's uneven steps.

"How'd you hurt your leg? Hockey?"

"I didn't hurt it." He detected a hint of bitterness.

"What happened?"

"Nineteen fifty-one."

He stopped. Dead. Turned her to face him. "The polio epidemic?"

She nodded. "I was lucky. My left leg's a bit short, but I didn't end up in an iron lung like some of the kids."

"Jesus."

She dropped his hand and took one step back. "I suppose I won't be hearing from you now? Men don't like women who aren't perfect." Her words were matter-of-fact.

He sensed that she had been hurt before, perhaps badly.

"I don't want pity," she said. He looked up and saw Orion, high, high, each star glimmering, bright and proud. He knew that to him, her short leg made no difference, none in the whole wide world.

"I'm not very good at pity," he said. "I don't give a damn about your leg, Patricia. I don't care at all."

"Do you mean that?" She stepped away from him, stared at him through to his soul.

He said nothing, just waited and watched her face, trying to read her expression in the dim starlight, hoping she wouldn't tell him that she didn't believe him.

"I shouldn't, Barry Laverty, I know I shouldn't, but I think I believe you."

He saw something silver beneath her left eye, and he wanted to taste the salt of it, but something told him he mustn't rush her. "Come on," he said, "let's get you home."

"All right," she said, "and Barry?"

"What?"

"I'd really like you to phone."

11

Deliver Us from Evil

"You look like the *Hesperus* . . . a total wreck," O'Reilly said, leaning forward in one of the upstairs armchairs and peering over the top of the *Sunday Times*.

Barry yawned. "Late night."

"I know. I heard Arthur. He sounded happy."

"I wish—" Barry began, intending to tell O'Reilly that something would have to be done about his sex-crazed Labrador, but O'Reilly interrupted.

"Must have been two o'clock. Good thing there's no surgery today. What kept you?"

Barry parked himself in the other armchair. "Fate," he said. "Kismet." He stared out the window, seeing not the church steeple but Patricia's face.

"Whatever it was, it's put a grin on your face."

Barry debated whether to tell O'Reilly about her but decided that now was not the time. She was his to relish in private. Just for a while. O'Reilly would probably make some crude joke, and Barry didn't want that.

His musing was interrupted by a rhythmic rending noise.

"Stop that," O'Reilly yelled, tossing the *Times* colour supplement in Barry's direction.

Barry ducked. "Stop what?"

"Not you. Her. Lady Macbeth."

The white cat that had been left on the doorstep had been so named by O'Reilly after she'd bloodied Arthur Guinness's nose and chased him back to his doghouse—twice. O'Reilly'd said she clearly had an ambition to rule the entire place and, like her namesake, might very well kill to do so.

She stood semi-erect on her hind paws, body arched like the downward sway in the back of a spavined horse. Her front claws raked and ripped at the fabric of Barry's chair with the enthusiasm of an out-of-control combine harvester.

"Stop it, madam." O'Reilly stood over the animal, who clawed away and condescended to give him one of those feline looks that asks, "My good man, are you by the remotest chance addressing *moi*?"

"Stop it." O'Reilly grabbed the cat, picked her up, and tickled her under the chin.

Barry watched as she fixed the big man with her green eyes, smiled, laid back her ears, and made a throaty sound. She held her tail straight out from her body. The tail's tip made circles, the amplitude of which increased in keeping with the deepening timbre of her growl.

"I don't think she's very happy, Fingal."

"Nonsense. Animals dote on me. Don't you?" He went on tickling her until she struck, fangs sinking into the web of O'Reilly's hand.

"You bitch," he roared.

Lady Macbeth sprang from his arms, landed nimbly on the rug, sat, regarded O'Reilly as she might have looked at a piece of limp lettuce in her food dish, and deliberately, nonchalantly, hoisted one hind leg and began to lick her bottom.

" 'Tyger, tyger, burning bright,' " O'Reilly glowered at the cat. " 'In the forests of the night. . . .' "

"Blake," Barry observed, trying to hide his smile.

"I know it's bloody Blake." O'Reilly swung one booted foot

backwards. "I've half a mind to give Lady Macbeth her arsehole to wear as a necklace."

"Here, hang on, Fingal." Barry rose and interposed himself between O'Reilly and the cat.

O'Reilly grunted and lowered his foot. "I'd not do it. She's only young." He glared at his punctured hand. "Just a love bite anyway."

"Maybe," said Barry, "but we'd better get it cleaned up. There's a thing called cat scratch disease, you know."

"And tetanus," O'Reilly remarked. "And you can disabuse yourself of any notion, Doctor Laverty, that you're going to stick a bloody needle in *my* backside. I've already been inoculated."

"Thought never entered my head," Barry lied, thinking of the Dettol that would have to be poured onto the raw punctures. "Not for a minute."

"Phew," said O'Reilly, "that Dettol stings." He waited for Barry to apply a dressing. "Maybe you should try it next time you cut yourself."

"No thanks."

"No, really." O'Reilly held out his hand. "It wouldn't be a bad thing if all of us quacks had to see things from the customers' point of view once in a while. Might make us a bit more empathic."

"You want to feel like one of your patients?" Barry clapped an Elastoplast on O'Reilly's puncture wounds. "You're a bit on the heavy side, Fingal, but I could try to chuck you into the rosebushes."

O'Reilly guffawed. "You can try any time you like, son."

Yes, Barry thought, and for an encore I'll have a go at tossing the Ballybucklebo maypole like a caber. "No thanks." Barry heard the front door closing.

"That's Kinky home from church," said O'Reilly. "Come on. We'll see if she can hustle up a cup of tea."

O'Reilly was once again ensconced in his living room. He nodded to where Lady Macbeth lay curled up in a patch of sunlight. "Now, before Her Ladyship remembered she was descended from a long line of albino sabre-toothed tigers, I was trying to find out what kept you out so late last night. You were muttering about kismet, which, as an aside, is probably what Lord Nelson really said to Hardy at Trafalgar. I can't see the old sea dog saying, 'Kiss me, Hardy,' can you?"

Barry had been wondering how to ask O'Reilly for more time off. Every other Saturday night was hardly sufficient time to give a blooming romance much of a chance. Unable to think of a suitable way to introduce the subject, he decided to let the conversation take this other tack. "It's in all the history books."

"Most books are full of rubbish. Kiss me? Kismet? Damned if I know about Nelson and Hardy . . . but I still want to hear what kept you out so late."

"I got on the wrong train. The ten o'clock doesn't stop at Ballybucklebo. I had to walk from Kinnegar. That's all."

O'Reilly chuckled. "The exercise'll do you good." He looked straight at Barry. "I'd hardly call getting on the wrong train 'destiny.'"

"Destiny?"

" 'Kismet,' from the Turkish *kisma,* meaning 'destiny.' And that comes from the Arabic *kasama,* meaning 'divide.' "

"You amaze me, Fingal."

"Sometimes, my boy, I amaze myself." O'Reilly leant forward. "What's her name?"

"What?"

"You've had a dreamy look all morning. You were muttering about fate. Two and two usually make four. I was a young fellow once myself." O'Reilly's voice held a distant wistfulness, as if he were remembering something gone, something precious.

Barry hesitated.

O'Reilly rose and walked to the window. Without looking at Barry, he said, "You're far too young to be getting involved with a woman. Take my advice. Medicine's a selfish enough mistress for any man."

"I think, Doctor O'Reilly, I can be the best judge of that."

"You'll see." For the first time in their week's acquaintance bitterness had crept into the older man's voice.

Mrs. Kincaid bustled in, carrying a tray.

"Tea," she said, "and a bit of toasted, buttered barmbrack, so."

Barry could smell the raisins and yeast in the hot, black loaf. "Thank you, Mrs. Kincaid," he said, "and how was church?"

"Grand altogether. He's a powerful preacher, that Reverend Robinson. When he gives the sermon, you can feel the shpits of him six pews back from the pulpit." She smiled and set the tray on the sideboard. "And how's my wee princess?" She bent over Lady Macbeth and stroked the cat's head. The cat stretched, rose, arched her back, shuddered, yawned, and began to weave against Mrs. Kincaid's shins. "You're just a wee dote. Y'are, so y'are."

"With sharp teeth," muttered O'Reilly, showing his Elastoplast.

"Huh," said Mrs. Kincaid, "if you lie down with dogs, you'll rise with fleas, and if you annoy cats you must take the consequences, so."

"Me?" said O'Reilly. "Have you seen what the beast's been doing to the furniture?"

"You'll just have to train her not to claw it."

"And how do you suggest we do that?"

"Don't look at me," said Mrs. Kincaid, turning to leave, "but Maggie MacCorkle knows as much about cats as you do about the doctoring."

"Now there's an idea," said O'Reilly, as he poured himself a cup of tea. "We'll ask her next time we see her."

Barry had only half paid attention to the discussion about the cat. He had been disturbed by O'Reilly's attitude towards women.

If that was how he felt, Barry's chances of having more time to see Patricia were probably slim, but if he didn't ask . . .

"Fingal?"

"What?" O'Reilly carried his tea to his place and sat easily in his chair. "You don't think we should talk to Maggie?"

"It's not about the cat." Barry swallowed. "I'd like to have more time off."

"So it *is* a girl." O'Reilly sipped his tea and looked steadily at Barry. "What's her name?"

"Patricia. Patricia Spence."

"And I suppose, to quote Ecclesiastes, if memory serves, she's 'a woman to make men run out of their minds'?"

"All I'm asking for is a bit more free time."

O'Reilly stared over his teacup. "How much?"

"An hour or two the odd evening, maybe every other Sunday."

O'Reilly put his cup on the saucer. "I thought you wanted to be a GP. It's not Butlins Holiday Camp here."

Barry's shoulders sagged. He should have known better than to expect any sympathy, but he wasn't ready to give up. He looked into O'Reilly's face. At least his nose tip was its normal colour. "Damn it, it's not a lot to ask for."

Barry could not meet O'Reilly's gaze and looked down. He was startled to hear O'Reilly say, "All right. Once I'm happy that you understand the running of the place, and when I can trust you not to kill too many customers, I wouldn't mind a bit of time off myself. I thought we'd take alternate weekends and have a couple of week-nights each off-duty."

Barry looked up. "Do you mean that?"

"No. I'm just talking because I'm in love with the sound of my own voice. I told you, difficult as I know you find it to believe, I wasn't always fifty-six."

Barry stood. He could have hugged the big man and nearly did when O'Reilly continued, "I suppose you'd like to take this after-

noon off? Go on then. I'll hold the fort." Barry could hear no sar-
casm, none of the earlier frostiness.

"I'd really appreciate that, Fingal."

"Go on. Phone your Patricia . . . that's her name, isn't it?"

"It is." Barry sped to the door. "Thanks, Fingal. Thanks a lot."
Kinnegar 657334. Her number rang in his head, over and over like
a Buddhist mantra as he took the stairs two at a time. He was just
about to lift the receiver when the double ring of the phone's bell
startled him. He lifted the phone.

"Hello. Doctor O'Reilly's surgery."

"Is that Doctor Laverty?" It was a woman's voice.

"Yes. Who's speaking?"

No voice came over the line, just a whimper that swelled to a
hoarse groan, then deep breathing.

"Hello? Hello? Are you there?"

"Doctor Laverty. It's Maureen Galvin. My waters bust three
hours ago, and the pains is every five minutes. I've sent for the midwife. Can you come now?"

"Of course. Doctor O'Reilly will be round right away."

"Thank you." The line went dead.

Barry raced back upstairs. "Fingal, that was Maureen Galvin. Her
membranes have ruptured, and she's contracting every five minutes."

"She'll be a while yet. I'll just finish my tea, then I'd better get
round there." O'Reilly drank, swallowed, stood, put his cup back
on the tray, and faced Barry. "She doesn't live far from here."

Patricia, Barry thought; then he said, "I'll get my bag."

"Good lad. I might need a bit of help."

O'Reilly rapidly organized his equipment: two heavy bags that
Barry assumed to be instruments, sterile towels, drugs, and rubber

gloves. Together they carried the gear to the car, and for once O'Reilly deflected Arthur Guinness's amorous advances by telling the dog to get into the back seat. "We'll give him a run on the beach when the smoke and dust have died down."

The short drive would have been more pleasant if Arthur hadn't insisted on standing up, draping his front paws over Barry's shoulders, and licking the back of his neck. He was so distracted that he couldn't pay attention to where they were going, and when the car stopped he found himself in a strange part of Ballybucklebo. By the look of the narrow-fronted terraces that lined the street he could have been in one of the slums of Belfast.

"Where are we, Fingal?"

"Council estate. Cheap housing for the less fortunate." O'Reilly hauled the packs from the car. "Here. Take these bags."

Barry grabbed the equipment. "Pretty grotty-looking place."

"Council voted the budget and chose the building contractor. Bishop sold them the land *and* finagled the contract. I told you he owns half the bloody village."

"Jerry-built?"

"Bishop cut so many corners it's a bloody miracle that these houses aren't circular. They don't even have inside bathrooms." O'Reilly slammed the door. "Come on. Let's get at it," he said, as he crossed the footpath and pounded on a front door.

A slim woman wearing the blue uniform of a district midwife answered. "Doctor O'Reilly."

"Miss Hagerty, this is Doctor Laverty."

She nodded.

"How's Maureen?"

"Grand. Three-minute contractions and the last time I examined her, the head was only a knuckle, and she's a good five shillings and fully effaced. The fetal heart rate's fine."

Barry mentally translated the antiquated system of assessing the progress of labour. One knuckle—the length of the last joint of the examiner's finger—meant that the baby's head was close to the pelvic floor. It also meant that the widest part of the head had successfully negotiated the narrowest part of the bony pelvic canal. Cervical dilatation of five shillings indicated that the neck of the uterus was halfway to being completely open, and because it was fully effaced, it had thinned out from being like a stubby carrot to the thickness of a piece of cardboard.

"She's tramping on," said O'Reilly. "The pains were every five minutes when she phoned."

"She'll not be long," Miss Hagerty agreed, turning back into the house.

"Right," said O'Reilly, charging down a narrow hall and onto a steep staircase. "Up the apples and pears."

There was barely space for Barry in the small bedroom. Maureen Galvin lay in bed. The midwife had spread a red rubber sheet under the labouring woman. No other bedclothes were in sight. O'Reilly and Miss Hagerty stood on opposite sides of the bed. O'Reilly finished tying the belt of a chest-high rubber apron, then he bent over and put his ear to a fetal stethoscope pressed to Maureen's belly.

"Uuunnnhhh," she groaned. Barry watched her face contort, her upper teeth driving the colour from her lower lip. Her eyes were screwed shut, and sweat glistened on her forehead.

O'Reilly straightened and took her hand. "Squeeze," he said. "You're doing fine."

Barry remembered the force that a woman in labour could exert in her grasp. He'd held enough hands during his obstetric training. He watched as O'Reilly's knuckles blanched. The big man showed not the least discomfort.

"Uuuunnnh . . ." Maureen sat forward and clenched her teeth. The muscles at her throat tightened like the ropes in the sheaves of a lifting gantry. "Uuunnnhhh."

"Pant, Maureen. Pant. Like this." Miss Hagerty began to puff. Short breaths through barely open lips.

Maureen huffed and stared at O'Reilly.

"Good lass," he said. "You're not quite ready to push yet."

The contraction passed. Maureen lay back on her pillow.

"Could you open the big pack there, Doctor Laverty?"

Barry set to work preparing the sterile towels, scissors, clamps, bowls, and a suturing kit.

"Now, Maureen, Miss Hagerty and I are going down to the kitchen to wash our hands. Doctor Laverty'll keep an eye to you." He jerked his shaggy head at the midwife, and together they left.

Barry moved closer and wished that O'Reilly would get a move on. It had been one thing to practise deliveries under the watchful eye of the midwives and medical staff when he'd been a student. He'd never been left alone with a woman in labour before.

Maureen grabbed his hand. "Oh, Jesus. It's coming, Doctor."

"Doctor O'Reilly." Barry heard his voice crack. "Doctor O'Reilly."

"Holy Mary, Mother of God . . . Aaaaa."

Barry tore off his jacket, flung it aside, and rolled up his sleeves. No time to scrub, not even time to put on gloves. Well, he thought, if taxi drivers can do this . . . "Can you bend your knees up, Maureen?"

She parted her legs and bent her knees. Barry stood beside her with his back to her head so he could watch closely as a black circle of damp baby's hair appeared at the opening of the vagina.

"Hail, Maaaary . . . ummmh." Maureen was pushing with all her might. The visible circle of the little head grew.

His hands went to work unbidden as he remembered what he had been taught. With his left hand he controlled the rate of descent of the baby's head. With the other hand he eased the skin between the anus and the bottom of the vagina down and away from the pressure above them. He gagged as a piece of stool dropped onto the rubber sheet.

The contraction passed.

"Are you all right, Barry?"

He looked up to see O'Reilly standing at the foot of the bed, Miss Hagerty behind.

"I think so."

Miss Hagerty moved to the top of the bed. She made soothing, shushing noises.

"I'll get the gear ready," said O'Reilly. "You carry on."

Barry hadn't time to decide whether he was flattered by O'Reilly's show of confidence or terrified because the older man hadn't immediately taken over. Maureen sat up now, supported by Miss Hagerty. "Come on, Maureen. Big puuush."

Under Barry's fingers the baby's head advanced. He let it come further, further, a little further. Now that the widest part was clearly in the open, he allowed the head to begin to extend. As it rotated, a wrinkled forehead appeared, damp and smeared with *vernix caseosa*, the greasy waterproofing that coats the skin of the baby in the uterus. A squashed nose came next, and in a rush a puckered rosebud of a mouth and a tiny pointed chin. Even before the shoulders were born, the baby gave its first, weak wail.

Barry used both hands to guide the slippery infant out of its mother and onto the rubber sheet, careful to avoid the reeking lump of faeces and conscious of the warmth of the body, the beating of the heart under his right palm.

He heard Maureen ask, "Is it a boy or a child?"

"It's a boy," he said. "He's fine."

The Galvin boy shrieked in protest against being forced from his cozy nest into the harsh, cold world.

"Here," said O'Reilly, reaching out with gloved hands to swathe the little one in a green sterile towel, "we'll just pop him on Mum's tummy."

Barry reached past the bundle and put his hand on Maureen's

belly. His fingers found the firm lump that was the top of the now shrunken uterus. Firm. Good. It had contracted. If it did not, the placenta would not be expelled.

"Move over," said O'Reilly, snapping two clamps on the umbilical cord and slicing through the twisted rope of jelly and blood vessels with a pair of scissors. "Come on, meet your mum." He lifted the baby and moved past Barry, who was busy watching the stump of the umbilical cord lengthen and a small gush of blood flow onto the rubber sheet.

"Can you manage one more push, Maureen?"

He felt her abdominal muscles harden, and onto the bed slid the placenta, all raw beef and glistening membranes. His hands were warm and bloody, his shirt splattered with amniotic fluid and smeared with *vernix*. He took a deep breath, stood up straight, and turned to see Maureen Galvin, baby content at her right breast. The smile on her face would have done justice to the Madonna to whom moments before she had been pleading for relief.

"Placenta all in one piece?" O'Reilly asked.

"I think so."

"Right. This'll sting a bit, Maureen." He stabbed a hypodermic needle into her thigh.

Ergometrine, Barry thought, to make sure the uterus stayed tightly contracted and to prevent the risk of postpartum haemorrhage, the killer of so many women not so long ago. He smiled at Maureen.

"Thanks, Doctor Laverty," she said. "You've a quare soft hand under a duck, so you have."

He laughed at the country description of gentleness. "You did very well, Maureen. What are you going to call the wee lad?"

"Well, I told Doctor O'Reilly that if it was the boy he promised me, I'd name him Fingal, but if it's all right with the pair of you, I'd like him to go by Barry Fingal Galvin."

"That's a mouthful for such a little lad," Barry said, grinning from ear to ear.

"What'll Seamus think of that?" Miss Hagerty asked.

"Seamus? He'll be happy enough. He's down at The Black Swan with his mates wetting the bairn's head."

Barry hardly noticed the time pass as Miss Hagerty busied herself tidying up the mess of the delivery and then went to make the new mother a cup of tea. O'Reilly expertly examined the newborn as Barry repacked the instruments.

"Right," said O'Reilly, "young Barry Fingal's fit as a flea." He gave the baby back to Maureen.

"Thanks again, Doctor," said Maureen. "He'll make a grand wee American, won't he?"

"Indeed," said O'Reilly, "a regular Abraham Lincoln."

Barry remembered that the Galvins intended to emigrate once the baby was born.

"Miss Hagerty'll be in tomorrow. She'll make sure you and the wee one are all right, and Maureen, if you're worried about any-thing, give us a call."

"I will."

"Now," said O'Reilly, "we'd better be going. Doctor Laverty could use a bath and a change of shirt. He's off somewhere tonight."

Barry nearly dropped the bag he was carrying. In the excitement of the delivery, the terror that things could go wrong in his inexpe-rienced hands, and the jubilation that everything had turned out perfectly, he had completely forgotten about Patricia.

"You run on, Doctor Laverty," said Maureen. "You did grand, so you did, and Doctor O'Reilly, I don't know how you fixed it, but Seamus'll be tickled pink that it is the wee boy you promised us."

How in hell, Barry wondered, could O'Reilly promise anybody what the sex of an unborn baby would be?

As soon as they were back in the car, Barry asked.

O'Reilly grinned. "That's one of the few useful things my predecessor taught me. The first time they come in to find out if they're pregnant, you ask them what they want."

"But we can't do anything about it."

"I know that, so you write down the opposite in the record."

"I don't understand."

"Look, say Mrs. Hucklebottom comes in in her third month and tells you she wants a boy. You write 'girl' in the record."

Barry frowned.

"Six months later if baby Hucklebottom is a bouncing boy, Mrs. H. is delighted."

"But what if she has a girl?"

"You show her the six-month-old record. What's written in it?"

"Girl."

"Exactly. You tell Mrs. H. you're very sorry, but she must have forgotten what she asked for when she saw you first."

"But that's dishonest."

"Indeed it is, but I've yet to meet a new mother who really cared about the sex of the child as long as it had all its fingers and toes, and it works wonders for your reputation."

Barry sniffed.

"Sniff away, son, but half of curing folks is getting them to have faith in their healer. . . . Sometimes we doctors aren't much better than a bunch of Druids. We might as well be casting the runes and chanting incantations to Lugh or Morrigan or any of the other old Celtic gods."

Barry recognized the truth of what O'Reilly had said, but every year new discoveries were made. If Jonas Salk had discovered his vaccine just three years sooner, Patricia and all the other victims of the 1951 polio epidemic need not have suffered. Since 1953 they'd known about the link between smoking and lung cancer. New antibiotics appeared regularly. O'Reilly must surely see that.

"But there is so much we can do that works," Barry countered.

"Thank God for that. But the whole thing still hangs on having the customers believe we know what we're doing . . . And if they think you're special, they're more likely to heed your advice, and anyway, unless it's something really serious, time cures most of them. Ambroise Paré had it right four hundred years ago. He said, 'I dressed the wound, but God cured the patient.' "

When O'Reilly said, "cured the patient," Barry remembered something that had been bothering him. Jeannie Kennedy. Jack had been going to Children's Hospital to re-operate on an appendix abscess.

"Fingal?"

"What?"

"Is Jeannie Kennedy home from the hospital yet?"

"No. She blew up an abscess. They opened her again yesterday, but she's on the mend now."

So Jack *had* been going to assist in Jeannie's reoperation.

"Aye," said O'Reilly, pulling into the lane at the back of his house. "I always phone the hospital to see how any of my lot are getting on. Sir Donald spoke to me this morning . . . when you were still asleep . . . so I was able to let the Kennedys know they mustn't be too worried."

"Decent of you."

"Rubbish." The car stopped. "I'll take Arthur for his walk, and you go and get cleaned up, make your phone call, and tell your lassie you'll not be able to see her until after supper."

"But—"

"No buts. You still have to go and tell the proud father."

"Could you not do that?"

"I didn't deliver the wean, you did, and son, you did well."

"I was scared stiff."

"Didn't look like it to me. Now bugger off, get organized, and walk down and meet me in the Mucky Duck."

"The what?"

"The Black Swan, known to all and sundry as the Dirty Bird or the Mucky Duck."

12

God's Holy Trousers

Barry undressed. His trousers as well as his shirt were blood-stained. He bathed, changed, and gratefully gave his splattered clothes to Mrs. Kincaid to be washed. Then he phoned Patricia. His hand shook just a little when he heard her voice, and he mouthed a silent, "Oh, yes," when she said she'd be happy to be picked up at seven. Where they'd go after that was anyone's guess, but he didn't care as long as she'd be with him.

He walked with light steps past the church and the row of thatched cottages. What a day. The sun shone; he'd delivered Barry Fingal Galvin *and* to Doctor Fingal Flahertie O'Reilly's satisfaction. Now he'd drop into the pub to congratulate the father, go home for a quick supper, and then . . . He skipped like a ten-year-old leaving school at the end of the summer term.

He paused at the maypole and waited for the light to change. He could see The Black Swan ahead. He didn't want to stay there long. It wouldn't do to show up at Patricia's the worse for drink.

He crossed the road and went into—what did the locals call it?—the Mucky Duck?

The bar, loud with competing voices and hoarse laughter, was a single timber-beamed, low-ceilinged room. To his left, bottles stood on shelves behind a counter where a bald-headed man, wearing a floral waistcoat over a striped shirt, pulled pints. Barry counted six half-filled straight glasses of Guinness on the marble bar top.

The place was packed. Men in shirtsleeves and collarless shirts, pints in hand, crowded round the bar. Seamus Galvin, left ankle strapped, stood swaying in the centre of the crowd. He had one arm round the shoulders of a ginger-haired youth. Donal . . . ? Donal Donnelly, that was it. Barry grinned. Already he could recognize some of O'Reilly's patients by name.

Through the fug of pipe tobacco smoke that made his eyes sting, Barry could see tables and occupied chairs crammed cheek by jowl in the small space. Either the Ballybucklebo natives took their drinking seriously, or news of the Galvins' baby had gone through the place with the speed of light. Barry suspected the latter. He peered through the throng but saw no sign of O'Reilly.

Councillor Bishop, seated at a table, beckoned with a crooked bandaged finger. The gesture reminded Barry of a patron summoning a tardy waiter. "Laverty, hey, you. Laverty, where the hell's O'Reilly?"

Barry, too content to let the councillor's dictatorial manner bother him, shrugged and held his hands out, palms up.

"When you see O'Reilly, Laverty, you tell the old goat it's time he had a look at my finger."

"It's *Doctor* O'Reilly, Bishop," Barry said civilly, "and you know when the surgery's open."

"It's *Councillor* Bishop to you, you young puppy." Bishop started to rise.

A man sitting at the table put a hand on the councillor's shoulder. "Don't you be getting your knickers in a twist, Bertie. Have another pint." The man winked at Barry. "Pay no heed, Doc. He's half-cut."

Barry turned away as the door opened and O'Reilly appeared, followed by a panting, tongue-lolling, sand-covered Arthur Guinness. Barry glanced anxiously at his corduroys, his last clean pair of pants.

"Good afternoon to this house," O'Reilly bellowed.

Conversation died. Every eye turned toward the door. The men who sat at the table nearest the door rose and joined those standing at the bar. Without a word of thanks O'Reilly took one of the chairs.

"Under and lie down."

Arthur obeyed, much to Barry's relief.

"Take the weight off your feet, Barry."

Barry sat, carefully tucking his legs under the chair out of the way of the drooling dog. "The usual, Doctor?" he heard the barman ask.

"Aye, and a pint for Doctor Laverty."

In moments, two pints of Guinness were delivered to the table.

"*Sláinte,*" said O'Reilly, sinking half of the contents of his glass in one swallow. "It's warm out there."

"*Sláinte mHath.*" Barry sipped the bitter stout.

The barman reappeared carrying a bowl. He bent and shoved it under the table.

"Arthur likes his pint," O'Reilly remarked, "but he only drinks Smithwick's bitter."

Barry heard lapping noises under the table. The buzz of conversation rose.

"Doctor Laverty's round," O'Reilly said.

Barry tightened his lips, but paid.

"Lovely," said O'Reilly, finishing his glass. "Come on, boy. Don't let yours go flat."

Barry swallowed more Guinness but was determined to restrict his intake to one pint. Someone was standing at his shoulder. He turned to see Seamus Galvin, a lopsided grin pasted to his narrow face. He bore a striking resemblance to a tipsy weasel.

"So's a boy, Doctors? S'a wee boy?"

O'Reilly nodded.

Galvin hiccupped. " 'Nother round here, Willy," he shouted to the barman. "On me."

"Easy, Seamus," O'Reilly said quietly, "you'll need your money now there's another mouth to feed."

Seamus tried to lay one index finger alongside his nose but managed to stick it into his nostril. "Ah, sure, I'm like Paddy Maginty; I'm going to fall into a fortune." He favoured O'Reilly with a drooping wink.

"Oh?" said O'Reilly, glancing at Barry. "And where would that come from, Seamus?"

"Least said, soonest mended." Seamus extracted his finger and squinted at the tip.

Two more pints appeared. Barry felt something stirring at his feet, and Arthur Guinness's square head appeared.

"One for Arthur," Seamus ordered.

The barman collected Arthur's bowl.

Barry drank from his first pint and eyed the second.

Seamus Galvin climbed onto a chair and stood, swaying like a willow in a high wind. He whistled, a piercing shriek like the blast from a tugboat's siren.

Silence.

"Just wanna say . . . just wanna say . . . to say." He wobbled and grabbed the chair back. "I just wanna—"

"Get on with it, Seamus," someone roared.

"Just wanna say . . . best two doctors in Ulster . . . in all of Ireland."

"Hear, hear."

Barry looked up. The last remark had come from Donal Donnelly, who was staring at O'Reilly. The ginger-haired youth had a look on his face that seemed to be a cross between adulation and terror.

"Balls," Councillor Bishop yelled. "That bloody O'Reilly couldn't cure a sick cat."

"Wheest, Bertie," his friend said.

Barry looked at O'Reilly, who lifted his glass to Bishop and smiled. There was enough ice in the smile, Barry thought, to put a hole in the *Titanic*.

"Are you not going to say something, Fingal?"

O'Reilly shook his head. " 'Revenge,' " he said, " 'is a dish best eaten cold.' I'll say no more today."

Barry stared at the corpulent councillor and thought, I'd rather not be in Bishop's boots when O'Reilly makes good on that promise.

The barman came back with Arthur's bowl. His subtable slurping was drowned out as Seamus Galvin roared, "Just wanna say . . . best doctors in Ireland. They got me a wee boy, so they did. Everybody have a drink to Farry . . . Bingal . . . Gavlin." He finished his pint to the cheers of the crowd.

Barry felt duty-bound to join in the toast. He regarded his empty glass with surprise. That stout had vanished quickly.

"A wee boy," Galvin continued when at last there was a semblance of silence. "And I'll tell you . . . *I'll* tell you, that's very smart because," he inhaled deeply and swept his gaze over the entire room, *"any ould tinker can put a hole in the bottom of a bucket . . . but . . . but it takes a craftsman to put a spout on a teapot."*

He clapped O'Reilly on the shoulder and, to the renewed cheers of the patrons, waved both arms over his head, hands clasped like a boxer who had just KOed his opponent. Then with great solemnity he fell off the chair.

"Jesus," said O'Reilly. "Drink. It's the curse of the land. It makes you fight with your neighbour. It makes you shoot at your landlord. And it makes you miss." He looked round. "Donal Donnelly, see if you can get the proud but paralytically pissed papa home."

"I will, Doctor, I will, so I will." Donal nudged a man beside him. "We'll need to oxter-cog him." Together they took the limp Galvin by his armpits and dragged him towards the door.

" 'Not in utter nakedness,/But trailing clouds of glory do we come,' " O'Reilly remarked to the passing group. He turned to Barry. "Drink up."

"Wordsworth, 'Intimations of Immortality,' " Barry said, taking a goodly swallow from his second pint, surprised by how much better than the first it tasted.

"Willy. My shout, and don't forget Arthur," O'Reilly roared.

Barry shook his head. "Fingal I have to—"

"See a certain young lady tonight. You have, haven't you?"

"Yes," said Barry, smiling like a mooncalf.

"Well. One more won't hurt you."

Someone started to sing.

> As I went out a-roving and a-rambling one day,
> I spied a young couple who so fondly did stray.
> And one was a young maid at the turn of her year,
> And the other was a soldier and a bold Grenadier.

Barry, off-key, joined in the chorus:

> And they kissed so sweet and comforting as they clung
> to each other.

And, by God he was going to kiss Patricia tonight. By God, the stout tasted good, and by God, wasn't Ballybucklebo the nearest thing to heaven on earth?

It had been a wonderful afternoon, Barry thought, as he accompanied O'Reilly and Arthur on the short walk back to O'Reilly's house. Wonderful. He giggled as he watched Arthur tacking along the pavement, the dog's forward progress being intermittently interrupted when he crossed his front legs like a show jumper in a dressage competition. You, Arthur Guinness, Barry thought, you are stocious. At least it's dampened your ardour, and my pants are safe. Barry stumbled and grabbed O'Reilly's arm.

" 'Steady the Buffs!' " said O'Reilly.

"The Duke of . . . ?" Barry struggled to remember.

"Wellington," said O'Reilly. "At Waterloo."

It dawned on Barry that he was not entirely sober. He'd better pull himself together. Nothing was going to spoil his evening.

"I wonder . . . ," said O'Reilly as he opened the back gate, "I wonder how Galvin's going to 'fall into his fortune'?"

"Why?" Barry closed the gate.

"I'd not like to think it'll be the cash Maureen's been saving for their emigration."

Barry might have been concerned too if Arthur Guinness had not begun to make a strange ululation as he sat on the grass, head thrown back, trying and failing to scratch his ear with a hind paw that flapped in the air like a flag with a broken halyard.

"Daft dog," said O'Reilly. "Come here."

Arthur wobbled to his feet, staggered over, and stood between O'Reilly and Barry. He cocked one leg, and with the unerring accuracy of a marksman at the army's rifle range at Bisley, he pissed all over Barry's trousers.

Barry left the parked Brunhilde, smoothed the tuft of hair on his crown, and looked down. He was a sight. Bloody dog. With one pair of pants still wet from the wash and his only others reeking of dog piss, he'd had to accept O'Reilly's offer of the loan of a pair. Wearing brightly checked trousers cut for a man of six foot two, even with the cuffs rolled up and the waistband cinched with a belt, he knew he looked like an escapee from Duffy's one-tent, touring circus. Nor was he convinced that a short nap, Mrs. Kincaid's liberal doses of black coffee, and the greasy fry she'd made him eat had restored him to complete sobriety. If they had, he probably wouldn't be standing here outside Number 9, the Esplanade, Kinnegar, giving a fair impression of Pantaloon.

He looked at the row of bell pushes, each accompanied by a hand-lettered card. Patricia Spence. Flat 4. He rang the bell and waited.

The door opened and Patricia came out.

"Hello, Barry Laverty." She turned to close the door, and her high ponytail danced impertinently as she turned back to him, her dark eyes wide, lips full, her dimple deep as she smiled. She wore a white silk blouse open at the neck, and a mid-calf green skirt above tiny, low-heeled black shoes.

His breath caught in his throat.

"What in the world?" She stared at his trousers.

"It's a long story." He felt the heat in his cheeks. "I'll tell you in the car."

"I can hardly wait."

He walked beside her as she limped along; then he held Brunhilde's door and waited until she was seated. He closed the door, rushed to the driver's side, climbed in, started the engine, and drove off.

"Now," she said, "tell me about those pants, Mr. Laverty."

"Mr. Laverty." He hadn't told her last night he was a doctor, hadn't wanted her to think he was trying too hard to impress her. "I only own two pairs. I got both of them dirty today, so I had to borrow these from a friend."

"A stilt-walker?"

Barry laughed. "No, but he's big."

"So's the Atlantic Ocean, and you're drowning in those." She put one hand on his arm. "Don't worry about it. Clothes don't always make the man."

He wanted to kiss her, but had to concentrate on his driving.

"Where are we going?"

"I thought we'd go to Strickland's Glen. Walk down to the shore."

"You'd ask a girl with a game leg to go for a walk?"

Was she teasing him? Was she being caustic? He couldn't tell from the tone of her voice.

"Patricia," he said levelly, "if you'd rather not go for a walk, say so."

She leant over and kissed his cheek. "I like you, Barry Laverty."

For the rest of the drive they chatted about the weather, about Maria Bueno's victory over Margaret Smith at Wimbledon (although she couldn't play herself, Patricia was a keen tennis fan), and about pop music. She liked the Beatles but wasn't sure about the new lot, the Rolling Stones.

We're like two strange dogs, Barry thought, stiff-legged, circling, sniffing each other out. Yet even with the confidence given to him by the remaining effects of the afternoon pints, he couldn't bring himself to take the conversation to a more personal level, and he wanted to so much. He wanted to know everything about her.

"Here we are," he said. "Hop out."

She took his hand, and he felt its dry warmth. He led her onto a path strewn with needles from the evergreens above, the air redolent with their piney scent. They walked past dark laurels and patches of late-blooming bluebells. Rays of sun filtering through the trees made pools of gold on the brown earth.

Other walkers were taking advantage of the sun-soaked evening. But Barry was barely aware of them.

"Listen," she said.

He heard the notes of a bird, high, rising, a piccolo tune.

"Song thrush," she said. "You can tell his song a mile away. I love birds."

"Do you?"

"My dad's an ornithologist. He taught my sister and me about them when I was little, growing up in Newry."

"Mine taught me astronomy."

"Bit of a stargazer, are you?"

"Yes," he said softly, and careless of passersby, he bent and kissed her lips.

"Mmm," she said, "nice, but we should move along if we're going to get to the shore."

"It's not far." He could still taste her.

A boy of five or six ran past, stopped, pointed, and yelled, "Mammy, look at the man in clown's pants."

He heard Patricia's laughter, warm as butter on fresh toast.

"Don't you be at it, Sammy," the child's mother said, smiling as she passed them. "Pay no heed, he's only wee."

"Come on, then, Pagliacci." Patricia tugged at Barry's hand.

"Pally who?"

"A clown. In an opera. The Beatles aren't the only ones I listen to."

"I'm not much up on opera."

"I'll teach you. I've tons of records back in the flat. I'm going to Queen's. Taking extra courses this summer. I want to graduate as soon as I can. It's too far from Newry to Belfast to travel up to town, and the rent's cheaper in the Kinnegar."

"I see. So you're a student and you like opera. Do you like to read?"

She frowned for a moment. "I've tried Hemingway, but he's too curt. I prefer John Steinbeck."

"*Cannery Row?*"

"And I love *Sweet Thursday*."

The path had begun to descend, and he had to help her over tree roots that sprang from the earth and lay like petrified serpents. He climbed over a fallen branch. "Can you manage?"

"I think so." She pulled herself up. "Catch me."

He did and held her softly to him, the belt buckle of his outsized britches digging into his belly.

"Thank you, sir." She kissed him. "I thought so," she said. "You taste of beer."

"I had to have a pint with my boss this afternoon."

"So you're a bit of a bowsey, Barry Laverty?"

"Never sober." He hiccupped loudly. "I'm usually pissed as a fiddler's bitch by lunchtime."

She laughed. "Stop acting the goat."

He took her hand. "Come on. Just over this bridge," he said, as he walked onto a small wooden arch over a stream. "Might be trout in there. In that deep pool under the bank."

"Or a hobbit under the bridge. I've just finished *The Lord of the Rings*."

She knew Steinbeck, Tolkien. "So, you're taking an arts degree?"

"No." She stopped walking. "Why would you say that?"

"I dunno. You certainly seem to know the kinds of authors that I'd expect an arts student to know."

"And women should take arts or nursing? Is that it? And there's plenty of work for good secretaries?"

"I—"

"I'm twenty-one and I'm the youngest student in my class . . . my civil engineering class . . . and there are only six of us."

"Six what? Engineers?"

"No. There are eighty-two in the class. Only six are women."

"I still don't understand. We'd ten women in our lot at university."

"What exactly don't you understand?" Her eyes were narrow, lips tight, arms folded.

"What are you making such a fuss about? Why shouldn't a woman be an engineer or a doctor?"

"A lot of people wouldn't agree. Have you any idea how hard it was to get in?"

"All professional schools are tough."

"A damn sight tougher if you're a woman." She took a step back.

"Well, they shouldn't be." Barry did not like the way this discussion was going.

"Do you mean that?"

"Of course I do." He saw her shoulders relax.

"Really?"

"If you want to be an engineer you ought to have the chance."

She pursed her lips and spoke, as if to herself. "Bloody right I should."

Barry moved closer to her and said, "But I thought you were going to be a civil engineer."

"I am."

"Good. You can start practising with me."

"What?"

"You just about bit my head off. Nothing civil about that."

"Look. I'd a hell of a job getting admitted. Women have to fight for their rights."

"Fair enough. But you don't have to fight with me."

"You're right."

"Right as rain," he said. Then he grinned at her.

Like a summer squall her anger passed. "I shouldn't have yelled at you, but . . . damn it. . . ." She grabbed him and kissed him hard. "Am I forgiven?"

He would have forgiven her for not one but all of the seven deadly sins and a few mortal ones thrown in for good measure.

"To the beach, woman," he said, with mock sternness.

"Yes, sir." She took his hand.

"Look at that," he said. Across Belfast Lough on the Antrim shore sat Carrickfergus Castle, squatted motte-and-bailley solid, granite-grim, built by the Normans, once shelter to Robert the Bruce, landing place in 1690 of William of Orange.

One of Kelly's Company's rust-streaked coal boats chuffed her way toward the quay in Bangor around the point. Smoke from her tall, spindly funnel smudged the clean sky and was torn to tatters by a breeze from the northwest.

"I used to walk round here when I was a wee fellow."

"It is lovely."

"In the summer, yes, but in the winter it can really blow up." Just like someone I'm getting to know, he thought.

She stood, glancing up, her ponytail tossed by the wind. Overhead two brown birds with long, curved bills glided on rigid wings down the wind's invisible road. Their voices were melancholy.

"Curlew," she said, turning to him. "Now you know all about me."

Like hell I do, he thought, and he saw the sunlight sparkling in her eyes.

"Tell me about Barry Laverty."

"Well, apart from my incurable alcoholism, and my unshakeable belief that women should never be admitted to faculties of engineering—"

"Just cut that out." She was smiling. "I'm sorry I got shirty with you."

"Fair enough." He looked down and then back at her. "I'm twenty-four, no brothers or sisters. I like to read, to fish. I used to sail, but I'm a bit busy now." He paused before looking her right in the eye and saying, "My dad's a consulting engineer."

"A what?"

"Mining. He and Mum are in Melbourne."

"And what does the son of a consulting engineer do?"

"Actually . . . actually, I'm a ballerina with the Sadler's Wells Ballet."

"What?"

"Well . . . why shouldn't a man be a ballerina?"

She struck him on the chest. "You bastard. All right. Touché."

He held her wrist. "I'm a doctor. I'm an assistant to Doctor O'Reilly in Ballybucklebo."

"You're a GP?"

"That's right."

She pointed at his ridiculous, oversized, baggy pants and giggled. "Well, Doctor, I hope to God none of your patients have seen you this evening." She snuggled against his chest as the sun slipped behind the Antrim Hills leaving one last molten streak across the darkening lough.

He kissed her, his tongue finding hers, and little shocks ran through him. "Now *that's* what I'd call civil," he said, and kissed her again.

Barry peeped through the double doors of the upstairs lounge. By the light of a single table lamp he saw O'Reilly, feet propped up on the coffee table, sprawled in his chair. A copy of Winston Churchill's *A History of the English-Speaking Peoples* lay spine-up on the table. O'Reilly's head drooped to the left. Lady Macbeth lay tucked into the angle between his neck and his right shoulder. O'Reilly snored sonorously. Lady Macbeth's purring could be heard only when he exhaled.

Barry was reminded of the proverb "And the lion shall lie down with the lamb." But which was which might be hard to tell, given Lady Macbeth's propensity for biting and O'Reilly's ability to become distinctly leonine when aroused.

O'Reilly opened one eye. "You're home."

"Sorry, Fingal. I didn't mean to disturb you."

"What time is it?"

"Eleven."

O'Reilly scratched his belly. His movements dislodged the cat, which slid down his waistcoat and curled up in his lap, rolling onto her side and twisting her head to that impossible angle only cats can achieve. Barry thought she looked as if she had turned herself inside out.

"Had a good evening?"

Barry savoured his memories of the slow walk back through the moth-fluttering gloaming, stopping to watch bats swoop and dive, laughing together at the bats' squeaks. Stopping to kiss her lips, her hair. The drive to Patricia's flat, her invitation in, and his polite refusal. He'd known from the minute he'd seen her that she was different, special, and after her flare of temper in the glen he'd sensed that if he were too hasty he would be rebuffed. Better to let things percolate than try to rush them to the boil.

"I presume by your dewy-eyed silence that the answer is yes." O'Reilly fondled the cat's head.

"It was wonderful."

"Huh. Women."

Barry glanced at O'Reilly, expecting from his tone to see distaste written on the big man's face, but instead Barry saw only sadness in his brown eyes.

"Come on, Fingal. You don't mean that."

"Don't I, by God?" O'Reilly rose. Lady Macbeth slipped to the carpet. O'Reilly paced to the window and stood, hands clasped behind his back, staring out. "Women? Nothing but grief." O'Reilly turned, and for a second Barry thought he could see moisture in O'Reilly's eyes.

"Jesus Christ, would you stop it?" O'Reilly swore at Lady Macbeth, who had happily returned to reducing the furniture to tatters. "Give over."

Lady Macbeth haggled one last strand loose, jumped onto O'Reilly's chair, and crouched, back humped, tail waving.

Barry was relieved that the animal had distracted them. Whatever was troubling O'Reilly was none of Barry's business. "Maybe Kinky's right. We should ask Maggie what to do about Her Ladyship."

"It's not Maggie we need. It's a bloody exorcist."

"What are you talking about?"

"I think she's possessed."

Barry laughed. "Go on."

"She doesn't like Stravinsky," O'Reilly said, perhaps pleased like Barry to have something else to talk about.

"How do you know that?"

"Watch." O'Reilly went to the pile of records and put a disk on the Black Box. The chords of Beethoven's *Pastoral* Symphony filled the room. Barry thought of the piney Glen and the sweetness of Patricia.

Lady Macbeth sat upright, whiskers pointing forwards, jumped to the floor, and tail erect, pushed herself against Barry's legs, weaving and thrusting.

"Looks like a happy cat to me."

"She is. She likes old Ludwig, but watch this." O'Reilly changed records.

Barry listened to the unfamiliar cadences that he thought bordered on the cacophonous.

Lady Macbeth's weaving stopped. Dead. Her pupils became so large that all Barry could see in her eyes was blackness. She growled. She spat. She waved her tail in circles and without further warning launched herself at him and bit his shin.

"Gerroff." He pushed her away and hauled up the leg of his borrowed pants. At least the skin wasn't broken.

O'Reilly lifted the gramophone's arm, and the music stopped. Lady Macbeth sat and started to wash.

"So much for *The Rite of Spring*. And if you think that's a fluke . . ." O'Reilly dropped the tonearm.

Lady Macbeth charged O'Reilly. She crossed the floor diagonally in a series of sideways hops, legs rigid, back arched, Barry thought, like a laterally leaping kangaroo, but a kangaroo with murderous intent.

"See?" O'Reilly stopped the music. "Possessed. Maybe Father O'Toole could do the rites."

"I've never seen anything like it." Barry stared at the now docile animal. "I wonder how she'd like the Rolling Stones?"

"Who?"

"The Rolling Stones. They're a rock band."

"Probably have a fit," said O'Reilly. He yawned. "Anyway. I'm off to bed. We'll be busy for the next few days."

"How come?"

"Thursday's the Twelfth of July, of 'glorious and immortal memory.' Unless someone's at death's door they'll not want to miss the parade, so anyone with blepharitis, a blister, a bunion, bursitis, or a badly broken heart will be bellyaching in the waiting room first thing tomorrow, Tuesday, and Wednesday."

"Oh."

"So you'll have to wait for a few days to go back and see the light of your life."

"Well, I—"

"Don't worry," said O'Reilly, as he left, "you can have Friday night off."

"Thanks, Fingal," Barry said to the departing back. He sat down. It was too soon to go to bed. He knew he'd not sleep. He'd too much to think about.

Patricia. Soft, warm, delicious, and with spirit. Patricia Spence. She was twenty-one now. He made a rapid calculation. That meant she'd have been eight when she'd had polio. Lots of kids—he'd seen them as patients—had lapsed into self-pity, used their handicap to their own advantage to garner sympathy. She hadn't. It was impressive that she was studying civil engineering. He'd phone her tomorrow and hope to hell she was free on Friday. Perhaps he could afford to take her to dinner.

Lady Macbeth jumped into his lap and startled him, broke his train of thought. Jesus, what a household. A killer cat, a Labrador with the canine equivalent of satyriasis and a touch of dipsomania to boot, and a senior colleague who for his own obscure reasons did not seem to think much of the opposite sex. Did Barry really want to join this menagerie?

"Excuse me, Doctor Laverty, but I've a pair of pants dry and pressed for you, so." He hadn't heard Mrs. Kincaid coming in.

"Thank you." He stood.

"You can get out of himself's bags now. You don't seem to fill them too well."

"I know." And, Barry thought, I don't think I'm ready to fill the big fellow's shoes either.

"You should be in bed, Mrs. Kincaid."

"I'm on my way. Was there anything else you'd want before I go?"

It was all a bit feudal. "No thanks. But . . ." Barry hesitated. "Mrs. Kincaid, would you mind if I asked a question?"

"You can ask."

"It's about Doctor O'Reilly."

He saw her stiffen, her lips narrow.

"I'm a bit worried about him."

She relaxed almost imperceptibly. "How so?"

"He gets very upset when I mention a young woman I've started seeing."

"Does he now?"

"I know it's silly, but earlier—now please don't laugh—I thought he was going to weep."

"Did you?" Her eyes softened, and she rocked gently on her heels. "Sometimes I wish to God he would."

Barry knew that it was not the time to interrupt.

"Can I sit down, sir?"

"Please."

She stuffed her bulk into an armchair, glanced at the closed door, lowered her voice, and said, "You'll keep what I'm going to tell you to yourself?"

"Of course."

"He doesn't know I know. He's a very private man, so."

Barry waited.

"Old Doctor Flanagan told me. In 1941, April, Easter Tuesday, them Germans, the bad bashtoons, dropped bombs on Belfast, aye, and Bangor." Her eyes hardened. She clenched her fists. "A young nurse was killed. They'd been married six months. He'd courted her hard for three years. He worshipped that girl, so."

"My God."

"Himself was away on that big ship. He didn't get told until June that she was dead." She looked up into his face. "It hurt him sore, Doctor Laverty."

"It still does," Barry whispered.

"Aye, so." She rose and stood before him. "I know he's happy for you and your girl, but I think he worries that you'll get hurt like him. He's taken quite a shine to you, Doctor. I can tell."

"Mrs. Kincaid, I thank you for telling me this."

"Not a word now, but . . ." She smiled at Barry. "There's only you and me to look after the big buck eejit."

"I understand."

"I hope you do, for I'll not see him let down again." Mrs. Kincaid stood like a guardsman, her three chins thrust out, eyes hot.

"Don't you worry, Mrs. Kincaid."

"Aye, so. Well, trot off to your bed. The pair of you'll be running round like bees on a hot brick for the next few days, and himself's not getting any younger." She put a hand in the small of her back. "I'm no spring chicken myself anymore."

She crossed the room and turned. "It's not my place to say it, Doctor Laverty, but I'd take it kindly if you'd think of shtaying on here. Permanently."

Barry rose. "I will think about it, Mrs. Kincaid. I promise."

"Well, you think hard," she said. "For he's a good man and he needs you here."

13

For Marriage Is an Honourable Estate

Although Monday morning's surgery started slowly, with three men waiting for tonic injections, their departure opened the flood-gates. It seemed to Barry that every case in Ballybucklebo of back strain, sniffles, cough, hay fever, and hangovers following the welcoming of Barry Fingal Galvin poured through the place. Several of the hangover sufferers had also needed attention for blackened eyes and skinned knuckles.

As the last of what he called the Mucky Duck Militia left, O'Reilly said with a grin, "Ah, agree by all means, boys . . . but fighting's more fun. Jesus, the natives haven't changed since the '*Scél Mucci Mic Dáthó*,' the tale of Mac Datho's pig, was written."

"Pardon?"

"It's one of the old sagas. There's a Celtic feast described in it: 'A good drinking bout broke out in the courtyard, with everyone striking his neighbour.' All good clean fun, I suppose. I just hope we don't get a rematch on the Twelfth, or we'll be here half the night stitching up the walking wounded." He stretched. "Never mind Thursday. Are there many more left today?"

"Two children and a young woman. I think that's it for the morning."

"Get them, would you?"

Barry brought them from the waiting room. He had assumed, incorrectly, that the woman was the mother of the two children. The boy, who Barry guessed was five or six, wore short tweed trousers and a grey shirt. One of his woollen stockings was held at the knee by an elastic garter; the other had slipped down his shin and lay crumpled round his ankle like the newly shed skin of a snake. He stood, one foot turned in, his left thumb firmly in his mouth. The blonde girl's pale blue pinafore dress matched solemn eyes that never left O'Reilly's face. She was probably a year older than her companion.

"Good morning, Colin Brown. Good morning, Susan MacAfee, and what can I do for the pair of you?" O'Reilly peered over his half-moons.

"Mr. Brown and I want to get married."

Barry watched O'Reilly's face to see how he would react.

"Indeed," said O'Reilly, without a flicker of expression. "Married?"

This, thought Barry, should be interesting.

"And how do you feel about it, Mr. Brown?"

The little boy looked down and tugged at the front of his pants.

"I see," said O'Reilly. "Well, marriage is an honourable estate not to be entered into lightly."

"Yes, Doctor O'Reilly," said the little blue-eyed girl. She twisted the hair of her bangs round one finger. "We know that, don't we, Mr. Brown?"

"Uh-huh," said Mr. Brown. He shifted from foot to foot.

I wonder, thought Barry, what O'Reilly's going to say when he gets to the bit about "the union of the flesh"?

"We've saved up," said the little girl.

"And how much have you got?"

"A whole shilling," she said.

"And sixpence." Mr. Brown squeezed his thighs together and pulled at his pant front.

"You know," said O'Reilly, "maybe you're a bit young to be getting married."

Mr. Brown nodded, yanked the girl's hand, and whispered into her ear.

"You'll just have to wait," she said.

"Before you see the minister?" O'Reilly asked, a smile beginning.

Mr. Brown hauled so hard on her hand that she had to take a step toward him. "I said, you'll have to wait. What . . . ?" She bent to him.

"Oh," she said when she straightened up. "Doctor O'Reilly, we'll have to be running along."

"Fine," said O'Reilly. "So you *are* going to wait?"

"No," she said, putting a hand on her hip and pouting at the little boy. "Mr. Brown here . . ." The little boy hung his head. "Mr. Brown here's just wet himself."

"Oh, well," said O'Reilly, "perhaps Mrs. Kincaid can help. Come on." He rose and took the girl's hand. "I think she's in the kitchen." O'Reilly turned to Barry. "Get the last one in, will you? Start taking her history."

"Right," said Barry, not moving. He waited until O'Reilly and his charges had left before he surrendered to the laughter that had been trying to overwhelm him. He was still chuckling when he reached the waiting room. "Will you come with me, please?" he asked a young woman who sat all alone staring at the floor. She wore a white raincoat and black high-heeled shoes. She clasped a patent-leather handbag with both hands. Her corn-silk hair was held in place by an Alice band, and when she looked up her eyes were dull and red-rimmed, and by the look of the shadows beneath, she must have been short of sleep. Whatever ailed her, this was no time for frivolity.

She stood. "Doctor O'Reilly?"

No one from Ballybucklebo would have mistaken him for Fingal. "No," he said, "Laverty. But Doctor O'Reilly'll be along in a minute."

She said nothing, even when she was seated in the patients' chair.

"Now," said Barry, spinning the swivel chair and reaching into one of the desk drawers to pull out a blank patient-record card. "I'll just get a few details. You're not from round here, are you?"

She shook her head. "Rasharkin."

"County Antrim?" Barry heard the lengthening of the vowels and the slight sibilance that marks the speech of the Antrim country folk, and Rasharkin was an even smaller place than Ballybucklebo. "You're a long way from home." He glanced at her left hand. No ring . . . "Miss . . . ?"

"MacAteer. Julie MacAteer."

"Is that Mc or Mac?"

"Mac."

He entered the name. "How old are you?"

"Twenty." There was a catch in her voice. "Next week."

"And what brings you to see us?"

A single tear fell from her left eye. She opened her handbag and brought out a handkerchief.

"That's all right. Take your time."

She dabbed at her eyes. Her shoulders shook.

Barry leant forward and took her hand. "I'd like to help, Julie."

She looked into his eyes, and in her own he saw sadness. "I'm late," she whispered.

"How late?"

"Three whole weeks. And I'm always on time."

Barry swallowed. The next question had to be asked. "Do you think you could be—?"

"I know I am." Her eyes flashed. "I've thrown up every morning for the last week, and I'm main sore here." She put her free hand to her breast.

"It could be something else. Hormones are funny things. It's not unusual for young women to miss a period if they're worried about something."

"Worried? I'm worried sick. What am I going to do?" She closed her eyes and tilted her head back.

Barry heard O'Reilly enter. He looked over to see the big man put a finger to his lips.

"Have you told anyone?" Barry asked her.

"Who could I tell? Da would kill me, so he would."

"Julie, you could be wrong. You could be worrying for nothing."

"I'm not wrong. I know I'm . . . pregnant . . . and I don't know what to do."

"I think we should find out for sure. Did you bring a urine sample?"

She pulled a small glass bottle from her bag. "Here."

Barry took the bottle. "I'll have to send it to Belfast for a test." From the corner of his eye he saw O'Reilly hold up a thumb. "We'll know for sure on . . . ?" Barry realized he didn't know how long it would take to get the results.

"Friday," said O'Reilly.

She swung and stared at him.

"This is Julie MacAteer," Barry said.

"It's all right, Julie. I'm Doctor O'Reilly."

She turned back to Barry and tried to smile. "I'll just have to wait then. Keep my fingers crossed?"

"I'm sorry," Barry said.

She lowered her head, clenched her fists, took a deep breath. "All right."

"Will you be going back to Rasharkin today?" Barry asked.

"No. I'm stopping here."

"Where?" Barry realized he had forgotten to take her address.

She tugged at the handkerchief. "I'm not telling."

"But—"

"It's not important." O'Reilly put a hand on her shoulder. "Doctor Laverty only needs it for the records. Just put 'local' on the card."

"Right."

"Doctor O'Reilly?" She straightened her shoulders and stared up into his face. "If I am . . . you know . . . I can't keep it."

"You'll not have to," said O'Reilly. "I promise."

Barry sat bolt upright. He could understand why a single woman would not want to consult a physician in her own small community, and he had assumed that was why she had travelled to Ballybucklebo. But was O'Reilly an abortionist?

"Do you mean it?" she asked.

"I do," said O'Reilly. "I promise."

She stood and hugged the big man.

"Get away with you, Julie," he said gently. "Everything'll be fine."

Good God. Barry could not believe what he was hearing. Abortions were illegal. The words came out before he could think about what he was saying. "Doctor O'Reilly, I won't—"

"Hold your horses, Barry. It's not what you think."

Barry spluttered.

"So, Julie," said O'Reilly, stepping back. "I tell you what. Wash your face at the sink there, and put on a bit of makeup. You'll not want people to know you've been crying."

"Thank you," she whispered.

"Och, for what? Take your time."

Barry, unable to trust himself not to say something he might regret, left the surgery, trying to ignore the young woman's words of gratitude. How the hell could O'Reilly tell her that everything would be rosy when the odds were that she *was* pregnant and there wasn't a damn thing they could do about it?

He almost bumped into Mrs. Kincaid as she let the two children out through the front door.

"Sorry," he snapped. "I wasn't looking where I was going."

"No matter."

The surgery door opened, and O'Reilly, holding Julie's arm, took her to the front door. Barry saw Mrs. Kincaid peer at the young woman's face, and a look of puzzlement cross her own. "Huh," she grunted.

Barry heard O'Reilly say, "Come back on Friday, and try not to worry. We'll take care of it, I promise." The front door shut. "Kinky. Lunch," O'Reilly said. "We've a lot of calls this afternoon."

Barry went into the dining room. He'd be damned if he was going to have a row with O'Reilly in front of Mrs. Kincaid.

O'Reilly came in and sat at the table.

"You promise, do you, Fingal?" Barry could barely stop his hands from trembling. "How can you promise her?" He leant forward, supporting himself on hands splayed on the tablecloth. "Do you do abortions here? In the surgery? Is that why she's come all the way from Rasharkin?" Barry remembered the human wreckage that flooded the gynaecology wards every Friday night when the men were paid and the women had the cash to make clandestine visits to backstreets somewhere off Shankill Road or Sandy Row. The unlucky ones came in in agony, haemorrhaging, raddled with infections that spread like wildfire. Some would never have to worry about falling pregnant again. The scarring and destruction of their Fallopian tubes saw to that. Some died, and all because they couldn't face another pregnancy and had no recourse but a filthy harridan who rammed a knitting needle or a bent coat hanger into the life they were carrying.

O'Reilly sucked in his cheeks, folded his arms, and looked levelly at Barry.

"Are you one of the charlatans who take money from the well-to-do ladies of Malone Road or Cherryvalley and make sure they can get rid of their little inconveniences?"

"At least," said O'Reilly mildly, "those fellows use a sterile technique."

"And you think that sterility's justification for what they do?"

"It's better than the backstreets."

"Christ." Barry stood straight. "I won't be party to it."

"You won't have to be."

"I suppose not. You've obviously managed quite well without me before."

"Yes," O'Reilly said, "I have."

Barry swallowed. He saw clearly that although he was now enjoying working in Ballybucklebo, he wouldn't, he couldn't, stay here. He could lose his licence. More to the point, he'd never be able to look himself in the eye. He half turned, fully intending to leave, when he heard O'Reilly say clearly and distinctly, "I don't do abortions."

Barry spun back. "What?"

"I said I don't do abortions. Mind you, I'm not sure they shouldn't be legal. I'd not want to be single and up the spout, would you?"

"No." Barry frowned. "But if you don't . . . how could you promise Julie she'd not have to keep it?"

"I didn't say she wouldn't have to have the baby."

"Come on, Fingal." Barry had been so sure a moment ago that he had been in the right. "How could a single woman go on living in a place like Rasharkin, or here in Ballybucklebo? The shame would kill her."

"Why don't you take a deep breath, count to ten, and sit down?" An edge of command laced O'Reilly's last few words.

Barry sat, slowly.

"If she's pregnant, and she probably is, I'll arrange for her to go to Liverpool."

"Liverpool?"

"Aye. There's a charity there. A home for the Piffys."

"Piffys?"

"PFIs. Pregnant from Ireland. Piffys. The people there will look after her until the baby's born and then arrange an adoption. The folks in Rasharkin can suspect, but they can't be sure that she's had a wee bastard."

"Oh." Barry could not meet O'Reilly's gaze. "Fingal?"

"Yes?"

"Look. I'm sorry. I shouldn't have jumped to conclusions."

"No. You shouldn't . . ."

Barry flinched.

"But I'll say one thing. I admire a man who has the courage to speak his mind."

Barry looked up and saw a soft smile on O'Reilly's face.

"So we'll say no more. Mind you, it would make life a lot easier all round if the babby's daddy would make an honest woman of her."

"Do you think that's likely?" Barry wanted to get off the subject of abortion.

"I don't think so. If he'd been going to, she wouldn't have come here in the first place."

"I wonder why she's here? In Ballybucklebo? I thought that she'd heard that you . . ." Barry bit back his words.

"Haven't a clue." O'Reilly ignored the implied question and looked over Barry's head to where Mrs. Kincaid stood holding two steaming plates. "What do you think, Kinky?"

"About what?"

"About why a pregnant young woman would come here from Rasharkin to see me?"

"So, the wee one's in trouble?" Mrs. Kincaid set the plates on the table.

" 'Fraid so." O'Reilly grabbed his knife and fork and set to.

"I'll need to ask about," said Mrs. Kincaid, frowning, "but I've seen that girl before."

"You do that, Kinky. I want to know by Friday." O'Reilly skewered a sausage.

"I will." Mrs. Kincaid handed over a piece of paper. "And here's your afternoon list. Now eat up. After lunch the pair of you will be healing more sick than the sainted Lord Jesus himself."

14

The General Comes Up to Scratch

Down the hall, through the kitchen, and into the garden. Barry looked for Arthur Guinness. The dog lay in his kennel, big head on his front paws, eyes shut.

"Arthur!" O'Reilly roared. "Wake up, you idle lummox."

Arthur opened bloodshot eyes, muttered a feeble *aaarrgh*, and went back to sleep.

"Serves you right, you drunken piss artist," O'Reilly said.

Piss artist in more ways than one, Barry thought, steering well away from the dog.

"Who've we to visit today, Fingal?" he asked, as they climbed into the car.

O'Reilly consulted his list. "Old Archie Campbell's arthritis is playing up, Katy Corrigan's bronchitis is getting worse, Mrs. Mallon thinks her Jimmy's broken his ankle . . . I doubt it, but we'd better drop by . . . and . . . that's very handy."

"What is?"

"The Mallons live near Maggie's place. We'll make our last call with her and see if she has any suggestions for what to do with Lady Macbeth."

The actual consultations hadn't taken long. Most of the time was consumed driving from place to place, and Barry now understood why O'Reilly had explained on the first day—was it really a week ago?—that it was important to know the geography of the place so that time wasn't wasted backtracking.

At their first stop O'Reilly examined Archie Campbell's twisted hands and knuckles, red and inflamed. He told the old man to keep soaking them in salt and warm water and to double his dose of aspirin. In the car, O'Reilly wondered aloud if perhaps it wasn't time to start giving the octogenarian cortisone, the wonder drug.

Katy Corrigan, lying in her bed, wheezing like a broken-down cart horse, agreed to inhale the fumes of Friar's Balsam three times daily, sent her eldest boy on his bicycle to the chemist's shop to collect a new prescription for penicillin V, and in no uncertain terms, assured O'Reilly that she had not the slightest intention of giving up her cigarettes.

Jimmy Mallon's ankle had made a remarkable recovery. When O'Reilly asked to see the patient, the mother said she'd have to call young Jimmy in from where he was playing soccer. Barry expected O'Reilly to blow a fuse, but the big man simply shrugged. He gave Mrs. Mallon a short lecture on how busy doctors were and asked could she please be certain in the future that a call was necessary.

"You have to make allowances," he remarked, as he pulled the Rover away from the Mallons'. "She's got eight kids and a husband who spends even more time in the Mucky Duck than Seamus Galvin. What we need is some decent kind of contraception . . . like this pill thingy."

"It's been available with a doctor's prescription in England for the last year."

"It's not available here, and it bloody well should be."

Barry had been wondering all afternoon when O'Reilly would

return to the subject of reproduction, the matter that had provoked
Barry's rebellion at lunchtime. Was this the opening shot? Perhaps
the air did need a bit more clearing. Metaphorically that was. Literally it certainly did. O'Reilly had lit his pipe. Barry said deliberately, "It would have saved that woman this morning a great deal of
grief."

"Julie MacAteer?"

"That's right." How the hell did he remember all their names?

"And us," said O'Reilly, "if that's what you're thinking."

"I said—"

"You were sorry, and I said we'd say no more about it. So,
Barry, let the hare sit. We've more important things to think
about."

"Like getting her fixed up in Liverpool?"

"No, you goat. That's easy. We've to hope to God that Maggie
has the answer to what to do with Lady Macbeth."

"Oh," said Barry, realizing that this was O'Reilly's way of
changing the subject. If Barry's outburst was a thing of the past,
Barry was happy to go along.

"We're here," said O'Reilly, pulling the car to the roadside outside Maggie's cottage. "Come on."

"Hello, Doctors dear," said Maggie, trowel in one hand, as she
turned from a window box. "Grand day."

It was. Out past her cottage, far out on the whitecapped lough,
Barry could see a fleet of yachts running down the wind. In the sun-
light their multihued spinnakers billowed like fairies' parachutes.
I'd like to be out there with them, he thought.

"How are you, Maggie?" O'Reilly asked.

"Grand, so I am." She wiped the back of her hand across her
forehead. Barry noticed that the geraniums in her hatband had been
replaced with marigolds. "I'm glad you dropped by. I need a wee
favour."

"All in good time, Maggie. *We've* come to ask advice."

"Oh? What about?"

"Cats," said O'Reilly. "I've just got a new one."

"Good. It'll be better company for you than that great lummox of an Arthur Guinness." Maggie looked gently at the big man.

Barry wondered just how accurate Mrs. Kincaid had been when she'd assured him they were the only ones to know of O'Reilly's loss.

"I'm having trouble training her."

Maggie cackled. "Sure you can't train cats."

"Oh," said O'Reilly, looking crestfallen. "So I'll just have to wave good-bye to my living-room suite?"

"Clawing is she?"

"Like a tiger with fits."

Maggie frowned. "You could try doing what I did for the General. Come inside and I'll show you." She led the way, leaving the front door open.

Barry watched and listened.

The General lay on a chair beside the unlit fire. Maggie went into another room and came back carrying a T-shaped piece of equipment. The base was a bit of flat plywood. A post, two by two by thirty-six and covered in old carpet, rose vertically from the base.

"One of these might do the trick," she said, offering it to O'Reilly. "It's a scratching post, so it is."

The General opened his eye, stared at the scratching post, and made a moaning sound. He crouched against the chair's seat.

Maggie held out her hands and took the post from O'Reilly. "You know this thing, don't you, General Sir Bernard Law Montgomery?"

The General whined. He slipped off the chair and scuttled, belly to the floor, under the table, and from there he peered balefully, his good eye never leaving the post.

"The General used to rip my bits and pieces, didn't you, you bugger?" She waved the post at the cat, who put a paw over his eye and retreated out of sight.

"How do you use it?" O'Reilly asked.

"When he was little, I set this beside the chair he liked to claw—"

"I see," O'Reilly interrupted, "and every time he tried to scratch the furniture you showed him the post, and he learned to use it instead. Brilliant."

"Not at all," said Maggie. She raised her voice. "When he tried it, I took the post . . . and I fetched him a right good belt on the head, didn't I, General?"

Barry was aware of an orange streak that rushed past him and out through the open door. He couldn't hear if the cat was still yowling. He couldn't hear anything except O'Reilly's rafter-ringing guffaws.

"Maybe," said O'Reilly, when he finally stopped laughing, "maybe a piece of rolled-up newspaper would work?"

"Maybe." Maggie looked thoughtful. "It's the best I can think of."

"Thanks, Maggie." O'Reilly walked to the door, stopped, turned, and said, "I nearly forgot. What was the wee favour you wanted?"

Maggie fidgeted, cocked her head to one side. "I sometimes take a dander up past Sonny's place."

Barry saw her cheeks redden.

"I don't go that way often, you understand?"

"Of course," said O'Reilly.

She looked O'Reilly in the eye. "But I was up there this morning, and I don't think the old goat's right."

"Why not?"

"He usually hides in his car if he sees me coming." She nodded quickly, as if reassuring herself that she was doing the right thing. "He just sat in his chair. 'Morning, Maggie,' says he, and he coughed. Not just a wee hirstle. A great big long hack. He looked terrible blue in the face, so he did. 'Morning, Sonny,' says I. You have to be polite. 'You all right?' 'Mind your own business,' says he, all hirstles and wheezles." She put a hand on O'Reilly's arm. "He never asks nobody for nothing, but would you maybe drop by and take a gander at him?"

"Of course. We'll head up there right now."

"Thanks, Doctor . . . and for the love of God, don't you be telling him 'twas me that sent you. He'd have a carniption."

"Mum's the word, Maggie."

Barry backed out through the door as O'Reilly strode towards him. Maggie followed. As he climbed into the Rover, he heard her growl, "He's nothing but an old eejit, but a Christian wouldn't ignore a sick animal." Barry saw her eyes glisten. "Make sure he's all right, won't you now?" Her voice was tremulous.

There was no sign of Sonny. Nor did he appear when O'Reilly bellowed the man's name. Four of his five dogs ran barking through the scrapyard to the gate in the hedge. The spaniel stood outside a derelict car, front paws on the sill of an open rear door.

"He must be in there," O'Reilly said, opening the gate. "Away to hell out of that." He brushed aside the dogs and made his way, Barry in tow, along a well-trodden path through weeds and rusting metal. He bent at the open car door.

"Are you there, Sonny?"

Barry heard a hacking cough and a feeble "Go away."

"It's Doctor O'Reilly."

"Leave me alone."

"Be buggered if I will," said O'Reilly, clambering through the open door.

Barry peered through the dirty windows. O'Reilly's back nearly blocked his view, but he could make out a figure curled up on the backseat.

"Ah, Jesus, Doctor, let me be." More coughing.

O'Reilly backed out, dragging Sonny. "It would be a hell of a sight easier if you'd cooperate," O'Reilly panted. "You're sick as a dog."

"All right. All right."

"Put your arm round my neck."

"Can I help, Doctor O'Reilly?"

"Get out of my way." O'Reilly straightened up. He held Sonny in his arms, the man's long legs dangling to one side, his head pillowed on O'Reilly's chest. Barry could see that Sonny's cheeks were slate grey. His nostrils flared like a scared horse's, and his neck muscles stood out like cords every time he tried to inhale. There was no need of a stethoscope to hear the damp rattling of each laboured breath. Had his heart failure suddenly worsened?

"Come on," O'Reilly said, "we'll have to get him to the surgery."

"Right."

The last thing Barry heard as they drove away was the doleful howling of Sonny's dogs.

O'Reilly laid Sonny on the examination couch. "Give me a hand with his clothes."

Barry helped O'Reilly remove Sonny's raincoat, a heavy sweater, and a collarless shirt. It took several minutes to peel away the layers of old newspaper that lay under the shirt. Although his arms were brown to just above the elbow—farmer's arms, Barry thought—and there was a deeply tanned V at his neck, the rest of his chest was pearly white. With each rasping inhalation, the muscles between Sonny's ribs were sucked inwards. With each rasping inhalation, Sonny whimpered.

"Hurts to breathe, does it?" O'Reilly asked, as he took Sonny's pulse.

"Yuh-huh." Sonny put a hand to his ribs.

"When did it start?"

"Just after . . . *hack* . . . the storm . . . *hack* . . . got soaked."

"Help me sit him up."

Barry put an arm round Sonny's shoulders. His skin felt as if it were on fire, and God, he was heavy, yet O'Reilly had carried the man as if he had been a small child. One glance told Barry that the jugular veins were distended right up to the angle of Sonny's jaw, a sure sign that blood was backing up behind a heart that lacked the strength to pump it further.

O'Reilly percussed Sonny's back. Barry could hear the sullen thumps where a resonant sound should have been. Either the lungs or the pleural cavities, the space between the glistening membranes that sheathe the lungs, were filling with fluid. O'Reilly stuffed his stethoscope in his ears and listened. A look of pure anger filled his eyes. "You daft old bugger. Why the hell didn't you send for me sooner?"

Sonny hacked.

"Right," said O'Reilly, pulling his stethoscope from his ears. "Hang on." He rummaged under the examining table and swung the upper end to an angle of forty-five degrees. "Let him lie back now."

Barry eased Sonny's head back onto the pillow.

O'Reilly hauled up the leg of Sonny's pants and thrust his thumb against the shin. When he pulled his thumb away, Barry saw that there was a deep depression. That meant there was oedema, fluid accumulating under the skin.

"Heart failure?"

"And pneumonia and pleurisy. Both sides." O'Reilly shook his head. "I suppose you didn't want to bother anybody. Christ on a crutch. It's the hospital for you, Sonny."

Barry saw the terror in Sonny's eyes. "My dogs . . . *hack* . . .
who'll look after . . . *hack* . . . my dogs?"

"Your dogs'll do a damn sight better if you're around to take care
of them," O'Reilly said, "and you won't be if we don't get you to
the Royal. And quick." He turned to Barry. "Go and call the ambulance. The number's by the phone. We need oxygen down here as
quick as we can get it."

"Right."

"I'll get Kinky to bring blankets." He started to turn away, but
Sonny reached out and grabbed O'Reilly's arm.

"Don't leave me alone."

"I won't."

"I'll get the blankets too."

"Good man."

Barry saw O'Reilly holding one of Sonny's hands. With his
other hand he smoothed the grey hair from Sonny's forehead. All
Barry could think of was a Victorian etching that had hung in the
students' mess hall. In the background of a cramped room the parents stood wringing their hands over a child sprawled on a rumpled
bed. A bearded, frock-coated doctor sat on the side of the bed, chin
on hand, tired eyes full of what? Compassion? Despair? Barry had
never been sure, but the look in that man's face had come through
time, and now it was there on the brown-eyed, bent-nosed counte-
nance of Doctor Fingal Flahertie O'Reilly.

"Sherry?"

"Please." Barry sat in his by-now usual chair in the upstairs
lounge.

"Here. Get that into you." O'Reilly gave Barry a glass, set his
whiskey on the coffee table, shoved Lady Macbeth out of his chair,

and sat. The cat leapt into his lap, and he fondled the animal's head. "Jesus," he said, "it never rains but it pours. What a day. Surgery packed to the gills, a pregnant lass from Rasharkin. I'll need to give the folks in Liverpool a call about her tomorrow . . . and that's not the half of it." O'Reilly frowned. "I'm worried as hell about Sonny and his place."

"Do you not think he'll make it?"

"Touch and go. Pneumonia, pleurisy, and a dicky ticker? Still he's a tough old bird. Anyway they'll do the best they can for him in the Royal, and if they can't fix him, that was in his stars. That's not what I'm concerned about."

Barry had learned, hard and painfully, that no doctor could care too deeply, not about any one patient. You *couldn't* cure them all, and unless you built a wall, a carapace of forced indifference to hide behind, you'd crack up. He couldn't fault O'Reilly for his apparent lack of concern about the clinical outcome, but why had O'Reilly mentioned Sonny's place? Barry looked at Lady Macbeth. O'Reilly had a soft spot for animals. No. It couldn't be.

"You're not going to go and see to his dogs?" Barry asked.

O'Reilly shook his head. "No. Maggie'll look after them if we ask her."

"I saw her face when we drove off. She's still carrying a torch." Barry instantly regretted his words.

"It happens," said O'Reilly, glancing out the window. "But it's more than his dogs that's got Sonny scared shitless."

"Oh?"

"Bishop." O'Reilly spat the word. "Bloody Bishop. Sonny told me when you were phoning for the ambulance. There's some council bylaw that if a property's derelict and the owner moves away, the council can get a purchase order and have it repossessed. Then they sell it to the highest bidder. And who do you think that might be?"

"Ah, no."

"Ah, yes. The bastard's been trying to get his hands on Sonny's place for years."

"Could we not have a word with Bishop?"

"Aye. With about as much chance of success as Moses when he had a wee word with Pharaoh about letting the Israelites go off for a long holiday. Unless you can think of a few plagues we could call down on the councillor's head?" O'Reilly ground his teeth. "I'm damned if I can see a way out, but Bishop may not hear for a day or two, and the Council offices will be closed for the Twelfth week. Maybe we can come up with something."

"I hope so, and I hope Sonny recovers."

"That," said O'Reilly, "goes without saying." He took a deep breath. "It's no use boiling your cabbage twice. We've done all we can, and we'll have to wait and see how things turn out." He moved as if to rise.

Lady Macbeth jumped to the floor. She put both front paws on the side of Barry's chair, looked sideways at O'Reilly, dropped to the floor without as much as having unsheathed her claws, and sauntered away.

"Bloody cat's psychic. Of course she's a female," said O'Reilly, lowering a rolled-up copy of the *Belfast Telegraph*. "And while we're talking about females, I said you could have Friday off. Do you think you should give that lass of yours a call?"

"I'd like to."

"Go on then."

Barry ran downstairs, dialled, and waited.

"Hello. Kinnegar 657334."

"Patricia? It's Barry. Look, I'm off on Friday. Would you like to go out for a bite?"

"I'd love to but I've got an evening seminar."

"Damn. It's my only night off." He felt the plastic of the receiver cold against his palm as he squeezed.

"I . . . I suppose I could ask someone to let me borrow their notes."

"Do it."

"It's an important class."

"All work and no play make Jack a dull—"

"Make *Jill* a dull girl." He heard her chuckle. "All right. What time?"

"Seven. We could go to my yacht club, in Bangor." The grub's cheaper there for members, he thought.

"Super. I look forward to it. Got to run now."

Before the line went dead, he thought he heard a kissing noise but couldn't be sure. It didn't matter. He'd see her on Friday. Only three days to go—well, four if he counted Friday's working hours. He hung up and started to climb the stairs.

The phone rang.

Bugger. Another patient. "It's all right, Mrs. Kincaid." Barry came downstairs again and lifted the phone. "Doctor O'Reilly's surgery."

"Can I speak to Doctor Laverty?"

Barry recognized the voice. "Jack? How are you?"

"Busy as bedamned, but I'm off on Friday. Fancy a jar?"

Barry laughed. "Sorry, mate."

"Working?"

"No. I'm taking a girl to dinner."

"Poor girl."

"Piss off. This one's different."

"I've heard that before, but good luck to you. Sorry we can't get together. I'm running round like a blue-arsed fly here. I don't know when I'm off again."

"Still enjoying it?"

"You remember we used to watch *Dr. Kildare* on the telly?" Jack assumed an American accent. "'How do you like the work, Kildare?' 'It's hell, Doctor Gillespie, but I love every gruelling minute.' What a load of cobblers, but yes. I'm pretty sure I made the right choice."

Barry chuckled. "Me too." And he knew his words were true.

"It's a great comfort to know you're out there stamping out disease," Jack said. "Listen. I found out about that appendix abscess. It *was* one of O'Reilly's."

"Jeannie. Jeannie Kennedy."

"I can't remember her name, but she's well on the mend. Should be out in a day or two."

"Great."

"Bugger." Barry could hear a beeping in the background. "My bleeper's going off. Got to go. Give me a bell sometime next week."

"Okay."

"And Barry? Friday night? Try to keep it in your pants."

15

The Stars in Their Courses

Tuesday and Wednesday sped by. Barry knew that if he were asked to pick the salient moments from hours of full surgeries and rushed home visits, he'd have been hard-pressed to recall, except for those events that later he would come to realize would shape the futures of Doctor O'Reilly's more prominent patients.

O'Reilly's phone calls to the Royal brought the news that Sonny was holding his own. He wasn't out of the woods, but his condition had not deteriorated.

Maggie had agreed to take care of his dogs.

Seamus Galvin showed up to have his sore, but immaculately scrubbed ankle looked at, and the source of the fortune into which he had fallen was revealed.

O'Reilly and Donal Donnelly had had a most peculiar conversation about a dog.

Somewhere in the village Julie MacAteer tried not to worry about the results of her pregnancy test, but failed.

Councillor Bishop's finger needed attention.

And despite the long hours, Barry began to feel truly at home in his choice of career in general and in the village in particular. Bally-bucklebo, where the orbits of people's lives swung on their orderly courses, preordained, highly individual, separate until nudged into a great planetary conjunction by the Fates—or by the Fates' local messenger, Doctor Fingal Flahertie O'Reilly.

Seamus Galvin came into the surgery on Tuesday morning. He sat in the patients' chair and pulled a cloth cap off his pear-shaped head. His eyes, small and close-set, lurked between hairline and jawline like a pair of timid brown animals, never still, never seeming to focus on anything in particular.

"Good morning, Doctor O'Reilly. Morning, Doctor Laverty."

"Morning, Seamus. How's young Barry Fingal?" Barry asked.

"Grand. Mind you, it's a good thing men can't feed wee ones. He has Maureen up half the night, so he has."

"Huh," said O'Reilly, "I don't suppose *you'd* think of giving the child a bottle once in a while?"

"Not at all. You don't buy a dog and bark yourself. That's Maureen's job, so it is."

O'Reilly looked at Barry over his half-moons and shook his head. "I'd not want you to rupture yourself, Seamus. A wiser man than I said, 'Work is the scourge of the drinking classes.'"

"Wilde," said Barry. "Oscar."

"The very lad," said O'Reilly, "but that's not why you're here, is it, Seamus?"

"Ah, no, sir. It's time for you to take a wee look at my ankle."

"Huh," said O'Reilly, "and I suppose you want a line?"

"Oh, indeed, sir, I do that. I'll have to go on the burroo."

Barry understood. Seamus wanted a medical certificate so he could draw disability insurance from the Bureau of Unemployment—"burroo" in the local dialect.

"We'll see," said O'Reilly. "Show me your ankle."

Galvin bent and unwound a tensor bandage.

O'Reilly sat back, knees together. "Put it up on my lap."

Seamus obeyed. Barry moved closer. The ankle in question looked perfectly normal. No swelling. No bruising.

"Can you bend it down?" O'Reilly asked.

Galvin made a show of trying to extend his foot. "Ah. Ooh."

"Up," said O'Reilly.

"Ooh. Ah."

O'Reilly grasped the foot between both of his big hands and, bending it to the left, asked, "Does that hurt?"

"Ah. Ooh. Ouch."

"You sure?"

"Indeed, sir."

"Hmm. Right. Let's see you walk on it."

Galvin stood and teetered across the room, hauling his allegedly wounded ankle behind him. He would have been giving a fair imitation of the mock-injury display of a mother plover trying to lead a predator away from her nest, except peewits don't usually moan "Ooh, ah" as they flutter across the moors.

"You're one for the textbooks, Seamus," said O'Reilly. "It seems you've managed to hurt the side that was fine when you showed that hoof to me first."

Galvin hung his head.

"Maybe we should be putting you up for an Oscar? Best actor in a nonsupporting role?"

"But it hurts, sir. If I try to stand on it, I get a terrible stoon all the way up to my knee."

"Seemed to hold you up at the bar on Sunday when you were spending your fortune."

Galvin smiled an ingratiating grin that made Barry think of Charles Dickens's Uriah Heep. "Ah, but sure you know, Doctor sir, that alcohol kills pain." For a moment Galvin's dull eyes sparkled. Barry's mental image was of Wile E. Coyote with a light bulb flashing on above his cartoon head. "I know I had one or two. That must have been when I hurt the other side."

"*Ecce Galvinus. Homo plumbum oscillandat*," O'Reilly remarked to Barry, who immediately understood. "Behold Galvin. The man's swinging the lead."

"Is that *plumbum* stuff bad, sir?" Galvin hobbled back across the room and sat heavily, his narrow face contorted into a rictus.

"All depends," said O'Reilly. "Put up your foot again." Galvin obeyed, and O'Reilly rapidly reapplied the bandage. "You want me to give you a line?"

Galvin brightened. "Yes, please, sir. For two weeks if that's all right?"

"I might," said O'Reilly, "but . . ."

"But what, sir?"

"But I'd need to know about the fortune you said you'd be falling into."

Galvin sat back in the forward-tilting chair. "Ach, you don't, sir. Ach, no."

"Ach, yes, Seamus, I do. Or it's no line."

By the wrinkling of Galvin's brow and the clenching of his teeth, Barry could tell that the man was having a gargantuan struggle with himself.

"No tickee, no laundry, Seamus."

Galvin took a deep breath. "Maureen gave me the money."

O'Reilly's nose tip blanched. "She what? The money for California?"

Galvin hung his head.

"You skiver. You unmitigated gobshite. Give it back to her, do you hear?"

"I can't, sir. It's spent. On ducks."

"In the Mucky Duck?" O'Reilly rose and towered over Galvin. "I'll kill you. I'll kill you dead."

Galvin held both arms against the side of his head nearest to O'Reilly and leant his body in the opposite direction. "No not *in* the Duck. Well, only a couple of quid. The rest of the money went *on* ducks. Rocking ducks."

One of O'Reilly's shaggy eyebrows rose. "What the hell are you talking about?"

Galvin slowly lowered his arms. "Rocking ducks, sir. I'm going to make rocking ducks. Just like rocking horses. There'll not be a kiddie in Ballybucklebo won't go daft to have one. The lumber and paint's all bought. I can sell them for twice what they'll cost to make. That's why I want two weeks off, so I can finish making them and get them sold. Then Maureen and me and the chiseller can go to America with a bit of the oul' do-ray-mi."

"And Maureen agreed to this half-witted notion?"

"Lord, aye, sir."

Barry was pretty sure from the way Galvin refused to meet O'Reilly's glare that the man was lying.

"How many will you make?"

"About a hundred, sir."

"Jesus Christ on a rubber crutch. And how many kiddies that would want a rocking duck do you think live in Ballybucklebo?"

"I don't know, sir." Galvin's Adam's apple bobbed up and down.

"Forty, maybe fifty. Do you reckon they'll buy them in pairs? Matched sets?"

"I never thought of that, sir. But it will all work out. You'll see."

O'Reilly said, "I doubt it."

Galvin pushed himself back up the chair, using, Barry noticed, a hearty thrust from his reputedly damaged ankle. "So you'll give me the line, Doctor sir?"

Barry was surprised when O'Reilly said, "A promise is a promise," and returned to the desk to scribble on a government form. Doctors were meant to be honest when supporting genuine claims for disability money.

"Here," said O'Reilly, handing Galvin the form. "Two weeks.

But you build those damn ducks. I might know a business in Belfast that'll take the lot."

Galvin tugged his forelock and rose. "Bless you, Doctor, and I will build them, so I will." He struggled to the door, accompanying himself with a lamentation of oohs and aahs.

"And Seamus," O'Reilly said softly.

"Yes, Doctor?"

"Get out of your bloody bed and give that wife of yours a hand. Do you hear me?"

"I do, sir. I will." Galvin left.

"Useless bugger," said O'Reilly. "I told you he was a skiver when you were going on about me chucking him into the bushes."

"So why did you give him a disability certificate when we both know he's faking it?"

O'Reilly sat in the swivel chair. "I was getting into too many fights with my patients when I wouldn't give them their lines."

"But that's part of our job."

"Balls. Our job's to look after them when they're sick, not behave like some bloody civil servant."

"I know, but—"

"What do you know about the medical referee?"

"Not much."

"The politicos aren't altogether useless. A few years ago they had the bright idea that maybe an independent doctor, a referee employed by the ministry, could examine anyone their local GP thought was working the system. Take some of the load off the GP. Sometimes the referee'd pull a certificate at random and invite the customer up for a visit. Kept a lot of people honest. Let the ministry doctor be the villain. He's never going to see the patient again."

"That makes sense."

"Didn't work. You were *still* the villain as soon as you told someone you were going to send them to the referee. They call him 'The Big Doctor.' They're scared stiff of him. It was as good as telling them to their faces that you thought they were pulling your chain."

"So what do you do?"

O'Reilly chuckled. "The Big Doctor is a classmate of mine. We worked out a code. Here." He handed Barry a blank certificate. "See where it says Signature of Referring Doctor?"

"Yes."

"If I sign it F. F. O'Reilly, my friend knows I believe the complaint is genuine. It saves him and the customers a lot of trouble. He doesn't have to send for really sick folks. But . . ." O'Reilly's chuckle became a full laugh. "If I sign it F. F. O'Reilly, M. B., B.Ch., B.A.O., the lead swinger's up in the ministry office before the ink's dry on the paper."

"You wily bugger."

"The customer doesn't know I blew the whistle. No more fights in here. Works like a charm."

"And how, may I ask, did you sign Galvin's line?"

"Ah," said O'Reilly, "let's just say my recommendation was unqualified. Now, be a good lad and see who's next."

"Might be a bit difficult to park the car on Main Street. They'll be getting it ready for Thursday," said O'Reilly, finishing his lunch. "We've to nip round to Declan Finnegan's. He lives over the grocer's. It's not a bad day. Let's walk. We'll pick up the car later."

"Fine." Barry would be glad of the exercise. He seemed to have done little recently but sit in O'Reilly's surgery or in the big Rover. He thought wistfully of his fly rod, propped up, unused in his attic. A couple of lines from the old song "The Convict of Clonmel" popped into his mind:

> At my bed foot decaying,
> My hurley is lying;

172 *Patrick Taylor*

Through the boys of the village
My gold-ball is flying.

He was hardly in gaol here in the practice, but never mind time off to go fishing—Friday and dinner with Patricia seemed to be such a long way away.

"Is it nice in there?" O'Reilly asked.

"Where?"

"Wherever the hell you've gone off to in your head. It's not spring, but I suppose your young man's fancy is lightly turning to thoughts of love?"

"Not *quite* how Tennyson put it, and if it's any of your business, I was thinking about fishing."

"Were you? I noticed you've a rod. You like to fish?"

"Very much."

"I'll have a word with His Lordship."

"Who?"

"The Marquis of Ballybucklebo. Nice old bugger. He owns a beat on the Bucklebo River. He'd probably let you on his water if I asked him."

"Would you?"

"Next time I see him."

"I'd love a day on a good trout stream."

"I'll see to it." O'Reilly rose. "But sitting here blethering won't get the baby a new coat. Come on."

At least, Barry thought, as he closed the green front door, going out this way avoids having to run the gauntlet past the canine world's answer to Casanova. "It's a great day, Fingal."

"It's too muggy. There could be a bit of thunder about," said O'Reilly, as he strode along the footpath, elbowing his way through knots of passersby. "Afternoon, Aggie. Afternoon, Cecil."

Barry kept pace, nodding at those who greeted him. The town was busy. Shoppers and children on their school holidays filled the narrow footpaths and spilled into the roadway to jostle with a farmer and the small herd of Aberdeen Angus bullocks he was driving along Main Street, seemingly oblivious to the horns of the cars stalled behind them.

A gang of men bent to their work, painting the kerbstones in bands of glistening red, white, and blue. The maypole had been touched up in the same Loyalist colours, and from its peak, drifting lazily in a sea breeze, hung a large flag: the Red Hand of Ulster centred on the red cross of Saint George set against a white background. It kept company with its smaller brothers and the Union Jacks that dangled from upstairs windows.

Other men struggled to erect an arch across the road.

"Would you look at that?" said O'Reilly.

Barry gazed at the structure. Plywood-covered posts supported a slim, quarter circle of the same material that curved across the street. In its centre was a picture of a man in seventeenth-century costume, feather drooping from his cocked hat, riding boots black and polished. He was mounted on a rearing white horse. One hand held the reins; the other waved a sabre over the rider's head.

"Pity," said O'Reilly, "that William of Orange's charger has a squint."

Barry looked more closely. O'Reilly was right. The artist had managed to have each glaring eye focus at a spot just in front of its flaring nostrils.

"Derry, Aughrim, Enniskillen, and the Boyne." O'Reilly read the names of battles that were lettered on painted scrolls on either side of the mounted man. "In 1690 or thereabouts. Old battles that should be forgotten, but the way some of the locals go on, you'd think they'd been fought yesterday."

"You said it was all sweetness and light between the Protestants and the Catholics in Ballybucklebo."

"There's nothing overt. Not like the taunting and ranting and roaring that go on in Belfast. But I don't like it," said O'Reilly. "I saw a newsreel once. Alabama or Mississippi. Bunch of eejits in pointy hoods and white robes burning a cross, just to remind the blacks that they are second-class citizens. It gave me the shivers."

"Surely a bit of decoration, a few flags, and a parade aren't the same as a Ku Klux Klan rally?"

"I was a boy during the Troubles . . . the Black and Tans and the Civil War . . . back in the nineteen twenties. I'd hate to see the Troubles come back, and when you keep on rubbing folks' noses in it with flags and parades . . ."

"I'm sure there'll never be anything like the Troubles again. Not here."

"I hope you're right," said O'Reilly thoughtfully, "but long memories are the curse of Ireland. The Twelfth's just a holiday to most folks, but there's a bunch of bigots that do go on stirring the pot, keeping the old hatred alive . . . like our worthy councillor. When he can spare the time from trying to drive a decent old man off his property, he'd be happy to string up the odd Fenian from a lamp-post."

"He really is a miserable man, isn't he?"

"He's a pure and unadulterated gobshite," said O'Reilly. "I don't know about you, but I'm no closer to sorting out how we can help Sonny, and now I have to find a way to get Maureen Galvin's money back for her."

"I thought you knew a company in Belfast that would buy the rocking ducks."

"I can phone a fellow I played rugby with, but would you want to try to sell the things?"

Barry shook his head.

O'Reilly started to cross the road. "Something will turn up," he said, stepping back up onto the footpath. "Just what the dickens do you think this is all about?"

Barry saw the ginger-haired Donal Donnelly waving at them as he forced his way across the street past the cow clap–splattered rump of one of the bullocks. He was accompanied by a grey dog. He and his companion stepped up onto the footpath.

"Doctor. Doctor O'Reilly, sir. Could I have a wee word?" Donal's buckteeth trembled against his long lower lip.

"Of course."

"This here's Bluebird." He tugged on a thin piece of rope. The dog raised its narrow muzzle and fixed Donal with a look of pure adoration from its liquid brown eyes.

"Bluebird?"

"Yes, sir. After your man's speedboat."

Barry looked more closely at the beast. It had long thin legs, and carried its skinny tail in an arc curved in underneath its belly. Every rib was as visible as the bones of an anatomic display specimen.

"Donald Campbell?"

"Himself. The very fellah."

"He's in Australia," said Barry. "He's going to have a go at the world water-speed record later this month."

"Races, does she?" O'Reilly asked, bending and examining the dog's flanks.

"She does, sir, but she hasn't won yet."

"So if she's slow, why do you call her Bluebird?" O'Reilly's brow wrinkled.

"Because, sir"—Donal's left upper eyelid drooped in a slow wink—"she runs on water."

O'Reilly started. "Water?"

Barry was baffled.

"But on Friday at Dunmore Park she'll be running dry."

"Will she, by God?" O'Reilly's eyes widened.

What the hell were they talking about?

"I thought you'd like to know, sir." Donal peered furtively around. "Not a word now."

"A wink's as good as a nod to a blind horse. Thanks, Donal. I'll keep it in mind. I might just take a trip up to Dunmore. Doctor Laverty could look after the practice."

Barry flinched. Oh, no. Friday was to be his night off.

"We'll be running on," said Donal, tugging at the rope. "Got to get you fit, girl."

"Fingal," said Barry. All his questions about the recent strange conversation had been driven away by the thought that he might not be able to see Patricia after all. "Fingal, you said I could have Friday night off."

"Did I?"

"Yes."

"Must have forgotten."

Barry steeled himself. "Look, Fingal—"

"Don't worry. We'll both get away. You just hold the fort 'til it's time for you to go."

"But who'll look after things when we're both out?"

"Kinky. I don't do it very often, but if no one's baby's due and the shop seems reasonably quiet, Kinky takes the calls. Either she asks the customer to wait until the morning, or if she thinks it is urgent, she arranges for an ambulance to take the patient up to the Royal."

"Oh."

"So you can see the light of your life, and I can have a bit of fun myself." O'Reilly chuckled. "The Lord might just move in a mysterious way his wonders to perform."

"You've utterly lost me."

"I do that sometimes," said O'Reilly, "and I've no time to explain now. We're running behind. Come on and we'll get Declan Finnegan looked at."

Declan Finnegan was a man in his fifties. He was sorely afflicted with Parkinson's disease. The diagnosis was instantly apparent the moment Barry walked into the small flat above the grocer's shop. The man's face was a mask, expressionless, immobile. A string of spittle hung from the corner of his mouth. His eyes held no questions for the doctors. Any hope he might have treasured of a cure must have been long gone. He held out one hand in greeting, and Barry saw the telltale rubbing of thumb against fingers, the uncontrollable pill-rolling movements.

His wife, a worried-looking woman who bore herself like a Victorian dowager, wore her hair, glossy as black Italian marble, pulled back into a severe bun in the style favoured by Spanish duennas.

"Bonjour, monsieur le docteur."

"Bonjour, Madame Finnegan. Comme il faut aujourd'hui?" O'Reilly replied in barely accented French.

"Je crois qu'il est encore plus mal. C'est très triste, ca."

Barry saw sadness in her eyes. He listened and watched, his schoolboy French barely sufficient to allow him to follow the questions and answers. It would appear that indeed the man's condition had worsened since O'Reilly's last visit. The pill rolling was increasing, and when O'Reilly asked Declan to walk for a few paces, he did so in tiny shuffling steps.

O'Reilly offered what little comfort he could, agreed that, yes, it would be a good thing to keep the appointment that had been made for several weeks hence with a neurosurgeon at the Royal. Perhaps indeed it might be time for stereotactic surgery to destroy the part of the brain with a mind of its own that caused the muscles to rebel. *"Au revoir, Madame. Nous vous verrions un jour pendant. la semaine prochaine,"* O'Reilly said as they left.

"I didn't know you spoke French," Barry said, as they walked back to the house to collect the car.

"Oh, aye," said O'Reilly, "and I used to have a bit of Italian. I picked them up when I was in the Med. On the *Warspite*. Comes in handy once in a while. Mind you, she's the only Frenchwoman I know of in Ballybucklebo. Declan was in the Tank Regiment. Met her somewhere in Normandy in forty-four."

"Poor bugger. It's a horrible disease."

"There are some really sick ones here. It's not all cuts and bruises. I just wish to Christ there was more we could do for folks like Declan." His voice had an edge like a new scalpel.

Barry had no chance to reply as O'Reilly put his head down, lengthened his stride, and ploughed like an angry bull through the pedestrians.

In local parlance O'Reilly went through Tuesday's afternoon calls—and most of the patients who had come to the surgery on Wednesday morning—like grease through a duckling. Barry could barely keep pace. He was glad of the respite when Mrs. Kincaid set his lunch plate on the table.

"Your list, Doctor. It's not too bad." She handed O'Reilly the sheet of paper.

"Thanks, Kinky." O'Reilly consulted it quickly. "Not bad at all. I don't know about you, Barry, but I'm feeling a bit ragged."

"Umh," Barry muttered through a mouthful of lamb chop.

"Kinky?" O'Reilly asked. "Any luck with finding out about Julie MacAteer?"

"I'm not getting very far. The wee girl is living somewhere here, but nobody knows where."

"Keep at it, will you?"

"I will—"

Her reply was interrupted by the jangling of the front doorbell.

"I'll see who it is, so." She left, and when she returned her colour was high, her black eyes flashing. "It's the wee Hitler man. His exalted excellence, Councillor Bishop. The Great Panjandrum says he doesn't give a . . ." She hesitated. "Well, he's not concerned that it's your lunchtime, and he wants to be seen now. Will I tell him to wait?"

"No," said O'Reilly, pushing his plate aside. "Pop these in the oven, Kinky. Come on, Barry."

"Right."

Councillor Bishop stood in the hall, legs astraddle, arms folded, eyes narrowed.

"You took your time."

"Ach," said O'Reilly mildly, "if the knitter is weary, the baby will have no new bonnet."

"What the hell are you talking about?"

"Doctor Laverty and myself have been just a toty bit busy for the last couple of days. We were at our lunch," said O'Reilly. "Could you not have come during surgery hours?"

"And wait forever with the unwashed? Don't be stupid."

Barry saw a spark deep in O'Reilly's brown eyes, a spark that reflected the fires of hell. The consultation should be interesting, he thought.

"Come into the surgery," said O'Reilly, crossing the hall and opening the door. He sat at the desk and waited for Councillor Bishop to take the patients' chair. "What can I do for you?"

As Barry made himself comfortable on the examining table, Councillor Bishop thrust his bandaged finger under O'Reilly's nose. "I told you on Sunday. I need this better for tomorrow."

"Right," said O'Reilly as he went to a tray of instruments and picked up a pair of scissors and a set of fine-nosed forceps. "I'd forgotten that the Duck doubles up as my consulting room. Nothing like giving medical advice when you're having a quiet pint."

"What?"

O'Reilly sat. "Show me your finger."

Bishop gave his hand to O'Reilly, who picked up the bottom end of the bandage with the forceps, slid one blade of the scissors beneath the gauze, and began to snip. When the dressing was divided from finger base to fingertip, O'Reilly grabbed one edge between the forceps blades and used his free hand to immobilize Councillor Bishop's wrist. O'Reilly gave a ferocious yank with the forceps.

Barry was sure he would have been able to hear the rending of material as it parted from the freshly healed flesh beneath had it not been for a deafening *yeeeow.*

"Sorry about that, Councillor," O'Reilly said. "I could have soaked it in Savlon for fifteen minutes and softened the old blood, but I know you're always in a rush."

Barry was glad that he was seated behind the councillor so that the grin that ran from ear to ear was not obvious.

"Go and rinse it in the sink," said O'Reilly.

The councillor obeyed.

"All set for the big day tomorrow?" O'Reilly enquired.

"Don't talk to me about big days. The sooner it's over, the better." Councillor Bishop held his finger under the stream of water. "I've bigger fish to fry."

"Oh?" said O'Reilly. He glanced at Barry.

"Sonny's in hospital and that parcel of land—"

"You wouldn't," said O'Reilly. "Och, no."

"I will," said the councillor.

Barry needed to hear no more. He slipped off the couch. "I think that's the meanest thing—"

"Nobody asked you to think," O'Reilly snapped. He shook his head.

Barry bit back his words. He felt heat in his cheeks. His breathing quickened.

Councillor Bishop turned off the tap and glowered at his fingertip. "Doesn't look too bad," he allowed. "Does it need another bandage?" He stumped over to O'Reilly, who peered at the digit.

"Looks fine to me."

"Good. I'll be off then. I've work to do."

"Fine," said O'Reilly, as he accompanied the councillor to the surgery door. "And how's Mrs. Bishop today?"

Barry followed, still smarting from the rebuke. He was amazed at O'Reilly's civility and disappointed that he had not argued Sonny's case. He heard the councillor's reply as they crossed the hall.

"She's fit to be tied. That new maid of ours. The Antrim girl. She's given her notice, and where in the hell can you find good help these days?"

"I wouldn't know," said O'Reilly, smiling at Mrs. Kincaid, who was busy in the dining room. He opened the front door and let the councillor pass. As the fat man marched down the path, O'Reilly called, "I beg your pardon?"

"I said nothing," the councillor yelled back over his shoulder.

"My mistake," said O'Reilly in a loud voice. "I could have sworn I heard you say thank you." Then he muttered, "Gobshite."

Barry, now standing at O'Reilly's shoulder, said, "You said not to let the customers get the upper hand. You were too damn civil to that man." The words spilled out. "And I thought we were going to have it out with him about Sonny's place. You were right. Bishop is going to take it. When I saw you weren't going to do anything and tried to help, why did you jump all over me?"

"Soft words butter no parsnips, son, but they won't harden the heart of a cabbage either," said O'Reilly. "Arguing with men like Bishop's never any use. All it does is stiffen their resolve. If we're going to sort him out, we need a lever. An argument he can't resist."

"And what the hell could that be?" Barry was not satisfied.

"I'm beginning to wonder, but I'm starting to get an idea. I didn't know his maid came from County Antrim." O'Reilly looked up at the sky as if seeking divine inspiration. "Jesus, would you look at that? I told you it was too muggy."

Barry stared at the sky. Although the lower reaches were azure, above the Antrim Hills, not ten miles away, ranks of cumulonimbus clouds marched like dark-cuirassed dragoons towards the little town of Ballybucklebo. Already the skirmish line was firing rifle shots; the distant thunderclaps were sharp as they followed the scattered lightning flashes.

"I think," Barry said, "we're in for a storm."

"Indeed," said O'Reilly, glowering at the distant departing back of Councillor Bishop, "you could be right."

16

Don't Rain on My Parade

O'Reilly opened the upper half of one of the sash windows in the upstairs lounge and said, "We'll watch from here."

Barry looked across to the church steeple, dark against a leaden morning sky, and on down Main Street where red, white, and blue bunting strung between lampposts drooped listlessly. The street was flanked by the citizenry. Many carried tiny Union Jacks or Ulster flags. Some women wore dresses made of the Union Jack and embellished with mother-of-pearl buttons. Youngsters were hoisted onto their daddies' shoulders. Older children tried to push between the legs of adults or scurried up and down behind the ranks lining the route. Stray dogs yapped. Rooks, disturbed from the yew trees in the churchyard, flapped and complained as they headed for the Ballybucklebo Hills. Borne on the humid air, the rattling of side drums and the distant wailing of bagpipes drifted into the room.

"That'll be the Ballybucklebo Highlanders warming up down at the maypole," O'Reilly remarked. "As brave a bunch of musical heroes as ever blew into a bag. Pipe major Donal Donnelly, bass drummer Seamus Galvin, and the rest." O'Reilly chuckled and lit a richly stained meerschaum pipe. "We could be busy when the parade's over and that lot have gone to the Field for the speeches and the hymns and a bit of good old neighbourly pope bashing. Bag-piping's a thirsty business."

"I know," Barry said. "I worked in the first-aid tent last year at the Bangor Field. It was all right when the marchers arrived. They behaved themselves during the prayers and the sermon and the speeches, but by the time the day was over and they'd all had a few, I'd put in more stitches than a shirt factory."

"And I'll bet some of the worst offenders were members of temperance lodges," said O'Reilly. "But maybe we'll get lucky today and that thunderstorm will break before they get too much of a head of steam up."

The pipe music faded from a vaguely recognizable rendition of "Rock around the Clock" to a series of wails and squeaks. Barry heard a faint dirge, a monotonous *owwowwll*.

"Arthur," said O'Reilly. "He likes the pipes about as much as Her Ladyship there likes Stravinsky." He nodded to where Lady Macbeth lay, curled up on the hearth rug. "He doesn't seem to mind flute bands or accordions, but he hates the pipes."

Never mind, Barry thought, he likes trouser legs and Smith-wick's bitter.

O'Reilly put another match to the bowl of his meerschaum. "There are Orange Lodges coming from Cullybackey and Broughshane to keep the Ballybucklebo Loyal Sons of King William company." He consulted his watch. "Eleven o'clock. Should be starting soon."

Tah-rah-rum, tah-rah-rum. The distant side drums broke into the double triple-roll that Barry knew signalled the start of a pipe band's advance. He could imagine the drum major's command— "By the left, quick march"—and sure enough the first ragged bars of "Boyne Water" meandered down Ballybucklebo's main street.

"Here they come," said O'Reilly. "That'll be the worshipful master Bertie Bishop on the horse at the head of them."

Barry could see a man riding an off-white horse. Behind him tramped the members of an Orange Lodge following its banner. Next came a drum major marching in front of a kilted pipe band, and twirling his silver-headed mace as if it were a windmill with a broken sail.

"Ballybucklebo's finest," said O'Reilly. "The Highlanders. No wonder George Washington's troops called the kilted Scottish soldiers 'ladies from hell.'"

Barry craned to see past O'Reilly. The pipe band was followed by the banners and men of another lodge, who in turn were pursued by a flute and drum band. "I wonder who designed the uniforms for the flautists?"

"Probably Christian Dior on a bad day. Why would anybody put red seams down the outside legs of sky blue trousers?"

"Or give them peaked caps like the ones that bus conductors wear?"

"Huh," said O'Reilly, "if you think *they* look a bit gaudy, wait 'til you see the accordion players. Which of course is the definition of a true gentleman."

"What is?"

"Someone who can play the accordion . . . but doesn't."

"Come on, Fingal, that one has whiskers."

"I know, but it's still true." He stabbed the stem of his pipe towards the street below. "Jesus, would you look at the great bollocks on that horse?"

"It looks more like a mare to me," Barry said uncertainly, as he strained to hear O'Reilly's reply over the rattle of drums, the howling of the pipes, and the cheers of the spectators.

"I wasn't referring to the elderly equine's genitals. I meant Lord Muck from Clabber Hill sitting on its back."

Barry recognized Councillor Bishop at the head of the procession, proudly guiding his steed immediately ahead of the rank and file of the Ballybucklebo Orange Lodge. A cocked hat with a plume of cockerel's tail feathers, which looked to Barry as though the previous owner had had a bad case of fowl pest, was perched on the councillor's head. Barry could see that the man was perspiring heavily. His corpulent body had been forced into a scarlet serge coat that clashed horribly with his orange sash, and he wore white breeches that disappeared into mud-spattered Wellington boots. The right one didn't quite reach the stirrup. By the way the horse's shoulders moved, Barry could tell that even for a Clydesdale plough-horse, which hardly had the sleekness of the original King Billy the Third's warhorse, the animal was making heavy weather of carrying the councillor's weight.

O'Reilly chuckled as the animal flapped its lips, snorted, lifted its tail—and by the reactions of the nearest ranks of the Orange Lodge—cut an enormous fart.

At either side of the road, two boys, who Barry guessed to be about six or seven, plodded along. Both wore miniature orange sashes. He recognized the pants-wetting Mr. Brown clutching a braided guy rope. The little lads' ropes were part of the arrangement steadying a great square of embroidered cloth, beneath which two bowler-hatted, white-gloved, orange-sashed men held the banner's poles.

"Thing of beauty, that," said O'Reilly.

Barry wasn't quite sure if O'Reilly was referring to the horse's recent statement of protest or the banner. It was fringed with golden tassels and bordered in orange. On a blue background reared the inevitable white charger and its princely rider. Immediately over the picture were the words "Ballybucklebo Loyal Sons of William, Lodge 747." On the left side, angled at forty-five degrees above the horseman's head, a slogan roared, "Remember 1690. No Surrender," and on the right, "Civil and Religious Liberty for All."

"Bit ironic that 'for all,' don't you think?" O'Reilly asked.

Barry nodded.

"And don't," said O'Reilly, "ever tell an Orangeman the truth."

"What about?"

"Their famous Battle of the Boyne was actually fought on July first, sixteen ninety. July twelfth, sixteen ninety-one, was the final fixture of the campaign. At the Battle of Aughrim."

"I didn't know that."

"Neither does most of that lot down there. They think they're celebrating the Battle of the Boyne today when 'the Orangemen with William did join.' "

" 'And fought for our glorious deliverance.' "

"Where? 'On the green grassy slopes of the Boyne.' Funny, isn't it, how we all know the words, but nobody really knows the history."

"I don't suppose it matters to the Loyalists, and King William did beat King James."

"Actually, neither one was present in sixteen ninety-one at the decisive Battle of Aughrim. Ginkel played substitute for King Billy, and Sarsfield captained the home team. Bloodiest battle ever fought in Ireland. Anyway, the Jacobites lost and the Williamites kept the cup, and we get to watch a parade every year. I wonder," O'Reilly said thoughtfully, "how long it'll be before some clever American anthropologist comes over here and writes a learned paper on the 'Tribal Customs of the Primitive Ulster Races.' "

"I think Brendan Behan said that too."

"Sensible chap, Behan. Pity about him and the drink, but honestly, just look at that lot down there. Swap their regalia for grass skirts and bones through their noses, and they could be wandering about on one of the cannibal islands."

Barry looked down on the members of the lodge as they marched by in four ranks, eight files deep. Every man wore his silver-bordered, orange sash over a dark jacket; white kidskin gloves; and his bowler hat, the latter as much a badge of office as the lord mayor of Belfast's chain. Barry noticed that despite attempts to march in military formation, two men were out of step and one in the nearest file ambled along with that peculiar gait where the right arm swings forward in company with the right leg.

"Look at those faces." O'Reilly shook his head. "Good, strong, country Ulster faces. Ruddy. Rough skinned. You'd think they shaved with emery paper. And every last one with the corners of his mouth turned down to twenty to four."

"They do look dour," Barry said, able to lower his voice now that the pipers' "South Down Militia" had been replaced by the flute band's tremulous rendition of "The Sash My Father Wore."

"You think those are miserable looks? You should have seen Bishop's face the day I told him there's convincing evidence that King Billy of 'glorious and immortal memory' was queer as a coot."

"Homosexual?"

"Bent as a two-penny nail. Mind you, I don't see why it should matter what anyone does in their spare time," said O'Reilly levelly. "The ancient Greeks didn't care."

"The Victorians jailed your namesake for it."

"Oscar Wilde? Silly bugger. He should have stuck to his writing and his green carnations and kept away from lawyers."

"Still—"

"Still be damned. People come in all shapes and sizes. If you're going to be any use as a doctor, you have to learn to accept that. It shouldn't matter to us 'what you do in the bedroom as long as you don't do it in the street and frighten the horses.' Mrs. Patrick Campbell said that, and I . . ."

His words were drowned by a series of shrill whinnies. Barry looked to the head of the procession to see Councillor Bishop's mount rearing on her hind legs, pawing at the sky with her front hooves. Like the Lone Ranger calling out, "Hi ho, Silver, away!" he thought. The animal bucked, twisted, unseated its rider, and galloped off down the road, pausing only to kick her hind hooves in the air in a gesture of unbridled defiance.

"I wonder," said Barry, "who was doing what in the street?"

O'Reilly doubled over, hands clasped to his ample belly. "Better," he said, laughing like a madman, "better than a bloody pantomime. If we could just sell tickets."

Barry watched the Ballybucklebo Lodge members cluster around their fallen worshipful master. "I hope he's not hurt."

"So do I. He's the last bugger I'd want to have to minister unto today. I think it'll be all right though. He's getting up."

Barry was suddenly aware that all was not well below. The pipers who had just launched into "Dolly's Braes" seemed to have lost their musical way—badly.

"Lord, Fingal. Look."

The councillor's mishap had brought the marchers of the lodge to an untidy halt, blocking the progress of the pipers. The drum major dropped his mace. He fell to his hands and knees trying to retrieve it. The front rank of pipers shambled to a halt, hauled the pipes' drones from their shoulders, and tried to stand at attention.

"That's Donal Donnelly there at the left of the front rank," Barry said.

"Pipe major. How do you like his uniform?" O'Reilly asked between gusts of laughter.

Donal wore a green caubeen with a red hackle. His bottle-green tunic, on the left breast of which shone a huge Celtic pin, was cinched with a broad belt of patent leather from which dangled a large, hairy sporran. His saffron kilt hung from his skinny hips. It ought to have ended at knee level but instead drooped to half-calf.

"Look out, Donal," O'Reilly bellowed, as uselessly, Barry thought, as kids at a cinema would try to warn the hero with loud yells of "Behind you!" when the villain appeared. He watched open-mouthed as the red-faced piper in the rank behind, his eyes closed, fingers running up and down the chanter, marched smack into Donal's skinny back.

Accompanied by the tuneless yodelling from the rapidly deflating pipes of the man behind him, Donal's kilt slipped off. Donal dropped his pipes, bent, and hastily hoisted his nether garment.

"I see," gasped O'Reilly, "that Donal's not dressed like a true Highlander. I wonder why he's wearing his Y-fronts back to front?"

Collapsing pipes wailed as rank tangled with file. The drum section, which marched at the rear of the band, had enough time to avoid the melee. Seamus Galvin, trying to peer over a huge bass drum that hung from a shoulder harness and nearly covered a mangy-looking piece of synthetic leopard skin, pounded out the rhythm.

"Now that's impressive," O'Reilly said. "Go, Seamus."

Barry doubted if Seamus heard O'Reilly, but it was clear that he needed no further encouragement to keep up his display of drumming virtuosity. The woolly heads of his drumsticks flew in counter-rotating circles above his head. Seamus held both arms straight out from his shoulders and spun the drumsticks like the tail rotors of a strangely configured helicopter.

He never missed a beat, now striking opposite sides of the drum's skin, then crossing his hands above its circumference to deliver a whack to its left side with his right stick, its right with his left. A crowd of spectators gathered, perhaps, Barry thought, uninterested in how the remainder of the stalled procession was faring.

"Go, Seamus." O'Reilly did a little jig. "Christ, he's wailing away like Gene Krupa on something stimulatory, aye, and quite possibly illegal."

The strap securing one stick to Seamus's wrist parted. The noise of shattering glass could have come only from O'Reilly's dining-room window.

"Shite," said O'Reilly, but his beaming grin did not fade.

As if in celestial solidarity with the ructions below, the heavens joined in. Last night's skirmishers with their distant fire had been reinforced by batteries of artillery. Howitzers and cannons grumbled and crashed, hurling their bolts in glorious flashes of screaming yellow and sulphurous blue across the ramparts of the clouds.

The deluge broke, lashing the participants and the spectators. Bandsmen scurried for shelter, the drummers trying to protect their drumheads from the rain. Pacamacs appeared as if from nowhere, and family groups shared the dubious protection of the transparent plastic held over their heads.

"I'd call this a humdinger too," said O'Reilly, closing the sash window. "No point getting this room soaked."

"What about downstairs?"

"Seamus Galvin's a carpenter by trade. He'll—"

The front doorbell rang.

"That'll be him," said O'Reilly. "He'll have it patched up in no time." He strolled to the sideboard. "How about a sherry?" he asked, as he filled his Waterford glass. "Bushmills for me today. Seeing it's the Twelfth I'll have a drop that's made up here in Ulster." He savoured his drink. "I know the sun's not quite over the yardarm, but I don't think there'll be much business for us today."

O'Reilly was almost right, but the first of the walking wounded appeared in the surgery at four o'clock.

"That doesn't look too bad, Constable Mulligan." O'Reilly sponged blood from a short gash in the officer's right eyebrow. "What happened?"

The officer, dark green uniform made darker by the rain that still hammered down outside, sat rigidly, polished boots firmly planted on the carpet. One hand rested on his holster, the other on the butt of his truncheon, a wicked-looking piece of ebony. He pursed his lips and seemed to believe that he was in court giving evidence. Barry fully expected the man to consult a notebook.

"At three twenty-four on Thursday, July the twelfth, I was proceeding in an easterly direction, sir, acting on information received that a civil disturbance had broken out outside the licensed premises known as The Black Swan."

"Indeed?" said O'Reilly, most civilly. "Do go on."

Barry was surprised. Usually O'Reilly interrupted anyone who embarked on a rambling history.

"Arriving at the said premises, I seen two male persons who was engaged in fisticuffs. . . ."

"Is that a fact?" O'Reilly wandered over to the instrument trolley, bent, and retrieved an Elastoplast.

"The first suspect was wearing nothing but a kilt and a flute bandsman's hat. The other was hatless but had on flute-band accoutrements."

"Bit of friendly uniform swapping?"

The constable snorted as O'Reilly stuck the dressing over the wound. "Suspect A had both fists raised in an aggressive manner. Suspect B had a bleeding nose. Several members of the public had gathered and were encouraging the belligerent parties. Suspect A said, 'See you, you couldn't knock the skin off a rice pudding.'"

"Fighting words," said O'Reilly.

The constable's naturally florid cheeks burnt scarlet as he muttered, "Suspect B said, 'Away off and fuck yourself.' I'm sorry, sir."

"I've heard worse," said O'Reilly. "So did you arrest them for a breach of the peace?"

"That was my intention, sir, but upon my stating these intentions the crowd surged forward." He pointed to his now blood-free eyebrow. "Some person or persons unknown threw a bottle."

"I see," said O'Reilly. "Still it could have been worse."

"In the resulting scuffle I was unable to apprehend the suspects. In accordance with regulations, I drew my truncheon." A steely gleam came into the officer's eyes. "I dispersed the crowd and came here, sir."

"The pugilistic pair of them are probably having a jar together by now." O'Reilly re-examined the policeman's dressed wound. "I'd not worry too much about them. Go on home and have a cup of tea. I'll have a word with the sergeant if he has any questions."

"Thank you, sir. I'm much obliged." Constable Mulligan rose and left.

"Not your usual style, Fingal," Barry said. "I thought he was going to go on forever."

"Bloody Arthur Guinness," O'Reilly rumbled. "I have to be extra civil to our local peace officer."

"Why?"

"Last year someone broke in here and stole a couple of bottles of whiskey. My Hound of the Baskervilles probably tried to beat them to death with his tail."

"Or . . ." Barry bit back the words.

"Arthur's protective instincts only went into full cry when Constable Mulligan arrived." He frowned. "I think his uniform upset the dog."

"He didn't—?"

"He bloody well did. Bit the arse out of Mulligan's trousers and got a fair chunk of the nether cheeks of the law as well."

"Oh, dear."

"I was lucky he didn't haul Arthur away, but Mulligan's a decent lad. I just have to be a bit careful."

"I can see why."

The front doorbell rang.

Barry opened the door to find a stranger standing in the rain. He wore a bus conductor's outfit and carried a flute. Rivulets of blood ran through an elaborate, Brylcreemed pompadour that would have made Elvis Presley proud. "Come in." Barry took the man into the surgery, relieved him of his flute, and parked him in the patients' chair. "What's your name?"

"Sammy Greer, from Cullybackey." The man's words were slurred.

"Nasty cut you have there, Mr. Greer," Barry said, staring at the middle of the man's head. It was dead centre and shaped like a cross. It looked as if someone had given a ripe orange a solid whack. "It's going to need a stitch."

"I don't give a shite. Get on with it."

Barry glanced at O'Reilly. "Carry on, Doctor Laverty. I'll get the gear."

"What happened?" Barry asked.

Sammy Greer giggled. "I chucked a bottle at a fucking peeler, so I did. I got him too." Greer folded his arms. "Pity he got me back."

So that's what Constable Mulligan's remark about drawing his truncheon and dispersing the crowd had meant.

"Jesus Christ, would you hurry up? I've a couple of pints going flat back at the pub." He hawed and spat on the carpet. "Mind you, I don't think much of that place."

"Charming," said O'Reilly, his nose tip ashen as he pushed the instrument trolley over beside the patient. "You scrub, Doctor Laverty. The instruments are ready."

Barry scrubbed and then dried his hands, pleased that he was allowed to do the suturing.

O'Reilly lifted a pair of scissors. "We'll have to clip off some of your hair."

"You be bloody careful." Greer half focused bloodshot eyes on O'Reilly. "Took me fuckin' years to grow that."

"All great achievements take time," said O'Reilly, "but you'd not enjoy having hair sewn into the wound."

"Indeed not," said Barry. He wondered how O'Reilly would prevent this surly customer from getting the upper hand.

"And I want it disinfected proper too. I know my rights, so I do."

"I'm sure you do," said O'Reilly, deftly snipping through the greasy, blood-clotted hair. "I promise you'll have the best disinfecting job in all of County Down."

"Fuckin' right."

Barry filled a syringe with Xylocaine, laid it on the trolley top, and loaded a set of sponge forceps with gauze swabs. "Dettol please, Doctor O'Reilly."

"No. That would sting too much. Use this." O'Reilly poured a dark liquid into a gallipot.

Barry dipped the swabs, turned to the patient, and then hesitated. O'Reilly had certainly cleared the surgical field. He had shorn a patch right on the top of Greer's dome, a patch of the size and circular configuration of a monk's tonsure. Barry glanced at O'Reilly's face. It was perfectly expressionless.

"Right," said Barry, "here we go." He used the soaked pads to paint the shorn patch. At the first stroke, when the man's scalp suddenly turned bright blue, Barry spun and stared at O'Reilly, who smiled gently and nodded. All right, Barry thought, and carried on.

Greer sat stoically as the needle slipped into the skin of the wound edges. "Didn't feel a fuckin' thing."

"You're one tough banana all right," said O'Reilly. "A real man."

"You're fuckin' aye. Tough as fuckin' nails."

And thick as two short planks, Barry thought, as he picked up a pair of forceps and a needle holder that O'Reilly had loaded with a curved needle armed with black silk.

"I'll cut for you," said O'Reilly.

Needle in one side, out the other, a rapid twirling of the thread round the forceps once and then repeated. The first knot was tied.

"Good," said O'Reilly, as he clipped the thread.

In what seemed to Barry like no time at all, the job was done.

"Nice," said O'Reilly. "Really pretty."

Barry wasn't sure if O'Reilly was referring to what were two tidily placed rows of black sutures in a wound that had now stopped bleeding. Perhaps he was alluding to his own unique contribution to the procedure.

"Can I go now?" Sammy Greer asked.

"Oh, indeed," said O'Reilly. "Don't forget your flute."

Greer grabbed his instrument.

"I'm sure your doctor in Cullybackey will be happy to take the stitches out for you next week. I don't suppose you'll want to come back here."

Barry had great difficulty keeping a straight face.

"Bloody right I won't."

"Off you go then," said O'Reilly.

As soon as the front door closed, O'Reilly began to laugh. "Oh dear, 'took me years to grow that.' It'll be weeks before the bald bit grows back."

"And," Barry himself was almost helpless, "and 'I want it disinfected proper.'"

"It was," said O'Reilly. "Oh, dear me. It was."

"I know, Fingal, but did you have to give me gentian violet?"

"Oh, yes. Oh, yes. And the beauty is that Sammy Greer can't see that the top of his head looks like a bright blue football with black cross lacing. And do you know what else?"

"No."

"The pair of us forgot to give him any painkillers, and oh boy, is he going to have a headache tomorrow."

"Couldn't happen to a nicer man." Barry began to bring his laughter under control.

"I do hope he's going back to Cullybackey tonight. I'd not want the poor lad to be travelling tomorrow."

"Why not?"

"Because tomorrow's the thirteenth. Friday the thirteenth."

"So it is. You're off to the dogs tomorrow night, and I'm—"

"Going to be left on your own here for a while. I think you're just about ready for that. You did a very good job of the suturing."

Barry's pride in O'Reilly's praise was tempered by the knowledge that he was supposed to be taking Patricia out.

"Don't look so worried, Barry. You'll get your dinner out tomorrow night. Friday the thirteenth? Pure superstition. Nothing's going to go wrong."

17

The Best Laid Plans of Mice . . .

By Friday the thirteenth the thunderstorm had passed and bright sunlight streamed in through one dining-room window. The day before, an apologetic Seamus Galvin had patched the other with plywood.

"Big day for the pair of us," said O'Reilly, finishing his breakfast.

"I know," said Barry, trying not to think too hard of his evening to come with Patricia. "You're going to the dogs."

"I'd hardly put it that way, but yes, I want to see how Donal's Bluebird runs."

"On water? That's what Donal said."

"Dry tonight." O'Reilly grinned. "The dog will be. I won't. I'm meeting an old friend."

"Not by any chance the one that might buy Seamus Galvin's rocking ducks?"

"The very fellah, and serious business always goes better with a bit of social lubrication," said O'Reilly. He rose. "But the dirt has to come before the brush. How'd you like to run the surgery this morning?"

"Me? Seriously?"

"Aye. I've been watching you, son. You did a grand job with Maureen's delivery, put in those stitches last night as well as I could."

"Honestly?" Barry felt a flush start under his collar.

"Time for you to fly solo. Well, dual control for a start. I'll keep you company, but you do the work. I'll not interfere."

Barry straightened his tie, smoothed the tuft of hair on his crown, rose, and said, "If you really think so, we'd better get at it." He started toward the waiting room.

O'Reilly stopped him. "I'll fetch the customers. Explain to them who's in charge today. There'll be the odd one will bugger off when they hear."

"Oh." Barry frowned.

"Don't take it personally. If the sainted Jesus Christ Himself was working here, some of the older ones would still rather see me."

"I understand." Barry realized that of course O'Reilly was right. No need for hurt pride.

"And you," said O'Reilly, grabbing Lady Macbeth, who was trying to get into the surgery, "can bugger off. Doctor Laverty will not be in need of your advice today. Into the kitchen. We'll have a word with Kinky. She was going to find out about Julie MacAteer. Julie should be in later today to get her results."

"That's right," said Barry. "How do we get them? Phone the lab?"

O'Reilly shook his head. "They'll be in the nine-thirty post." He headed for the kitchen, stuffing a protesting Lady Macbeth under his arm like a rugby football. "I'll bring the first customer back with me."

With each case Barry's confidence grew. True to his word, O'Reilly offered no advice unless asked, and sat quietly on the examining couch. The morning passed quickly and, as far as Barry was concerned, enjoyably.

Just before lunchtime, O'Reilly brought in Maureen Galvin, carrying baby Barry Fingal wrapped in a blue shawl.

"Good morning, Maureen," Barry said. "It's a bit early for your post-natal visit. Is everything all right?"

"Doctor Laverty, I'm worried about Barry Fingal's wee willy."

"We'd better have a look. Can you put him on the table?"

Maureen laid the little lad on the table, unwrapped his shawl, and unpinned a bulky towelling nappy. She smiled at him and he cooed gently. "At least he's clean," she said.

"What has you worried?" Barry asked.

"It's under here," she said, gently retracting the foreskin. "It doesn't look right."

Barry bent over to get a better look at the boy's tiny penis. "Ah," he said, smiling. "Nothing there to be upset about." He could see that Maureen looked dubious. "That's what we call a hypospadias. It's quite common."

Maureen frowned. "Hypo . . . ?"

"Spadias. The urethral meatus, the little hole the pee comes through, is just a bit underneath the glans instead of in the centre. Won't make a bit of difference. It's to do with the way a baby develops in your uterus."

"You mean I did something wrong when I was pregnant?" Maureen let the foreskin slip back into place.

"No. Of course not." Barry glanced at O'Reilly, then ploughed on. "The urethra—that's the tube that brings the urine from the bladder—is formed in the fetus from different tissue than the rest of the penis. Sometimes the tube doesn't quite make it all the way to the tip."

"I don't know," she said, repinning the nappy. "I don't think it's right."

"Are you worried, Maureen?" O'Reilly asked.

Barry watched as the big man put a hand on her shoulder, and she looked into his eyes and nodded.

"You'll be a damn sight more worried in sixteen years when he's after anything in California that wears a skirt."

She smiled.

"He'll be knocking rings round him. Up and down like a whore on hinges."

Barry flinched. There was no need to be quite so crude.

"Thank you, Doctor O'Reilly," said Maureen, her smile widening. She lifted Barry Fingal from the couch and cradled him. "You'll just be a randy wee goat, won't you?"

"He will that," said O'Reilly. "He'll be banging away like a buck rabbit."

Fingal! Barry thought, but then he saw Maureen's clearly satisfied expression. O'Reilly had set her fears to rest, which was half of what being a good doctor was all about. Barry was annoyed that he hadn't understood the real nature of her concern: how the boy would be able to function sexually when he grew up. She'd be too embarrassed to blurt it straight out. But O'Reilly had gone right to the heart of the matter, and in a language she clearly understood. No wonder he himself had baffled her, using words like "hypospadias."

Maureen laughed. "That's all I need to know."

"Good," said O'Reilly, "but I should have spotted it the day he was born."

"Och, we're none of us perfect," said Maureen. "There's no harm done."

"Thank you," said O'Reilly. "I appreciate that."

So do I, thought Barry. It takes an honest man to admit that he can make mistakes.

"Barry Fingal and me'd better be getting on, Doctor," said Maureen.

"Right. How's Seamus by the way?"

"He said he'll pop round later with the glass for your window, and he's dreadful sorry he broke it, so he is."

"Tell him not to worry. Accidents happen."

"He's very busy. Him and his rocking ducks." Her green eyes

sparkled. "He says we're going to make a mint. That you've fixed it up for him to sell the whole lot of them to a firm in Belfast."

"Umm," said O'Reilly. "Maybe."

"I know it'll all work out, Doctor. Me and him and wee Barry Fingal out there in all that sunshine."

"I hope so," said O'Reilly, taking her by the arm and leading her to the door. "We'll see you in five weeks."

"If we're still here," she said, and as she left, Barry heard her in the hall singing to Barry Fingal. "California here we come, right back where we started from . . ."

O'Reilly closed the surgery door. "I hope to God she's right. I'll just have to put the screws on my friend tonight, or think of something else." He folded his arms and stroked his chin with his left hand. "And we're going to have to sort out Julie MacAteer. She's next."

"What did the test say?"

O'Reilly grunted. "Bloody typical." He pulled an envelope from his jacket pocket. "Look at that."

Barry read the results of an Aschheim-Zondek pregnancy test. " 'Urine toxic. The mice died.' Oh, great."

"Right, and Mrs. Kincaid's no further on finding out about the mystery woman of Ballybucklebo." He blew out his cheeks. "I'll go and get her."

He returned moments later and offered Julie MacAteer a seat.

She sat, knees together, feet flat on the carpet, hands folded in the lap of her tartan skirt. "Am I?" she asked, her voice steady.

"We don't know. The test didn't work. I'm really very sorry," Barry said.

"My period's not come."

Barry swallowed. "Julie, we can do another test. It'll only take a few days."

"I know I'm pregnant," she said flatly.

"You may be right," Barry said, "but let's make sure."

"I suppose so. Mind you, if I just wait another few months I'll know for certain, won't I?" She sniffed and used the heel of one hand to dry her eyes.

O'Reilly spoke quietly. "That's true."

She spun in the chair to face him. "What'll I do?"

"Doctor Laverty's right. We'll repeat the test. But in the meantime we've made arrangements for you to go to Liverpool. Just in case."

"Liverpool?" She sat back in the chair. "In England?"

O'Reilly nodded. "They'll take good care of you there. No one here need know."

"I'd have to have the baby. Give it up?"

"Yes."

"Oh, Jesus." Her tears flowed, smearing her mascara.

"It'll be hard on you," O'Reilly said. "I know that."

Barry watched her shoulders shake. She took two deep breaths. "I've no choice, have I?"

"I'm sorry," O'Reilly said gently, "unless—"

"Unless?"

"Unless you can tell us who the father is."

She shook her head, tossing her corn-silk hair. "No."

Barry, shifting in the swivel chair, was about to speak when he caught O'Reilly's glance. Barry realized that if he interfered it would seem to the young woman that they were ganging up on her.

"I can't do that," she said. "I just can't."

"That's all right," said O'Reilly. "I understand."

"No, you don't. Nobody does." She gave two more deep sobs and stiffened her shoulders. "Can I bring in a specimen this afternoon?"

"Yes," said O'Reilly. "Go on home now. Give it to Mrs. Kincaid when you come back."

"All right."

"She'll make you a cup of tea. Would you like that?"

Julie nodded. "Liverpool. Jesus, Mary, and Joseph." She sniffed deeply.

Barry offered her his handkerchief.

She took it, blew her nose, and returned it with a small smile. "Here."

He stuffed it in his pocket.

She stood. "I just knew I'd have to go away. I just knew. I've already given my notice."

"Oh?" said O'Reilly. "And who's your boss?"

"I'm not telling."

"Fair enough." O'Reilly held out his hands, shoulders high, palms out. "None of my business."

"I'd better be going." She rose. "Can I wash my face, please?"

"Of course."

Barry watched as she tidied herself up.

"I'll tell Mrs. Kincaid to expect you," O'Reilly said, as he opened the door. "You'll like her."

"Liverpool" was the last thing Barry heard Julie MacAteer say as she left.

"Four o'clock. Time I was going," said O'Reilly, leaning against the mantel in the lounge, his briar belching.

Barry shifted in his armchair, coughed, and wondered if the captain of HMS *Warspite* had ever asked Surgeon Commander O'Reilly to lay down a smoke screen for the entire Mediterranean Fleet. "Aren't you leaving a bit early?"

"I've to pick up Donal and Bluebird and drive them up to Dunmore Park; then I'll take a run-race over to the Royal. See how Sonny's getting on."

"He should be on the mend by now."

"I hope so, but what we're going to do with him when he gets out of hospital is beyond me. He can't go on living in his car."

"Maybe he'll be so grateful to Maggie for taking care of his dogs that he'll fix his roof and ask her to marry him . . . and she'll say yes . . . and let him move in with her until his place is fixed up."

"Aye. And Councillor Bishop will buy all of Seamus Galvin's rocking ducks and use the lumber to do the job at Sonny's. The father of Julie MacAteer's wee bastard will turn out to be Sean Connery, who'll whisk her off to Hollywood and make her his leading lady in the next James Bond film . . ." O'Reilly knocked the dottle of his pipe into the fire-place. "And the Reverend Ian Paisley will enter a Jesuit novitiate."

Barry laughed.

"I don't think the pair of us are going to unravel the riddles of the universe today." O'Reilly stuffed his pipe into his jacket pocket. "You just keep an eye on the shop until it's time for you to go out yourself."

"I'll do my best."

"I know that," said O'Reilly, looking Barry in the eye. "I told you I've been watching you, son. You've the makings of a damn good GP."

"Thanks, Fingal." Barry knew he was grinning, but why not? Praise from O'Reilly was praise indeed. "I will do my best."

"God," said O'Reilly, "you sound like a fornicating Boy Scout. Well, you stay here and do your good deed for the day, Baden-Powell. I'm off, and you have fun tonight. You've earned it."

Barry sat back in his chair. O'Reilly had been right. There *was* a great deal of satisfaction to be gained from the routine of a busy general practice, and it was gratifying, very gratifying, that O'Reilly was pleased with Barry's work and trusted him sufficiently to leave him in charge. Still, being left alone was a little unnerving. He stood and walked to the window just in time to see the black Rover roar off along the Belfast Road.

He heard the front door close and looked down. Julie MacAteer walked down the front path. She must have brought her urine specimen. Poor lass. It was a hell of a thing for her to be pregnant by a— what was O'Reilly's word?—a gobshite who refused to take responsibility. And all the secrecy. Why wouldn't she tell her physicians who she worked for? Something worried away at the back of Barry's consciousness. Something that somebody had said about a maid giving her notice. An Antrim girl.

He hadn't heard Mrs. Kincaid come in, and he jumped when she said, "Would you like some tea, Doctor Laverty?"

"Please."

"It's a bit stewed." Mrs. Kincaid set a tray on the sideboard. "I made it for that nice MacAteer girl, the wee lamb."

"How is she, Mrs. Kincaid?"

"She puts up a brave front, so. Very private. Himself asked me to try to find out about her." She handed him a cup. "Milk's in it, the way you like it."

"Thanks." Barry took the cup. "And what have you discovered?"

"Not much. No one in the village seems to know her. But she works somewhere here, or out in the country a ways. Her hands are soft, so she'll not be working on a farm."

"So what could she be doing?"

"Maybe she's in service. Lord Ballybucklebo still has a gamekeeper and a couple of maids."

And then Barry remembered that it was Councillor Bishop who'd said his wife was fit to be tied because their maid had given her notice.

"Mrs. Kincaid?"

"Doctor Laverty, I'd be very pleased if you'd call me Kinky, like himself."

Barry felt flattered. "All right, Kinky."

She smiled.

"Kinky, could Julie MacAteer be working for the Bishops?"

Kinky's small black eyes narrowed. "Aye, so."

"Could we find out?"

"On Monday I'll be going to the Women's Union. Mrs. Bishop's a member."

"Could you ask her?"

"I will, so."

"Good. What kind of woman is Mrs. Bishop anyway?"

"She's no oil painting but she's a decent soul. What she sees in Ulster's answer to Adolf Hitler is beyond me. I suppose she didn't want to end up as one of nature's unclaimed treasures."

"She must have been pretty hard up to take him."

Mrs. Kincaid's chins wobbled as she chuckled and said, "Hard up? Maybe for a husband, but she'd inherited a parcel of money from her father. Adolf didn't have two pennies to put on the eyes of a corpse before he married her."

"Interesting," said Barry, finishing his tea. He heard the front doorbell.

"I'll see who that is," said Kinky.

"It's all right, Kinky. I'll go." It might just be my first patient, Barry thought, looking at his watch. "I've plenty of time before I've to get ready."

"Aye, so," said Kinky, as the bell jangled again. "You're just like himself when he started here. Raring to go like an angel of mercy on roller skates."

As he left the lounge he saw her smile like a mother whose youngster has just won a Sunday-school prize.

A large, familiar-looking woman stood on the step. She wore a straw hat and a floral-patterned dress with the dimensions of a small bell tent. Barry noticed her white court shoes, over the edges of which the flesh of her ankles drooped.

"Doctor Laverty?"

"Yes."

"Could I have a wee word?"

"Certainly, Mrs . . . ?"

"Sloan. Cissie Sloan. I'm one of the tonics." Her voice was coarse and rasping.

"Come into the surgery." Barry stood aside to let her squeeze past. She was the one who'd been wearing her stays when O'Reilly had tried to inject her with vitamin B_{12}.

"What can I do for you?" He closed the door and went to the swivel chair.

She perched her bulk on the patients' chair. "Cold in here," she said.

Barry was surprised that she felt cold as the room was overly warm.

"I feel the cold something chronic."

"Do you? Is that why you came?"

She shook her head. "I've been under Doctor O'Reilly for six months, and he's doing me no good."

Barry controlled his smile despite his mental picture of the gargantuan Mrs. Sloan being mounted by an enthusiastic, but clearly outclassed Doctor F. F. O'Reilly.

"I come for a second opinion. He's away, isn't he?"

"Yes." News travelled so fast in Ballybucklebo, Barry thought, that it must practically attain the speed of light.

"Donal Donnelly's my nephew. Him and his dog and Doctor O'Reilly's away to Belfast. Donal told me. The day you come here, Doctor O'Reilly said you was the youngest doctor that ever won a prize for the learning."

"Well, I—"

"So I want *you* to tell me what's wrong with me."

"I'll try. Can you give me a few clues?"

She pushed herself back into the uneven chair, folded her meaty arms, and grunted. "I thought you were an expert. Finding out's your job."

"I know, but I do have to take your history, perhaps examine you."

"Ask away then."

Barry, with great patience and with growing concern that the consultation would make him late for Patricia, managed to mine a few nuggets of clinically relevant information from the slag heap of Cissie's detailed reminiscences; reminiscences delivered in a husky, drearily slow monotone. "I first took poorly on a Thursday. No. No. I'm wrong. It was the Wednesday that Donal's other dog died. The one with the wee short tail . . . So I said to Aggie, that's Aggie Arbuckle that was . . . now she's Mehaffey. Married to Hughie, him that's Maggie MacCorkle's second cousin . . . on the mother's side . . . Anyway, Doctor O'Reilly says to me . . . you know what he's like . . . you'd think he was Jehovah giving out the Commandments to Moses . . . he says to me, 'You're run down, Cissie. You need a tonic.' And here's me taking the tonic every six weeks for six months and I'm no better—"

"Right, Mrs. Sloan." Barry finally managed to stem the tide. "Let's see if I've got this right. You've been tired for six months and it's getting worse?"

"Aye."

"You feel the cold?"

"I do."

"Muscle cramps?"

"Desperate. In my legs. And you'll not believe this, Doctor. I've been putting on weight."

"Never," said Barry, inwardly congratulating himself for being able to keep a straight face. "Has any of your hair fallen out?"

"How did you know that?"

Barry ignored her question but asked, "Are you constipated?"

"Constipated? I've been like an egg-bound hen for months"— she dropped her voice to a whisper—"and I haven't seen my monthlies since January."

Barry tapped his pen against his teeth, leant forward, and peered at her face. Her eyebrows stopped about two-thirds of the way to the corner of her eyes. Her complexion was pasty yellow, and there were puffy bags beneath both eyes.

"Let me have a look at your neck." He stood and moved behind her chair. "It's all right, I'm not going to strangle you," he reassured her, as he placed his fingers over the front of her throat. Underneath the fat he could feel a solid, rubbery mass. Barry stepped back. She was right. She wasn't simply tired. She had all the classical manifestations of an underactive thyroid gland. Fingal had missed the diagnosis.

"What do you think, Doctor?"

Barry coughed. He was unsure how to answer her honestly and at the same time preserve O'Reilly's professional reputation.

"I'm not sure," he said. "We'll need to arrange a test at the hospital."

"The hospital?"

"I'm afraid so."

"Have I cancer?"

Barry flinched. It was possible, but her thyroid gland was smooth, not hard and craggy. "I don't think so." He saw her relax. "I think your thyroid is a bit underactive."

"Why'd O'Reilly not do the test?"

"Um . . ." Lord. The truth was that he'd probably been in a hurry and had missed the diagnosis. "It's new. I only heard about it this year."

"See. I *was* right to come and see you."

"But if the test shows what I think it'll show, we'll need Doctor O'Reilly to prescribe your treatment. He's much more experienced than I am." Two weeks, Barry thought, it had taken only two weeks for him to start bending the truth, but he couldn't let O'Reilly down. "Would you like me to explain to you about the thyroid and the test?"

She shook her head. "Not at all. I'd not understand a word. Just you fix it up. You can tell me when you get the results."

"I'll go and make a phone call," he said. "Wait here."

The laboratory was still open when Barry phoned. Yes, they'd arrange for her to have a radioactive iodine uptake test. Could he fill out a requisition and ask her to bring it with her to the metabolic laboratory at ten o'clock on Monday morning?

"Here," he said, handing her the form. "Monday morning at the Royal. Go to the information desk. They'll show you how to get to the lab."

"Thank you, Doctor Laverty, sir." She rose and left.

"My pleasure," he said, and he meant it. He had been worried about being left all on his own, but unless something dramatic happened between now and half past six when he would leave to pick up Patricia, he would be quite happy to feel just a little smug.

18

The Best Laid Plans of Mice and Men

Barry took one last look in the mirror. He probably hadn't needed to shave for a second time that day. He winced as the Old Spice aftershave stung. He brushed his hair, knowing that it was a futile gesture. Before long the tuft would be sticking up again like the crown of a broken hat, but at least he'd tried. He tied a half Windsor knot in his Queen's University tie. He glanced down. His shoes were newly polished and his corduroys pressed. He silently thanked Mrs Kin . . . no, Kinky.

He ran downstairs and into the lounge. Before he collected his sports jacket from where it hung on the back of a chair, he pulled out his wallet. One thing about being so damn busy, it didn't leave much time for spending money. He had almost thirty-five pounds. Plenty.

He slipped into his jacket. "You behave yourself, Lady Macbeth."

The white cat, who lay on the hearth rug, opened one eye.

"I'm off," he said.

The telephone began ringing as he cleared the last stair. He hesitated. O'Reilly had said to let Kinky take care of any calls.

He lifted the receiver. "Hello?"

"I want to speak to Doctor O'Reilly."

"I'm sorry. He's in Belfast."

"Is that young Laverty?"

"It's Doctor Laverty, yes. Who's speaking?" He could overhear a conversation at the other end of the line: "O'Reilly's away." "I want to see O'Reilly." "You can't. You'll have to make do with Laverty."

He snorted and raised his eyes to the heavens at Kinky, who had appeared from her kitchen.

"Are you still there, Laverty?"

"Yes."

"This is Mrs. Fotheringham. It's very urgent."

"I see."

"I want you to come at once. The major's been taken ill. Very ill."

"What seems to be the trouble?" He glanced at his watch. Six fifteen.

"It's his neck. He's got a terrible pain in his neck."

He *is* a terrible pain in the neck, Barry thought. "Could it wait until the morning?"

"I want him seen now."

Barry knew he couldn't justify sending for an ambulance for a man with a stiff neck. "Very well," he said. "I'll be right over."

"Don't be long." The line went dead.

Barry replaced the receiver. "It's all right, Kinky. Major Fotheringham has a stiff neck. I'll just nip round there. It's almost on my way."

"Why don't you telephone your wee girl? Tell her you might be late?"

"I will." He lifted the phone and dialled. Damn it, the line was engaged. "Busy," he said. "I'd better get my bag."

"You run on, Doctor, and don't you worry. I'll take care of things here. What's her number?"

"Kinnegar 657334." Barry charged into the surgery, grabbed his bag, and started to head for the kitchen. He stopped. Although

Brunhilde was parked in the lane, he'd be damned if he was going near Arthur Guinness. He turned and left by the front door.

Gravel crunched underfoot as, bag in hand, Barry left the parked Volkswagen and walked to the house with the imitation coach-lamps in the porch. Mrs. Fotheringham opened the door. She was wearing low-heeled, laced, brown brogues, thick lisle stockings, and a two-piece jacket and skirt of tweed Heather Mixture. An amethyst formed the head of a silver thistle brooch in her left lapel. Around her neck hung a single strand of pearls.

"Mrs. Fotheringham."

"Come in, Laverty. The major's in the drawing room." Her tone was haughty.

Barry followed her. He was amused by her changed attitude. The last time he had been here she had fawned over O'Reilly; now she was treating Barry like an underling. Mrs. Fotheringham must have clear views on the caste structure of Ballybucklebo. She was certainly dressed like the wife of a Scottish laird, and her "drawing room" was an upper-crust term for what most people called the lounge.

"Laverty's here, dear," she announced, moving aside to let Barry precede her into a spacious room.

A fireplace, on the mantel of which stood an ornate ormolu clock, was flanked by two antimacassar-covered armchairs. Barry was disappointed not to see a potted aspidistra in a corner. The clock said six thirty-five. He'd better get a move on.

"Major Fotheringham," Barry said to his patient, who lay on a long sofa between the armchairs. "How are you?"

The major put a limp hand to the left side of his neck, between the jawline and the top of an immaculately tied cravat. "It's my neck," he said.

"What seems to be the trouble?"

"It's awfully stiff."

"When did the stiffness start?"

"This morning, so we thought we'd better ask Doctor O'Reilly to visit before it got too late."

In case he might want to do another all-night test, Barry thought. "Were you doing anything when the stiffness started?" he asked.

"He was carrying stepladders," Mrs. Fotheringham said. "I told him to wait for the gardener, but not my husband." She sniffed.

"You've probably just strained it." Barry laid the back of his right hand on the major's forehead. Meningitis was one serious cause of neck stiffness. But if such were the case, the patient would have a fever, and the major's skin was cool and dry. "Could you sit up and take off your cravat?"

Mrs. Fotheringham moved forward to help her husband and blocked Barry's view of the clock on the mantel. He reached out and took the man's wrist. It wouldn't hurt to take his pulse, and it gave Barry an excuse to consult his watch. Six thirty-seven and the pulse rate was normal. "Fine," he said. "Excuse me, Mrs. Fotheringham." Barry moved past her. "Just look into my eyes," he said to the major. Both pupils were the same size. No early clues of increased pressure inside the head there. "Show me where the stiffness is worst."

"It hurts when I try to put my chin on my chest. Mostly on the left."

Barry put a hand on the side of the major's neck. He could feel the tension in the *sternocleidomastoid*, the strap of muscle that runs from the clavicle to the base of the skull. It was probably a simple sprain or more probably *torticollis,* spasm of the muscle which was frequently a manifestation of hysteria. He could see the clock. Twenty to seven. "You've got a wry neck, Major Fotheringham."

He saw Mrs. Fotheringham's shoulders tense, her lips purse.

"Its correct name is *torticollis*," he said, and he watched her relax. That was interesting. Technical terms had confused Maureen Galvin, but in Mrs. Fotheringham's case it seemed that the old adage was true: bullshite *did* baffle brains. Perhaps *torticollis* had a better social cachet than a wry neck. "We'll soon put it right." He opened his bag and pulled out an aerosol canister of ethyl chloride. "This is pretty cold." He depressed the red button and a cloud of vapour hissed out onto the skin.

"Wheee." The major flinched as a thin rime of frost formed. "That is very cold."

"Sorry, but it makes the muscles relax." He stuffed the can back into his bag. "If it's no better in the morning or if it gets worse, give us a call."

The ormolu clock wheezed, clicked, and began to sound the third quarter of the Westminster chimes. *Bing-bong, bing-bong* . . .

"I've another call to make." Not quite true but what the eye couldn't see, the heart wouldn't grieve over. "I'll see myself out."

The fact that Mrs. Fotheringham called him Doctor Laverty when she said good-bye was not lost on Barry.

***

Barry drummed his fingers on the steering wheel. Rural Ulster at its pedestrian best. It was nearly seven and he was going to be late. He could only hope that Patricia would understand that not only was a doctor's time not always his own, but also that people did get stuck behind tractors on country roads. As the car crept along, Barry thought about the recent consultation. O'Reilly would approve of the way he'd handled it, particularly the use of ethyl chloride. No one had the faintest idea why it might work as an antispasmodic, but it certainly had "keep the upper hand" properties. The only thing that bothered him was a niggling worry that perhaps his examination had been a bit hurried. He hadn't made a full neurological evaluation, testing skin sensation and reflexes, but that would have taken at least half an hour and almost certainly would have shown absolutely nothing. Stiff necks could have sinister causes, but most were rare as hen's teeth, and as one of his teachers had been fond of remarking, "Any bird sitting on a telegraph pole is much more likely to be a sparrow than a canary."

And that bloody tractor up ahead was going at the speed of a badly damaged snail. His watch said seven. Blast. He saw the tractor's driver stick out his right arm, the right-turn signal. Barry braked. The tractor swerved right and then, as if having second thoughts, turned a good one hundred and twenty degrees and went into a field on the left-hand side of the road. At least the road ahead was clear.

He trod on the accelerator. Brunhilde's engine's clattering increased, spluttered, wheezed—and died. Damnation. He knew he could have written his entire knowledge of the working of the internal combustion engine on a postage stamp. He turned the key to be rewarded by a grinding of the starter motor—a grinding that steadily became fainter as the battery began to expire—and as he released the key, the silence was broken only by the grumbling of the nearby tractor.

Lips pursed, he climbed out.

The tractor, which moments before had turned into a field, was nosing back out onto the road. Perhaps, Barry thought, perhaps the driver might have some mechanical experience. "Hello," he yelled, gratified to see the Massey-Harris halt. "My engine's stopped."

The driver, a middle-aged man with an acne-scarred face and hair like a haphazard hayrick, touched the peak of his flat cap, climbed down, and walked across the road. Barry recognized the man from his rolling gait, the result of a pair of spectacularly bowed legs. He'd come in last week for some linament for his sore knees.

"Sorry to bother you, Mr. O'Hara, but do you know anything about engines?"

"Aye."

"Could you take a look at mine?"

"Aye." He leant into the car, and Barry heard the click of a catch being released. O'Hara rolled to the front of the car and lifted the bonnet.

He sprang back. "Boys-a-dear." His eyes were wide, his mouth agape. He turned and stared along the road. "Boys-a-boys-a-boys, Doctor dear. Your engine's fallen out."

Despite his frustration Barry had to smile as he said gently, "The engine's in the back in a Volkswagen. Let me show you." He walked to the back of the car and lifted the louvred engine cover. O'Hara peered over his shoulder.

"There's a power of architecture about thon," he said. "I'll just give her a wee try." He moved to the driver's door and peered inside. "Excuse me, Doctor, but would you take a look at thon gauge?"

Before Barry could reach the open door, he heard Mr. O'Hara say, "Engines go better if there's a wee taste of petrol in the tank."

"No?"

"Aye. You're out."

"Damn. And I'm late."

O'Hara scratched his head. "I could give you a lift to Paddy Farrelly's garage."

"Would you?"

"Aye." He set off and Barry followed. His watch said ten past seven. Now he was going to be much later. He could only hope that Patricia would understand.

19

Love Comes as a Butterfly Tipped with Gold

Eight thirty. Barry's pants were stained with cow clap from the tractor's iron seat, his hands stank of petrol, and God only knew if his tie was askew. He rang the doorbell of Patricia's flat and waited, one hand clasped in the other. The door opened.

"I'm sorry I'm late."

She laughed. "It's all right. Your Mrs. Kincaid phoned. Said you had to make an emergency visit and you'd asked her to let me know."

He silently blessed Kinky as he looked at Patricia. She'd let her hair down, and it fell like raven's wings, glossy and smooth to her shoulders. She wore a cool pink lipstick and the tiniest trace of eye shadow that accented her almond eyes.

"Cat got your tongue?"

"No. I was just thinking. It's no wonder Mark Antony took a shine to Cleopatra. If she had eyes like yours."

"Thank you, sir," she said lightly. Then she kissed his lips, a short chaste kiss like brother to sister, yet he closed his eyes and savoured the perfumed taste of her. "So did you save a life?"

"A life? One life? I eradicated bubonic plague from the hinterland of Ballybucklebo, brought a moribund malingerer back from the brink, gave three pints of my own blood—"

"Stop it." She laughed. "I don't think you can ever be serious."

"Yes, I can."

"No, really," she said. "You are very late. It must have been an important case."

"Not exactly. Some hypochondriac with a stiff neck." Bloody Major Fotheringham, he thought. "It didn't take long to sort him out."

"So what kept you?"

"My car ran out of petrol."

"No."

"Yes. I had to get a lift on a tractor. That's why . . ." He gestured at his dirty trousers. "Look, we'd better get moving. The kitchen at the club closes at nine."

"No need. I phoned them and cancelled. I've made us a bite." She took his hand and pulled him into the hall.

What a girl. Beautiful, self-possessed, and well able to accept and adapt to changing circumstances. Not, he thought wryly, like his last one, who would fly into a tizzy if he were held up on the ward and threw her plans out of kilter.

"You really don't mind?"

"I like cooking. It's hardly your fault you had to do your job. People's jobs are important." She brought him into a small room. "And it's the first time I've heard of a fellow running out of petrol on his way *to* a date."

"I know. I usually arrange that for the drive home. On some dark, unfrequented byway."

"Well, you'll not be able to try that one on tonight."

"Me? Try it on? Never." He reached for her but she moved away. He did not pursue her. He knew he had all the time in the world. He looked around the room.

Books were neatly stacked on shelves improvised from planks laid on piles of bricks. Many were engineering texts, but he also saw works of Steinbeck, Tolkien, and—what a strange title—*The Femi-*

nine Mystique—by a Betty Friedan. He wondered if it was anything like a most peculiar book, *The Second Sex*, by that Frenchwoman de Beauvoir that he'd tried to read but had found too dense. A table was set for two, close to a window overlooking Belfast Lough.

"Nice place you have here."

"Thank you."

She put a record on a gramophone. Barry listened as a soprano sang in what he guessed was Italian. The notes swelled, rose, and fell in cadences that touched something deep in him.

"What's that? It's beautiful." And so was she, standing there, backlit by the light reflected from the lough's calm waters. Her pure-white silk shirt subtly emphasized the darkness of her eyes and hair, as the setting of a diamond ring complements the stone.

"Mozart," she said. "It's 'Voi che sapete' from *The Marriage of Figaro*. Do you like it?"

"It's amazing."

"I hope you like lasagne," she said.

"I had one once . . . but the wheels fell off."

"What?"

He laughed. "I've never heard of it."

"Idiot." She chuckled. "It's Italian cooking."

"Oh."

"Right. Italian music. Italian food and Italian wine." She handed him a corkscrew. "Open it, would you?" She indicated a bottle on the table. "Valpolicella."

"All we need now are a couple of strolling mandolin players to make this *la bella notte.*" He knew his stage Italian accent was good after all his years of friendship with Jack Mills, the archmimic.

"You speak Italian?"

"Not at all, but I've seen *Lady and the Tramp*."

"Eejit." Her hair swung gently as she shook her head, and her laughter, deeper than the soprano's notes, filled the little room. "I read once that women should beware of men who make them laugh. I'll have to keep an eye on you, Barry Laverty."

And I'll keep mine on you, Patricia, he thought, seeing the curve of her breast and the slimness of her waist and not noticing her limp, not noticing it at all, as she went, still chuckling, through a doorway that Barry guessed led to her kitchen.

"That," he said, laying his knife and fork on a tomato-smeared plate, "was great." He sipped the dark red wine, tasting Tuscan sunshine as the Ulster sun slipped beneath the sea's edge. "Great."

"Glad you liked it." She lifted their plates. "I'll just be a minute. Sit where you are. These can soak in the sink."

Barry, replete with lasagne and two—he looked at his glass—no, nearly three glasses of wine, stretched his legs in front of him. Although the evening could have turned out disastrously, everything in his own universe seemed to be unfolding as it should, apart from just the tiniest worry that perhaps he should have taken more time examining Major Fotheringham. What would Fingal say? "No use boiling your cabbage twice." He dismissed all thoughts of his patient when Patricia reappeared and bent over the gramophone.

"This is my very favourite," she said. "Listen."

It was a duet. Two sopranos with voices like liquid silver and molten gold, now flowing together, now parting, always in harmony.

"It's 'The Flower Duet,' *'Viens, Malika,'* from *Lakme*."

He stood and crossed the floor to where she stood swaying, her eyes closed. He put his hands on her waist, and she leant against him, head on his chest. He lifted the hair from the nape of her neck and kissed her where only the finest down grew. He heard her breathing quicken as he turned her to face him, holding her close, feeling the softness of her. He kissed her slowly, deeply, and felt her teeth nibble at his lower lip. He folded her into his arms as the music embraced them softly, and the fading light dappled the walls of her room in watercolours painted with a fine brush.

His hand found her breast, firm through the silk, and she whimpered, her breath warm as fresh buttermilk, sweet as new-mown clover. He fumbled with the top button. He felt her hand on his wrist as she moved away.

"Not yet, Barry. Please."

"Patricia—"

"Not yet. Don't spoil it." Her voice was low.

Barry swallowed. Hard. Her eyes were wide, soft as velvet, shining through a thin sheen of moisture.

"All right." Had he scared her? Had he been too fast? That's what Ulster girls called a fellow who made advances too quickly. Would she—please, no—would she ask him to leave?

"I'm sorry, Barry. I want to, but . . ."

He made soft shushing noises. Stroked her hair.

"But not yet. Not tonight."

"I understand." The hell he did. So what if he wasn't very experienced with women? He'd known—he'd absolutely known that she wanted him as much as he wanted her. "It's all right."

"Thank you." She took his hand and led him to a small sofa. "Sit beside me? Don't be angry."

He sat. "I'm not angry."

"Barry." She hesitated. "Barry, I think I could fall in love with you. I'm not sure I'm ready."

"Why not?"

"I want to be an engineer."

"I know that."

"I haven't time to fall in love."

"I have." He could tell by the set of her jaw that arguments would be futile. He knew by the racing of his pulse, the dampness in the palms of his hands, the way that his thoughts raced like an out-of-control sailboat in an overpowering wind, that he was in love, in love to the depths of his soul.

As the last sad notes of "The Flower Duet" fell with the dying of the light, he sat, holding her hand, lost for words.

"You *don't* understand," she said. "It's not about sex. It's about me. I want to do a man's job in a man's world, so I have to work twice as hard. You know what it took for you to get through medical school."

"I bribed the examiners," he said, taking refuge as always in facetiousness. Could he see the beginning of a smile?

She shook her head. "It took hard work, dedication." The last of the dusk's glow outlined her face in silhouette.

"But I still had time for a bit of fun."

"I cut a class tonight to see you, and you said yourself that medical school was a bit busy." Her breasts rose and fell.

"I did have time for a girlfriend."

"I don't . . . a boyfriend, I mean. Not a serious one. I daren't fall behind." She stood, arms folded, and he wished that he could see her eyes, but the room was too dark.

"I'd better go." His words were more clipped than he had intended.

"Please . . . please don't be angry. I like you a lot, but I don't want you or anybody else to—"

"I understand." He stood. "Did you ever hear that old song? 'Dance, ballerina dance, and just ignore the chair that's empty in the second row'?"

"What are you trying to say?" A tiny edge crept into her voice.

"The dancer gave up the man who loved her for the sake of her career. She regretted it."

"And you think I will?" She moved away from him.

"Honestly, Patricia, I don't know . . . but I will." I'll regret it like a death, like a loss too bitter to bear, he thought.

"I'm sorry."

"So am I." He waited for her to say something, anything, but she had half turned to stare into the dark night.

"All right." He walked to the door. "Thank you for a lovely dinner." His words were politely cold.

"Barry, I . . ."

"Yes?"

"I'd still like to see you again." She moved closer to him, and he was aware of her scent.

To tell me that your career is more important? To hold out a hope and dash it again? He remembered the advice of the professor of surgery: "When you try to treat cancer, catch it early, cut wide, cut deep. Get rid of it all." Better to heed that advice. And yet . . .

"I'll not be free again for a couple of weeks."

"Will you phone me?"

He hesitated. No. There'd be no future in getting his hopes up.

"Please?" She moved closer still, but he simply held out his hand. She ignored it and kissed him, and he held her.

"I'll phone," he said and swallowed, telling himself he was being stupid. But there could never be another Patricia. Not for him. That was something else he'd learned from the prof. "As long as there's any hope, any hope at all, don't give up the fight."

"Thank you," she said softly. "Please try to understand."

"Good-night," Barry said, and closed the door behind him.

20

I Fall to Pieces

"You've a face on you like a Lurgan spade," O'Reilly said, referring to the extra long turf-cutting implements peculiar to that town in County Armagh. "Bad night?"

"Not really." Barry sipped his tea and stared out through the putty-smudged pane of new glass that Seamus Galvin had installed in the dining-room window. Yes, it had been a bad night. Things had not gone at all the way he had been hoping with Patricia, and as a result he had slept badly, but he saw no reason to confide in O'Reilly.

"Kinky said that you were busy."

"I saw Cissie Sloan." Barry hesitated. He was in no mood for a debate if the older man didn't approve of what had been done.

"And?"

"I think you're wrong about her." Barry studied O'Reilly's face. Senior physicians could become bloody-minded if they thought their expertise was being challenged.

"Is that a fact?"

"I'm sure she has hypothyroidism."

"Why?"

"Well . . ." Barry quickly listed her symptoms.

"You might just be right." O'Reilly went to the sideboard and helped himself to a second kipper. "Good lad."

Emboldened, Barry said, "I'm sending her for a radioactive iodine uptake on Monday."

"Better and better." O'Reilly tucked into the butter-dripping
smoked herring. "If you *are* right, it'll do wonders for your reputation."

"What about yours?"

O'Reilly grunted. "I'm big enough and ugly enough to look after
myself."

And generous too, Barry thought. "I'd not mind another kipper," he said rising, realizing that although he was still disappointed about Patricia's attitude, perhaps things might work out if
he gave her time. And in the meantime there were the compensa-
tions of doing his job here to the best of his ability.

"Kinky said you went to see Major Fotheringham."

Barry rolled his eyes. "Another false alarm. *Torticollis.* I gave
him a squirt of ethyl chloride and told him to call us if there was no
improvement."

"Jesus," said O'Reilly, wiping his mouth with his napkin. "One
day that man *will* have something wrong and we'll miss it. He'll not
have just cried wolf. Since I've known him, he's roared on as if he
was being attacked by Akela, Mowgli, and the rest of the whole
bloody pack."

"Kipling," said Barry, returning to the table.

"*The Jungle Book,*" said O'Reilly. He chuckled. "I always liked
the wolves. *Canis lupus,* to give them their Latin name."

"I know. You've one of their descendants, *Canis familiaris,* in
your backyard." Far too familiar, Barry thought.

"Good old Arthur," O'Reilly said fondly. "And by God, I'd a lot
of fun with another canine last night."

"Donal's Bluebird?"

"The darling dog. She excelled herself."

"Oh."

"She won in the third at twenty to one."

Barry's fork stopped on the way to his mouth. "And I suppose you'd backed her."

"Wouldn't you have if you'd had inside information?"

Barry popped a bite-sized lump of kipper into his mouth, savoured the salty taste, swallowed, and said, "All that business about running on water, then running dry?"

"That's it."

"Fingal, would you mind explaining?"

"About racing greyhounds?"

"No. Einstein's theory of relativity."

O'Reilly chuckled. "Actually, greyhounds and relativity are pretty much the same thing."

"I'm not following you."

"Look. At the races a bunch of dogs rush round an oval track chasing an electrical hare. Their relative speeds dictate which one wins. And after a few races the bookies figure out the relative likelihood of any given dog winning and on that basis offer odds."

"Go on."

"When there's money involved, people will always try to fiddle the system. It's not been above some of the doggy fraternity to help their contender along a bit."

"How?"

"Stimulant drugs. That's why all dogs that place are immediately tested." He held one thick finger alongside his bent nose. "But they don't test the losing animals."

"Why bother?"

"What do you think the odds will be like after a dog has come last in half a dozen races?"

"Relatively good."

"Relatively. See, you're beginning to understand."

"The hell I am."

"Water," said O'Reilly conspiratorially.

"Water?"

"When Donal told me the dog had been running on water, he meant that he'd kept her thirsty until immediately before each one of her previous outings. Just before the race he let her have all she wanted to drink. No dog can run when it's waterlogged."

"So the odds go down?"

"Right," said O'Reilly. "You're not as green as you're cabbage-looking."

"And when Donal said the dog would run dry last night . . ."

"Exactly. No water. No handicap. Great odds and not a thing to show up on a drug test."

"But isn't that dishonest?"

"Totally, absolutely, and utterly, but it keeps the bookies humble, and they've had enough of my hard-earned money over the years."

"You like a flutter?"

"Only on the dogs and the so-called sport of kings. A man has to have the occasional vice."

"How much?"

"Twenty quid."

Barry whistled. That's almost as much as I make in a week, he thought. He then did the mental arithmetic. "But that means you won four hundred pounds."

"Indeed," said O'Reilly, "but it's going to a good cause."

The Fingal Flahertie O'Reilly Benevolent Fund, Barry thought.

"Donal did well too," said O'Reilly. "All in all a very satisfactory evening."

"And I suppose to top it off, Sonny's better and your friend is going to buy Seamus Galvin's rocking ducks. You said you were going to see Sonny."

"And so I did. He's off oxygen. Temperature's normal. Worried as hell about his dogs but gracious enough to say that once they let him out, he'll go and see Maggie and thank her for looking after them."

"Good." Barry's words held just an edge of bitterness. "Maybe romance will be rekindled."

"Mmm," said O'Reilly, looking out the window. "Unfortunately my business friend doesn't want Galvin's ducks. He's probably still laughing about them. Can't say I blame him really."

Barry's thoughts had strayed back to Patricia. "What?" He wondered why O'Reilly was beaming.

"I'm sure something will turn up for Seamus." He winked at Barry, who tried to guess what O'Reilly meant. He was nowhere close to an answer when O'Reilly said, "I did have one other bit of good luck, and so did His Lordship, and that should please you."

"Why me?"

"The old boy likes a night at the dogs, an afternoon at the horses. I gave him the nod about Bluebird, and when he'd collected his winnings I asked him if you could have a day or two's fishing on his water. 'Anytime,' he said."

"Thank you, Fingal."

"I presume you'll be spending a bit of time there soon."

"Why do you say that?'

O'Reilly pushed his plate away. "Young fellows who've been out on dates with beautiful young women generally beam a bit the following morning. You were decidedly deficient in the beaming department. Happy chaps are usually pleased about other folks' good fortune in the romance stakes."

Barry regretted his sourness when he'd spoken of Sonny and Maggie.

"I'd guess you and Patricia didn't hit it off."

Barry was about to tell O'Reilly to mind his own business, but when he looked at the big man he saw nothing but kindness in his eyes. "You could say that," he said quietly.

"I just did. You'll get over it. But it'll take time. I know."

I know you do, Barry thought, but remembered Kinky's admonition to respect O'Reilly's privacy. He sighed, and as he wondered how to reply he heard the telephone ringing in the hall.

"If it's one of the customers, I'll go, Barry."

"Thanks, Fingal, I—"

Mrs. Kincaid burst in. "It's Mrs. Fotheringham. She says to come at once. Her husband's unconscious."

Barry glanced at O'Reilly, who was heading for the door. "Wait for me, Fingal."

"Front door," said O'Reilly. "I parked the car on the street last night."

O'Reilly hurled the long-nosed Rover along the narrow road. Barry tried to answer O'Reilly's questions and keep an eye on the road. As the car slid out of a blind corner onto a straight section, Barry noticed a cyclist in the distance.

"Tell me again. Exactly what did you find when you examined him?" O'Reilly's fists grasped the steering wheel, and he stared ahead.

"Not much. Bit of spasm in the left neck muscles. His pupils were equal in size, not dilated or constricted."

"What about his reflexes?"

Barry was temporarily distracted. As the car came within a few yards of the cyclist—Barry recognized Donal Donnelly's ginger hair—the rider's mouth opened in a silent yell, and he hurled himself and his rusty machine into the ditch.

"Fingal, you nearly hit Donal Donnelly."

"Nearly doesn't count. What about Fotheringham's reflexes?"

"I . . . I didn't test them." Barry cleared his throat. "I thought Fotheringham was up to his usual tricks."

"I'd probably have done the same."

"Would you?"

"Probably." O'Reilly stamped on the brakes, and Barry was thrown forward. "Out. Open the gate."

Barry obeyed, waited for the car to pass, and ran up the now familiar gravel drive, past the parked Rover with the driver's door still wide open, and on into the Fotheringhams' house. He caught a glimpse of O'Reilly disappearing into the upstairs bedroom and raced up the stairs. He was short of breath when he arrived.

Mrs. Fotheringham stood at the foot of the bed. O'Reilly sat on the side of the four-poster taking the pulse of a clearly unconscious Major Fotheringham and barking questions at his wife.

"Doctor Laverty came and examined your husband, sprayed his neck, and the pain got better?"

"That's right."

"He told you to phone if it got worse?"

"Yes. Basil said the spray was working, but his head had started to feel funny so he thought he'd go to bed. He was still asleep when I got up to make the breakfast. I was going to bring his up to him, but I heard him calling for me." She clasped her right fist in her left hand. Tears slid down her cheeks.

"When did he vomit?"

Barry was aware of the acrid smell, could see half-digested carrots, little red islands in an ochreous lake on the pillow beside Major Fotheringham's head. Stiff neck, headache, vomiting, coma. God almighty. It couldn't be.

"I'm sorry I didn't have time to clean it up before you came."

"Doesn't matter," said O'Reilly. "When did it happen?"

"I came back up, and he said he thought someone had hit him on the head." She sniffled. "I told him not to be silly . . . I wish I hadn't."

Barry could see the lines in the textbook, word for word, the ones he'd memorized before his finals: "and headache may be so abrupt in onset as to make the patient think he has been struck." Christ.

"Go on." O'Reilly produced a penlight and bent to examine the major's eyes. Barry knew, he just knew, that one pupil would be widely dilated and would not respond by constricting when O'Reilly directed the thin beam under the eyelid. Barry held his breath.

"Then he boked. Grabbed his head and . . ." Her sobs came in gusts.

"Right pupil's fixed," said O'Reilly.

Barry exhaled. He didn't need O'Reilly to demonstrate that there were no muscle reflexes in the patient's left arm or leg, or that when a key was scraped along the sole of his left foot the great toe would curl upwards—the so-called Babinski sign—not down as was normal. Major Fotheringham had suffered an intracranial haemorrhage. And his stiff neck last night had been the earliest sign.

O'Reilly stood, moved to the end of the bed, took Mrs. Fotheringham by one arm, and led her to a velvet-covered, button-back armchair. "Sit down."

She sat and looked up silently at O'Reilly.

"I'm afraid your husband's had a kind of stroke."

She crossed her arms in front of her stomach and rocked back and forth, all the while making little keening noises.

And if I'd not been in a rush, hadn't been so busy congratulating myself for catching O'Reilly out about Cissie Sloan's thyroid disease . . . Barry's thoughts were interrupted when O'Reilly said, "I'm sorry Doctor Laverty didn't make the diagnosis last night."

Barry stiffened. He couldn't believe that O'Reilly was trying to— an old naval expression that his dad was fond of came to mind— keep his own yardarm clear.

"But I doubt if anyone could have." O'Reilly stared at Barry and nodded once, almost imperceptibly.

"I know. He was very nice." She forced a tiny smile.

Barry half accepted O'Reilly's unspoken reassurance, but inwardly he shrank. "Nice" wasn't good enough. What O'Reilly had said, and Barry blessed the older man for his support, would have been true if last night's examination had been thorough, if he had tested the reflexes and found them to be normal. But that hadn't happened.

"Right," said O'Reilly. "We'll have to get him to the Royal."

"Is he going to die?" Mrs. Fotheringham asked.

O'Reilly nodded his shaggy head. "I'll not lie to you. He could."

Barry was only too aware of the statistics. At least half the number of patients like Fotheringham would not recover.

Mrs. Fotheringham yelped and stuffed a fist into her mouth.

"He could live but be paralysed."

"Oh, my God."

"But until the specialists have done a test called a lumbar puncture, maybe take special X-rays, we'll not know what's caused it."

Maybe it's just a bleeding aneurysm, Barry thought, and heard O'Reilly echo the idea.

"If it's just a leak from a thin-walled blood vessel, they can usually operate. Some patients make a complete recovery."

"Really?" Barry saw hope in her eyes.

"Yes. But I won't make any promises."

Her eyes dulled again. She took a deep breath, stood, and exhaled. "Thank you, Doctor O'Reilly, for telling me the truth."

O'Reilly grunted. "Doctor Laverty, could you phone for the ambulance?"

"Right." Barry rummaged in an inside pocket for a notebook where he kept important telephone numbers. When he opened the book at random, he found himself staring at Patricia's number. As if he needed to be reminded why he had slipped up so badly last night. "I'll go and see to it," he said.

21

The Compleat Angler

"I wonder where Lady Macbeth is?" O'Reilly remarked, walking directly to the sideboard in the upstairs lounge.

Barry neither knew nor cared.

"Get that into you," said O'Reilly, handing Barry a cut-glass tumbler of Irish whiskey.

"I'd rather have a sherry." Or perhaps some hemlock, Barry thought. It had been more than an hour since Major Fotheringham's intracranial bleeding had been diagnosed and he and his wife dispatched to the Royal. O'Reilly had driven back home. They had exchanged few words.

"That's a medicinal whiskey. Sit down, drink up, and shut up."

Barry sat. The Irish was peat-flavoured, sharp on his tongue.

O'Reilly fired up his briar, took a pull from his own glass, lowered himself into the other armchair, looked Barry straight in the eye, and said, "I'm disappointed."

Barry flinched. He wasn't surprised that O'Reilly felt he'd been let down, but did he have to be so blunt about it? Of course he did. That was the mark of the man. And the damnable thing was that he was right to be upset. "There's no point making excuses. So I won't."

"Excuses? What for?"

"Come on, Fingal. I told you I was in a hurry last night. I didn't do a complete neurological examination."

"And if you had, what do you think it would have shown?"

"Enough so that I could have got him to a hospital before the bleeding into his head got any worse."

"Maybe, but what did his wife say?"

"What do you mean?"

"Everything blew up this morning. Hours after you were there."

"But—"

"If he'd had a decent bleed last night, don't you think it would have been as plain as the nose on your face? A second-year student could have seen what was wrong. But he hadn't bled and it wasn't plain."

"I was wrong last night."

"And that's why I'm disappointed."

"Because I didn't do my job right?"

O'Reilly stood and loomed over Barry. "No, you buck eejit. You knew your patient's history of malingering. You went to see him, and you didn't have to. You put him before yourself, and there was no need to. I know how much you wanted to see that wee girl. You could have been late for your big date."

"I was."

"You didn't have to be. I told you Kinky could have handled things. Fotheringham would have been no worse off if you hadn't been conscientious enough to go last night and we'd not gone out there 'til this morning."

"It's still no excuse."

"Christ, man. Who do you think you are? Sir William Osler? Hippocrates? Jesus Christ All-fornicating-Mighty?"

"No. But doctors have certain responsibilities."

"You're a sanctimonious young—"

"I don't have to take this." Barry started to rise, but the pressure from the hand that O'Reilly had clamped onto Barry's shoulder forced him back into his seat.

"By God, you do. Listen, what makes you think you're the only physician to make mistakes? Do you think missing Cissie Sloan's buggered-up thyroid and the Galvin baby's hypospadias are the only bollocks I've ever made?"

"Well, I—"

"Of course not. And not living up to your own personal standards last night may seem like the end of the world to you. It's not. You'll make mistakes. Even when you've done absolutely everything right, you'll still ask yourself questions when somebody falls off the perch in spite of you. But none of us is the Pope in Rome speaking ex cathedra."

"What?"

"Ex cathedra. That's when your man's being infallible. You're beating the holy bejasus out of yourself because you think you should be infallible. That's why I'm disappointed. You should know better than that." O'Reilly released Barry's shoulder and stepped back. "Let up, boy. Go easy on yourself." Barry looked up at the big man. The hint of a smile was at the corner of his lips as he said, "How long have you been here?"

"Two weeks."

"That's long enough for me. I've told you, Laverty, you've the makings of a damn good GP. But you'll never last if you insist on taking everything to heart."

"I still think I could've done a better job."

"Yes," said O'Reilly levelly, "you could, but you recognize it and that's to your credit. What happened can't be helped. Learn from it, and put it behind you."

Barry could not honestly say that he felt as if a weight had been lifted from his shoulders, but somehow the pressure seemed to be less.

A huge grin erupted on O'Reilly's face, and Barry had to smile back.

"Good man, Barry." O'Reilly finished his whiskey. "Do you know what I do when this bloody place gets to be like the seventh circle of Dante's *Inferno*?" He crossed to the sideboard and refilled his glass.

Barry resisted the temptation to say, "get pissed." "I don't know."

"I take old Arthur down to Strangford Lough."

"To go wildfowling?"

"That's the excuse, but the ducks don't really matter. Nothing like a day in the open air, away from whatever the hell you do for a living to give you a chance to get your mind straightened out."

"I used to go fishing."

O'Reilly looked at his watch. "It's only two o'clock. Why don't you grab your rod and head down to His Lordship's? There'll probably be a good trout rise this evening. And there's still the odd salmon in the Bucklebo River."

"I'd like that, Fingal."

"So finish your whiskey. Kinky'll make you some sandwiches. Off you go. Forget about Fotheringham. Forget about your broken heart. Girls are like buses. There's always another one along soon."

"Do you believe that?"

"No," said O'Reilly, "but there's no reason you shouldn't."

"I see."

"I'll look after the shop, and Barry, would you do me a favour?"

"Of course."

"Take Arthur Guinness with you. He loves a day down at the river."

Barry, rod in hand, wicker creel half-full of Kinky's ham sandwiches slung over his shoulder, and hip waders buckled to his belt, let himself out through the back door. At least if the dog had a go at Barry's leg, this time he was well dressed for the occasion.

"Here, Arthur."

The big dog, tail going at thirteen to the dozen, lolloped from his doghouse, poised ready to mount Barry's leg, hesitated, sniffed the rubber boots, and turned away with a look of disdain.

"Heel."

Arthur looked at Barry, seemed to be having some difficulty making up his mind, and sat.

"Don't *sit. Heel.* Heel, you great lummox." That's what O'Reilly called his dog. To Barry's surprise the big Labrador rose and stood behind Barry's left leg. He kept his muzzle there as Barry walked the length of the garden and into the lane. Barry opened Brunhilde's door and tipped the seat. "Get in."

"Aarff," said Arthur, obeying immediately. Barry shut the door, climbed in, and drove off. He followed O'Reilly's instructions. Out of Ballybucklebo and along the shore road. He was just about to pass Maggie's cottage when he saw her, sitting in a canvas-and-wood deck chair surrounded by Sonny's dogs. He braked and wound down the window.

"How are you today, Miss MacCorkle?" He noticed she had fresh snap-dragons in her hatband.

"Is it yourself, Doctor dear?"

"Doctor O'Reilly saw Sonny last night. He's on the mend."

Maggie said, "I should hope so. Then he can come and take these flea-ridden beasts away." But her words were out of place with the way she fondled a dog's head and grinned toothlessly.

"How does General Montgomery like having the dogs about the place?"

She cackled. "You'd not believe it. The ould General's made up with Sonny's spaniel. They're best friends just like David and Jonathan now, so they are." She rose and strolled over to the car. "Is that Arthur you have in there?"

"It is."

"Keep him in. The General's got used to having Sonny's ones here, but I don't think he'd take too kindly to Doctor O'Reilly's big lad."

"I'll be running on anyway. Just wanted to let you know about Sonny."

"Huh." She scratched her cheek. "He's on the mend?"

"Very much so."

"I suppose we should be grateful."

"I am." At least, Barry thought, some of them do recover.

"I wonder did the pneumonia cure his stubborn streak?"

"Now that I couldn't tell, Miss MacCorkle."

"If it did, it would be like the day Himself turned the water into wine. An honest-to-God miracle."

Barry laughed. "We'll have to wait and see."

"Is that a rod in the motorcar?"

"It is."

"Well, if you're going fishing, go on with you, and thanks for dropping by."

"My pleasure." Barry put the Volkswagen into gear and pulled away.

He drove past a red-brick gatehouse that stood guard over two high wrought-iron gates, each bearing the crest of the marquis of Bally-bucklebo. A long drive led to the Big House with its Georgian façade and ornate planters ablaze with nasturtiums and pansies. At the head of an immaculately manicured lawn, the topiarist's work on five evergreens was clearly visible, although Barry had some difficulty determining whether one was meant to be a horse, a rabbit, or a ruptured duck.

O'Reilly had said that the first fork to the right led to the river—a rutted lane that disappeared beneath huge elms. The car jolted along. Arthur gave voice to a series of excited yips. Tree branches scraped the windows until, leaving the small wood behind, Barry found himself in a broad meadow. The path crossed the field and led to what must be the banks of the Bucklebo, where willows, some drooping silvered foliage, others polled and knobby-headed, wandered in a meandering line, presumably, Barry thought, following the curves of the stream.

The lane petered out. Barry parked and lifted his gear from the car. Arthur leapt out and began to quarter the ground ahead of Barry, running to the left, then to the right, nose to the ground, tail thrashing. Barry followed the dog through knee-high grass until he could see up ahead the waters of the Bucklebo. He lengthened his stride, clumsy in the waders.

A clattering of wings startled him when a pair of mallard strained to gain height as they leapt from a patch of bulrushes, chased out by a now soaking Arthur Guinness. The dog trotted back to Barry and looked at him as if to ask, "Why didn't you shoot?"

"Heel, Arthur." Barry did not want the dog to disturb the water. Trout, he knew from long experience, were easily scared. To his surprise Arthur obeyed instantly and followed, tucked in behind Barry's leg as he covered the last few yards to the riverbank.

"Sit." Down went Arthur's backside. His pink tongue quivered as he panted. I'm not surprised, Barry thought. Galloping about the way the dog had in the afternoon's bright sunlight would be warm work.

He stood and studied the water. The current flowed gently from his left to his right. Upstream a wide curve swirled with the current, and sunlight dappled, extended from the far bank to the centre stream. There might be a fish at the tail of the ripple. Across on the far side—Barry had no doubt that he could reach there with a cast—he saw the still, dark waters of what must be a deep pool shaded by the branches of a willow. Trout would lurk there, waiting hungrily for any insects unlucky enough to fall from the tree.

"Come on, Arthur." Barry walked slowly upstream. O'Reilly was right. Something was soothing about the solitude of a river-bank. Was it the gurgling of the water, the distant lowing of a herd of Aberdeen Angus grazing on the far bank, the susurration of a slight breeze in the leaves of the willows? Perhaps it was simply the knowledge that no one could call him there, nothing could force him to make any decision more important than which artificial fly to choose. Whatever it was, the riverbank—he thought of Moley and Ratty in *The Wind in the Willows*—was a place for reflection. It was a haven where Barry could look into his thoughts and decide whether O'Reilly was right about learning from a mistake and about moving on. Or whether the calamity, as Barry saw it, of Major Fotheringham was a clear indication that general practice was the wrong choice, that perhaps pathology or radiology, specialities with little or no contact with patients, might suit his temperament better.

He was close to the run at the curve of the river. Barry unslung his creel, propped his rod against a willow, and sat on the grass beneath, back against the tree's bole. Arthur flopped down beside him.

And what about Patricia? O'Reilly was wrong on that account. As far as Barry was concerned, despite their short acquaintance—a train journey, a walk, and a disastrous dinner—he knew with com-plete certainty that while there might be more fish in the sea (or in the Bucklebo River), for him there could never be another Patricia. Bloody typical. He could make up his mind about the only part of his life over which he had no control, but he still was confused about the professional part, the part that was his to do with as he saw fit.

He sensed movement on the river's surface. A series of concentric rings had appeared and were spreading outward, exactly where he had anticipated that a fish might be lying. He saw why. The river's surface was dappled with tiny spots, each marking the place where an insect, newly released from its larval stage, had struggled to the surface, to rest there to dry its diaphanous wings and then take flight.

If he was going to catch a trout, this was the time. They would feed, rising again and again to take the mayfly. He would have to make sure that his artificial fly matched the natural ones exactly. He rose, ignored Arthur's gruff *aarf*?, and went to the water's edge. Time to concentrate now, time to stop thinking about careers and women.

He smiled, recognizing that he enjoyed being enmeshed in the day-to-day life of Ballybucklebo. Even so, Sonny's housing difficulties, Seamus Galvin's rocking ducks, Julie MacAteer's pregnancy, and Cissie Sloan's thyroid could wait. The mayfly were hatching.

He bent and scooped up a handful of cold water. He let it dribble away between his fingers until he could see, resting in the palm of his hand, a single mayfly. He studied it closely and knew he had several well-tied imitations. He opened a small aluminium box, took out a fly, and tied it to the tip of his line.

"How did you make out?" O'Reilly asked when Barry walked into the kitchen.

Barry grinned, parked his rod, opened the creel, produced two shining brown trout, and dumped them into the sink.

"Not bad," said O'Reilly. He opened a drawer, took out a knife, and handed it to Barry. "You caught 'em. You gut 'em."

"Fair enough." Barry turned on the cold tap, took the first fish, and expertly slit it open, dragging the guts out with the fingers of one hand. A steady stream of bloodstained water ran through the fish's belly cavity and drained down the plughole.

"That was slick," said O'Reilly. "Ever consider a career in surgery?"

Barry shook his head. "No, but I did think over what you said." Barry laid the cleaned fish aside and reached for the other. "I didn't do all I could have for Fotheringham, but you're right. I will try to put it behind me."

"Good lad. 'To err is human.'"

"'To forgive, divine.'" Barry sliced into the second fish. "Alexander Pope."

"And you'll be pleased to hear that the Divinity must have been keeping an eye on you."

"What do you mean?"

"Fotheringham had a small aneurysm. The neurosurgeon reckons he got it tied off all right and that the major should make a reasonable recovery."

Barry's fingers stopped moving. He turned and saw that O'Reilly was smiling.

"Honestly?"

"Honestly." O'Reilly darted forward and flapped a big hand at the counter where Lady Macbeth, who had appeared from nowhere, sat eyeing the two trout. "Get to hell out of that."

She sprang lightly to the floor and began to weave around Barry's legs.

"Bah," said O'Reilly. "Cupboard love." He handed Barry a plate. "We'd better stick the fish in the fridge before Her Ladyship gets at them."

"Right." Barry put the fish onto the plate.

"Now," said O'Reilly, "tomorrow's Sunday. No surgery. I'd like to nip up to Belfast . . . see if I can't do something about those damn rocking ducks. Think you could manage on your own?"

Barry hesitated.

"Best thing you could do. Just like falling off a horse. Most riders—and I exclude Bertie Bishop from that category—think it's a good idea to get back into the saddle as soon as possible." He turned. "I'm off upstairs. Come and have a jar when you've cleaned yourself up."

Barry stood holding the plate of fish, feeling the insistent pressure of the cat against his legs, grateful to O'Reilly for his understanding earlier in the day. Barry sensed that the business of O'Reilly's going to Belfast tomorrow might simply be an excuse so that he would *have* to cope single-handedly.

He opened the door of the Electrolux fridge, took a deep breath, and looked up to the ceiling. He'd put religion behind him years ago, had not been able to reconcile the suffering he had seen as a student and houseman with the concept of a merciful deity, but today just in case he was wrong, he muttered a silent thank-you, unsure whether the thanks were for Major Fotheringham's good fortune or for his own second chance.

22

Sunday Morning Coming Down

Barry stood in the recess of the bay window. It was pouring outside, the rain lashing down in stair-rods, blackening the tiles of the
steeple opposite, and drenching those members of the congregation who scurried to their cars. Most hurried away on foot, looking
from his vantage point like umbrellas with legs. He saw Kinky cross
the road and felt the door slam as she let herself in.

He heard the phone jangle below. The ringing stopped. Kinky
must have taken the call. If someone needed him, he hoped it
would be a simple case. O'Reilly had left an hour ago.

"Doctor Laverty."

He walked to the door.

"There's some foreign gentleman says he has to speak with
you, so."

"Right." Downstairs. He took the receiver. "Doctor Laverty."

"Crikey. Is it being the great, healing sahib?" The man's muffled
voice had the singsong cadence of what was known as Bombay
Welsh. "I am very much tinking that I am wishing to consult the
man of medicine, Doctor Lavatory."

"It's Laverty."

"That is what I am saying, Lavatory, and I am knowing it is yourself, Sahib. All the time I am saying to myself, I am wondering how

the bringer of hygiene and healing to the untouchables of Ballybucklebo is faring."

Barry started to laugh. "Stop buggering about, Mills. You're not Peter Sellers."

"But I am tinking it is a pretty damn good impression of his Mr. Banerjee, isn't it?"

"Jack. Stop it."

"All right, mate. How the hell are you?"

"Pretty fair."

"What are you up to today?"

"I'm on call."

"I'm not . . . for once. I thought I'd take a run-race down and see you."

"That'd be great. Hang on." He turned. "Kinky, could you manage lunch for two?"

"Aye, so."

"Come and have lunch."

"Great. How do I get there?"

Barry gave the directions.

"Fair enough. I'll see you in about an hour."

"I *am* on call, so if I'm not here, Mrs. Kincaid, the housekeeper, will let you in."

"I'll wait for you." He slipped again into Bombay Welsh. "I must be running away and driving like a fleet he-goat running over the Hindu Kush Mountains, isn't it? *Namaste*, Sahib."

The phone went dead. Barry chuckled and said to Mrs. Kincaid, "Jack Mills is an old friend of mine. He'll be here in about an hour. Look after him, will you, Kinky, if I have to go out?"

"I will, so." She bustled off to her kitchen, pausing only to ask, "Would you like them fishes for your lunch?"

"Yes, please." Barry went back upstairs. He lifted the *Sunday Telegraph* from the coffee table, found the cryptic crossword puzzle, and sat down, brow furrowed, and stared at the first clue. One across: "Rag's made very tatty underwear—it's most serious! (7)"

Stupid way to pass the time, he thought, but he'd been addicted to trying to solve the things since his mother had introduced him to them years ago. And that was something else he'd better do. He really did owe his folks a letter. Perhaps he'd write tonight after Jack had gone. He settled into the chair and welcomed Lady Macbeth when she jumped into his lap. Rag's made very tatty? So he had to use a combination of the letters of "rag." Arg? Gra? Underwear. Knickers? Singlet? Vest? G-r-a-vest? 'Most serious? Gravest. Bingo! He wrote the word into the squares, only mildly hampered by the cat who wanted to play with his propelling pencil.

He put the paper aside. Except for six down, "Refuse to boast about how old you are," he had managed to finish the cryptic. "Go on, cat." He stood and let Lady Macbeth slip to the floor. Outside, the rain had become a steady mizzle. Ballybucklebo lay grey and gloomy under its damp shroud. It certainly looked better when the sun shone but, and he was damned if he could remember who'd said it, "Into every life a little rain must fall." No sign of Jack Mills yet.

Barry hunted through O'Reilly's record collection. Beethoven, Beatles, Bix Beiderbecke, Glenn Miller, *Il Nozze di Figaro,* Frank Sinatra. He thought about putting *This Is Sinatra* on the Black Box, but realized that Ol' Blue Eyes crooning, "The Gal That Got Away" would be too close to home, and certainly "I've Got the World on a String" hardly described how he felt about Patricia. *Il Nozze di Figaro*—surely that was the opera she'd been playing on Friday night? He lifted the sleeve and read the table of contents, looking for "Voi che something or other." There it was. He put the record on the turntable and swung the needle over the wider groove that separated the tracks.

The notes filled the room, bittersweet, matching his mood. Perhaps he'd phone her tonight.

"If that one would stop standing on the cat's tail, maybe it would stop howling."

Barry turned to see Jack Mills standing in the doorway.

"Your housekeeper let me in. Jesus, what a miserable day." Jack shook his head, scattering droplets from his dark hair. He ran his fingers through his mop, sat in a chair, crossed his legs, pulled out a cigarette, and lit up. "Good to see you, mate."

"And you."

"Could you turn that thing off?"

"Sure." Barry pushed the button. The aria died. "It's a pretty piece."

"Sounded like a sick cat to me."

Barry laughed. "You've no culture, Mills."

"Yes, I do . . . but it's agriculture." Jack glanced over to the sideboard. "Any chance of a jar?"

"What would you like?"

"That John Jameson's looks good."

Barry poured. "Here."

"You not having one?"

Barry shook his head. "The customers take a dim view if you show up smelling of booze."

"Just like back home in Cullybackey," Jack said, sipping his drink. "One whiff and they think you're a piss artist." He gazed round the room. "Looks like your boss knows how to look after himself."

"He's a decent man. Damn good doctor."

"That's the word at the Royal. The drill-the-dome boys reckon he was pretty quick off the mark getting that aneurysm in the other morning. Another couple of hours and . . ." Jack drew one finger across his throat.

Barry pursed his lips. "Actually it was my fault. I misdiagnosed Major Fotheringham."

"Who?"

"The bloke with the aneurysm."

"Don't be daft."

"No, it's true. The night before I'd seen him for a stiff neck. I never even thought that he might be bleeding into his head. He could've died."

"I wouldn't worry about it. We can't get them right every time."

"That's what Fingal said."

"Sensible chap." Jack rose and walked to the window. "Remember the day I walked through a packed waiting room with that book of medical humour in the pocket of my white coat? Caused no end of a fuss. All the silly buggers could read the title."

Barry laughed. He remembered the incident clearly. Poor old Jack had ended up on the carpet with the professor of surgery, a Yorkshireman.

Jack's accent changed. "Ah tell thee, Mills, thou'll not do ought as daft as that again, not to my patients you won't."

"It was a bit careless."

"It wouldn't have mattered if the damn thing had been *A Surgeon's Handbook*."

"But it wasn't."

"I suppose letting the customers see me wandering round in a white coat with *Kill as Few Patients as Possible* sticking out wasn't exactly tactful."

"True."

"But it's probably the best we *can* do. Kill as few as possible. I've had three or four pop their clogs in the last couple of weeks. I thought we were going to lose that appendix of yours."

"Jeannie Kennedy?"

"I'd never seen anything like the pus in that abscess. It's a bloody good thing somebody invented those new tetracycline antibiotics. Had her on her feet and out the door in no time."

"Would it not have bothered you?"

"If she'd died?" Jack swirled the whiskey round in his glass. "Honestly?"

"Honestly."

"I don't really think so. I'd have been annoyed that the surgery hadn't gone as planned, but when they're asleep under the sterile drapes you don't really think about them as people. You can't."

"Why not?"

"It would be too damn difficult to stick the scalpel in and rummage about in their innards as if you were gutting a fish."

Barry had a vivid mental image of last night's trout's intestines, slippery gobs of tissue, being washed down the sink. "I don't think I'm cut out to be a surgeon."

Jack groaned. "That's awful. 'Cut out to be a surgeon.' " His face wrinkled into a great smile, and Barry couldn't help smiling with his friend.

He heard Kinky calling, "Lunch is ready, Doctors."

"Coming, Kinky." He nodded toward the lounge door. "Bring your drink. Kinky can be a bit owly if we let her cooking get cold."

"Can't have that." Jack rose. "I could use some decent grub. The hospital kitchen hasn't improved."

"That there trout," said Jack in the accents of Belfast's dockland, "was cracker, so it was. Dead-on. Bloody wheeker."

"I take it you approve?" Barry smiled. Jack Mills hadn't

changed, not since they'd met eleven years before. Solid. Dependable. Never able to be serious for long.

"Isn't that what I just said?"

"I caught them yesterday."

"So you get a bit of time off?"

"A bit."

"Have you seen that bird you were telling me about?"

Barry's smile faded. "Patricia?"

"That her name?"

"Yes, and I don't think she'd be too happy to hear you call her a bird."

"Oh?"

"She's an engineering student."

"Good God. What's the world coming to? The next thing you know women'll be playing rugby."

"I doubt it. Mind you, she's pretty single-minded about her engineering."

"She'll grow out of it."

Barry shook his head. "Not Patricia. She told me on Friday night that she didn't want to get serious. Her career was too important." He glanced over at Jack.

"And you did? Want to get serious?"

Barry nodded.

"Oh, Jesus. Is it getting to you, mate?"

"A bit."

Jack rubbed the web of his left hand over his upper lip. "How many times have you seen her?"

"Three."

"And it's that bad?"

"Yes."

"Engineer or not, she must be something special."

"Very."

"You poor bugger." Jack stood. "So what are you going to do about it?"

"I'm not sure. She asked me to phone her. I thought I might tonight."

"I wouldn't."

"No?"

"Let the hare sit. Either she's giving you the brush-off—in which case you're stuffed, mate—or maybe she really does want you to phone. She's playing a bit hard to get."

"So why wait?"

"Do you remember when you tried to teach me about fly fishing?"

"Yes."

"You said that trout would be scared off if we rushed up to the riverbank, that we'd have to stalk them, move up quietly, take our time?"

"So I should take my time with Patricia?"

"Definitely. Let her stew for a while. If she's serious and doesn't want to see you again, you'll not hear from her. If she does want to see you again, she'll call."

"Do you really think so?"

"It worked for me with that blonde staff nurse. Remember?"

Barry did remember. "Are you still seeing her?"

"Not at all. I took her out for a couple of months. She was a hot wee number, but she started hinting about marriage, and you know me. Why buy a cow when you can get a pint of milk at the store?"

"You don't get any better, Mills."

Jack laughed. "I've nearly four more years training ahead. You know what they pay junior staff. I'll be buggered if I'm going to be some kind of celibate for the greater glory of the priesthood of surgery. And I'm certainly not ready to settle down yet. Can you see me with a pipe and slippers and a bunch of rug rats?"

"Not exactly."

"Not one bit. If you want to get your knickers in a knot over a girl, I can't stop you, but there's a lot to be said for not getting too involved."

Barry said quietly, "Sometimes you can't help it. It just happens."

"There's no hope for you, Laverty. First of all, you seem to think that you have to take every one of your patients to heart. Then you can't look at a girl sideways without deciding she's a cross between Venus de Milo and Raquel Welch."

"Come on, Jack."

"Come on, nothing. You're a hopeless romantic. That's why I like you." Jack rose and handed Barry a now empty whiskey glass. "And I'd like you a lot better if you could find the other half of this. A bird can't fly on one wing."

23

Marching to a Different Drummer

"It's like Paddy's market." O'Reilly closed the door to the packed waiting room. "We'll have to do something about that. I'm not up to facing all the woes of the world this morning."

Barry wasn't surprised. He'd gone to bed last night at ten-thirty, after a surprisingly call-free day, before O'Reilly had returned. Nor had Barry been graced with the big man's presence at breakfast. He didn't usually oversleep. No doubt the little red veins in the whites of his eyes, the bags underneath, bore silent testimony to the reason he'd not appeared until moments before the surgery was supposed to open.

"What can we do? Ask some of them to go home?"

O'Reilly grunted, opened the door wide, and asked, "Who's first?"

"Me, Doctor sir." A short, cloth-capped man rose. He wore a red scarf round his throat and had a torso like a small beer barrel. He had a cough, dry and hacking.

"Come on then, Francis Xavier."

Barry led the way.

"Your turn," said O'Reilly, hoisting himself up onto the couch, massaging his temple with one hand as he did so. "I've a bit of a strong weakness today."

Barry took the swivel chair. "What can I do for you, Mr.—?"

"Francis Xavier Mac Mhuireadhaigh."

Barry looked helplessly at O'Reilly.

"Francis Xavier Murdoch," O'Reilly translated.

"Frankie it is, sir," said the little man, whipping off his cap to reveal a bald pate. "Frankie it is. But I've the blood of gods in my veins, so I have." He wheezed and rubbed his throat.

Barry immediately wondered if this was to be another psychiatric consultation, but he remembered his first day when he had misjudged Maggie MacCorkle.

"Gods? Which ones?"

The stocky little man shoved himself back up the tilted seat. "My forbear, William Mac Mhuireadhaigh, invented gas lighting back in 1800 and something. The oul' shah of Persia, a fellah called Nassred-din, reckoned Willie Murdoch was the reincarnation of Merodac, the Persian god of light."

"It's a fact," said O'Reilly wearily. "I looked it up."

"Very interesting," said Barry, pleased that he had not jumped to the wrong conclusion. "What brought you here today?"

"I walked. My bike's broke, so it is."

"Why have you come to see us?" Barry knew that some Ulsterfolk could be literal in their thinking.

"I've a terrible wheezle in my thrapple." He coughed.

"Sore throat?" Although Barry might not speak Irish, the local dialect posed no difficulties.

"Aye. For about a se'nnight."

"A week? Anything else bothering you?"

"Just my nut. I tried rubbing it with salt herrings but it was no use."

"I don't think there's much we can do for baldness, Frankie."

"Aye, but if a storm's lifted the thatch, it lets the cold in and that goes to your thrapple." One knobby hand massaged his pate, the other his throat.

"Let's have a look." Barry lifted a tongue depressor. "Open wide. Say aah."

The man's throat was red, flecked with yellow spots. It looked like a ripe strawberry. Barry removed the tongue depressor. "It's a bit infected, Frankie."

"It's suppuratin' like?"

"Not as bad as that. There's no real pus. Here . . ." Barry scribbled on a prescription pad. "There's a script for penicillin. Take one four times a day for a week."

The little man eyed the prescription dubiously and turned to O'Reilly. "Do I not get the black bottle, sir?"

"Oh, indeed," said O'Reilly. "Put some *mist. morph. and ipecac.* on that, would you, Doctor Laverty?"

Barry retrieved the slip of paper and added the orders for the famous black bottle. He should have thought of that. The *morph*—morphine—was a good cough suppressant, and the *ipecac*—ipecacuanha—had no medicinal qualities at all. It simply made the mixture taste horrible, and of course the fouler the taste, the more curative the potion. "Here you are, Frankie. Pop in in a week if you're no better."

"I will, sir." Frankie rose.

Barry hadn't noticed O'Reilly slip down from the couch. O'Reilly took Frankie by the elbow and steered him out of the surgery. Barry did not hear the front door closing, and when O'Reilly returned, he carefully shut the surgery door. He held a finger to his lips and grinned at Barry.

The hairs on the nape of Barry's neck twitched when O'Reilly started howling, a moan that started low and ran through at least two octaves. The screeching was interrupted by O'Reilly's yells of "Jesus, Doctor, give over," and "You're murdering me, so you are," and "Jesus. Jesus, that's enough. Mercy. Mercy." O'Reilly strode out of the surgery. The front door slammed mightily, and there was no gentility in the way he closed the door to the surgery on his return.

"What—?"

O'Reilly's finger went back to his lips for a moment; then he pulled out his briar and lit up. "We'll just wait five minutes," he whispered. "Then when you go back to the waiting room, it'll be just like the 'Teddy Bears' Picnic' song."

"Pardon?"

"You'll be sure of a big surprise. Half the ones with nothing better to do and less wrong with them will have taken to their heels." He rubbed his forehead. "I told you I couldn't face those multitudes today." He walked to the door. "You'll have an easy morning of it now. I'm off for a while."

Barry watched the big man go. Fingal Flahertie O'Reilly, he thought, two weeks ago I'd have considered you the greatest charlatan unhung. Now? Well, there's no doubt you're different, but it's certainly not dull working here.

When he opened the door to the waiting room only a handful of patients remained, and all eyed him with looks of silent fear. He could tell that not one of them, not one, stood the remotest chance of getting the upper hand.

O'Reilly's temper had improved somewhat by the time they left to make the afternoon's home visits, but he had been incommunicative during what for Barry had been a foreshortened lunch. Even though the number of patients to be seen in the morning had been drastically reduced by O'Reilly's histrionics, Barry had taken extra time with every one. He'd have no more Major Fotheringhams to burden his conscience.

"Get a move on," O'Reilly growled. "We haven't got all day."

Barry gulped down the last of his tea.

"The car's at the front of the house."

"Right."

Their itinerary took them high into the Ballybucklebo Hills to see a farmer who was recuperating after being crushed several weeks previously when his tractor had rolled over; O'Reilly was satisfied with the man's recovery. Their route back down passed the Six Road Ends. Crops that had still been green when Barry sought directions from Donal Donnelly were golden now, whiskery barley bowing and shining in the afternoon sunlight. A magpie, white and black and long-tailed, swooped over the car.

Barry saluted it. For all his book learning even he was not immune to the country superstitions. A rhyme about magpies went, "One for sorrow / Two for joy / Three for a girl / Four for a boy." The single bird could presage sorrow, but saluting it was guaranteed to ward off the evil eye—so it was said. He wished there had been three birds. There was only one girl that he wanted.

O'Reilly slowed down as the car passed Sonny's junkyard. The roofless house looked forlorn, and weeds were higher among the scrap metal and aging cars. The purple heads of thistles had gone, to be replaced with fluffy seed cases that the wind scattered like tiny parasols among the brown-headed ben-weeds, nettles, and broad-leaved dock.

"Funny that," said O'Reilly, "how nettles that sting and dock that soothe the sting always seem to grow together. I wonder what the pharmacological agent is in those leaves?"

"No idea." Barry stared at Sonny's washing machine standing mute at the roadside.

"What we need," said O'Reilly, "is some sort of dock to soothe that old nettle, Councillor Bertie Bishop, worshipful master of the Orange Lodge . . . and all-around gobshite. Make him come to some accommodation with Sonny. He'll be discharged in a few more days." O'Reilly accelerated into a blind corner. "There's an old folks' home in Bangor. We could try to get Sonny in there, but then Bishop would take over the property, and Sonny would go into a decline if he thought he was going to be there for the rest of his life. It would be the end of him."

"Fingal! Look out for that cyclist."

O'Reilly swerved.

Barry lifted the foot that he had shoved against the floor in the unreasonable hope that it would brake the car. "You told me, not in as many words, that we can't fix all the troubles of the universe."

The car came back on course.

"You're right. But it's still a bugger about the old boy." O'Reilly lapsed into silence, and Barry decided to say no more until they reached their destination.

Barry recognized the council housing estate as they drove through it. Two-storey terraces scowled at each other across streets so narrow that at three o'clock the sunlight had gone. Children had tied ropes to the top of a lamp-post and swung round it, laughing and chirping in high-pitched voices like a flock of starlings—which along with some dusty sparrows pecking in the gutters, and flocks of feral pigeons, were the only birds that frequented the slum.

He remembered that Patricia was a bird-watcher, how she'd known the bird that was singing the evening they'd gone for a walk. She'd not get much joy bird-watching here.

O'Reilly braked. "You'll not have seen what I'm going to show you next."

"Oh?"

"Come on."

A woman wearing a calico apron and fluffy slippers let them in. Barry noticed that her bare shins were mottled with a network of brown lines, tangled like a fishing net on reefs of varicose veins. *Reticularis ab igne,* he thought, a network from the fire, a sure sign of poverty. With no other heating in the winter for their draughty, damp houses, the poor huddled in front of tiny, smoky coal fires that in some mysterious way provoked the mottling on the fronts of the legs.

"How's Hughey today?" O'Reilly enquired.

"He's out in the backyard, Doctor. There's still a wee taste of sunshine there, and he loves the warmth, so he does."

Barry wondered as they passed through a small kitchen why the woman picked up a tin tray and a spoon.

The backyard was typical: a cramped slab of cracked concrete hemmed in by low red-brick walls. Overhead a clothesline, washing hung out to dry, sagged and swayed. Although the shadow of the house darkened most of the concrete—a shadow that lengthened as Barry watched—the far end was still in light. A man in a frayed cardigan and moleskin trousers stood there, bent over a wooden box where impatiens bloomed, red and white and violet. He didn't turn as they approached, which surprised Barry because O'Reilly's boots clattered on the concrete.

The woman went up to the man and tapped him on the shoulder. He spun round and looked at O'Reilly.

"How's about ye, Doctor O'Reilly?" The man's face, leathery brown but for several irregular white puckered scars, broke into a grin.

"How are you, Hughey?"

The man cupped a hand behind one ear. Barry noticed the tufts of hair sticking out from the auditory canal.

"What?" Hughey frowned and shook his head. "Hit the bloody tray, Doreen."

Barry jumped when Doreen belaboured the tray with the spoon. He glanced at O'Reilly and saw him put a hand to his head. The horrid clangour must have been working wonders for O'Reilly's hangover. It had certainly disturbed the equanimity of a pair of pigeons, which had taken flight from their perch on a chimney-mounted television aerial.

"I said, How are you, Hughey? Are you managing with your medicine?" O'Reilly was roaring at his patient.

"I'm bravely. But them eardrops aren't worth a tinker's damn."

Barry could hardly make out the man's words above the constant clanging. What was going on?

"Sorry to hear that," O'Reilly yelled. "Maybe you'd better stop using them. Pity they didn't work."

"Och, what can't be cure must be endured." Hughey gave Doreen a sideways glance. "At least I don't have to pay any heed to her craking on."

"Away off and feel your head," she said and pecked his cheek. "I'll not bang this wee drum for you anymore." And mercifully she stopped. "So is that it, Doctor O'Reilly?"

"I'm afraid so, Doreen. I asked the ear doctor in Belfast, and he says he's done the best he can. It's a shame that he can do no more."

"It is. But I still have my man, the oul' goat." Once again she started to bang away. "The doctor says he can do no more, Hughey."

The man nodded. "Just like the old song. 'I'm too old to work, but I'm too young to die.'"

"Away off and chase yourself. I'm puttin' a big fry on for your supper, and there's a couple of bottles of stout in the house. You'd not die before you got those into you, would you?"

He shook his head.

"I'll see the doctors out then. Away you, back to your flowers."

He nodded and turned back to the little blooms as the sound of clanging and the last of the sunlight died.

"He loves his wee flowers, so he does," she said, and Barry saw the moisture in her eyes.

"I've never seen anything like that," Barry said, as he closed the Rover's door.

"Bloody shipyards," said O'Reilly, driving away. "Hughey was a riveter. Did you see the scars on his face? You can't work with red-hot metal all your life and not get a few burns."

"But what was the business with the tin tray?"

"Have you ever heard riveters at work?"

"No."

"I have. In Valletta Harbour in Malta during the war. They were fixing up the *Ark Royal* after she'd been bombed. A thousand men with rivet guns pounding away? It's like the proverbial hammers of hell. It's a wonder more men don't lose their hearing." He pulled the car to the side of Main Street, before the maypole and the traffic light. "Hughey's deaf as a post. Riveters' deafness."

"But he can hear if someone hammers on a tin tray?"

"Right. Don't ask me why, but it's true."

"Amazing."

"It is," said O'Reilly, opening the car door. "Now that's all the calls for today, and I need a wee cure."

"A what?"

"A hair of the dog. I wasn't quite abstemious last night."

"Oh," said Barry tactfully.

"I'll buy you a pint in the Duck."

"Fine."

"Just one, mind. The pair of us'll have to be in top form tomorrow. Half the ones I chased away this morning will show up, and you've to see Cissie Sloan about her thyroid. Her results should be back."

"That's right."

"And if the bloody mice haven't died again we should know for sure about the wee MacAteer girl's pregnancy."

"We might even know more than that, Fingal. Kinky's going to the Women's Union tonight."

"What has that to do with the price of corn?"

"I forgot to tell you. Kinky thinks that Julie could be a housemaid at the Bishops', and she'll try to find out from Mrs. Bishop tonight."

"Interesting," said O'Reilly, "but I'm drier than the bottom of an empty flour sack. You can tell me all about it in the Duck."

24

All Professions Are Conspiracies Against the Laity

Barry was disappointed that he'd not had a chance to speak to Kinky the previous night after her return from the Women's Union, but he and O'Reilly had been called out to attend another confinement. He grinned as he knotted his tie. If many more mothers expressed their gratitude by calling the baby after him, it would be tricky trying to decide which little Ballybucklebo Barry was which.

He wasn't going to complain. It worked wonders for the morale to see a baby safely delivered by a grateful, healthy woman. It might not be as challenging as brain surgery, as intellectually stimulating as being a cardiologist or an endocrinologist, but—Barry was irritated that he could not express his own thoughts more coherently—it felt right. And that was a good feeling.

He headed for the dining room.

"Morning, Fingal."

"You look like the cat that got the cream." O'Reilly glanced up from a plate of devilled lambs' kidneys. "Feeling pleased with yourself?"

"Well, I . . ."

"So you should. You've a knack for midwifery."

Barry helped himself to a small portion, inhaling the steam from another of Kinky's mysterious but inevitably delicious sauces.

"I know," said O'Reilly. "You came down here to give general practice a try."

Barry turned from the sideboard.

"I'd not want to force you to stay." O'Reilly's gaze was level. "You might do better if you specialized in obstetrics and gynaecology."

Barry wasn't sure what to say. He had wondered last night about that very possibility.

"You have to do what's right for yourself, son."

"That's generous of you, Fingal."

"Balls."

"It is."

O'Reilly took a deep breath. "I wanted to be an obstetrician. Bloody war came along, so like a buck eejit I volunteered. After it was over, I was too old to spend another four years training. I'd to make a living. And it's not been so bad here."

Barry remembered his dad saying that the casualties of war couldn't be counted only among the dead and wounded. "I didn't know."

"Why would you?" O'Reilly's words were gruff.

Barry shook his head. "No reason. I'm flattered that you would tell me."

"Bollocks. I'm only telling you so you'll not think I'm being— what did you say—generous?"

Silly old bugger, Barry thought, you'd die of mortification if you let anyone suspect you'd a soft side. "Perhaps that was the wrong word. I meant you were being fair."

O'Reilly seemed to be mollified. "It's up to you. Now eat and shut up. I've a lot I want to think about." O'Reilly hunched over his plate, shovelled in another mouthful, and chewed fiercely.

Barry sat. He too had a lot to think about. Obstetrics and gynae-cology had much to recommend it. He had no doubt that he'd enjoy obstetrics. Plenty of satisfied patients when things went well—and they usually did. The snag was gynaecology. Days in clinics dealing with women with vaginal discharges and heavy periods. Or having to break their hearts because they cannot conceive. The poor things had a pathetic belief that their doctors could help, but he knew that in most cases little or nothing of any proven value could be done. It was a damn good thing so many *did* conceive—usually despite their doctors. And then there were the cancer cases. He shuddered. Ovary. Cervix. He'd seen women die of both, despite heroic radical surgery, despite massive doses of horribly debilitating radiotherapy.

"Your kidneys are getting cold," O'Reilly said. "Kinky'll kill you."

"What?"

"Shove those bloody things back in the chafing dish. Maybe she'll not notice."

"Right." Barry rose and was scraping off the last of the congealed mess when Kinky strode in, took one look at what he was doing, and sniffed—a sniff of such force that, as she would say herself, might suck a small cat up a chimney.

"And was there something the matter with the kidneys, so?" she asked, arms folded, chins wobbling.

Barry scuttled for cover like a mouse scared by a flashlight. "Not at all. My eyes were bigger than my belly. I couldn't finish what I took."

"Huh."

"It's a fact," said O'Reilly. "Greedy bashtoon. Mind you, I can't say I blame him." He handed her his plate, which was so thoroughly cleaned that Barry thought O'Reilly had probably ingested some of the pattern as well. "They were heavenly." He forced a small belch. "Beg pardon."

"Granted, so," she said, unfolding her arms and accepting the plate. She peered at the chafing dish. "There's the makings of a good-steak-and-kidney pie there if you'd not mind kidneys again for your supper."

"That would be wonderful," said Barry. "Kinky?"

"What?"

"Did you get a word with Mrs. Bishop last night?"

Kinky beamed. "Aye, and you were right. The wee Rasharkin lassie *is* a housemaid at the Bishops'. Only a poor wee skivvy, so."

Barry smiled. The class distinctions among those in service were as rigid as the caste system of India. A housekeeper was as far above a housemaid—a skivvy—as a Brahmin was above a sweeper.

"How long has she worked there?" O'Reilly asked.

"Three months."

O'Reilly counted on his fingers. "Interesting. And how does she get on with the Bishops?"

"Mrs. Bishop's heartbroken that Julie's given her notice. The wee girl wouldn't give a reason for a while. Now she says she has a sick sister living in Liverpool."

O'Reilly glanced at Barry.

Kinky sniffed, more gently. "Mrs. Bishop's fit to be tied. She's crosser than a wet hen, so. She thinks that there's no such thing as a sister in England."

"What *does* she think?"

"That Bertie Bishop's always had an eye for the ladies. Mrs. Bishop can't be sure, but she thinks her husband maybe pinched the wee lass's bottom once too often."

O'Reilly eyes were wide. "Now there's a thing."

Barry was not quite sure what O'Reilly might be hinting at, and trying to find out who the baby's father was seemed to be more important. "Do you happen to know, Kinky, if Julie has a boyfriend?"

Kinky frowned. "I did ask."

"And?"

"Mrs. Bishop didn't know, but once or twice a fellow with ginger hair had come round to the servants' quarters at night."

"Did she know who it was?"

Kinky shook her head. "She only caught a glimpse of him."

"Damn."

"Don't let that bother you, Barry." O'Reilly was rubbing his hands with, Barry thought, the enthusiasm of Ebenezer Scrooge surveying a heap of gold sovereigns. "Thanks a million, Kinky. You're a better spy than your man James Bond. And he can't cook."

"Go on wit' you, Doctor dear." Kinky chuckled. "I went to see one of those double-oh-seven films." She lowered her voice and much to Barry's surprise said, "I'd not mind having that Sean Connery's slippers under my bed, so."

"You're a powerful woman, Kinky Kincaid," said O'Reilly.

"And you're full of blarney for a man with work to do."

"How much?"

"Not too much. Half a dozen of the regulars. Julie MacAteer'll be in later." Kinky's brow furrowed. "And Cissie Sloan's here and it's not her tonic day."

Kinky was right. The waiting room was half empty. As Barry and O'Reilly peeped through the barely ajar door, Barry whispered, "That must have been a better performance yesterday than you thought, Fingal. They haven't all come back."

"They will," said O'Reilly. "Like His sainted self should have said, The poor, *and* the weary, walking wounded are always with us."

"Actually it's 'For the poor always ye have with you,' Saint John 12:8, at least it is in the King James Version."

"I stand corrected," said O'Reilly. He then threw the door open and yelled, "Right, who's first?"

Cissie Sloan rose.

"Sorry, Cissie," O'Reilly said, "your results won't be in for another half hour. I'll come and get you as soon as they're here."

She sat ponderously.

"Anyone else?"

"Me, sir."

Barry followed O'Reilly and the patient to the surgery. He was a tall, lugubrious-looking, middle-aged man, dressed in a black three-piece suit. His dark hair was sleek, oiled, and split by a centre parting of such precision that Barry thought the man must have used callipers to find the exact meridian. Either that or the man had simply painted his cranium with black enamel.

His cheeks, sunken beneath high cheekbones, would have given his face the characteristics of a skull had it not been for his nose. Its last two inches had blossomed into a craggy and pitted tomato. Barry recognized the condition—*rhinophyma*—the result of a blockage of oil glands; the buildup of their secretions caused the skin to swell and become distended.

The unfortunate man could have passed for Chuckles the Clown wearing only one piece of his stage makeup, or a skinny W. C. Fields on a particularly well-lubricated day.

"Sit down, Mr. Coffin," O'Reilly said, taking the swivel chair. "What seems to be the trouble?"

"Ah'm no at myself." His voice was as gloomy as his demeanour. Barry knew that Mr. Coffin meant that he just felt generally unwell. Had no specific symptoms.

"Still?" O'Reilly asked.

"Aye." The word was spoken slowly, weightily, and only after much deep thought. It sounded like "aaaaaaaye," its pitch gradually rising.

"And you've seen the two specialists I sent you to?"

"Aye." As ponderous as the first.

"Neither one could find anything wrong with you?"

"Aye." The same tonal inflection.

Some countrymen could be a tad on the reticent side, but Barry thought, this Mr. Coffin could represent Ulster if there ever was an international competition for taciturnity.

O'Reilly asked several more questions. All were answered with polysyllabic "aaaaaaayes." Finally O'Reilly said, "I think we're at a bit of a loss, Mr. Coffin. Would you consider taking a wee holiday?"

The patient, frowned, looked at the ceiling, took a deep breath, started to speak, reconsidered, and then to Barry's amazement, said one word. His "ayes" had climbed the scale. This time he slid down it in a baleful glissando, in keeping with the descent of his narrow bottom along the seat of the forward-tilting chair.

"Nooooo."

Barry had great difficulty keeping a straight face.

"Well," said O'Reilly, rising, "all I can suggest is get lots of fresh air, eat a healthy diet, and get plenty of sleep."

"Aye?" Plaintive.

O'Reilly sighed. "I suppose you could try something my grandmother used for folks that were a bit low."

"Aye?" This time there was a hint of interest.

"You collect up a wheen of Saint John's wort, chop it up, and make a tea to drink."

"Aye?"

"Aye," said O'Reilly.

It's catching, Barry thought, as O'Reilly ushered Mr. Coffin to the door.

"Give the wort a try, but come back and see us if you're still worried," O'Reilly offered.

"Aye," moaned Mr. Coffin as he left.

"Poor old bugger," said O'Reilly after he had closed the door. "Bet you can't guess what he does for a living."

Barry shook his head.

"It's no wonder that the waiting room was half empty. The locals are scared stiff of him. Think he's bad luck," said O'Reilly. "Mr. Coffin is our undertaker."

"He's not."

"He is, and did you see his nose? Talk about having a cross to bear. Nothing will persuade the locals that a big red nose isn't the mark of a boozer . . . and poor old Coffin is actually the head Pioneer in Ballybucklebo."

"Pioneer?"

"They're a temperance organization. They take the pledge at thirteen. Avoid the demon drink like the plague." O'Reilly shuddered.

"Oh."

"It's no wonder he's 'no at himself.' Would you be with a job and a nose like his . . . and not even the solace of a jar once in a while?"

"It must be a bit tough."

"We can't fix his nose. He can't afford to give up his job." O'Reilly sighed. "All we can do is sit and listen. Who knows, maybe my granny's herbal tea will work."

"Aye," said Barry.

"Lord," said O'Reilly, "don't you start. Go and see if the post has arrived. If you're right, there *will* be something we can do for Cissie."

Two reports in the buff envelope: Cissie's and Julie MacAteer's. Barry read both. His sharp pleasure when he saw that the radioactive iodine uptake test had indeed confirmed his diagnosis was dulled by one word on the second piece of paper: "Positive."

He tried to smile at Julie, who sat in the waiting room. "Just be a minute, Julie." He avoided meeting her gaze. "Will you come in, Mrs. Sloan?"

Cissie followed him to the surgery, rolling along in his wake like a battleship following a tugboat.

"Morning, Cissie." O'Reilly raised a questioning eyebrow, and Barry nodded. "Here," said O'Reilly, standing. "You sit here." He vacated the swivel chair.

I see, Barry thought, if you are actually ill you don't have to sit on the tilted one. He watched O'Reilly's placatory gesture nearly going astray as Cissie struggled to cram her bulk between the arms of the chair.

"So, Doctor Laverty?" O'Reilly held out his hand. Barry handed him the pink laboratory form. O'Reilly rummaged in his breast pocket, pulled out his half-moons, and set them firmly on the bridge of his nose. He peered at the form, then gave it to Barry. "You'll have to tell me what this newfangled stuff means."

Was O'Reilly serious? Could he not interpret the results? Barry cleared his throat, and although he then spoke to Cissie, he kept his eyes on O'Reilly's face. "Mrs. Sloan, I'll not blind you with science. In a nutshell, a gland in your neck isn't making enough of a little thingy it releases into your bloodstream."

O'Reilly's face was deadpan.

"The little thingy's supposed to help you feel full of get-up-and-go, so it's no wonder you've been feeling frazzled."

A slight smile from O'Reilly at that. She'd understand "frazzled" better than "run down."

"And it's there to help you use the food you eat. You know when you light a fire but you keep the damper closed?"

"I do," she said. Barry glanced at her. She was leaning forward— as far as her girth would permit—looking into his face, clearly taking in every word.

"When that happens you can pile on the coal, but it won't burn very quickly. Thyroxine . . . that's what the little thingy's called. . . ." He deliberately avoided using the word "hormone," knowing that its mere mention would scare the living bejesus out of any country patient. "Not having enough thyroxine's like having the damper shut all the time."

She put two hands on her belly. "And this here's like half a hundredweight of nutty-slack?"

"Exactly."

"I'll be damned," she said, eyes wide. "Who'd of thought it?"

"I told you," said O'Reilly, "he's full of the learning, our Doctor Laverty."

"He is that. Just you wait 'til I tell my husband that I'm all clogged up with slack because me damper's shut." Her tone was absolutely serious.

Barry looked at O'Reilly, who said, "Do you think some thyroid extract might do the trick, Doctor Laverty?"

"Indeed. Will you write the prescription?"

"I will," said O'Reilly, scribbling away.

"I told you," said Barry, "Doctor O'Reilly's the expert on the treatment."

"And amn't I the lucky one having the pair of you to look after me?"

"Oh, I don't know. . . ." Barry began modestly.

"This'll put that there Aggie in her box. She said you near killed that snooty Major Fotheringham."

Barry flinched.

"I told her a thing like that could've happened to a bishop. She said the last time she looked the pair of you weren't bishops. You were meant to be doctors. Says I to her, 'Nobody's perfect, Aggie.'" She looked directly at O'Reilly as she delivered those oblique words of forgiveness.

He inclined his head.

"Aggie . . . that's my cousin twice removed on the father's side . . . she's the one with the six toes. . . ."

Lord, she's off again, Barry thought, remembering the trouble he'd had on Friday when he'd tried to take her history.

"She said the pair of you didn't know the difference between a corn plaster and an anenema."

"A what?"

"An anenema. You know. The thing you stick up your back passage when you're bound? God knows I tried enough of them things in the last six months."

"This'll fix that too," said O'Reilly, handing her the scrip. "You'll be running round like a spring chicken, with a figure like a sylph."

"Like a what?" she asked, looking puzzled.

"Sorry, Cissie. A skinny minnie." He turned and winked at Barry. "Just what I've been trying to teach you, Doctor Laverty. Always use language the patients'll understand."

You bugger, Barry thought, but returned the wink.

"Now, Cissie . . ." He gave her instructions for using the medication, explained the most important symptoms of overdose that should be reported to her doctors at once, and accompanied her to the door.

"I'll tell Aggie and the others we've a regular professor here in Ballybucklebo."

"There's no need for that, Cissie," Barry said.

"Is there not? That Aggie," she said, "she's the one that needs an anenema." Cissie lowered her voice but still managed to sneer. "She's always full of shite."

"Well done," said O'Reilly when she'd left. "I mean it. That was a smart diagnosis, and you're getting the hang of explaining things. I liked the analogy about the damper and the fire. And thanks for that bit of professional courtesy, letting on that I know more about the treatment."

"There's honour among thieves," Barry said, smiling.

"Sure, 'All professions are conspiracies against the laity.'"

Barry frowned. "Who said that?"

"Fooled you that time. George Bernard Shaw in *The Doctor's Dilemma*."

"One to you, Fingal. And speaking of dilemmas"—Barry handed O'Reilly Julie MacAteer's results—"she's next."

"I'd like you to come in here, Julie," said O'Reilly, holding the door of the dining room open. "Have a seat." O'Reilly pulled a chair away from the table and waited until she was seated, facing the window. "Park yourself, Dr. Laverty."

Barry closed the door and sat with his back to the window, facing a worried-looking young woman. O'Reilly lowered himself into a chair at the head of the table.

"It's a bit cosier in here than in the surgery."

Barry watched her closely as she folded her hands and rested her forearms on the tabletop. She showed no curiosity about her surroundings but merely looked down at her hands.

"I'm sorry, Julie. . . ." O'Reilly began.

"It's positive, isn't it?" She looked up.

He nodded. "I'm afraid so."

She squared her shoulders. "I knew it." She took a deep breath. "So that's me for Liverpool?"

"Not for a while, but yes. Before you start to show . . . unless—"

"Unless what?"

"The father—?"

"He can't."

O'Reilly scratched his chin. "Do you mind me asking why he can't?"

"I don't mind you asking, Doctor . . . but I'm not going to tell you." Barry saw a hint of a smile at the corner of her lips. She certainly had spirit.

"Fair enough. I had to ask."

"I know. Is that all?"

"We should start your prenatal blood work. I'll go and get the laboratory forms," O'Reilly said. As he passed her chair, he put a hand on her shoulder and squeezed gently.

She turned and looked up at him. "Thanks, Doctor O'Reilly."

O'Reilly grunted and left.

"So, Doctor Laverty," she said.

Barry hesitated. Kinky had gone to the trouble of finding out about the young woman, and he suspected that there was a simple reason why the father could not marry her. He decided to take the bull by the horns. "Julie, do you enjoy working for the Bishops?"

She jerked back in her chair. "How did you know where I work?"

"It's a small village."

"Just like Rasharkin. The sooner I'm out of here, the better."

"Is Councillor Bishop the father?"

"What? That lecher?" Her brow furrowed and her cheeks reddened. She rose and stood, hands on the table top, resting her weight on her forearms. "I've better taste than that."

O'Reilly came back, pink laboratory forms held in one hand. He looked at Julie and then across to Barry, who shook his head.

"If he is," Barry ploughed on, "we could at least make him pay for—"

"Not him." Her lip curled.

"Who's him?" O'Reilly enquired.

"Councillor Bishop. I asked Julie if he could be the father."

"And I told Doctor Laverty. . . ." A single sob interrupted her words. "He tried to have a go at me. I'd not let him anywhere near me."

"It's all right, Julie," O'Reilly said gently. "Doctor Laverty was only trying to help."

"I know that." She dashed the tears away with the back of one hand. "But just thinking of that man gives me the creeps." Her green eyes flashed.

"We'll say no more about it." O'Reilly waited.

She twitched at the front of her skirt and held out her hand. "Give me them forms. Where've I to go to for the tests? Can I get them done here?"

O'Reilly gave her the requisitions. "You could, but if you want to keep this to yourself maybe you'd be better to nip down to Bangor to the health clinic there."

"I'll do that," she said, her chin firm, her eyes dry. "Would tomorrow be all right?"

"Of course. We'll have the results by Friday."

She shook her head. "I can't get any more time off this week. Could I come in on Monday?"

"Of course, and we'll have all the information you'll need about Liverpool."

She forced a smile. "I hear there's so many Paddies living there that it's really the capital of Ireland."

"That's right," said O'Reilly.

"Well," she said, "when it's all over, maybe my poor wee bastard'll find a good Irish home."

"I'd hope so," said O'Reilly.

She stuffed the forms into her handbag. "It'll not be too bad. I'm not the first girl to get put in the family way . . . and I won't be the last." She held out her hand to O'Reilly, who hesitated.

Barry was surprised. Women didn't usually offer men a handshake.

O'Reilly smiled and shook her hand. "You'll be all right, Julie MacAteer." His arm encircled her shoulder, and he hugged her. "You will, you know."

She looked up into his face and back to Barry. "I appreciate what you've both done for me." She swallowed, then turned back to O'Reilly. "If the wee bastard's a boy, I might call him Fingal." She stepped back. "I'd better be off. I'll be in on Monday."

"She took it well, Fingal," Barry said, after she'd left. "I hope I didn't upset her too much, asking her about Bishop, but I did think—"

"I know exactly what you thought, Barry," O'Reilly said. "I'd the same half-notion myself, but it's given me an idea. I'll need your help, and we'll have to bend a few rules, but . . ."

Barry's eyes widened as O'Reilly unfolded his plan. It might just work—indeed the more he thought about it, the more he was sure it would work—and if bending a few rules would help, well . . .

"Bend the rules, Fingal? I'll help you twist them so far out of shape they'll look like one of those German pretzels." He knew that if they could pull off O'Reilly's scheme, Councillor Bishop was in for a fall—a fall that hadn't been seen since "Joshua fit the battle of Jericho and the walls came tumbling down."

25

The Stranded Fish Gaped Among Empty Tins

As soon as the morning surgery was finished, O'Reilly began to make telephone calls. He drummed his fingers on the hall table. "Come on." The drumming grew faster. "Jesus, I'd hate to be bleeding to death and try to get through to a hospital switchboard. You'd need a transfusion just while you waited. It would be damn near as quick to drive up to Belfast." He switched the receiver to his other ear. "Will you come on?" He tapped his foot, whistled off-key, and finally growled, "Hello? Royal Victoria? I wanted to be sure. You took so long to answer I thought maybe I'd got through to the White House. No, not the ice-cream shop in Portrush. The place where the president of America lives. Put me through to Ward Six. Of course I'll hold on." He glanced at his watch. "Christ, you'd not need a watch to see how long you've to wait. You'd need a bloody calendar."

"Maybe they're busy," Barry suggested.

"Ward Six? Doctor O'Reilly here. Can I speak to Sister? Yes, I'll hold on."

Barry noticed a hint of pallor in O'Reilly's nose tip. "I think Sister must be on holiday in the south of France and they've sent a boat to fetch . . . Hello? Sister Gordon? Fingal O'Reilly here. I'm grand. How's your bad knee?"

Typical, Barry thought, how O'Reilly could switch from temper to cordiality in the blink of an eye.

"I'm delighted it's on the mend. How's Sonny? My customer with the pneumonia and heart failure. I see . . . right . . . right . . . another week? Fine. I think we can fix things up for him at this end, but it'll take a while . . . Has she? That's grand. Now you look after yourself." He hung up. "I learnt that when I was a student. The consultants like to think they're in charge, but you'd better be on the right side of the ward sister."

"I know."

"Anyway, Sonny's on the mend . . . they'll discharge him on Saturday. The almoner's been to see him . . . nice word 'Almoner' . . . some bloody bureaucrat wants to change it to 'medical social worker' . . . and she won't let him go back to his car. She's got a bed for him in the convalescent home in Bangor, and he'll be all right there until we get things sorted out. And to do that . . ." He opened the telephone directory, flipped through the pages, found the number he was looking for, and dialled. "Doctor O'Reilly here. I want to speak to Councillor Bishop." He winked at Barry. "Noooo. I was quite precise. I didn't say I'd like to speak to him; I didn't say I would consider it a privilege to be allowed to speak to him. I said"—his voice rose to a roar—"I *want* to speak to him . . . and I meant right now." He waited.

"Councillor. Sorry to bother you." O'Reilly's voice oozed solicitousness. "Yes, I'm sure you must be frightfully busy. I won't keep you a minute. It's about Sonny's property. I know you want to acquire it. I think perhaps I can help." He held up one hand, finger and thumb forming a circle. "Not on the phone. Could you drop in about six? Splendid." The hellfires that Barry had seen once before in O'Reilly's brown eyes flared brightly. "I'll look forward to it." O'Reilly replaced the receiver. He cut a little caper on the carpet. " 'I gloat!' " he roared. " 'Hear me gloat!' "

"*Stalky and Co.*, Rudyard Kipling," Barry said. "So he's taken the bait?"

"He's risen like a trout to a mayfly. All we have to do is play him a bit . . . I'm going to enjoy that . . . then we'll gaff the gobshite and land him."

"Now," said O'Reilly, "he'll be here in a minute or two. Just follow my lead. Agree with everything I say."

"Like the first night we went to the Fotheringhams'?"

"No. With enthusiasm. You tried to contradict me that night."

"Sorry about that."

The front doorbell rang. Barry looked at O'Reilly, who said, "Kinky knows to bring him up here."

Barry heard footsteps on the stairs. Kinky showed Councillor Bishop into the upstairs lounge. "It's the councillor, so." She had a look on her face as though she had found something unpleasant on the sole of her shoe. She left.

"Come in, Councillor," said O'Reilly, rising. "Have a seat. Would you like a wee . . . ?" He inclined his head towards the decanters on the sideboard.

"I've no time for that. I'm here on business, so I am." Councillor Bishop lowered himself into O'Reilly's recently vacated chair. Barry sat opposite. O'Reilly, briar in mouth, leant against the mantelpiece.

"How's your finger?"

"What? It's fine."

"Oh, good," said O'Reilly.

"So," said the councillor, "is the old bugger going to die?"

O'Reilly shook his head. "Sonny? He's very much on the mend."

"Pity." Bishop crossed his short legs and began to swing the upper one up and down, up and down, in short jerky arcs. "Him and them scruffy dogs."

O'Reilly glanced at Barry.

"I tell you, O'Reilly, Ballybucklebo would be a damn sight better off if we could see the back of the lot of them." Little flecks of spittle appeared at the corners of the councillor's mouth.

"You're probably right," said O'Reilly, "but I think old Sonny'll be around for a day or two yet."

The frequency of Bishop's leg swinging increased. "All right. How much?"

"How much for what?"

"Sonny's place."

"I'm only a country GP. I've no idea."

Barry had difficulty believing that O'Reilly could assume a look of such total innocence.

Bishop's eyes narrowed. He steepled his fingers. "I'm a fair man."

"Oh, indeed," said O'Reilly, "everyone knows that."

"Two thousand pounds."

Barry's knowledge of land values was limited, but the figure seemed low.

"I'm sure that would be very fair," said O'Reilly, "but we're not actually talking about selling Sonny's land."

"Am I here on a wild goose chase? You said you could help me get the property."

"Not exactly," said O'Reilly. "I said I knew you wanted to acquire the property and that perhaps I could help."

"It's the same thing."

"No. Not quite. I didn't say I could help *you*."

"What the hell are you talking about, O'Reilly?"

"I meant I thought I could help prevent you from getting within a beagle's gowl of the place."

Barry smothered a smile. He'd always liked that expression, although why distance should be measured by the baying of a hound had never been quite clear to him.

Councillor Bishop's face turned scarlet. His leg swinging

stopped. "And you wasted my time, dragging me round here? Listen, you stupid country quack, there's not a fuckin' thing you can do to stop me. I'll have Sonny's place, lock, stock, and barrel by the end of next week, so I will. And there's not a damn thing you can do."

"Oh, dear," said O'Reilly.

"Two thousand pounds. Take it or leave it. I don't give a shite."

"I think we'll leave it." O'Reilly blew a cloud of smoke toward the ceiling.

"Right." Bishop stood. "I'm for home."

"I hope Mrs. Bishop will be pleased to see you."

"What are you on about?"

"And little Julie MacAteer. She's up the pipe, you know."

Barry clenched his teeth. This bending of the rules, this breach of a patient's confidentiality, bothered him a lot.

"What's that wee guttersnipe being poulticed got to do with me?"

"I thought you'd know," said O'Reilly, the first suggestion of an edge creeping into his voice.

"Why the hell should I know? She's given her notice. Good riddance to bad rubbish."

O'Reilly took a long three-count, then said softly, "She says you're the daddy."

Barry winced. He knew O'Reilly was acting from the best of motives, but still. Perhaps he shouldn't have been so quick to agree to go along with this plan, but it was too late now.

Councillor Bishop rocked back on his heels. "She what? The wee bitch. I'll kill her. I'll kill her dead, so I will."

"I don't think so," said O'Reilly. "I don't think so at all."

Councillor Bishop's face went from scarlet to puce. He gobbled like a turkey that had just been informed that tomorrow was Christmas Eve. He took a deep breath, clearly pulling himself together, secure in the knowledge that indeed he was not the father. "If she's a bun in the oven, it's no concern of mine. Mind you . . . I wouldn't have minded giving her a wee poke."

"You did, Bertie."

"Balls. Lying slut. She'll have no reference from me. She'll never get another job—"

"Our tests don't lie." O'Reilly moved closer to the perspiring councillor.

"What tests?" Bishop's narrow forehead wrinkled. "What tests?"

"Pus," said O'Reilly cryptically. "You left some pus on a couple of swabs from the night I lanced your finger."

"So what?"

"You tell him, Doctor Laverty."

Barry stood. "I think you'd better sit down, Councillor."

Bishop looked from O'Reilly to Barry and back to O'Reilly. Then he slowly sat. "What about the pus?"

"It's a new test," said Barry.

"I'd not heard of it," said O'Reilly, "but modern science is a wonderful thing."

"I never laid a finger on her."

"It's not your finger that did the damage." O'Reilly stared at Councillor Bishop's crotch, then at his pudgy hands. "Mind you, I'm sure your fingers are bigger than your willy."

"You bastard."

"No," said O'Reilly. "It's *your* bastard. The one that Julie's carrying. Tell him, Doctor Laverty."

Barry shoved his hands into his trouser pockets and intoned, "This may be difficult for a layman to understand, Councillor, but if you take a blood sample from a pregnant woman and mix it with pus, even old dried-up pus, from the putative father, there can be an anaphylactoid progression of the polylobed acidophilic granulocytes." Barry knew he was spouting gibberish, but it was what O'Reilly wanted. "Blind the councillor with science," he'd said.

"A what?"

"Pay attention," said O'Reilly.

"An anaphylactoid progression of the acidophilic granulocytes.

It's absolutely . . . pathognomonic." Barry stumbled over the last word. It came hard to lie to a patient or about a patient to a third party.

" 'Pathognomonic' means that it's money in the bank," O'Reilly said helpfully. "You're the daddy all right, and to tell you the truth, Councillor, I'm proud of you. I wouldn't have thought a wizened-up, miserable gobshite like you would have had it in him."

"There's got to be some mistake." Bishop fiddled with one finger under the knot of his tie. "I never . . ." He took a deep breath. "Your stupid test's wrong. I can prove it. . . ."

"How?" asked O'Reilly.

"It's her word against mine."

"Not exactly," said Barry. "It's your word against hers . . . and two qualified medical men . . . and some highly sophisticated science. Acidophilic granulocytes never lie."

"But you doctors . . . and I know this for a fact, so I do . . . you doctors can't discuss a patient in public."

You're right, Barry thought. He looked over to O'Reilly, who bowled serenely along, saying, "Normally you'd be right, Bertie, but in your case we'd be prepared to make an exception. Old Hippocrates would understand."

I hope so, Barry thought.

"Oh, Jesus." The councillor buried his face in his hands.

"Of course, Bertie, there's an outside chance . . . what would you say it was, Doctor Laverty?"

Barry hesitated.

"Doctor Laverty?" O'Reilly's eyes were twin agates as he fixed Barry with a glare.

"About . . . about one in five hundred."

"That the test *could* be wrong," O'Reilly said.

"Could it?" Councillor Bishop's bluster had gone completely. "Could it?"

O'Reilly fiddled about, relighting his pipe.

"Could it, for God's sake?"

"I suppose so, but we wouldn't know for at least two weeks." O'Reilly exhaled smoke. "By then I imagine your loyal brethren down at the Orange Lodge would have had something to say. I hear they can get a bit right-wing about Orangemen who indulge in extramarital hanky-panky. Tend to ask for resignations. The town council could be a tad upset." He pulled the briar out of his mouth and stared into the bowl before saying, "I might just run myself for the vacancy your departure would create."

Bishop made one last attempt to bluster. "You're bluffing, so you are. Just bluffing."

"And then," said O'Reilly sweetly, "there's Mrs. Bishop. She told Kinky she'd seen you having a go at Julie MacAteer. I'm sure Mrs. B. wouldn't be hard to convince. . . ."

"Aaaah."

"Let's see, Bertie. You are a Protestant . . . of course you are . . . you couldn't be in the Orange Lodge if you weren't . . . and I don't think the Protestant church is as picky about divorce as the Romans."

"Honest-to-God, I only ever tried to feel Julie's tits. Just the once."

"Dirty old man," said O'Reilly. His voice hardened. "I might just believe you, Bertie Bishop, but I'll take a lot of convincing."

Bishop looked up at O'Reilly. "How?"

"Not much. A wee favour. That's all."

Barry saw a look cross Bishop's pudgy face as if to say, "Bargaining? I'm good at that." Then the councillor said, "And what would that favour be?"

With his pipe stem O'Reilly counted off the points on the fingers of his other hand. "You'll fix Sonny's roof, and the rest of his place . . . free of charge."

"What?" Bishop whimpered.

"You'll settle five hundred pounds on Julie MacAteer. That's two hundred and fifty per . . . what did you call them? Tits?"

"Oh, Jesus."

"You'll write her a letter of reference that would get her through the pearly gates . . . and if you breathe a word that she's pregnant—"

"I won't. I swear to God, I won't."

"Good," said O'Reilly. "Very good . . . and just one other small, little thing."

"Jesus, there's not more?"

"Seamus Galvin is looking for someone to buy a clatter of rocking ducks. About four hundred quid would see him right."

Barry chuckled inwardly. He'd completely forgotten about the Galvins.

"Do you know," O'Reilly said, "I think that's about it."

"I'll be fucked," Bishop muttered. "Ruined."

"Indeed you will be, Bertie, if you don't do exactly as I've told you, chapter and verse."

Bishop hung his head.

"And if you've any notion to try to tell people that Doctor Laverty and myself made all this up, there's the two of us to swear . . . regretfully, of course . . . that you came in here tonight hallucinating."

"A classic case of paranoid schizo-hebephrenia if ever I saw one," Barry added. In for a penny, in for a pound.

"Can I go?" the councillor asked.

"If you must," said O'Reilly. "And I'm sure when the laboratory retests the sample, it'll all turn out to have been a horrible mistake."

Councillor Bishop looked pleadingly at his persecutor.

"Just one more thing, Bertie."

"What?"

Hardened steel was in O'Reilly's voice. "If you ever call me a quack again, if you ever forget that Doctor Laverty and I worked hard for our degrees, I'll gut you like a herring. You'll be so unpopular in Ballybucklebo that you'll only find peace hiding behind a false beard, digging peat for a living on the west coast of Inishmore, which I believe is the most westerly of the Aran Islands."

"I hear you, *Doctor* O'Reilly," said Councillor Bishop. "I hear you, so I do."

"Thought you might." O'Reilly knocked the dottle from his pipe into the fireplace. His tone softened. "Cheer up, Bertie. Play your cards right when you fix up Sonny's roof, and your stock will soar in Ballybucklebo. You can pretend to be the greatest philanthropist since Dale Carnegie."

The look that appeared in Councillor Bishop's eyes reminded Barry of the dim yet cunning gaze he had seen in the orbs of Gertie, the Kennedys' pet sow. "I could, couldn't I?"

"The citizens would build a statue to you."

"Go on. They never would."

"That's 'Go on, *Doctor*,'" O'Reilly said, "but I'll forgive the oversight . . . this time." He put a big hand under Bishop's arm and hoisted the councillor to his feet. "Off you trot, Bertie. Just think how you'd look on a granite horse."

"I will, Doctor." Bishop sidled to the door. "I think I could maybe get a start made on Sonny's tomorrow. . . ."

"Close the door behind you," said O'Reilly. "There's a good chap."

Barry was able to contain his laughter, just, until the door was firmly shut. Finally he said, "That was brilliant, Fingal."

O'Reilly went to the sideboard and poured himself a whiskey. "Sherry?"

"Why not?"

"Here you are. *Sláinte.*"

"*Sláinte mHath.*"

"No doubt about it, Barry. No doubt about it at all. The pair of us make a grand team."

26

If You Can Meet with Triumph and Disaster ...

Wednesday morning surgery and lunch were over. O'Reilly consulted his list.

"Great," he announced, "not one sick one."

"So we can put our feet up?" Barry rose from the table. "I'm off
to have a go at today's crossword."

"The hell you are," said O'Reilly, shaking his head. "We need to
drop in on a few folks that we've been neglecting."

Barry sighed. "Sometimes, Fingal, I wonder about you."

"And why would that be?" One of O'Reilly's shaggy eyebrows
rose.

"You've been telling me since I came here that we can't carry all
the woes of the world on our shoulders. That we've to get away
from the customers once in a while."

"True." O'Reilly blew a perfect smoke ring. "Jesus," he said,
poking his index finger through the hole in the middle of the circle.
"I never knew I could make rings."

"Man of many talents," said Barry. "You'll be telling me you can
do spherical trigonometry next."

"As a matter of fact I can. The navigator on the *Warspite* taught
me." The smoke ring rose, twisted, and drifted away.

Barry shook his head. "What the hell can't you do?"

"Walking on water's a bit tricky." O'Reilly grinned. "And by God, I wish I could turn the stuff into wine."

"Or John Jameson's."

O'Reilly's grin widened. "Now that's an idea." He watched the blue-grey tendrils slowly vanish. He tried to repeat his feat but merely succeeded in producing a small mushroom cloud.

"And you can raise the dead . . . the farmer who keeled over in church when you first came here."

O'Reilly jabbed at Barry with his pipe stem. "Stick with me, son. I told you you'd learn a thing or two."

Barry was serious when he said, "I already have."

"Good," said O'Reilly, "and when we've finished seeing a few folks this afternoon, maybe you'll have learned a bit more."

"All right. Who do you want to go see?"

"The Galvins. I want to hear if Bishop's kept his word. The Kennedys. See how Jeannie's doing; then we'll have a word with Maggie. Let her know about Sonny."

"That shouldn't take long."

O'Reilly's expression clouded. "They're the easy ones. We'll have to make a stop with Mrs. Fotheringham."

Barry swallowed. He'd been trying not to think about that particular case. "Do we have to?"

O'Reilly nodded. "She'll be worried sick, and I'll bet she won't have a clue what's going on. The specialists at the Royal are too busy to talk to relatives. You know what visiting hours are like, and if she did get through on the phone she'd be told by some ward clerk, 'He's comfortable,' or 'He's resting,' or 'I'm sorry we're not allowed to give out information on the phone.' "

Barry was only recently removed from the bustle of the great teaching hospital. He could well remember how much time was spent on the technical aspects of the patients' cases—and how little on their and their families' worries. Visiting hours were regimented.

Immediate family only. Two 'til four in the afternoon. No visitors on Wednesdays. And he now recognized that most of the relatives had been too overawed by their surroundings to ask questions. It had all seemed perfectly natural to him—back then.

"Right," said O'Reilly, "I'll phone the ward. Check up on Fotheringham's progress. It'll only take a minute to see his wife. Set her mind at rest."

Barry steeled himself before saying, "Could I do that? It should be me who tries to explain things to her."

O'Reilly cocked his head on one side. "You know, I hoped you'd say that." Barry heard the satisfaction in his senior colleague's voice as O'Reilly continued, "You'll need to get put through to Ward Twenty-one. You make the call. I'll see you at the car. Out front again."

Barry spoke to one of the junior medical staff on the ward and was gratified to hear that Major Fotheringham's recovery, although slow, was progressing as anticipated. He'd be left with some impairment of his speech and weakness of his left side, but he should be able to live a fairly normal life. He'd have his stitches taken out on Friday and be discharged for outpatient follow-up and physiotherapy the following week.

"Thank you," Barry said, and was about to hang up, when—why not? "Could you reconnect me with the switchboard?" he asked. He got through at once.

"Could you page Doctor Mills please?"

"Hold on."

Barry waited. He could imagine the look on Jack's face when the *bleep-bleep-bleep* went off in the pocket of his white coat. More bloody work. That's what his friend would think.

"Mills here." Jack's voice was clipped. Businesslike.

"Jack? Barry."

"It's yourself, is it? I thought Sir Donald Cromie was after my hide when my bleeper went off. I'm running a bit late. What's up?"

"Nothing. I'll not keep you, but I had to phone the Royal so I thought I'd see if you were about the place."

"I'm on my way to theatre. It's lumps and bumps this afternoon. Minor cases, warts, sebaceous cysts, the odd ingrowing toenail. Good training for young surgeons, according to Sir Donald."

"And a good excuse for you to do the work while he—"

"Plays golf. That's one of the advantages of surgery. When you do get a senior position, you can turn over the trivia to your juniors. Get a bit of time off. You still as busy as ever?"

"Not too bad."

"Have you heard anything from that wee bird of yours yet?"

"Patricia?" Barry shook his head. Somehow the crisis with Major Fotheringham, Cissie's thyroid disease, and Julie MacAteer's pregnancy had all served to drive Patricia from his thoughts—most of the time. "No. Not a peep."

"She blew you out last Friday. That's only four days. Give her time."

"But if she doesn't call?"

"Then, my old son, you're just like the Christmas turkey . . . right, regally stuffed."

"I suppose so." Barry knew that his friend was right. It certainly looked as though she'd just been letting him down gently. Her insistence on the importance of her career had been a convenient way of letting him know that no matter how he felt, she was not as taken with him. And damn it, smitten as he was, it was up to her to make the next move.

"Time's a great healer," Jack said, "and so is the produce of Mr. Arthur Guinness and Sons. Any chance of getting together again?"

"I'll call you later in the week if I'm free . . . and if I haven't heard from Patricia."

"Do that. I've got to run. Can't keep the lumps and bumps waiting . . . and if I don't see you through the week, I'll see you through the window." The line went dead.

Barry hung up and smiled.

"Are you coming?" O'Reilly bawled from outside.

Barry closed the front door and trotted to the car.

"Well?" O'Reilly asked. "How's the major?"

"On the mend."

"Good." O'Reilly eased the car away from the kerb.

"Isn't it grand, Dr. O'Reilly?" Maureen Galvin, eyes bright, showed O'Reilly a pile of twenty-pound notes. "Some fellow came round first thing this morning. Seamus was out. Says your man to me, 'I hear your husband's got a load of rocking ducks for sale.' 'Right,' says I. 'I'll take the lot,' says he. And would you look at that? Four hundred quid."

"I'm delighted," said O'Reilly.

"You never saw such things in your life," said Maureen. "Not one of them looked like any duck I'd ever seen."

"Must have been things of beauty to behold," said O'Reilly. "I'm sure they'll sell like hotcakes."

Maureen pursed her lips. "I'm not so sure, but that's for the fellow that bought them to worry about."

"Oh, indeed," said Barry. If the rocking ducks were as odd as Maureen had said, he wondered, exactly what would Councillor Bishop do with his new acquisitions?

"Anyway," said Maureen, "we got our money back and a bit of a profit. I don't know how you fixed it, Doctor, sir, but . . ."

O'Reilly brushed her thanks aside. "So when are the three of you off to sunny California?"

"Just as soon as I can get the tickets bought. And . . ." She hesitated. "Would you do me a wee favour?"

"Ask away."

She handed him the money. "Would you take care of that?"

O'Reilly took the notes.

"I'd be happier if Seamus—"

"Don't you worry your head about them," said O'Reilly, stuffing the notes in his trouser pocket. "They'll be safe as houses."

She smiled at him, cocked her head to one side, and asked, "Would you be free on Saturday, Doctors?"

Barry had hoped he might be allowed some time off. He wanted to see Patricia if she ever did phone, or perhaps he'd meet Jack if she didn't. He looked questioningly at O'Reilly.

"We might," said O'Reilly.

"We're having a wee going-away party. We'd like for you both to come."

"What do you think, Doctor Laverty?"

"We'd have it here. In the afternoon," said Maureen.

Barry could tell by the way she looked up into O'Reilly's face that the presence of her medical advisors was important. "I don't see why not," he said. He might still be able to get an hour or two off after the party.

"Grand," said Maureen.

O'Reilly glanced round the tiny parlour. "How many folks were you thinking of having?"

Maureen shrugged.

"I tell you what," said O'Reilly, "could you or Seamus get your hands on the marquee the Ballybucklebo Highlanders use at the Field on the Twelfth?"

"I'll ask Seamus."

"Just in case it rains," said O'Reilly. "There'd be a lot more room in my back garden."

Maureen beamed. "You wouldn't mind, sir?"

"Not at all. You never know how many'll show up at a Ballybucklebo *céili*."

"Seamus'll get the big tent. He's not pipe major for nothing. We'll put it up on Saturday morning."

"Right," said O'Reilly. "Now, we'll need some grub. Mrs. Kincaid'll take care of that. I'll get a couple of barrels of stout over from the Duck."

"But that'll cost a fortune."

"No," said O'Reilly, "Willy the barman'll have to charge the guests. I'm not made of money."

Barry remembered the difficulties he and Jack had had when they wanted to throw a party in the students' mess. The Ulster licensing laws were a little on the confusing side. If anyone wanted to sell alcohol anywhere but in a registered public house they had to apply for a special permit. It usually took a week or two for one to be issued. "We'll not have time to get a permit," he said.

"We'll not need one," said O'Reilly. "We'll not sell drink . . . we'll sell glasses of water."

"What?"

"Water," said O'Reilly with a huge grin. "Grand stuff. Works wonders for greyhounds, you don't need a permit to sell it, and there's nothing to stop you giving away a free drink with every glass of water sold."

"Are you serious?"

"Absolutely."

"So you *can* change water into wine . . . well, beer."

O'Reilly nodded. "And just to be on the safe side we'll invite Constable Mulligan. If there *is* a law being broken, and him at the hooley, he'd have to arrest himself."

Barry laughed and his laughter woke young Barry Fingal, who let the world know of his presence in no uncertain tones.

"I'd better see to the wean," said Maureen. "Saturday it is, Doctors."

"Right," said O'Reilly. "Come on, Doctor Laverty. We've more calls to make."

To Barry's great relief the lane to the Kennedys' farmhouse was dry. He still lacked a pair of Wellington boots. For all he knew the pair he'd bought on the day he'd met Patricia were still rattling up and down on the train between Bangor and Belfast.

Jeannie was playing in the farmyard, throwing a stick for her Border collie.

"Hello, Doctor O'Reilly." She took the stick from the dog, who immediately flopped to the ground, front paws stretched out before her, head between her legs, alert gaze never leaving the stick in her mistress's hand. "Stay, Tessie." The dog glanced once at the new-comers.

"How are you, Jeannie?" O'Reilly walked over from the car. Barry followed.

"Much better now, thank you."

Barry could see that this was a different little girl from the one he'd met three weeks ago. She had colour in her cheeks, and her eyes were as bright as Tessie's porcelain blue ones. He thought she might have lost a little weight, but considering how sick she had been, that was to be expected.

"She's really on the mend." Mrs. Kennedy appeared in the door-way of the farmhouse. Her grey hair was neatly tied up in a bun. Her apron was clean. She walked to where Jeannie stood and put a protective hand on the girl's shoulder. "We were main worried about her for a while, but them doctors at Sick Children's were smashing, so they were." She looked into O'Reilly's eyes. "There was a young one, a Doctor Mills. He said if you and Doctor Laverty hadn't been so quick of the mark . . ." She swallowed.

" 'All's well that ends well,' " said O'Reilly. "And don't bother to tell me that's William Shakespeare, Doctor Laverty. I know."

Barry grinned and thought how critical he had been of his senior colleague's seemingly slapdash methods of diagnosis. He recognized that when O'Reilly said that sometimes country GPs could make a difference, he had been absolutely right.

O'Reilly said, "Lots of fresh air, plenty to eat, and she'll be fit as a flea in no time. Ready for school in September."

Jeannie scowled. "I hate math."

"So did I when I was your age," said O'Reilly. "Go on. Show me how you can throw the stick."

Jeannie threw the small branch across the yard. Tessie, body pressed to the ground, gaze fixed on Jeannie's face, trembled but did not move one inch from where she had been told to lie down.

"Smart dogs, collies," O'Reilly remarked.

"Fetch," Jeannie said, and the dog took off like a whippet.

"You'll not be needing us again," O'Reilly said to Bridget Kennedy.

"Dermot'll be sorry he missed you, Doctor, but he's out combining."

"A farmer's work's never done," said O'Reilly. "Just like a doctor's." He opened the car door. "If the three of you have nothing to do on Saturday afternoon, we're having a bit of a ta-ta-ta-ra in my back garden for Seamus and Maureen Galvin. They're off to America soon."

"I'll ask himself," said Bridget. "I'll bring some barmbrack."

"Great," said O'Reilly. He lowered himself into the driver's seat. "Hop in."

Barry climbed aboard.

"We were lucky with that one," said O'Reilly, as the car jolted down the rutted lane. "It would have been the death of Bridget if the wee lass hadn't pulled through."

"Mrs. Kennedy must have been a fair age when Jeannie was born."

O'Reilly pulled onto the main road and stamped on the accelerator. "Usual story. They couldn't afford to get married until old man Kennedy died and left his son the farm. I think Bridget was forty-two then. Took her forever to get pregnant. That wee girl's the light of her life."

O'Reilly leant on the horn and swerved across the centre line. "Bloody bicycles. Move over."

Barry's head swung round as he watched the unfortunate on the bike wobble, stop, and hurl himself and his conveyance into the ditch. "Have you ever hit one?" he asked.

O'Reilly shook his head. "Not yet. They all know the car."

And they all know you very well, Fingal Flahertie O'Reilly, Barry thought, and at least some of them are getting to know me. His pleasure at that idea was shattered when O'Reilly took both hands off the steering wheel to light his pipe and said, "Fotheringhams', next stop."

◈

"Would you like some tea and scones?" Mrs. Fotheringham asked when O'Reilly and Barry were seated in the antimacassar-draped armchairs. She wore her Heather Mixture two-piece and her pearls. Not a hair was out of place on her head.

"No, thank you," said O'Reilly. "We can stay for only a minute. Doctor Laverty has something to tell you."

She sat on the settee, knees together, hands clasped in an attitude of prayer resting on the lap made by her skirt. "Yes, Doctor?" she asked through thin lips.

Barry swallowed. "I've had a word with the hospital about the major. He's doing as well as can be expected."

"And how well would that be?"

"He's fully conscious. Weak on his left side. His speech is a bit slurred. He's never going to be quite right, I'm afraid, but the speech therapists and physiotherapists can work wonders . . . with time."

"I see." Her face was expressionless. "Perhaps if he'd gone to the hospital sooner?"

Barry glanced at O'Reilly, who was examining his fingernails intently. No help would be forthcoming from that quarter. Barry inhaled. "Yes. He might be doing better if I'd recognized what was wrong when I came to see him on Friday." Barry wondered if someone at the hospital had sown these seeds of doubt in her mind. 'If only we'd seen him sooner' was a common complaint of the medical staff there. "What did they tell you at the Royal?" he asked.

Her lips were so narrow they had almost disappeared. "They barely acknowledged my presence."

Barry wondered if there was anything more he could say in self-defence and decided that nothing short of total honesty would do. "I didn't think he'd done more than sprain his neck."

"But you were wrong, weren't you?"

"Yes, Mrs. Fotheringham. I was."

"I'm glad you admit it, young man."

Barry flinched.

"Ahem," O'Reilly grumbled. "You know, Mrs. Fotheringham, I don't think I would have done any better. There wasn't a lot to go on on Friday."

She sniffed haughtily. "Of course you medical men always stick together."

"You could say that," said O'Reilly levelly, "but what I've told you is the truth as I see it."

"I've had time to think this over," she said, rising, "and I have decided that my husband and I will be seeking our medical advice elsewhere in the future."

"That is of course your choice, Mrs. Fotheringham. I hear Dr. Bowman in Kinnegar is very good." O'Reilly's tone was measured.

Barry clenched his teeth. She was perfectly within her rights to change doctors, but he had hoped that by his being completely honest she might have understood.

"In that case," she crossed the room and held the door open, "perhaps you would be good enough to transfer our records to him?"

"With pleasure."

Barry, his head held low, walked slowly to the hall. "I'm sorry. . . ."

" 'Sorry' won't give me back a healthy husband."

Barry looked at O'Reilly, who shook his head and said, "You're right."

"I'm glad you admit that much," she said. "Now . . . ?"

"Good afternoon, Mrs. Fotheringham," O'Reilly said from the front step. "I hope the major makes the best recovery possible."

"Huh," she said and closed the door.

Barry walked slowly to the car. He felt the springs sag as O'Reilly joined him.

"Don't let her get to you," said O'Reilly, starting the engine. "She's upset, angry."

"And right," said Barry. "I might have—"

"Don't start that again." O'Reilly braked. "Open the gate."

Barry obeyed, waited for the car to pass, and closed the gate. It was all very well for O'Reilly to be philosophical. He wasn't the one who'd missed the diagnosis.

"Get in," said O'Reilly, "and for God's sake, buck up." O'Reilly accelerated. "You were spot-on about Cissie Sloan; between the pair of us we sorted out Jeannie Kennedy, and we got old Sonny put to rights." He made a screeching left turn onto the shore road. "You have to take the good with the bad. For the last time, I agree perhaps you could have done better with the major, but Mrs. Fotheringham's not just angry . . . she's feeling guilty."

"What about?"

"She's intelligent enough to recognize that maybe if the pair of them hadn't cried wolf so often you might have taken his stiff neck more seriously."

"Yes. I might."

"And when people are guilty . . . they often need someone to lash out at . . . to blame instead. You came in handy. Perfect scapegoat."

Barry thought about that. Certainly there was some truth in what O'Reilly said.

"Just remember," O'Reilly continued, " 'If you can meet with Triumph and Disaster/ And treat those two impostors just the same . . .' "

"Rudyard Kipling's 'If.' My dad gave me a framed copy when I was at school. 'If neither foes nor loving friends can hurt you; / If all men count with you, but none too much. . . .' "

"Precisely," said O'Reilly, " 'but none too much.' And that's another rule of practice besides 'Never let the customers get the upper hand.' "

"Oh?"

"Abraham Lincoln said something about fooling all of the people some of the time but not fooling all of them all of the time. It's the same with patients. No matter what you do for some of them, you'll never satisfy them."

"I know," Barry said quietly.

"So," said O'Reilly, "the sooner you come to the parting of the ways from those ones, the better."

"Like Mrs. Fotheringham wanting to see Dr. Bowman in future?"

"Exactly. She'll never trust us again. It's a pity, but that's the nature of the beast. But for every Mrs. Fotheringham, every Bertie Bishop, there are the Cissies and the Jeannies and the Maureen Galvins and . . . the Maggies that do make it all worthwhile." He pulled the car to the verge outside Maggie MacCorkle's cottage. "Come on. Let's tell Maggie about Sonny."

Dogs spilled out of Maggie's front door and clustered round the car, tails wagging, the air full of the sounds of their happy yapping. Maggie thrust her way past them. Barry noticed the fresh pansies in her hatband.

"You're just in time, Doctors dear. The kettle's boiled."

"Great," said O'Reilly, "a cup of tea would hit the spot."

"Yes, indeed," said Barry, following them both inside.

"Bugger off, General Montgomery." Maggie shooed the ginger cat off one of her chairs. "Have a seat, Doctor O'Reilly. Light your pipe."

She bustled round her stove, warming the teapot, dumping out the boiling water, spooning in tea leaves from a tin caddy with a picture of the coronation of Elizabeth II painted on the side, and adding more boiling water. "We'll let that stew a bit," she said.

"Grand," said O'Reilly.

"I'm glad you came," she said. "I've run out of them wee pills, and I'd another of those eggycentwhat-do-you-muhcallum headaches the other night, so I had. Would you have any more tablets with you?"

O'Reilly shook his head. "'Fraid not, Maggie. Eccentric headaches can be funny things. Could you pop in tomorrow? I'd like to take another wee look at you before I give you any more pills. Just to be on the safe side."

Barry smiled. He wasn't the only doctor in Ballybucklebo who would be taking a complaint of headaches more seriously in the future.

"I'll be round," she said, pouring tea into three china mugs, one commemorating the Relief of Mafeking, one with a picture of Sir Winston Churchill, and the third carrying a portrait of John F. Kennedy surrounded by black flags.

"Milk and sugar?"

"Just milk," Barry said, as O'Reilly nodded.

She gave each a cup. The tea was so strong that Barry wondered if it might dissolve the teaspoon. There was nowhere to dispose of the brew. He soldiered on, hoping that the tannic acid wouldn't turn his stomach to leather.

"We just popped in to let you know about Sonny," O'Reilly said.

Maggie cocked her head to one side like a thrush looking at the ground where it had just spotted a tasty worm. "So how is the oul' eejit?"

"He's getting out on Saturday," O'Reilly said.

"Told you," said Maggie, "they'll have to shoot that one." She sipped her tea. "That means he can have his dogs back."

"Not exactly," said O'Reilly. "He'll have to go to Bangor to convalesce for a while."

"How long's a while?" Maggie asked.

O'Reilly glanced at Barry before saying, "Until his roof's fixed."

Barry watched Maggie closely.

She sat bolt upright. "Until what?" Her eyes widened.

"His roof's fixed. Councillor Bishop told me he's had a change of heart."

"Jesus, Mary, and Joseph. That bugger Bertie Bishop? That man has a heart that would make Pharaoh's hard one look like a marshmallow, so he has."

"It's true, Maggie," Barry said. "Honestly."

"I'll believe it when I see it," Maggie grunted. "I've seen no stars in the east, and the last thing Bertie Bishop said to Sonny was that he'd only fix the roof after the Second Coming."

O'Reilly laughed. "Keep your eyes peeled for a bunch of wise men on camels, Maggie. It's true."

She squinted at him. "Cross your heart?"

O'Reilly did.

"Huh," she said primly, "and what has Sonny to say about that?"

"He doesn't know," said O'Reilly, "but I've a bit of a notion."

"Oh?" said Maggie.

"Aye," said O'Reilly. "I'm going to go up to the Royal on Saturday."

That was news to Barry, but it no longer came as a surprise that O'Reilly would be happy to ferry his patients about.

"I'll run him down to Bangor, but first we're having a bit of a *céilí* at my place. To send the Galvins off to America. Sonny'll be fit enough to drop in for a wee while."

"Go on," said Maggie.

"How'd you like to pop by and tell him about the roof?"

Barry watched as from somewhere deep under Maggie's leathery cheeks a glow rose and spread. "Away off and chase yourself," she said. "Him and me barely give each other the time of day."

"I know," said O'Reilly, "but the last time I saw him, Sonny said he wanted to have a wee word . . . to thank you for taking care of his dogs."

"That would be civil of him, right enough."

"So you'll come?"

"I'll mull it over," she said. "If I do, I'll bring one of my plum cakes."

"That," said O'Reilly, "would be great. Your plum cake, Maggie?" O'Reilly crossed his eyes at Barry. "It's as famous as your cups of tea."

27

Now Is the Time for All Good Men to Come to the Aid of the Party

O'Reilly had left for Belfast to collect Sonny. Barry yawned and toyed with a slice of toast. He looked through the dining-room window. The weather forecast had been right. Sunshine and a few low clouds. Perhaps the marquee that was being erected in O'Reilly's back garden might not be needed. Barry supposed he should be looking forward to today's going-away party for the Galvins, but he was tired and disappointed.

He rolled his shoulders. God, but Thursday and Friday had been hectic. Droves of patients, and last night there had been a traffic accident. Two men—one with a broken arm, one with a fractured femur, both with minor lacerations—had needed to be given morphine, splinted, and sutured before being sent to the Royal. It had been four in the morning when he and O'Reilly got into their beds.

A bit of a sleep-in wouldn't have gone amiss, but he had been woken by the sounds of Seamus Galvin and his team putting up the big tent. The steady pounding of wooden mauls on tent pegs accompanied by the barking of Arthur Guinness had made sleep impossible.

Barry sighed, picked up his dirty plates and cutlery, and carried them through to the kitchen. Perhaps his tiredness somehow made his disappointment more real. It seemed that Jack's advice to wait for Patricia to phone had been well intentioned but wrong. Not a peep from her and it was eight days now since. . . . Face it, he told himself, she doesn't want to know you.

Kinky straightened up from the oven. "Pop the dishes in the sink," she said. "I'll see to them after I get the last of the sausage rolls done, so." She brushed stray hair from her forehead with the back of one arm. "Grand day for the hooley."

"I suppose so." Barry put the plates in the sink.

"You don't seem too pleased." She squinted at his face.

"I'm not in much of a party mood."

"And why would that be?"

Barry shrugged.

"You're looking down in the mouth, so. Would another cup of tea help?"

"No thanks, Kinky." The pounding of mauls outside grew louder. "Lord, I wish they'd get a move on. Are you not nearly deafened with that racket?"

"Me? Not one bit, but Lady Macbeth didn't like it at all. She's gone off to hide someplace."

"Sensible cat."

"May I ask you a question, Doctor Laverty?" Kinky stood solidly, feet planted on the kitchen's tiled floor.

"Sure."

"It's none of my business, but—"

"But what, Kinky?"

"Is it that wee girl that has you sore tried?"

Barry wondered how she had seen through him so easily. He considered telling her that it *was* none of her business, but one look at her big open face told him that she was asking from concern, not idle curiosity. "A bit," he admitted.

"I thought so. You went off last week like a liltie. Now I know she's not phoned here and you've not been out with her since."

Barry sighed. "Things didn't work out. She told me she didn't want to get too involved."

Kinky tutted. "Silly girl. If you don't give, you'll not get back. I know that for a fact, so."

Barry had wondered what had happened to Mr. Kincaid. After all, Kinky wouldn't be Mrs. Kincaid if she hadn't been married. "You were married, Kinky, weren't you?"

She nodded slowly. "I was and it was grand, so. But I lost himself."

"I'm sorry."

"There's no need for you to be, but it's nice of you to say it."

Barry hesitated.

Kinky put her hands into the pockets of her apron. "I was only eighteen. He was a Cork fisherman. He was lost at sea and I was lost on land. It was like half of myself gone," she said, moving to the counter where a bowl of sausage meat stood beside a wooden board on which was heaped a mound of pastry dough. "But life has to go on." She grabbed a rolling pin and with steady strong strokes began to flatten the dough. "I thought I'd see the world." She chuckled. "It was a brave step from Cork to County Down before the war, so I took a job with old Doctor Flanagan here in Ballybucklebo . . . just for a wee while . . . just 'til I found my way again. I told you I was lost when my Paudeen was drowned."

"And you never left?"

"I never met another lad like Paudeen." She sprinkled flour onto the now flat pastry. "After a year or two of feeling sorry for myself, I looked hard for another lad but I never did find one."

Barry thought he felt the same way about Patricia, but at least Kinky had made an effort after she had been widowed. Perhaps he should get a grip, quit moping, and see if other girls were out there.

"Are you content here, Kinky?"

She brushed the hair back with her forearm, leaving a trail of flour on her forehead. "I am. I've had a good life, so. I'll not complain, but it pains me to see a young man moping."

"It's daft, isn't it?" And damn it, he was starting to believe it. It *was* daft.

She smiled. "Sure there *are* times the heart rules the head." She sprinkled flour on the sheet of pastry. "The newspaper's in the hall. Go you up to the lounge. It'll be quieter there. I'll call you if there are any patients."

"I'll do that."

"And who knows? Maybe things will turn out for you after all."

"I wish."

Kinky's eyes narrowed. She frowned. "Do you know what 'fey' means, Doctor Laverty?"

"The second sight? The gift?"

"More like a curse," said Kinky.

"It's only a superstition."

"You can believe that if you please, sir, but things *are* going to be fine. I know."

Despite all his scientific training, Barry felt the hairs on the back of his neck prickle. "Are you sure?"

She spooned lumps of sausage meat onto the pastry. Her big fingers deftly rolled it to enclose the filling. "Away on upstairs and read your paper," she said, "and while you're there, see if you can find the cat."

He looked at her hard, but she was bent over her work. "All right, Kinky," he said, knowing full well that as far as she was concerned the subject was closed.

He collected the paper and went upstairs. He didn't try hard to find the cat. He "push-wushed" a few times, then settled in one of the big chairs. He ignored the news and turned to the crossword, but despite his attempts to concentrate, his mind kept wandering to what Kinky had said.

No wonder, considering her own loss, she was sympathetic to O'Reilly, and yet, Barry began to wonder, was she perhaps a little disappointed in the big man's refusal to try again? If she was, she didn't let it show.

He'd been sorry for O'Reilly when Kinky explained how he'd lost his new wife all those years ago. You know, Barry Laverty, he told himself, it's all very well to admire O'Reilly—to try to emulate much of his style of practice—but you don't have to turn yourself into a living replica. Just because O'Reilly had turned his back on women, you don't have to. Patricia is golden. Maybe you'll never ever find anyone like her, but why not be like Kinky and try again?

It must have been terrible for her to have been widowed so young. Barry knew that many men from the small fishing villages were drowned—so many that often the villagers became half inured. In the Arran Islands, the famous local sweaters all had recognizable patterns that appealed to American tourists. The visitors didn't know that each pattern was particular to a family, so that if a man was lost at sea and washed ashore the corpse could be identified by the sweater.

The country folk believed that the sudden death of a loved one could confer the gift of second sight. Was Kinky fey? That was a hard one to answer. He could remember his own grandmother sitting bolt upright in her chair and announcing solemnly, "My sister Martha just died." Great-aunt Martha lived in England. The phone call that came several hours later had confirmed her passing. How had his grandmother known? He shook his head.

He'd like to believe Kinky was right about Patricia, but if she wasn't, he'd better be like the Cork woman. He could start looking for another girl. Certainly that's what Jack Mills would do.

The god-awful pounding in the back garden stopped. He rubbed his eyes, stretched, lay back in the chair, and nodded off.

Barry dreamed of Patricia, and the drowned eyes of Kinky's

Paudeen, and Kinky herself, like one of the witches from *Macbeth*, casting her spells, foretelling the future.

Barry wrinkled his nose. Something was tickling his nostrils. He was dimly aware of a gentle whiffling and a persistent rumbling. A weight was on his chest. He blinked, opened his eyes, and shook his head. Still not fully awake, he made out a dim white blur. Lady Macbeth was crouched on his chest. Her front legs were tucked under her body in that attitude that cats assume only when they feel they are secure.

The tickling in his nostrils and the whiffling noise, he now recognized, had been caused by the cat putting her pink nose close to his and directing her exhalations into his nose. The rumbling was her steady purr. This he knew from past experience was Her Ladyship's way of saying, "Wake up, you. I demand the pleasure of your company."

He wriggled in the chair, blinked, fondled the cat's head, and asked, "What time is it?" He looked at his watch. Good Lord. One forty-five. He yawned and stretched, eyes screwed shut, fists clenched, shoulders hunched. He felt Lady Macbeth spring to the floor, disturbed by his sudden movements.

He trotted upstairs, pursued by Lady Macbeth, who sat on the laundry hamper watching intently as Barry washed his face and combed his hair. She preceded him down the stairs and into the kitchen, sweet with the smells of newly baked pastry, where Kinky was busy loading plates of sandwiches onto a large tray.

"Did you have a nice nap?" she asked.

Barry nodded and asked, "Is Doctor O'Reilly back yet?"

She shook her head.

Barry tried to steal a sandwich. She batted his hand away.

"Leave you them be," she said. "They're for the guests. There's a plate on the shelf I've left for you, so." She pointed to a platter of ham sandwiches, sausage rolls, and devilled eggs. "Eat up how ever little much is in it."

"Thanks, Kinky." Barry helped himself. "I found Her Ladyship, by the way."

"So I see," said Kinky. "Go on, you wee dote, get down off that shelf. Sausage rolls is bad for pushycats." She shoved the cat off the shelf and lifted the tray. "I'd better be getting these outside."

Barry held the door open. Kinky, burdened by the tray, moved sideways through the doorway. Tail high, Lady Macbeth slipped past and strode out into the back garden.

Barry was curious to see what arrangements had been made. He followed Kinky out into the bright sunlight. The tent stood in the left side of the garden, close to the house. It was a two-poler with the central supports sticking through the canvas roof, in the midline, one pole at each end. Guy ropes ran from the corners of the structure and were anchored to stout wooden pegs that stuck up above the grass. The back and side walls had been lowered, but the canvas at the front was rolled up to the eave line and held in place with a series of straps, looking, he thought, like the furled sails of a square-rigger.

The interior was pleasantly shady, with small patches of light on the grass where the sun's rays slipped in through eyeholes and—he looked up—through two rents in the roof.

Willy the barman stood ready for action behind a trestle table that occupied the greater part of the rear wall. He wore his floral-pattern waistcoat, and his shirtsleeves were hoisted by a pair of black velvet–covered, elastic garters. He needed only a green eyeshade to be the epitome of a Mississippi riverboat gambler, Barry thought.

"How are you, Doc?" Willy called. "Ready for your first?"

"Not yet, thanks, Willy. I was just having a look-see."

"Look away to your heart's content. We're all set and rarin' to go."

Barry could see that Willy was right. There were four aluminium kegs, each with an array of hoses that led to taps on the table top.

Pint and half-pint glasses, glasses for whiskey, and glasses for wine stood there in ranks, foot soldiers in front of the heavy cavalry of spirits and wine bottles. A skirmish line of lemonade and orange squash for the children was flung out on both sides of the main array.

The side walls of the big tent were lined with more tables, covered with plates of sandwiches, sausage rolls, cheeses, barmbracks, a ham, and a cold leg of lamb. Kinky finished depositing her burden. She turned to him.

"I think there should be enough, so."

"Enough? I thought a few folks were coming over. You could feed five thousand."

Kinky smiled. "A few folks? The word'll be out. It'll be like a flock of locusts in here in the next couple of hours, and I have to be sure no one goes hungry."

"It's like 'The Galway Races,' Kinky."

"What do you mean?"

Barry quoted the old song. He didn't try to sing it. He knew that although he was fond of music, when it came to singing he couldn't carry a tune in a bucket. " 'Lozenges and oranges, and lemonade and raisins / And gingerbread and spices to accommodate the ladies . . .' "

" 'And a big *crúbin* for thruppence to be pickin' while you're able.' " Kinky finished the line. "Mind you," she said, "I've not much use for *crúbins* myself. I never fancied the look of boiled pigs' feet. Now Cork *drúishin* . . . that's a different matter altogether, so."

Barry tried to hide his shudder. He'd once and only once tried the Cork City delicacy, a sausage made of a mixture of pigs' blood, cows' blood, and oatmeal. The smell of it had almost turned his stomach.

"Not everybody likes it," said Kinky with a sniff, and Barry knew his revulsion had not gone unnoticed.

"You've done a wonderful job," he said.

"Aye, so," she said. "I've still one plate to get." She bustled away.

Barry wandered out of the tent. Rows of wood-and-canvas

folding deck chairs were lined up from the side of the tent to the back fence. An open space lay between the house, tent, and chairs.

He noticed something at the far end of the garden, near Arthur's kennel under the chestnut tree. An irregular shape covered in a tarpaulin. "Any idea what that is, Willy?"

The barman stopped polishing a glass. "That lump?"

"Yes."

"No idea and don't you go near it, Doc. Seamus Galvin brought it over. It's to be a surprise for Doctor O'Reilly."

"Oh," said Barry, almost tripping over one of the guy ropes. As he struggled to regain his balance, he was jolted from behind.

"Aaarf," said Arthur happily, wrapping his front legs round Barry's thigh, humping away, and panting like a steamroller with an overloaded boiler.

"Gerroff, Arthur. Sit, you great lummox."

Arthur looked baffled, paused, and subsided onto the grass, tail flattening wide swaths through the vegetation, tongue lolling.

"That's better," Barry said. "Now behave yourself."

He turned and started to walk back to the house. From behind he heard a hissing like a pit full of vipers followed by a sudden yelp. Barry spun on his heel. Lady Macbeth, back arched, tail fluffed, pupils fully dilated despite the bright sunlight, made what must have been her second attack on Arthur Guinness's nose. Her paw, claws unsheathed, flashed forward in a rapier thrust that drew a howl from Arthur and blood from his nose. Arthur put his tail between his legs and slunk off towards his kennel, only looking back over his shoulder to Barry with an expression that said, "Why you put up with that hellion is beyond me."

"It's a tough old life, Arthur," Barry said, and as the dog wandered away, Lady Macbeth deflated and started to wash. Barry heard the back gate creak and looked up to see the guests of honour: Seamus, Maureen, and Barry Fingal Galvin.

Seamus wore his best suit. Rusty black pants that by the creases had been freshly ironed, a shirt with a collar, and a tie that Barry recognized as bearing the regimental colours of the Brigade of Guards. He doubted that Seamus had served with that regiment. Seamus's attempt to look dapper was only partly spoiled by a flat cloth cap perched at a rakish angle on the top of his pear-shaped head.

Maureen was having difficulty walking on the soft grass. Her high heels sank into the earth with every step. She wore a yellow, pleated skirt, pale green blouse, floppy hat, and white gloves. She pushed a perambulator, a massive contraption, high sprung on tall, spoked wheels, the sort of vehicle that had been popular with the nannies of the Victorian upper classes.

"Good afternoon, sir." Seamus touched the peak of his cloth cap.

"Seamus. Maureen." Barry moved to the pram. "And how's wee Barry Fingal?"

"Grand, so he is," said Maureen, her green eyes smiling fondly into the vehicle. "Growing like a weed."

"Mother of God, would you look at that?" said Seamus, taking in the contents of the marquee with one all-encompassing sweep of his arm. "Feast fit for a king."

"Can I get you something, Maureen?" Barry asked.

"I'll see to it," Seamus said, gaze fixed on the aluminium kegs, tongue tip flickering over his lips. "I might just have a wee wet myself."

Maureen wobbled. Barry took her arm to steady her and guided her to the nearest deck chair. "Sit down, Maureen."

She sat, steadying her hat with one hand, holding the pram's handle with the other. Barry Fingal gurgled happily as she rocked him. "It's a great day for the party," she said, looking round the garden, gaze resting for a moment on the mysterious tarpaulin-covered lump. "Where's himself?" she asked.

As if her question had worked to summon Doctor Fingal Flahertie O'Reilly, the big Rover pulled into the back lane and juddered to a halt. O'Reilly opened the passenger door and helped Sonny out. "Open the back gate," O'Reilly roared.

Arthur Guinness stuck his head out of his doghouse. Lady Macbeth, who had perched herself on the kennel's roof, leant forward and dabbed at the dog's nose. He retreated inside. She washed.

Barry opened the gate. "How are you, Sonny?" he asked, as O'Reilly guided the old man into the garden. His grey hair was neatly combed, and his weathered cheeks had not the slightest hint of the ominous blue tinge that Barry had noticed the first time he met Sonny.

"I am very well, thank you, sir," Sonny said.

"You'll be even better when you take the weight off your feet," O'Reilly said, helping Sonny to sit in a chair beside Maureen Galvin. "Do you know Mrs. Galvin?"

"I've not had the pleasure," Sonny said, starting to rise, hand automatically rising to doff a hat.

O'Reilly put a hand on Sonny's shoulder. "Sit down. You've not all your strength back yet."

Sonny sat. "Forgive me," he said, making Barry smile at the man's old-world gallantry.

"This is Sonny," O'Reilly told Maureen.

"The motorcar man?"

"Indeed," Sonny said, lowering his head in a short bow.

"Afternoon, Doctor sir." Seamus Galvin appeared, balancing a glass of lemonade on a plate piled high with sandwiches in one hand, clutching an already half-empty pint of Guinness in the other. "Here you are, love." He gave the plate to Maureen and looked up at O'Reilly. "I never got you thanked proper, sir, for getting them Belfast folks to take the rocking ducks. Could I buy you a jar?"

"No," said O'Reilly, with a huge grin, "I've a thirst like the Sahara desert. You can buy me two." He headed for the tent with Seamus, paused, and said to Barry, "Would you look after Sonny?"

Barry nodded. "Can I get you something, Sonny?"

Sonny nodded and then wrinkled his nose. "After the food in that hospital . . . ," he looked at Maureen's plate, ". . . a bit of that ham would be much appreciated, and do you think I'd be allowed a small glass of stout?"

"Of course," Barry said. "I'll get them."

By the time he'd brought Sonny his plate and glass, the party had grown. Kinky had been right when she'd said she'd have to be ready to feed five thousand. The garden was filling up. Groups of women arrived, each lady dressed in her Sunday best. Barry had to jostle past knots of men, some of whom he recognized as members of the Ballybucklebo Highlanders.

Mr. Coffin, red nose bright in the sunlight, stood deep in conversation with Constable Mulligan, who was in civilian dress.

"It was quite upsetting," Barry heard Mr. Coffin say. "When the sexton dropped the first shovelful onto the casket, he uncovered a skull in the pile of earth that had been excavated from the grave." He shook his head ponderously. "It was in a family plot, you see."

"A skull?" Constable Mulligan asked, eyes wide.

"The sexton, and I must say he did it very dexterously, nudged the thing with his spade. It rolled down the pile into the grave and rattled off the mahogany coffin lid."

"My God." Constable Mulligan shuddered.

"Now you'd expect old bones to shatter. . . ."

"I'll take your word for it, Mr. Coffin."

"Oh, indeed, you'd expect them to, but the skull just bounced twice and sat there. All the mourners peered down, and you'll never believe what the recently departed's brother said."

Barry saw just the hint of a smile on the undertaker's face.

"What did he say?"

"'I think that was a bit of Aunt Bertha that was put in here ten years ago. She's sticking the pace bravely, so she is.'"

The constable gasped, but then he must have seen Mr. Coffin's smile broaden. "You're pulling my leg?"

"Oh, no, it's perfectly true." He managed to make a dry tittering noise.

My goodness, Barry thought, perhaps that stuff O'Reilly had suggested, the Saint John's wort tea, *had* helped to cheer up the lugubrious Coffin. Barry nodded in greeting at the two, both now openly laughing, as he forced his way forward. A thought struck him. What he had just heard had to be the best example ever of what could be called, quite literally, graveyard humour.

He'd read that the best parties were the ones that just happened. Judging by the length of the queue leading into the tent, the standing-room-only crush in the garden, and the still swelling number of new arrivals, this one was happening with a vengeance.

The bowlegged Mr. O'Hara, who'd given Barry a lift on his tractor, was in animated conversation with Francis Xavier MacMhuir—Barry stumbled over the Gaelic pronunciation—Murdoch. By the way the man was yelling to be heard over the din, there was little doubt that his sore throat was better.

Adult voices, laughter, and children's piping tones mingled in one ever-swelling drone. Someone tapped him on the shoulder. He turned to see the open country face of Jack Mills.

"How's about you, Barry?" Jack said.

"What the hell are you doing here?"

"Your boss was up in the Royal today. He was having a crack with Sir Donald Cromie. I was there and got introduced. Seems O'Reilly saw me play rugby for Ulster. He asked me if I was your Jack Mills and said I should come on down to the party."

"I'm delighted," Barry said, clapping his friend on the shoulder.

Jack adopted the tones of John Wayne. "Ah'm purty pleased mahself, pilgrim, but a man could die of thirst in this here corral."

Barry laughed. "Come on then. Let's get a drink."

"Mighty fine, pardner." Jack lowered one shoulder and started to clear a way toward the tent. He stopped. "Good Lord." He had reverted to his own voice. "What in the name of God is that?" He pointed at a woman making her way in the opposite direction.

Barry had to look twice before he recognized Maggie Mac-Corkle. Her skirt was ankle length, but instead of being its usual sombre black it was scarlet.

"It's like Mammy's petticoat in *Gone with the Wind*," Jack said.

As usual Maggie wore layers of cardigans, each one buttoned only at the neck. All were of different colours and resembled the icing on a layered sponge cake. The entire ensemble was crowned by a hat of such dizzying proportions that Barry thought it could have been left over from Cecil Beaton's costumes for the Ascot scene in *My Fair Lady*. And as ever, there were fresh flowers in the hatband, this time a bunch of orange lilies. She carried a bundle in one hand, and Lady Macbeth under an arm.

"There you are, Doctor Laverty," she said as she arrived. "Here." She thrust the cat into his arms. "This wee one doesn't like the crowds. You should take her inside."

"All right, Maggie," Barry said.

"Now," she said, waving her bundle, "I'll just go and put this plum cake on the food table." She scanned the crowd. "Someone said that oul' goat Sonny was here. Have you noticed him about the place?"

"He's sitting under that apple tree," Barry said, distracted by a squirming Lady Macbeth.

"Right," said Maggie, "and would you for God's sake get that wee scared moggie away to hell out of here. This is a Ballybucklebo ta-ta-ta-ra, and it's not hardly even got started yet."

28

Multitudes, Multitudes

O'Reilly, pint glass in hand, beamed down to where Jeannie Kennedy was playing on the grass with the pants-wetting Colin Brown and his bride-to-be, Susan MacAfee. "How are you, Jeannie?" O'Reilly asked. Her smile widened. "Grand," he said, turning to Jack. "See how your appendix abscess made out, Doctor Mills?"

"I hardly recognized her," said Jack.

O'Reilly patted Jeannie on the head. "Come on," he said to Barry, "I want to hear what's happening with Maggie and Sonny." O'Reilly winked at Barry and sidled across the lawn. Barry followed. They stood behind the chestnut tree, unashamedly eavesdropping.

"I have to thank you for looking after my dogs, Miss MacCorkle."

"It was no bother. I'll keep then 'til you get home, so I will."

"That would be most generous."

Barry noticed that neither Maggie nor Sonny would look each other in the eye. Sonny cleared his throat.

"Are you sure you're all right, Sonny?" Maggie asked, the concern in her voice plain to hear.

"Just a little tickle. A frog in my throat."

"I hope so. No wonder you near caught your death, living in that old car."

Sonny sat stiffly. "It suits me, and I'll not pay that despicable man, Bishop."

Maggie's toothless grin was as radiant as the sunlight that streamed through the tree's leaves.

"And what's so amusing, Miss MacCorkle?"

Maggie chuckled. "You'll not need to. Pay him, that is."

Sonny frowned. "Why not?"

"Because, and don't ask me how it happened, Councillor Bishop started fixing the roof yesterday."

Sonny's eyes widened. "I'll not pay. Not a penny."

O'Reilly stepped forward. "You'll not have to, Sonny."

"Doctor O'Reilly, I don't understand." Sonny tried to rise.

"Sit where you are."

"But . . ."

"The worm," said O'Reilly, "has turned. Bertie Bishop came to see me a few days ago. Said he'd had a change of heart, he was sorry you were so sick, and he'd fix your roof for free."

"I don't know what to say." Sonny looked from O'Reilly to Maggie and back to O'Reilly.

"I do," said Maggie, leaning over and planting a great wet kiss on Sonny's forehead. "And if you'd ask me as nicely as you did all those years ago . . . I'll say 'I do' properly when the reverend asks the question, so I will."

Sonny took Maggie's hand in his arthritic grip and raised it to his lips. He smiled up at O'Reilly, who turned to Barry and said, "This calls for a jar. Come on." He lowered his voice. "I think that pair of turtledoves would like to be left alone."

"Right," said Barry, nodding to Jack.

"What was that all about?" Jack asked, as the trio made its way back toward the tent.

Barry smiled. "The Lord and Doctor Fingal Flahertie O'Reilly both move in mysterious ways their wonders to perform. It's a long story. . . ."

His explanation was interrupted by a ferocious wailing. Barry swung round to see Seamus Galvin, bag under his arm, drones over his shoulder, cheeks puffed, foot tapping in time to the lively notes of "The Rakes of Mallow." Arthur Guinness sat at Seamus's feet. The dog had his head thrown back at an impossible angle. His eyes were tightly shut, and his ululations quavered and rose and fell. In the space at the house end of the lawn, men now coatless and women with their Sunday hats cast aside had formed a set and were dancing a reel.

"Jesus," said O'Reilly, "it's like 'The Galway Races.'" He sang in a surprisingly melodious baritone. "'And it's there you'll see the pipers and the fiddlers competing; the nimble-footed dancers and they trippin' on the daisies.'" As O'Reilly sang, Constable Mulligan, perhaps less nimble than the rest, managed to get his boots entangled and went down in a heap. "Must have been a big daisy," said O'Reilly with a grin. He finished his pint. "Who needs another one?"

"Me," said Jack. Barry shook his head.

"Come on then, Mills," said O'Reilly. He glanced at the yodelling dog. "Arthur'll be thirsty with all that singing. I'll see if Willy the barman has a can of Smithwicks."

Barry stood and watched the dancers.

"Doctor, sir."

Barry turned to see the bucktoothed, ginger-topped Donal Donnelly grinning like a mooncalf. "Could I have a wee word, Doctor sir?" He had to shout to be heard over the row of the pipes, the bellowing of the dog.

"Certainly." Barry's mouth fell open. Donal was holding tightly to Julie MacAteer's hand.

"Julie and me here wanted to say thank you to you and Doctor O'Reilly for being so decent."

"Don't tell me . . . ," Barry started.

Donal blushed to the roots of his ginger hair. "We couldn't afford to get wed," he said, scuffing his boots on the grass, "and Julie wouldn't tell nobody I was the daddy."

"So what happened to change things?"

Donal swallowed, his Adam's apple bobbing in his scrawny throat. "I won a wheen of money on Bluebird."

"So did Doctor O'Reilly, but that was a couple of weeks ago."

"It wasn't enough, but Julie here got a parcel of cash for severance from Councillor Bishop."

"I'm sure," she said with a wry smile, as she looked deeply into Barry's eyes, "I'm sure the doctors don't know anything about that."

"Not a thing," Barry said, wondering if he was blushing. He glanced away.

"Anyroad," said Donal, "I've a new job now. I'm labouring on Sonny's house for the councillor."

"So you're getting married," Barry said. "I'm delighted. And Doctor O'Reilly will be delighted too. There he is. You should go and tell him." Sometimes, he thought, the ends *do* justify the means. Sonny and Maggie. Julie and—hard to believe as it was—the bucktoothed Donal Donnelly. Neither pair would be together if O'Reilly, with Barry's complicity, hadn't broken the rules of confidentiality. Indeed, there wouldn't be a reason for this party at all if O'Reilly hadn't forced Councillor Bishop to buy Seamus Galvin's rocking ducks.

Barry watched Donal and Julie, still hand in hand, walk over to O'Reilly, who clapped Donal on the shoulder and whose cheerful "Bloody marvellous!" boomed over the end of the music.

Barry was pleased for the young couple, pleased for Maggie and Sonny. A Frank Sinatra song buzzed in his head: "Everybody's hand in hand, swingin' down the lane." He looked at his empty sherry glass. Damn it, it was a beautiful day. Everyone was having a hell of a time. He'd make the most of it.

He wandered back to the tent, acknowledging the greetings of the partygoers. It was a pleasant feeling to know he was becoming accepted in the village. A fiddle started to play. Someone had a pennywhistle. A large man rattled out the percussion on a *bodhrán*, the Irish drum of parchment stretched over a circular frame. Barry recognized the tune, "Planxty Gordon." He hummed a few off-key notes as he waited for the queue to reach the bar table.

"Another sherry, Doctor?" Willy asked.

"No. I'll have a pint."

"Good man, my da," said Willy, building the Guinness. "Get you round that. It'll put hairs on your chest, so it will." He handed Barry the straight glass. "One and six for your water please, sir," Willy said, with a wink. He handed Barry a can of Smithwick's. "Would you see to Arthur, sir?"

Barry paid, took the can, sipped the bitter stout, and made his way back into the sunlight.

Seamus Galvin had taken the *bodhrán* from its owner and was beating out a fierce tattoo. The buzz of conversation died. "Ladies and gentlemen," he yelled. "Ladies and gennlemen." He wobbled and grinned. "I'd like to call upon our senior medical man, Doctor Fingal Flahertie O'Reilly, for a song."

Cheers and yells of "Go on, Doctor!" rang out as Barry stooped over Arthur's bowl and poured the beer. Arthur eyed Barry's pants but must have decided that as the day was warm he'd settle for his second drink.

Barry looked up to see O'Reilly, standing, one leg before him, hands gripping the lapels of his tweed jacket, head thrown back.

"I'm a freeborn man of the travelling people. Got no fixed abode, with nomads I am numbered. Country lanes and byways were always my ways. Never fancied being lumbered . . ."

And who in their right mind, Barry thought, would try to lumber you, Fingal O'Reilly, with anything?

Seamus Galvin was at his elbow. "You're up next, Doc."

"Oh, no," Barry said, trying to back away. "Not me."

"Yes, you. You'll have to do your party piece."

"But I can't sing."

"Doesn't matter. We like a good recimatation, so we do. You're a learned man. I'll bet you do 'The Boy Stood on the Burning Deck' or maybe 'The Man from God Knows Where.'"

"Well, I—"

"Great," said Seamus. "Your man's near done."

". . . Your rambling days are over." O'Reilly finished to a chorus of cheers and whistles.

As soon as the row quieted down, Seamus marched Barry to the centre of the cleared space. "Silence for our other doctor. Young Doctor Barry Laverty."

Barry looked round the circle of expectant faces. Cissie Sloan smiled at him and said, mopping her brow with a hanky, "Warm today, Doctor." If she was no longer feeling cold, her thyroid medication must be starting to work. Barry didn't recognize a blonde with Jack, but his hand rested on her hip at a level just slightly below the polite. He squeezed and she giggled.

"Get on with it, Doctor Laverty," Jack yelled and raised his glass. Barry glanced helplessly at O'Reilly, who stood there, face more florid than usual, pipe belching smoke.

Someone started to sing "Why are we waiting? Why-hy are we waiting?" And other voices took up the refrain.

Barry held up both hands. "All right. All right."

The singing died.

He cleared his throat. "'The Charge of the Light Brigade,'" he announced, and to his amazement, hardly stumbling at all, he recited the poem.

When he'd finished, applause swelled, and he accepted a series of good-natured slaps on his back. Someone thrust a fresh pint into his hand.

"You," said O'Reilly, "in the immortal but hardly grammatical words of my old boss, Doctor Flanagan, 'done very good, son. Very good indeed.'"

And Barry let himself bask in the glow. He was just about to put his pint to his lips when Kinky, whom he hadn't noticed approaching, whispered, "Would you come into the house, Doctor Laverty? There's someone wants to see you, so."

"Could they not wait?"

"Ah, no. I can tell that this one is an urgent case. And they particularly asked for yourself."

"Very well." He handed his glass to a grinning Jack Mills. "Look after that for me. I've a case to see."

Jack's accent was pure American midwest. "Neither sleet, nor rain, nor heat of sun . . . not even a pint of stout going flat . . . can keep them from their appointed rounds."

"Bugger off," said Barry with a smile, as he followed Kinky.

"In the surgery, sir."

Barry grunted, walked down the hall, opened the surgery door—and stopped dead.

"Hello, Barry," Patricia said. "I thought you were going to phone me."

Barry's mouth hung wide open. He remembered a line he'd read somewhere: "If you find a jaw on the carpet—it's mine."

"You did, you know." Her voice was deep, just as he remembered. "You said you'd call."

"I know," he said, trying to collect himself, wondering if he was shocked because she was there or because her presence gave the proof to Kinky's claim of being fey. Whatever it was, he was delighted to see her. "I thought you were being polite . . . letting me down gently."

She shook her head, dark hair swinging, almond eyes laughing. "No. I meant exactly what I said. I wasn't sure that I was ready to get deeply involved."

"Oh."

"And," she said levelly, "before you start getting any notions, I'm still not sure."

"Then why are you here?" Barry felt his fists clench. Dear God, but she was lovely.

"Because . . ." She limped close to him and looked into his eyes. "There's something about you, Barry Laverty, and don't ask me what it is, that I think I'd like to get to know better."

"Really?" His grip relaxed. "Do you mean it?"

"I'd not be here if I didn't. And it just seemed that if you wouldn't phone me, then I should come and see you."

He took her hand. "I'm so glad you did." Jack had been right, Barry thought a bit smugly. He determined not to rush things now, much as he wanted to take her away, to have her all to himself. He said, "And you picked the right day. There's a bit of a party going on."

"I'd never have guessed," she said with a smile, as the sounds of the pipes, Arthur's *oooowl,* and a burst of applause echoed from the back of the house. "Can I come?"

"In a minute." He pulled her to him and kissed her in O'Reilly's surgery, beside the rolltop desk, the swivel chair, the patients' seat with the uneven legs, the old examining table. He was kissing her in a room that in three weeks had become as familiar to him as his old bed-room back in his folks' house in Bangor. And he might as well have been kissing her on the far side of the moon, so lost was he in her kiss.

Their lips parted. She moved back. "Now," she said, and he no-ticed that she was, like himself, a little breathless. "What about that party?"

"Follow me," he said, and still holding her hand, he led her through the house and into the kitchen where Kinky was lifting yet another tray of pastries from the oven.

"Mrs. Kincaid, I'd like you to meet Patricia Spence."

"We met at the front door, so." Kinky put the tray on the counter and shook off her oven mitts. "Nice to meet you, Miss Spence. Now, I've work to do, so run along with the pair of you."

"Right," said Barry, heading for the back door. Barry looked from Kinky to Patricia and back to Kinky. He saw something in her eyes, something unknowable, and he knew that whether it was second sight or woman's intuition he understood that she'd been right all along. It *would* be all right. He tugged on Patricia's hand. "What can I get you from the bar?" he said, holding the back door open.

He barely noticed Lady Macbeth slip past him out into the sunlit back garden.

29

Happy Days Are Here Again

Barry forced his way to the drinks queue. "Sorry about the scrum," he said. "What would you like?"

"Beer, please."

"If we ever get to the head of the queue," Barry said, watching two men who were in a heated argument blocking the further progress of those waiting behind.

"Not at all, Sammy. It's my turn to pay."

"Your head's cut. You bought the last ones, so you did."

"I never did."

"Did too, you great glipe."

"D'you wanna step out of this here tent and call me a glipe?"

"Ah, for God's sake, your mother wears army boots."

O'Reilly, stripped down to his rolled-up shirtsleeves, appeared and thrust his way to the head of the line. He grabbed each of the belligerent parties by a shoulder and roared, "You, you daft buggers, quit your argy-bargy. If you want to fight, get to hell out of my garden, or else one of you pay up and both of you shut up." His voice rose by what Barry thought must have been ten decibels. "And then get to hell out of the way before all these other folks die of thirst."

"That's Doctor O'Reilly," Barry said to Patricia.

"Is he really such an ogre?"

Barry shook his head as O'Reilly roared, "Pint, Barry, and what's your friend having?"

"It's not your turn," the man who would have been next in line complained.

O'Reilly did not dignify the remark with a reply. He fixed the complainant with a glare that Barry thought would have done justice to the mythical basilisk, whose glance could turn a man to stone. The protester blushed and muttered, "Sorry, sir. I didn't recognize yourself."

"Rank," O'Reilly roared, "has its privileges. Now, Willy. Two pints, and what for your friend, Barry?"

"A beer," Barry yelled.

"A beer," O'Reilly echoed. "No, you goat. A pint, not one of those piddly little glasses." He juggled three pint glasses between his hands and drove a way through to Barry and Patricia. "Here you are." He gave each a glass.

"Fingal, this is Patricia Spence."

O'Reilly smiled at her and extended his hand. "She's far too good for the likes of you, Laverty. How do you do, Miss Spence?"

She took his hand. "I'm very well, thanks."

"Good," said O'Reilly, waving his free hand in a circle. "And what do you think of the party?"

"Very nice," she said.

"I'll tell you," said O'Reilly, lowering half of his pint in one swallow, "parties are like those rockets the Americans and Russians fire into space. Once they leave the launching pad they either soar for a few moments, then wobble and blow up, or with ever-increasing speed they roar off into the ionosphere, out into space, and head for the stars."

"I think that's called escape velocity," Barry offered.

"It is," said Patricia. "A rocket has to achieve a critical rate of speed to overcome the gravitational pull of the earth."

"Patricia's an engineer," Barry explained.

"Is that a fact?" O'Reilly remarked. "Good for you. Escape velocity? Well, the last time I saw Seamus Galvin he was definitely flying, but poor old Mr. Coffin's succumbed to earth's pull. He's asleep in the vegetable patch."

"I thought he was a Pioneer," Barry said.

"He is, but I've a notion that Constable Mulligan has been spicing Coffin's tea up a bit."

"It was only the men from Crossmaglen that put whiskey in my tea?" Barry enquired, in the words of an Ulster song.

"Probably vodka," O'Reilly said. "He'd be less likely to taste that. Anyway. It's cheered him up, and the rest of the assorted multitude seem to be having a grand old time. Just look at them."

Barry surveyed the scene.

Seamus Galvin swayed gently in time with the music. He and a couple more Ballybucklebo Highlanders were piping for sets of dancers. Not a man among them wore a jacket or a tie. The fiddler and his small ensemble stood closer to the house providing the backup for half a dozen men who, arms round each other's shoulders, were well on their way into what Barry vaguely recognized as one of the later verses of "The Rocky Road to Dublin."

Doreen stood close by, belting away with her spoon on Hughey's tin tray. Barry heard her yell, "Do you want another pint?" And Hughey's reply, "What the hell are you going on about, woman? I want another pint."

Sonny and Maggie were back in their deck chairs under the apple tree.

"Begod," said O'Reilly, nodding toward them, "the pair of them are like Adam and Eve in the Garden."

"All we need is the serpent," Barry said.

"I didn't invite Councillor Bishop and he's the only snake St. Paddy didn't drive out of our wee country," O'Reilly remarked, looking wistfully at his now empty glass. "Now, Barry," he said, "before the worthy Seamus drinks himself utterly beyond redemption, I think it's time we got any formalities over and done with."

"What formalities?"

"It's the Galvins' going-to-America party. Someone should say a few words."

"Right," said Barry, glancing to the tarpaulin-covered heap at the end of the garden and remembering that Willy had said it was a surprise gift for O'Reilly. "What do you want me to do?"

"Get hold of that friend of yours, Mills. Between the pair of you, take one of the smaller tables from the tent and cart it up to the house end of the garden." He eyed Barry's glass. "And give that to me. You'll be too busy to drink it."

"Right," said Barry, handing over his drink and looking around for Jack Mills.

"Now, Miss Spence . . ."

"It's Patricia."

"Patricia . . . come with me," said O'Reilly. "I want you to meet Arthur Guinness. Then I'll find you a chair."

Barry found Jack, who apologized profusely for having misplaced Barry's earlier drink. From the flush on his friend's cheeks Barry reckoned he had a fair idea where the pint had gone. He explained to Jack what was required, pried him away from the blonde, and did his best to carry out O'Reilly's instructions.

They lugged one of the smaller tables to the end of the garden to make an improvised dais in front of the rows of chairs. O'Reilly appeared, holding Kinky by the arm and would hear none of her protestations. "There you are, Kinky Kincaid," he said, "and there you'll stay." Jack's blonde and Patricia had deck chairs of honour beside Maureen in a chair and Barry Fingal Galvin in his pram. Jeannie Kennedy and the want-to-be-weds, Susan MacAfee and Colin Brown, found spots on the grass.

"Would the Ballybucklebo Men's Choral Society care to join us?" O'Reilly roared. The fiddling and whistling stopped, and the singers drifted across the lawn. "Nip over and bring Seamus, will you, Barry?"

Barry skirted the apparently tireless dancers. "Seamus." He tugged at Seamus's sleeve. "Seamus."

Seamus stopped his pipes and raised a questioning eyebrow.

"Doctor O'Reilly would like everybody to gather round up there."

"Right, sir." Seamus giggled. "I'll see to it."

From the corner of his eye Barry caught a glimpse of Lady Macbeth sidling into the now empty marquee; then he made his way to where the entire congregation stood rank upon rank, waiting expectantly for the next part of the proceedings. Now that the piping had stopped, all that could be heard was a gentle murmur of conversation, the clattering of a spoon on a tin tray, and a woman's voice shouting, "The doctor's going to say a few words." To which came the audible reply, "I don't give a bugger what the oul' fart's going to say, I want another pint."

Barry jostled through the throng and stood behind Patricia's chair. He put a hand on her shoulder and she turned and smiled up at him.

"Here," said Jack from behind the blonde's chair. "Look what I found." He handed Barry a pint of stout.

"Thanks, mate." Barry took the glass and watched as O'Reilly hoisted his bulk onto the unsteady table. He spread his arms to his sides, hands cocked up, fingers splayed. "Ladies and gentlemen," he said. "Ladies and gentlemen, we are here today to bid farewell to three of Ballybucklebo's more illustrious citizens. Seamus and Maureen and wee Barry Fingal are off to start a new life in the New World."

"Will Seamus be working?" a voice enquired from the depths of the crowd.

"I will, so I will," Seamus yelled back.

"Mother of God," said the voice, "miracles still do happen."

"Now," said O'Reilly, "you all know I'm a man of few words—"

"And the Pope's a Presbyterian," a man called.

"Watch it, Colin McCartney," O'Reilly said. "I have my eye on you."

"How many of him do you see, Doctor sir?" someone else asked.

Barry laughed long and hard with the rest of the crowd, but stole a look at O'Reilly's nose. Florid as ever. The big man was taking the ribbing in good part.

When the hubbub died down, O'Reilly continued. "All right, fair play. But all I want to say today is every one of you that has a glass to lift, hoist it with me and wish the Galvins a safe journey and a grand new life." He held his own glass aloft. "To the Galvins."

"The Galvins" echoed back from the crowd.

"May God bless them and all who sail in them," Fergus O'Malley roared and sat down with a heavy bump.

"Jesus," said O'Reilly. "There's one at every hooley that wants to be the centre of attraction. If this was a wake, Fergus wouldn't be happy unless he was the corpse."

"Corpse? Where?" asked a clearly befuddled Mr. Coffin, just awakened from his slumbers.

"Never mind," said Constable Mulligan, taking the undertaker's arm. "Just sit you down there on the grass like a good gentleman."

"Come on, Seamus. Speech!" Donal Donnelly shouted.

"Speech! Speech!"

O'Reilly beckoned to Seamus. "Up here, boyo, and give us a few words of wisdom." O'Reilly leapt from the table.

"Right." Seamus had to be helped to climb up. He swayed, and Barry immediately thought back to the afternoon in the Mucky Duck following the birth of the Galvins' baby.

"Said it before . . . an' I'll say it again. Best couple of doctors in Ireland. Best village in Ireland. Best country in the whole world." Seamus's voice cracked.

"Whoops," said O'Reilly, who had moved beside Barry. "Next thing he'll say is . . ."

"I don't want to go to America," Seamus said, a tear dripping from one eye. "Don't want to go at all. Leave all my friends. . . ."

"Told you," said O'Reilly.

"We're going. The week after next," Maureen announced. "Doctor O'Reilly's holding the cash, and the tickets are ordered. Me and Barry Fingal's going anyhow."

"And I'm coming with you, love," Seamus announced, blowing her a sloppy kiss.

"You've a job to do right now, Seamus Galvin," Maureen said, handing her husband a parcel.

"Right. Right. Nearly forgot." Seamus held the parcel over his head. "This here's for Doctor Laverty." The crowd applauded. "You'se folks is very lucky he came to work with Doctor O'Reilly."

"Hear, hear!" yelled Cissie Sloan.

Barry knew he was grinning fit to bust.

"Go and get your present," Patricia whispered.

Barry, glass in hand, walked to the table.

"Here you are, Doc." Seamus bent forward and handed Barry the gift.

"Open it," said Seamus.

Barry ripped off the paper. Inside was a burnished aluminium box. When he opened the lid he could see it was full of beautiful, hand-tied flies. He knew he should say something, but a lump was in his throat. He nodded and turned away. He felt he was being ungracious, but didn't trust himself to speak.

He took a deep breath before facing the crowd and saying, "Thank you, Seamus and Maureen. Thank you all." He struggled to find something more appropriate to say, but his thoughts were interrupted by a sharp, deep bark and a screech that sounded as if there were a banshees' convention in O'Reilly's back garden.

Lady Macbeth tore past, made a beeline for the chestnut tree, and went up the trunk in a white blur. Hot on her heels, Arthur Guinness galloped past, bashing into Barry's legs and knocking him arse over teakettle. He felt the dampness of his spilled drink soaking into his pants. It wouldn't be Ballybucklebo, he thought, if that bloody dog weren't making a mess of my trousers. He felt O'Reilly pulling on one arm. "Up with you, m'son."

Barry struggled to his feet.

"Do you know," said O'Reilly, "I thought she'd go too far one day. Stupid cat tried to claw his nose, and I reckon the Smithwick's gave him a bit of Dutch courage."

Seemingly unaware of the mayhem all around him, Seamus said, "One more thing. This here's a token of our undying esteem for Doctor O'Reilly." He jumped from the table and stood by the canvas-covered object. "I'd like for himself to open it."

"Go on, Fingal," Barry said. "Your turn."

As O'Reilly strode across the grass, Barry returned to stand by Patricia. She was laughing as she stared at his sodden pants. "I think that's what I find most interesting about you, Barry."

"What?"

"Your trousers. I've only ever seen you once in a clean pair."

Barry, feeling as confident as the cat-chasing Arthur Guinness, and for the same reason, laughed. But then he looked Patricia in the eyes and said, "And I'm the one who wears the trousers."

"We'll see about that," she said, but still smiled. She stood and kissed him. "Could you by any chance get away tonight? I'll cook you dinner."

He looked into her smile and saw the promise there. "Come hell or high water," he said. "And I'll wear a clean pair of pants."

"Can we come too?" Jack Mills asked.

"Not on your life," said Barry, laughing. He saw Arthur Guinness staring up into the branches of the chestnut. He watched

Kinky try to shoo the dog away and heard her calling, "Come on down now, you wee dote."

He heard Seamus say, "It's like one of those unveiling jobs that the queen does. You've to pull this rope here."

"This one?" O'Reilly asked, holding a piece of frayed hemp.

"The very fellah," said Seamus. "Now, on the count of three, Doctor. One . . ."

"Two," Barry roared in unison with everyone else. "Three."

O'Reilly tugged. The tarpaulin slithered to the ground, and there, revealed in all its garish splendour—three feet tall by three feet long, green head and yellow beak bright in the afternoon sunlight, brown saddle painted on its beige back—was a rocking duck.

"Holy Mother of God," said O'Reilly, as gasps of pure amazement rose all around. "It's a thing of beauty, Seamus."

"Give her a try," Seamus said, grabbing O'Reilly by the arm. "You sit on here."

O'Reilly straddled the rocking duck.

"Ride 'im, cowboy."

O'Reilly lowered himself, hesitated, and said, "I think I'd be a bit heavy for it." He dismounted, crossed the grass, lifted up Jeannie, and sat her in the saddle. She started to rock back and forth, laughing and fending off a line of children who were noisily demanding their turns.

"See," said a beaming Seamus, "I told you they'd go down a treat with the kiddies."

"You might just be right," said a thoughtful O'Reilly.

"Whoever bought them'll make a fortune," Seamus added.

Barry had no difficulty understanding why there was a hint of pallor in O'Reilly's nose. Barry wondered if his timing might be poor, but he left Patricia and walked up to O'Reilly. "Fingal?"

"What?"

"I don't suppose I—"

"Could have the night off?" O'Reilly stared hard at Patricia.

"That's right."

"Buy me a pint and I'll say yes."

"You're on." Barry started to head for the tent before the queue grew too long. He felt O'Reilly's hand on his arm and turned back.

"Take tomorrow off too. I can manage without you. Although I'd like you to stay here for the long haul . . . as an assistant . . . partner in a year."

Barry hung his head, looked back into the big man's brown eyes, and said, "I'd need to think about it, Fingal. I really would. But you know I might just do that."

"You think about it," said O'Reilly, "but for the love of Jesus, get me a pint like a good lad . . . and a Smithwick's for Arthur."

"I'll be back in a tick," Barry said to Patricia. Then he turned to make his way to the makeshift bar.

He waited his turn in the queue, knowing that although he was becoming accepted by most of the villagers, he hadn't yet attained O'Reilly's commanding presence or earned the right to go to the head of the line. Ah, well, he thought, they also serve who only stand and wait.

He glanced over to where Patricia was deep in conversation with O'Reilly. Sunlight dappled her hair, and her eyes were bright. She must have noticed him staring because she waved to him and smiled. He waved back. Right, he told himself, he'd get the drinks for O'Reilly and his daft dog; then he'd make his excuses and leave. With Patricia.

"Ahem?"

Barry turned.

Donal Donnelly stood there. "Ahem? Doc, I know you must have been thinking of something important . . . but the queue's moved a bit."

"What?"

"I think we could maybe get a wee bit closer to the bar."

"Right." Barry shuffled ahead. Something important? Nothing was more important to him at the moment than Patricia.

"So, sir," remarked Donal, "I was just thinking about that day you asked me for directions to Ballybucklebo. Do you remember?"

"Yes, I do." Indeed he remembered—the yellow gorse, the drooping fuschia, the blackbird's song, the instructions *not* to turn at the black-and-white cow, how anxious he'd been about his interview with Doctor O'Reilly, and how Donal had fled at the mere mention of the man's name. He'd not understood why Donal had pedalled away back then, but by God, he did now.

Donal nodded his head to indicate that the queue had moved on again. Barry took several paces forward.

Donal tilted his head to one side and said, "Can I ask you a wee question, sir?"

"Fire away."

"You've been here a fair while now. How do you like Ballybucklebo . . . and working for himself?"

"I like it fine," Barry said, without a moment's hesitation. He thought about the little, quiet village with its maypole, pub, and thatched cottages on the shores of Belfast Lough, and of course its inhabitants: Kinky, Donal, Julie MacAteer, Jeannie Kennedy, the Galvins, Maggie, and Sonny.

Barry was distracted by O'Reilly's laughter roaring through the softness of the Ulster summer evening. Doctor Fingal Flahertie O'Reilly, odd as two left feet, but Barry knew that if he himself were ever ill there was no one he'd rather have to look after him.

He smiled at O'Reilly and Patricia, and murmured to himself, "I don't think 'like' is the right word. I love it here." And Doctor Barry Laverty knew it was the truth.

AFTERWORD
by
Mrs. Kincaid

You'd think a poor Cork woman with himself, Doctor O'Reilly, and young Doctor Laverty to look after had nothing to do but sit here at the kitchen table writing out my recipes. I've been busier than a bee on a hot brick, so, keeping young Laverty in dry pants for the last month. Filling the stomachs of the Ballybucklebo Highlanders today would have used up all of the two loaves and five small fishes, and divil the twelve baskets of scraps would have been gathered up. But then my name's Kinky Kincaid, not Jesus Christ Almighty, and although Doctor O'Reilly says I work miracles in the kitchen he's an awful man for exaggeration . . . but I do love to cook, so.

I learnt it from my mother down in *Béal na mBláth*—that means "the mouth of flowers"—in West Cork . . . the very place that Michael Collins, God rest his soul, was shot. My ma learnt it from her ma.

Doctor O'Reilly says the old ways are going, and now that fellah, Patrick Taylor—that should be Padraic Mac an Tàillier, but he's an Ulsterman and doesn't have the *Gaeilge*—has started telling these stories about life here in Ulster, Doctor O'Reilly reckons it wouldn't hurt for me to pass on some of my recipes before they get lost too.

I told him I'd start with *crùbins*, but he says he doesn't think there be much market in America for pickled pigs' trotters. "Just,

Kinky," says he, "put down some of the ones you've learnt here in
Ulster and none of your *drishin*." My mouth waters thinking of it,
made in Cork City, a grand blood pudding, but Doctor O'Reilly
says the smell of it cooking would gag a maggot, so. Says he, "Once
the world gets your instructions you'll be as famous as that American woman, Julia Child."

"Och," says I, "what's fame but a plant that soon turns to ashes,
but a good full belly is a thing of beauty."

So here you are.

Barmbrack's first; that's from the Irish *aran breac*, "speckled
bread." It'd not be Halloween without it, and in it a wedding ring, a
silver coin, and a button for telling fortunes. Then there's wheaten
bread. Himself says the Americans call it soda bread. They can call
it what they like, so. It's still called "wheatie bread" up here in the
Wee North. I'll finish up with my liver paté. Now it's just possible
my ma's ma got the recipe from an Englishwoman, but that's no reason not to make the thing if it's really good . . . and it is, so.

I've given you the instructions the way I'd write them in Ulster,
but I've had a friend of mine who's been to the States give me the
American equivalent measures and I've stuck them in.

Ulster Recipes

BARMBRACK

1 pound sultanas (2 cups)
1 pound brown sugar (2 cups)
1 pound flour (4 cups)
1 pound raisins (2 cups)
3 cups milkless tea
3 eggs
3 level teaspoons baking powder
3 teaspoons mixed spice (optional)

Soak the fruit and sugar in the tea overnight. The next day, add alternately 1 pound flour and 3 beaten eggs. Finally add 3 level teaspoons baking powder and the dried fruit. If you like it spicy, add 3 teaspoons of mixed spice. Turn into 3 greased tins, and bake for 1½ hours in a slow oven (300° F). When cool, brush the top with melted honey to give a fine glaze.

Normally eaten toasted with butter. The traditional Ulster cook will use yeast, but this is an easier recipe.

WHEATEN BREAD

2½ cups whole wheat flour
1 tablespoon granulated sugar
1 teaspoon baking soda
1 teaspoon salt
1¾ cups buttermilk

Mix dry ingredients very thoroughly. Then add 1¾ cups of buttermilk to make a thick paste—not too dry. Turn it into a well-greased loaf tin. Bake at once at 400° F for 15 minutes until risen; then bake a further 45 minutes at 350° F. If top gets too brown, cover with parchment paper.

Eaten with butter or with chicken liver paté (as follows).

Chicken Liver Paté

1 onion, chopped
2 cloves garlic, chopped
6 ounces butter (1½ sticks)
12 ounces chicken liver (1½ cups)
½ teaspoon ground mace
2 tablespoon brandy
½ teaspoon dried thyme
salt
pepper

Fry onion and garlic with 2 ounces butter until soft. Add livers and simmer for 7 minutes until cooked but still pink. Liquidize, then blend in remaining butter, mace, brandy, and thyme. Add plenty of salt and pepper, then turn into dish. Keep cool until served. Spread on wheaten bread (see previous recipe), eat, die, and go to heaven.

Freezes well.

Source: Kate Taylor, home recipe.

So there you are. Try making them, and when they're done, eat up however little much is in it. I just threw this next one in for a bit of a laugh. It's what I heard some English Professor call "black humour."

Irish Potato Famine Soup

Take a gallon of water, and boil the bejasus out of it until it's very, *very* strong.

Now that's enough for tonight. I'm getting the writer's cramp and I'm no great fist with a pen, so. But if that Taylor fellah ever gets round to telling more stories about Ballybucklebo, maybe I'll give you a few more recipes.

Enjoy the recipes here, and if you're having a wee glass of *uisce beatha* with them, I wish you *míle sláinte*.

MRS. KINKY KINCAID,
Housekeeper to
Doctor Fingal Flahertie O'Reilly, M.B., B.Ch., B.A.O.
1, Main Street
Ballybucklebo
County Down
Northern Ireland

GLOSSARY

The Ulster dialect, properly called Ulster-Scots, is rich and colourful but can be confusing. In my mind I hear the expressions used by my characters as clearly as if I were living back in the north of Ireland; I was, after all, immersed in the northern speech patterns for thirty years. For those unfamiliar with the idiom, however, I have appended this short glossary.

acting the goat: Behaving foolishly.

apples and pears: Cockney rhyming slang for stairs.

argy-bargy: Voluble disagreement.

arse: Backside (impolite).

away off and chase yourself: Go away.

away off and feel your head: You're being stupid.

away on: I don't believe you.

banshee: Female spirit whose moaning foretells death.

barmbrack: Speckled bread (see Mrs. Kincaid's recipes, page 340).

bashtoon: Bastard.

beagle's gowl: Very long way; the distance over which the cry of a beagle can be heard.

bigger fish to fry: More important matters to attend to.

bit my head off: Expressed anger by shouting or being very curt.

bloater: Salted and smoked herring.

blow you out: Tell you to go away.

bodhrán: Irish. Pronounced "bowron." A circular handheld drum.

boke: Vomit.

bollocks: Testicles (impolite). May be used as an expression of vehement disagreement or to describe a person you disapprove of: for example, "He's a right bollocks."

bonnet: Hood of a car.

both legs the same length: Standing about uselessly.

bowsey: Dublin slang, drunkard.

boys-a-boys, boys-a-dear: Expressions of amazement.

brass neck: Impertinence, chutzpah.

bravely: Feeling well.

buck eejit: Imbecile.

bun in the oven: Pregnant (impolite).

caubeen: Traditional Irish bonnet.

céili: Irish. Pronounced "kaylee." Party, usually with music and dancing.

chiseller: Dublin slang, small child.

clabber: Glutinous mess of mud, or mud and cow clap.

colloguing: Chatting about trivia.

cow's lick: Tuft of hair that sticks up, or hair slicked over to one side.

cracker: Excellent (see also *wheeker*).

craking on: Talking incessantly.

crúibins: Irish. Pronounced "crubeen." Boiled pigs' feet, served cold and eaten with vinegar.

cure, wee: Hair of the dog.

dab hand: Skilled at.

damper: Device for restricting the flow of air to a coal or turf fire to slow the rate of burning.

dander: Literally, horse dandruff. Used to signify either a short leisurely walk or anger. For example, "He really got my dander up."

divil: Devil.

divil the bit: None. For example, "He's divil the bit of sense." He's stupid.

doddle: A short distance or an easy task.

dote: Something adorable.

dote on: Worship.

do with the price of corn: Irrelevant.

drill-the-dome boys: Medical slang, neurosurgeons. See also *Nutcrackers.*

drouth, raging: Pronounced "drewth." Alcoholic.

drúishin: Irish. Pronounced "drisheen." Dish made of cows' blood, pigs' blood, and oatmeal. A Cork City delicacy.

dulse: A seaweed that when dried is eaten like chewing gum.

eejit: Idiot.

egg-bound hen: A hen with an egg stuck in the oviduct that cannot be laid. Applied to a person, it suggests extreme distress.

fag: Cigarette.

fall off the perch: Die.

Fenians: Catholics (pejorative).

Field, the: A place where Orange Lodges and bands congregate after the Twelfth of July parade.

finagle: Achieve by cunning or dubious means.

fit to be tied: Very angry.

flying: Drunk.

get on one's wick: Get on one's nerves.

give over: Stop it.

glipe, great: Stupid or very stupid person.

gobshite: Dublin slang used pejoratively about a person. Literally, dried nasal mucus.

good man ma da: Expression of approval.

grand man for the pan: One who really enjoys fried food.

great: The ultimate Ulster accolade; can be used to signify pleased assent to a plan.

grotty: English slang. Run-down and dirty.

guttersnipe: Ruffian.

half cut: Drunk.

hand's turn: Minimum amount of work.

having me on: Deceiving me.

heart of corn: Very good-natured.

heifer: Young cow before her first breeding.

hirstle: Chesty wheeze.

hit the spot: Fill the need.

hold your horses: Wait a minute.

hooley: Party.

houseman: Medical intern.

how's (a)bout ye?: How are you? Or good-day.

humdinger: Something extraordinary.

I'm your man: I agree to and will follow your plan.

in soul, I do: Emphatic.

jar: An alcoholic drink.

knackered: Very tired. An allusion to a horse so worn out by work that it is destined for the knacker's yard, where horses are destroyed.

knickers in a twist, in a knot: Anxiously upset.

knocking: Having sexual intercourse.

Lambeg drum: Massive drum carried on shoulder straps by an Orangeman and beaten with two sticks, sometimes until the drummer's wrists bleed.

length and breadth of it: All the details.

let the hare sit: Leave the thing alone.

like the sidewall of a house: Huge, especially when applied to someone's physical build.

liltie: A madman. An Irish whirling dervish.

load of cobblers': In Cockney rhyming slang, "cobblers' awls" means "balls." Used to signify rubbish.

lough: Pronounced "logh," almost as if clearing the throat. A sea inlet or very large inland lake.

lummox: Stupid creature.

main: Very.

make a mint: Make a great deal of money.

moping: Indulging in self-pity.

muggy: Hot and humid.

mullet, stunned: To look as stupid or surprised as a mullet, an ugly saltwater fish.

my shout: I'm buying the drinks.

near took the rickets: Had a great shock.

no dozer: Clever.

no goat's toe, he think's he's: Has an overinflated sense of his own importance.

no spring chicken: Getting on in years.

not as green as you're cabbage looking: More clever than you appear to be.

not at myself: Feeling unwell.

nutcrackers: Neurosurgeons (medical slang).

nutty slack: Fine, slow-burning coal.

Orange Order: Fraternal order of Protestants committed to loyalty to the British crown.

ould goat: Old man, often used affectionately.

out of kilter: Out of alignment.

oxter: Armpit.

oxter-cog: To carry by supporting under the armpits.

pacamac: Cheap, transparent, plastic raincoat carried in a small bag.

Paddy hat: Soft-crowned tweed hat.

Paddy's market: A large, disorganised crowd.

peat (turf): Fuel derived from compressed plant matter.

penny bap: A small bun usually coated in flour.

piss artist: Alcoholic.

poke: Have sex with; a small parcel.

pop one's clogs: Die.

poulticed: Pregnant (usually out of wedlock).

powerful: Very.

quare: Ulster pronunciation of queer. Very; strange.

raring to go: Eager and fully prepared.

recimetation: Malapropism for recitation.

rug rats: Children.

run-race: Quick trip to, usually on foot.

sheugh: Bog.

shirty: Short tempered.

shit: The action of defaecation.

shite: Faeces.

skiver: Corruption of scurvy. Pejorative. Ne'er-do-well.

skivvy: From scurvy. Housemaid.

snotters: Runny nose.

soft hand under a duck: Gentle or very good at.

sore tried by: Very worried by or very irritated by.

spavin: A disease of horses resulting in a sway-back.

spavined: Suffering from spavin.

stays: Whalebone corset.

stocious: Drunk.

stone: Measure of weight equal to fourteen pounds.

stoon: Sudden shooting pain.

stout: A dark beer, usually Guinness.

strong weakness: Hangover.

take a gander: Look at.

taste, wee: Amount. Small amount, not necessarily edible.

ta-ta-ta-ra: Dublin slang for party.

thick: Stupid.

thon: That.

thrapple: Throat.

throw off: Vomit.

toty, wee: Small, very small.

turf accountant: Bookmaker.

up the spout; up the pipe: Pregnant.

wean: Pronounced "wane." Child.

wee: Small, but in Ulster can be used to modify almost anything without reference to size. A barmaid, an old friend, greeted me by saying, "Come on in, Pat. Have a wee seat and I'll get you a wee menu, and would you like a wee drink while you're waiting?"

wet, wee: Alcoholic drink.

wetting the baby's head: Drinking to celebrate a birth.

whaling away at: Beating.

wheeker: Very good.

wheest: Be quiet.

wheezle: Wheeze in the chest.

whippet: Small fast-racing dog like a mini-greyhound.

willy: Penis.

your head's cut (a marley): You are being very stupid, and your head is as small and as dense as a child's marble.

your man: Someone who is not present but who is known to those who are.

you're on: Agree to a suggestion, or indicate acceptance of a wager.

youse: Ulster plural of you.

About the Author

Dorothy Timman

PATRICK TAYLOR, M.D., was born and raised in Bangor, County Down in Northern Ireland. Dr. Taylor is a distinguished medical researcher, offshore sailor, model-boat builder, and father of two grown children. He lives on Saltspring Island, British Columbia.

patricktaylorauthor.com